No Need to
Regret and
Nineteen Other
Twisted Tales

No Need to Regret and Nineteen Other Twisted Tales

Amy Kristoff

To order additional copies of this book, contact:
Xlibris Corporation
1-888-795-4274
www.Xlibris.com
Orders@Xlibris.com
1077

CONTENTS

"NO NEED TO REGRET"

Small and old. That was how Miriam Grunder's daughter Alyssa made Miriam feel. This was not the way she preferred to feel. (Should she add, she also felt inadequate?)

Oh, Miriam could get by with the "small" part. It was better to be that, at least according to society, than to be fat.

Even if Alyssa was overweight (she was simply big-boned) she wouldn't care. To be happy with herself, that was all that mattered. She had that philosophy mastered. Miriam must have done something right, raising her.

Stunningly beautiful, Alyssa more than made up for the fact she wasn't "petite." She exercised just enough to keep the flab at bay.

For a 36 year-old woman who joked (but wasn't joking as much as her accompanying laughter would indicate), "Michael messes around on me, and I'll kill him—or have him killed," she was remarkably casual about her appearance. Genetics was on her side.

However, Alyssa knew that her husband did his share of carousing before they married, and it was doubtful a man ever got those wily ways, out of his system. One way or another, one time or another, his true colors would show through.

So too, their marriage recently reached its ten-year mark, and Alyssa knew of a couple friends whose marriages crumbled at that point, due to infidelities.

Miriam wondered why her lovely, intelligent daughter, married that fool. Oh, he gave every appearance of being a great husband and father, with his job at Centurex (he was really no more than a glorified traveling salesman). He shuttled back and forth between Phoenix, the West Coast, and the Pacific Northwest so often, you'd think by now, he would have had his own plane to fly. He was in fact (finally) going to start taking flying lessons. It was a matter of finding time. He also just so happened to have "discovered" the game of golf.

Anyway, Miriam thought Alyssa and "Playboy" (he thought he was) just celebrated their tenth anniversary (February 14th), but she might have been mistaken. Was it their 11th? She could have spent the whole day adding and subtracting years, and she still wouldn't know the answer. She had no ability in math, not that she was particularly intelligent, to begin with.

Heck, her granddaughter Lasandra was better in math, and she was only in kindergarten. She was one smart girl, and Alyssa proudly recounted how her teacher, Miss Lindstrom, predicted Lasandra would be skipping a grade "or two." That was outrightly daunting, actually. Lasandra's three year-old brother, Colin, was still a little too young for anyone to say he too perhaps was "gifted."

Both children inherited their intelligence, whatever it amounted to, from their mother. Maybe that went without saying since Michael was merely a typical man—dumb.

But there were exceptions to the rules, Miriam knew that as well as anybody, and her beloved, deceased husband Kenneth, bless him, rest his soul, was indeed one of those.

Alyssa's intelligence was also of the shrewd, cunning kind, when it happened to suit her. Yes indeed, she was wicked. Lasandra had that very same attitude, and you could tell she didn't take no for an answer, if she didn't want to. She'd just figure out a way to do what she wanted, and she would manage to make you say yes.

Wicked. That word really did appropriately describe Alyssa. She was also sexy as could be, Miriam fairly blushed to admit it. She had that big, bronzed body, those golden brown ringlets (courtesy of Miriam, mostly, although Kenneth did have wavy hair, himself), those beautiful teeth, and that easy smile.

You wouldn't have known Miriam had naturally curly hair (gray by now, but once golden-brown) because this past year, ever since she lost the only man she ever loved (next to her father Edward, whom she didn't love, anyway) to a most unfortunate car accident, she'd been wearing a wig.

There were a number of reasons she took such a liking to her black bob hairstyle. (She even had three of the same, rotating them, so each one was always fresh-looking.) It granted her a certain amount of anonymity—primarily from herself.

At the same time, she couldn't get herself to make the final break and cut her hair, although she would still have to deal with its curliness, which was a pain. Maybe she would someday be finished mourning this terrible loss and would be able to show her real hair, in public. Right now, however, it was one day at a time.

Kenneth loved her hair, and it was the feature of hers, which first attracted his attention. What could she say? Tall and buxom never did describe her, even in the prime of her life.

Kenneth loved her for who she was, and Miriam loved him ten-fold, in return. No, it was more than that. Just like some possessions were priceless, there was no way to gauge her love for him. She loved him beyond reason, truthfully.

He died when he was still in his prime. His demise was so pointless. He was driving his silver Lexus down the mountain, returning from a business trip in Flagstaff. Oh, how Miriam wished his consulting work didn't force him to travel so much. But that was what he liked best about the job. And he absolutely loved to drive. At the expense of making much more money than he did, he drove, whenever possible. He believed too much efficiency was actually counter-productive.

Kenneth was also an excellent driver. Sure, some accidents weren't preventable, but Miriam didn't buy the investigators' conclusion. According to them, Kenneth lost control of his vehicle because he took a turn too fast, a gust of wind came up, it was late at night, he was physically exhausted . . .

Admittedly, this scenario *could* have indeed taken place, but Miriam still remained incredulous. And he wasn't drunk, by the bye. He knew better than to drink and drive. Besides, the most he liked was a couple glasses of wine, when Miriam and he went out to dinner. Indeed, the medical examiner verified the absence of any alcohol in his system.

Someone ran him off the road. That was what happened. The

very certainty of as much, was a lot of why Miriam felt she was being driven insane, especially since no one else believed it, including Alyssa—and why not. She was as efficient-minded as she was efficient and didn't see any reason to question a conclusion that authorities on the subject, had only reached after a thorough investigation.

Alyssa, by the way, was a superlative driver and loved to drive. That came in handy, considering all the chauffeuring and errand-running she did for her family.

Miriam regarded driving as an unpleasant necessity and never felt at all comfortable behind the wheel. She obviously lacked whatever natural desire it took, to actually enjoy navigating a load of steel around town—not that she'd rather walk the five miles to the grocery store.

Alyssa was a natural at everything she did. Even her look was naturally gorgeous. She was "bien dans sa peau," all right, as the French would say. She didn't look French, but she could have passed for a South American beauty, with that easy manner (or the appearance thereof). But just like any upright woman, no matter the country or continent, she had her morals intact. That wasn't to say Miriam had any doubt her daughter had plenty of boyfriends when she was single. (She kept her personal life very private, even as a teenager.) Alyssa was the mastermind of discreetness. She probably gave lessons on the subject, to all her girlfriends.

Alyssa would have made (or still could, for that matter) the perfect poster-girl-woman for just about any worthwhile cause. She possessed a certain magnetism, and it went far beyond her fresh-scrubbed looks, her open smile, her expressive green eyes, and that head of golden-brown curls (which she wore much longer than her mother ever could).

Alyssa's long hair was one of the many benefits of relative youth, not that Miriam would even look good with long hair, as short as she was. As for her wig, she often wondered if people were actually fooled into thinking it was her real hair.

One short year. Miriam didn't know how long it would take before it no longer felt like Kenneth passed away only yesterday.

How many years *would* it take? She loved him so much. Unless you too lost someone you loved, as much as Miriam loved her husband, you could never truly empathize with how much her heart ached—literally, at times. And she was not a hypochondriac, either. She lacked the inherent strength Alyssa seemed to have an abundance of, but she did pretty well for herself.

Not for the life of her, could Miriam part with even a single stitch of Kenneth's clothes, nor could she discard anything else of his, namely his toiletries. (This was a tacitly sore point with Alyssa.) She was in Miriam's bedroom but one time since Kenneth passed away. It was occasioned by the fact she wanted to change the sheets on the bed. She knew her mother had spent two weeks, doing little more than laying around, feeling sorry for herself. Alyssa showed up out of the blue because Miriam wouldn't answer the phone. She didn't have a key with her, but her mother had absentmindedly left the kitchen door unlocked. It was accessible by a gate that latched but didn't lock.

Anyway, Alyssa caught but a glance of the array of bottles by Kenneth's side of the double vanity-sink. The look of repulsion on her face was so intense for a moment, Miriam didn't even recognize her own daughter.

Time and again, ever since that day, Miriam kept expecting Alyssa to tell Miriam exactly what she thought of that bottle collection. In this case, Miriam felt like a naughty little child, anticipating inevitable punishment. She also knew Alyssa could catch her mother off-guard, clever woman that she was. Truthfully, Miriam couldn't even fathom the extent of her daughter's capabilities.

Meanwhile, Alyssa took the dirty sheets home with her, having put clean ones on the bed. She brought the other ones back a few days later. They were so fresh-smelling and perfectly pressed, Miriam was more jealous than appreciative of the effort. And no, Alyssa did not have a housekeeper, for a number of reasons, not the least of which, her fanatical attention to details.

Miriam should have been proud. This was her own daughter of whom she spoke. Instead, most of her pride was clouded by fear.

Yes, Miriam was afraid of Alyssa Grunder-Briscol, her very own blood and kin.

However, Miriam wasn't fearful of any sort of physical harm, not inflicted upon Miriam herself. She doubted she could ever be Alyssa's prime target. (Didn't Miriam already mention she felt small and old? Alyssa didn't need to waste her time on her mother.) Alyssa needed a reason, and a good one, before she did things. She was Ms. Efficiency, to a T. (Miriam was somewhat like that, but Alyssa was so much more of an intense individual. And the projects she undertook were more demanding than most normal, everyday people could imagine.)

Miriam always did think of Alyssa as an untamable, wild animal. And in later years, her teens, Miriam perceived in her an otherworldliness, as well. She was not a girl that Miriam would have wanted the burden of raising alone. Miriam never did feel up to the task of motherhood, as it was.

Kenneth was the one who wanted kids. Yes, that's the plural. He wanted several, but Miriam was the party pooper. After twelve hours of labor and delivering a 9 ½ lb. baby girl, once was enough.

Looking older than a newborn, Alyssa was a disturbing sight for her mother. Alyssa even had some hair. The other new mothers in the neighborhood were jealous of Miriam and her baby. All they had to nurse were soft-limbed, fuzzy-headed noisemakers. Alyssa never cried, not once. She would very soon grow into a loquacious little girl, so there was no cause for alarm. She was an extraordinary creation, actually.

This robust baby girl named Alyssa, completely changed Kenneth's notion of the "best" child to have. He found the real beauty really did lie in having a girl because here was this gorgeous, vibrant bundle of joy, who would only become more beautiful with age.

The fact Alyssa could work her magic on Kenneth was no small feat, because he was one of those people who had certain beliefs, and they were set in stone. He was that way, right down to his favorite kind of cologne.

Don't misunderstand. Miriam was proud of her daughter and

her undeniable strength of character. Alyssa proved the female species didn't need the male species for much more than procreation, not to sound facetious. Miriam's son-in-law Michael was an ample provider for his family, but if Alyssa had to go back to work, she would. She chose to be a full-time Mom, in keeping with her fanatical attention to details.

Did Alyssa love Michael? In the romantic sense, Miriam hadn't any idea. She married him for better or for worse, of that much Miriam was certain. Like her mother, she considered divorce taboo.

Miriam wasn't even sure how much love Alyssa had in her. Most of what she did have, went to her kids. She genuinely loved them. Thank God for that much. And she'd do just about anything to keep the marriage together. It wasn't especially for the kids, either. It was the principle of the matter. Michael spent an awful lot of time traveling, and although Alyssa never actually said so, she was getting tired of him being a father-husband, "in absentia." There was a point at which he only earned more money as an excuse to work, not because it was a favor to his family.

And recently, he finally hung up his tennis racket for good, due to the never-ending injuries he would get from playing. As already mentioned, he replaced it with golf and "is positively obsessed with it," according to a slightly miffed Alyssa. It would be a little while longer before he got to those flying lessons. In fact, he was taking a slew of golf lessons, using what tiny bit of spare time he had, usually Saturday afternoons.

Unfortunately, that was when the pro and his assistants didn't customarily teach, at Quail Brush Country Club. It was too busy. Michael, however, was so lucky as to have an assistant who was willing to break the protocol and give him a lesson at a public driving range, near his house in Alemada. Saturday happened to be the assistant's day off.

Finding time to visit with his mother-in-law seemed impossible for Michael, but Miriam didn't feel shunned, not at all. Alyssa had taken to bringing the kids over, and they'd play in the yard for awhile, before the four of them would head to the Pizza Pitstop, apparently the only restaurant they liked.

What they also liked was the mere possibility of being able to play miniature golf afterward, as the restaurant was part of the Phoenix Funtime Complex. The Pizza Pitstop overlooked both the miniature golf course and the driving range. It also overlooked the go-cart track, lending the restaurant its appropriate name. However, since Lasandra and Colin were too small and young to drive the go-carts, they didn't really care about them.

No, Michael had yet to accompany his family on a visit to Grandma's house. There existed a tacit agreement between the two of them, he was doing more of a favor, by staying away. (He may have been to Miriam's since Kenneth's death, but if he was, it was blotted from her memory.)

The first two times Miriam went out with Alyssa and the kids, it was on a Friday, and Michael was in town but he had to work late.

Now, this was a Saturday and as far as Miriam knew, he was having his golf lesson, and nothing in the world stood in the way of that. Before heading over, Alyssa called to say, "We're leaving now," but Miriam didn't have any idea whether that included Michael. She doubted it did, but it nonetheless put her on edge until their arrival.

The second she saw Alyssa's red Volvo station wagon, with her at the wheel, the kids in the back seat, Miriam was left to assume Michael was indeed having his golf lesson. Alyssa would never say so because it secretly pained her, her husband and her mother didn't really get along.

There were worse fates, Miriam would think. After all, Michael loved his mother Nancy, and no man could be all bad if he loved his mother. So there was a personality-clash between Michael and Miriam. It made no difference to her. It never did. She just wanted her daughter to be happy, and she hoped Michael was the man she really wanted in her life. Miriam hated to sound like the selfish mother, but she truly didn't feel as if he even deserved a woman as lovely and perfect in every way, as Alyssa was.

Kenneth seemed to like Michael just fine, although the talking and joshing they did at the wedding was hardly any indication of just what kind of "friends," they could have been. They never really got together much, after that. Alyssa and Michael always lived in Alemada, although they only recently moved into that cookie-cutter, two-story white stucco house of theirs. It was a good forty-minute drive, each way, and it always seemed like either Kenneth or else Michael was out of town, on business.

Then Alyssa had Lasandra, and of course, as anyone starting a family can attest, having her changed everything. The two couples essentially led completely separate lives. To be paid a visit by Alyssa and her two beautiful children was something that only happened on occasion, even before Kenneth passed away. Sure, Miriam and she talked on the phone quite a lot, but they would never get together, not the two of them, alone. They weren't "friends," like some mother and daughters were. (Yes. Miriam's own daughter was almost too much to take, and only in the company of her kids, did Miriam not feel threatened by her.) Still, as she mentioned before, on a day like this, there was no stopping feeling small and old and totally inadequate. The best part was Alyssa wasn't even in the house. Miriam was standing by the kitchen sink, watching Alyssa fooling around in the back yard with Lasandra and Colin.

Miriam didn't go out to dinner, since Alyssa came to the rescue and started making this habit of bringing the kids over and then going out. Formerly, Kenneth and Miriam would go out almost every night of the week—at nothing less than a gourmet restaurant.

If nothing else, what Miriam needed was a support group, or some sort of travel/activity group, perhaps? She couldn't even imagine traveling alone. She couldn't in fact imagine doing anything alone because she never did (aside from living alone, these days).

Nonetheless, she did try to go out to dinner, alone—once. It was a disaster. It wasn't a gourmet restaurant, nor was it one Kenneth and she frequented—a place between one of those and the Pizza Pitstop.

Maybe going somewhere she'd never been, wasn't such a good idea. Maybe she picked the wrong day of the week. She didn't want to drive far (nor give herself time to change her mind), so she ended up at the Italian bistro Ricci's, on a Thursday night.

Located among Scottsdale's Main Street art galleries, Miriam had the distinct pleasure of eating dinner and then proceeding to emerge from the restaurant, only to collide with all the well-heeled couples, enjoying the Thursday night "art walk."

The most depressing part was she ate way too much and felt ten pounds heavier than when she went in the door. Worse, the food wasn't even very good. She was usually a picky eater, so she had no idea what got into her, that night. She certainly wasn't hungry.

That evening, she realized that things would never be the same again, and she would have to learn to accept that fact.

And here came the troop, in through the kitchen door, Alyssa, trailed by Lasandra and Colin. Mom was laughing uproariously, looking more like a child than her two very precocious children.

Miriam felt awful. Alyssa and her family lived in rather cramped quarters, regarding their house's proximity to their neighbors' (identical houses). There was hardly a yard to speak of, and the size of the pool was a joke. Here, even with the large pool and the recently-added guesthouse, the yard was spacious. Alyssa wouldn't even promise the kids a dog (she wanted one that was medium in size) until/if they ever lived where there was more room for the animal to run and play. The kids barely had enough room for that, themselves.

Miriam ought to will "the Briscols" her house. She really should. Shamefully, she couldn't do it. Her own daughter and her family! Alyssa probably didn't even think about the matter, one way or another, but she'd definitely have an opinion to voice if she did know what was stopping her mother from being charitable—Michael Z. (Zachary) Briscol. He was the reason. Miriam was not about to make life easy for him. He already had it too good, married to Alyssa.

Michael's parents, Frederick and Nancy, had a lot of money, much more than Kenneth and Miriam had. They didn't do a darned thing to help their son and daughter-in-law, with their mortgage payments and other, assorted debts.

Kenneth and Miriam had yet to spend (and now, of course,

never would) an actual Christmas with the kids and their parents, as they (Kenneth and Miriam) went to Hawaii every year, for the holidays. Nonetheless, they came through with a tidy monetary "gift." You could bet the stingy Briscols didn't give them but a mere pittance, a couple hundred dollars, probably stuffed in one of those special cards, made just for the occasion. How thoughtful.

Indeed, Kenneth was a generous man, but at the same time, he was very subtle about it. He in fact built that guesthouse as a subtle gesture to his mother Winifred, to come stay with them. He knew her health was failing her, but it wasn't something she wanted to admit. Anyway, it turned out she really didn't want to stray from her home in Palm Springs, where a veritable army of doctors was treating her various ailments (both real and imagined).

Her one true ailment, however, was she never got over the death of her husband Kermit, nine years prior to when the guesthouse was completed. (And not one year after that, she died, too.)

Anyway, she was married to that man for something like 45 years and lived every single one of them in Duluth, Minnesota, the last place on earth she wanted to be.

But she stuck it out and when he died of "natural causes," as his death certificate reads, she moved to her dream destination, Palm Springs, California.

Still, Winifred was restless and truly missed her husband. Miriam always tut-tutted the old woman for not being happy and content. At least she no longer had to suffer through those long, snowy, winters. Kenneth's brother Vince used to visit her often, thinking his company would appease her. Finally she outrightly told him to save his plane fare money and just stay back in Duluth, where he ran a dry-cleaning business. That was about the same time Kenneth scurried to have the guesthouse constructed.

In all truth, Miriam was glad her mother-in-law never came to live with them. Even residing in so-called "separate quarters," she would have made a nuisance of herself.

"Mom! Hello!" Alyssa called to Miriam. It appeared she was

lost in thought—or space. Alyssa never could tell for sure if her mother had the smarts to ever be really thinking about something. Alyssa already knew that for all her father's bravado, he wasn't smart at all.

Miriam had been alone too long. A year, now. Alyssa would have been more than happy to find her mother a caring, wealthy handsome gentleman-companion, but Alyssa could tell her mother preferred to hold onto the ghosts of the recent past.

Proof of as much were those goddamned bottles of her dead husband's, which she kept meticulously arranged, by what used to be "his" bathroom sink.

The black wigs she wore, well, those were bad enough. But one thing you had to keep in mind about a mother as deeply devastated as Miriam, you had to be prepared for just about anything.

And so, when Alyssa finally got through to her (Miriam came back down to earth), it was not in the least bit surprising to Alyssa, she was asked, "Have you seen an almost-empty bottle of Chaps cologne? I could have sworn I saw it just this morning, when I was dusting in the bathroom. Now it seems to have disappeared."

Alyssa was positive, in that moment, her mother had really gone off the deep end, this time. It was all Alyssa's fault, having waited too long to try and rescue her.

There was only one thing for her to do, given the touchy situation. She whirled around, bent over, picked up Colin, and held him close, saying, "Colin, were you playing in Grandpa's old bottles, 'cause you know your daddy likes to wear Chaps too, and you wanted to pretend you were him?"

Poor Colin looked like he not only hated to be suspected of something for which he was completely innocent, but he didn't appreciate his mom's joke. He was the more sullen child of the two, taking after his pouty-lipped, curly-haired father—except Papa had black curls and Colin had dark blond ones—for the time being, anyway.

Lasandra didn't want to be left out of what she considered more fun and games, moved from the back yard to Grandma's kitchen. She tried, with the kind of innocence only a five year-old could have, to lend her advice: Mummy, I think Grandpa came down from heaven and took it back there with him, don't you?"

"No, Lasandra, I don't," Alyssa returned. "If there's such a thing as ghosts, Grandpa's spirit would have taken the full bottle."

Lasandra nodded, satisfied with the remark, which she obviously took seriously. Meanwhile, Alyssa got a laugh out of her mother. The day could be saved, yet.

Both her parents were so serious-minded. They were also very traditional and conservative, but did that mean you couldn't have a sense of humor about life? It was absolutely no wonder Alyssa's mother took her husband's death so hard. The woman couldn't even lighten up about life. Death was as certain of an issue, was it not? Alyssa saw no difference between the two.

Alyssa was born fearless and at this point, she didn't know how else to be. Her mother acted like she was scared of her own shadow. Her husband really was her only salvation, and Alyssa always did regret what could happen if he went before her. It was a shame he had to die of something besides natural causes, although there was some dispute if he had the heart attack prior to or after he swerved off the road. Either way, Alyssa chalked up the mishap as the result of old age. He just didn't react to split-second surprises, like he used to be able to do.

No one was in a position to blame Miriam for missing her husband. Any woman would, even independent-minded Alyssa herself, and she wasn't saying that because he was her own father. With him, every day of the week was a reason for celebration (or almost, anyway). He'd take Miriam out to the best restaurants in town, not that Alyssa was dying to go someplace fancy, with Michael. She liked the Pizza Pitstop just fine, with her kids' company—and every other time, lately, at least, with Miriam along, too.

But anyway, she, Alyssa, hadn't been to a gourmet restaurant since her parents took her. Yes, on occasion, they did. What Alyssa remembered most distinctly were the compliments the waitresses would make. (The waiters never said anything. They just looked shyly at her, wishing she was 26, not 6.)

The waitresses' comments would in fact be directed at her parents, as if Alyssa were some sort of circus freak, all because she could keep quiet and still for two hours, while her parents carried on their conversations, hardly paying any attention to her. That was fine with her. She'd lose herself in her imagination, which was better than real life, any day.

Miriam got such a kick out of dressing Alyssa in these frilly, lacey dresses, ones Alyssa was most grateful she never had to wear to school. She stuck out there as it was, given how much bigger and taller she inevitably was than the rest of her classmates—in about every grade, as it turned out.

Now that she thought about it, Alyssa was certain she hadn't dressed up, really did the whole dress/hair/make-up thing, since her wedding. (And look what it got her.) No, but seriously. (She really did have a wicked sense of humor.) How else could you get through life if you couldn't see a little humor in things? Otherwise you'd be reduced to wearing black wigs. (It was very difficult for Alyssa to keep her thoughts to herself, concerning what her mother was doing to herself.) If Alyssa didn't have plenty of her own problems (even smiling, fresh-faced Alyssa herself had her share), she would have been unable to keep from telling her mother exactly what she thought (or close enough). But alas, her own problems served to keep things in perspective.

Miriam would not have asked the question concerning the sudden disappearance of the bottle of cologne, if she could have avoided it. The last thing she wanted was to have her daughter and grandchildren know just how obsessed she actually was, with keeping tabs on all those toiletry bottles. It was her own form of therapy, although practical-minded Alyssa thought it was precisely what was driving Miriam insane, to the point of no return.

Nonetheless, it was none of their business; it didn't need to be. Miriam was still self-sufficient, she still had her wits about her, etc., etc. And for someone like her to make that sort of pronouncement, was no small feat, in and of itself (because now she would be expected to live up to it, day in, day out).

The problem was, she was so obsessed with knowing the exact whereabouts of the errant bottle, she put her pride on the line by even mentioning it. No, she herself did not believe in ghosts, nor did she think she was guarding Kenneth's spirit, by keeping those bottles. She just felt as if it were a responsibility of hers. It was much better to go through life with a sense of purpose, than not having anything to do. That was when you *really* lost your mind.

It was entirely possible she somehow misplaced the bottle. She was known (lately, anyway) to become absent-minded out of the blue. If she was doing something like dusting the living room, she'd pick up a knickknack and go put it in a closet or even toss it out. But until today, she had not done such a foolish thing with one of Kenneth's bottles—she didn't think. And she already did a thorough search of the entire upstairs, but she came up empty-handed. When she momentarily went back up to change into something a little nicer than the old cotton pants she had on (even the Pizza Pitstop deserved better), she would double-check a couple places, including the cabinet underneath the sink.

Was it possible either one of her grandkids was playing upstairs and happened to move and/or hide the bottle? Kids loved to hide things, didn't they.

Miriam didn't think they'd traipsed upstairs, not that it was off-limits, but they customarily hugged Grandma hello and ran back to the car, to get whatever they'd brought, to play with. Besides, they would have spoken up, when their mother was making her jokes about the missing bottle. They knew perfectly well not to mess with their no-nonsense mommy. You certainly couldn't have accused Alyssa of spoiling her kids. Yes, they had a good life, but she made sure they were respectful and took nothing for granted. (Darned if she wasn't raising them like Kenneth and Miriam raised her—but it worked. She was a wonderful woman.)

Oh, Miriam failed to include Michael. She didn't mean to

leave him *out*, but Alyssa really was the one most involved with raising their kids.

Alyssa must have told Lasandra and Colin about Grandma suddenly having short hair because they never once looked at her strangely or inquired about whether it was really hers or not.

Miriam said "must have" because she couldn't imagine two little kids as curious and naturally inquisitive as they were, merely accepting Grandma's "new look." The one and only child Miriam ever knew, who behaved as well as those two, if not better, was Alyssa herself. It gave Miriam goose bumps, to think such perfection really could be passed from one generation to the next.

Rather than worry about a silly, nearly empty, designer cologne bottle, Miriam told herself she should be happy as could be, feel like the luckiest grandmother on the earth (there was undoubtedly a lot of competition for that), and go upstairs to change.

Miriam just felt so confused. To lose Kenneth like she did without any kind of warning, was so unfair. She was sure all this would have been more bearable if she'd lost him to a lingering illness, as morbid as that sounded. At least she could have done her grieving by degrees, getting some of it out of the way *before* he died.

For right now: "I'm going upstairs to change, I'll be ready in a few minutes," she told Alyssa, to which none other than Lasandra piped up: "Can I play in the guesthouse?"

"Goodness sake, Lasandra, let Grandma have some peace," Alyssa admonished her daughter. She was turning out to be hyper-active—and annoying.

But Miriam didn't mind, really, not when she wanted a few minutes to collect her thoughts and attempt to relax, something she never seemed to do anymore. She was a ball of nerves.

She told Lasandra, "Dear, you're more than welcome to play in there. In fact, I do believe it's unlocked because I was cleaning in there, earlier" (only because she had nothing better to do).

Alyssa said, "I'll go with her, so she doesn't make a mess." Then she took hold of Colin's hand, saying, "Come with us, Colin." She also asked Miriam if she would like the guesthouse door locked, once they were ready to leave, to which Miriam said, "Yes, please." She needed all the help she could get, remembering the little things. She felt both resigned and defeated by this ongoing case of absent-mindedness.

Miriam ascended the stairs—slowly. It seemed to take all her physical and mental energy just to move her legs. The stairs really were becoming a pain. This wasn't a house for an old woman, living alone, without even a pet to keep her company. Alyssa's kids would love it here, Miriam was certain of it.

Miriam scoured the master bedroom one more time, in search of the missing Chaps bottle. She tried telling herself the darned thing was just a figment of her imagination. It was definitely easier on her psyche to say she'd bought the new bottle because Kenneth threw the old one out, than to go on maintaining she'd been dusting it for the past 370-plus days.

It would make Alyssa feel better if her mother pretended it didn't even exist. Alyssa. Yes, Alyssa. Now, wait a minute. Miriam stopped her rummaging around to think. Alyssa'd made a comment about those bottles of Kenneth's, and Miriam let it slip by. Whatever it was, Miriam was pretty sure she couldn't have said it unless she knew the exact inventory of the bottles, herself. Yes! She remembered. Lasandra mentioned she thought her grandfather's ghost came down from heaven and took the bottle back there with him. She had been referring to the one that was almost empty. Alyssa joked, if there was such a thing as ghosts, Grandpa's would have taken the *full* bottle.

Of course, Alyssa knew already, how Miriam liked to keep things well-stocked, especially something that Kenneth was fanatical about using, exclusively.

It was impossible Alyssa took any sort of actual inventory, however. There was just no way she did. Even as a little girl, she could have cared less about getting closer to her parents' bedroom than the doorway. Miriam couldn't imagine her daughter, at age 36, suddenly taking a keen interest in snooping in her parents' room, especially with one of them dead. The only time she was in here was two weeks after the funeral, when she'd shown up unexpectedly and insisted upon changing the bed sheets. She never went *near* the sink. She saw enough from a distance.

Then again, Miriam never could have predicted this show of concern from her, either, not that she was a selfish woman. Nonetheless, a person as independent as she was, usually didn't go too far out of his or her way to be helpful. Inevitably time was always of essence to them. In some ways, however, she really didn't go out of her way at all, to be generous. She came and picked Miriam up to go to the kids' favorite restaurant, which helped shut them up—not to be facetious, but it *was* true.

Oh shoot. Miriam needed to get ready, quit dawdling. That was seemingly all she did these days.

With separate, his and hers walk-in closets, Miriam didn't have to see Kenneth's clothes, every time she went in search of something to wear. (Clothes were a big deal to her.) Anyway, for some reason, she couldn't even peek at one of his tailored suit coats, without getting all teary-eyed. He had such a great build and a nice frame, and his posture was so wonderful, and, oh, she really couldn't even think about him in a suit, on his way to work, without getting miserably upset.

Miriam wanted to wear a skirt. Rather than look through the sporty "separate" ones, she found herself going through her skirt and jacket ensembles, the ones she formerly wore to all those restaurants, with Kenneth.

There was a day (before he died) when Miriam was a sensible shopper, finding the things she looked best in, and she didn't ever have to spend a lot of money. Anymore, she couldn't even go to the grocery store without having it turn into a long, drawn-out-affair. She was unable to decide whether to buy the frozen corn or the frozen peas, the microwave lasagna or the spaghetti (she no longer cooked, even occasionally, not that she did a lot of it, before, with all those stupendous meals out). Everything was a monumental decision. And she'd only buy a few things because she hated putting it all away, once she got home. Besides, going to the store was about her only reason for leaving the house.

One day, recently, in fact, more recently than when she made the mistake of trying to go out to dinner, she made herself go to the mall. If nothing else, she just wanted to see if she could stand being out for awhile. She didn't expect herself to do any shopping.

After a few minutes, she got it in her head that everyone was pointing and staring and making fun of her and her wig. She found herself ducking into stores for relief, hiding behind racks and display cases.

She ended up spending about $300.00 dollars, making the most stupid, irrational purchases of her entire life. They included: One pair of black suede, open-toe, lace-up platform sandals; one fuchsia, lacey, silk, above-the-knee, spaghetti-strap nightgown; and one pair of corn cob yellow, linen pedal-pushers.

Did she look in the mirror that morning and think she was 25 again? Really, she never would have worn any of this silliness, even at that age.

As for returning any of it, she just wouldn't return shoes or lingerie. Maybe you couldn't, she didn't know the rules on those. She would have been more than happy to hand it all over to Alyssa, but she was so much bigger than Miriam. And they certainly didn't have the same-sized feet, although Alyssa's shoe size was not, in fact, much bigger than her mother's.

But the pedal-pushers, now those she felt she ought to exchange. Money was money, and she wasted enough, even if she did end up giving the rest of the frivolous items to charity. That was where Kenneth's clothes would eventually be going, once she could bear to go through with boxing it all up. Even if some of it might have fit Michael, she wasn't about to give him one stitch of it.

As for all the toiletry bottles, she would someday empty the ones she could, and they would meet the same fate as any she had to toss out "as is." That would be a day of celebration for Alyssa, as she would feel Miriam was finally "well." Miriam already knew that was highly unlikely. The best she could ever be was *accepting* of her "new" life.

Miriam needed to go through her own clothes as well, and give away any she no longer wanted. She had a number of fancy

dresses and skirt ensembles that she seriously doubted she'd ever
again have a use for.

But for now, here she was, stealing this ocean blue silk skirt
away from it's colorfully-spangled, short-sleeved top. She intended
to wear the skirt with a casual-looking, salmon-colored, ribbed
cotton sweater.

She would allow herself to cheat like this, this one time and
then no more. It was high time she took a critical look at her
clothes and eliminate anything that was only creating clutter.

Miriam didn't want to give that errant cologne bottle any credit,
but it was possible it helped her reach this juncture. It made her
see she'd been going way overboard with her emotions, trying to
extract sentiments when/where she could no longer expect herself
to even *want* to feel them.

Tears came to her eyes, but not tears of sorrow. They were tears
of relief. Perhaps she'd inadvertently tried to drive herself insane,
but the experiment failed. She was still her same old self, not wanting
to accept change, despite how inevitable it was. She'd been entirely
unrealistic with herself, that was all there was to it.

"Knock-knock," came Alyssa's voice from the hallway, as she
tapped lightly on Miriam's bedroom door. Alyssa was getting very
concerned. Her mother wasn't one to primp and fuss for any length
of time (an attribute Alyssa was grateful to have inherited from
her—and from both parents, the complexion and entire "look"
that enabled her to look good, without doing a damned thing).

Alyssa sincerely hoped her mother wasn't sitting by the vanity-
sink, taking her one-hundredth "bottle inventory" of the day. Either
that or she was sitting there staring off into space. She was definitely
in a strange kind of mood, and it was making Alyssa uneasy.

As it was, it gave Alyssa the creeps to know her mother was
holding onto every single last remnant of her husband's. Who could
have predicted she would react this way, to his death? She was
otherwise (or used to be) a sane, rational, extremely practical-minded
woman.

Momentarily Miriam opened the door, sporting a simple but striking skirt and sweater, a purse in one hand, a Dillard's bag, in the other. She said, "I thought after dinner, if there's time—I'm not sure how late the stores are open at Desert Terrace Mall, on Saturday, but maybe we could stop in, and I could run in Dillard's, to exchange some pants."

All Alyssa could think was, *How much farther out of the way did she want to drag everyone, before the day was through?*

Admittedly, Miriam was a sort of guest of theirs, and the least Alyssa could do was accommodate her. Hell, if she had to do her mother a hundred favors in one day, if that would help to ease her sorrows, Alyssa would do every single damned one. Sometimes Alyssa had to remind herself that every little bit, might possibly do some good, even though it seemed like her mother was living on another planet.

No man was worth destroying yourself, Alyssa didn't think. And it just so happened *Kenneth* didn't die, quite the saint her mother had herself deluded into believing. Take it from Alyssa, the daughter, versus Miriam, the mother, the wife of that man. What people said was true, about the wife being the last to know. However, Miriam was better off if she didn't know too much of the truth, any truth. Alyssa noticed over the years, her mother was like that about everything.

Meanwhile, Alyssa presented Miriam with the "surprise" she'd been carefully hiding behind her back. It was courtesy of Lasandra, actually. She was nosing around like she was so good at doing and discovered the missing cologne bottle in the medicine chest of the bathroom in the guesthouse. Little sneak that Lasandra was, she got hold of that bottle before her mommy could reprimand her for crawling up on the marble sink-top. So, the naughty girl escaped punishment (again) all because she lucked out and saved the day. (Boy, did she remind Alyssa of herself.)

Alyssa told Miriam, "Thank your granddaughter, the little sleuth, for this," handing the bottle over.

Miriam took it graciously and felt quite embarrassed. That was strikingly apparent, and Alyssa couldn't help thinking it kind of served her mother right. Hopefully, sooner or later, she'd realize the ridiculousness of some of her obsessions. It was interesting. Alyssa never would have thought her mother was the obsessive type. But sadly, something in her common sense and good judgment must have snapped. It was entirely possible it was too late for her.

Nevertheless, Alyssa was an optimist. She didn't like to conjecture for even one moment, in negative terms.

Descending the stairs, Alyssa heard the squeals of her two little rabble-rousers, before she actually saw them playing what looked like jungle-gym, using the family room sofa. They were working on their second, if not third wind by this time.

Alyssa was screaming mad at them, for being disrespectful of the sofa (she was into furniture), not to mention being ignorant and heedless of the potential damage they could do to their craniums, when they clunked them on the Saltillo tile. Trying to hold her temper, she ordered, "That is enough, you two, of jumping all over the furniture!" It was hard to stay cool, but it was imperative she did. Ever since her mother became so emotionally fragile, Alyssa felt like she needed to tiptoe and whisper in her mother's presence.

There came an indication Miriam's mind was warming up, if only be a degree of two (if Alyssa ignored the fact Miriam was behind her and couldn't really see a thing). Anyway, Miriam said "Don't worry. I need a new sofa."

That statement alone was almost enough to induce Alyssa to do a jig, once she reached the bottom of the stairs. She kept her immense relief to herself, however. It was possible her mother's "lightening up," was only momentary. Besides, the kids would start dancing too and get completely out of hand. She was hungry and wanted to get this show on the road.

One look at the Dillard's bag and Lasandra wanted to know, "Did you go shopping, Grandma?" to which Alyssa told her, "You goofy girl. She's been upstairs, getting ready to go out with us. If the store's still open after dinner, we're taking Grandma there, so she can exchange something."

"Does that mean we won't get to play miniature golf?" Lasandra asked. Meanwhile Colin hung back, awaiting the verdict. It was plain Lasandra was always the one to do the talking, when they were together.

This time, instead of expecting or even wanting Alyssa to make a reply, Miriam did, thinking she was otherwise the probable party pooper: "Not especially. We don't have to stop at the mall."

Alyssa added, "We don't have to play miniature golf, either. Don't you two remember we played it the last time we ate there?"

Lasandra shook her head. Colin just stood there.

Alyssa said, "Oh, come on. Sure you do. Lasandra, you almost got a hole-in-one on that hole that has the purple turtle standing in the middle of it, wearing that straw hat with the petunias."

Lasandra nodded, evidently not excited by the flashback to that memorable moment in time. She preferred to be open to the possibility of playing miniature golf, again today.

Finally, the entourage was on its way to the Pizza Pitstop. Alyssa's Volvo station wagon would be the vehicle of choice. That went without saying, if only because it was parked in the middle of the driveway.

More importantly, Alyssa would have to drive because Miriam certainly couldn't, when her daughter was in the passenger seat. She would be so self-conscious, she'd probably have an accident.

The most recent occasion on which Miriam drove Alyssa anywhere was when she was pregnant with Colin and had to go to the doctor's for a check-up. There was no one to watch Lasandra because both the "regular" babysitter and the "back-up" one, were unavailable. It was a last-minute cry for help from the typically very organized, efficient Alyssa.

It seemed easier on everyone if Miriam simply picked Alyssa up and took her to the doctor's office, and Lasandra accompanied them.

That day, Miriam drove all the way to Alemada, drove Alyssa and Lasandra to the doctor's office, which was in the northern part of the Phoenix Valley (even in regard to where Kenneth and Miriam lived), drove them back to Alemada, and then drove home. That was the most driving Miriam ever did in one day. For most people it wouldn't have been that much, and unlike Alyssa (and Kenneth), Miriam never did feel at home, behind the wheel. The few times she went a significant distance in a car, she was a passenger.

Anyway, that day, Miriam wasn't nervous or self-conscious with Alyssa in the passenger seat because Miriam knew Alyssa appreciated the favor too much to bother with being her critical self. She was also too tired and too pregnant to even really take notice of Miriam's driving skills. (Alyssa found the second time around, wasn't easier than the first.)

However, it deserved to be mentioned, Miriam never had an accident, nor did she ever get a speeding ticket.

Now, Miriam noticed a couple faint scrape marks on the right side of Alyssa's car, between the front passenger door and the headlights. It looked like the kind of thing that would happen, pulling into or backing out of a tight place. This car was only a year old and Alyssa usually took meticulous care of her vehicles. It made Miriam wonder if Alyssa even knew these scrapes were here. She was always in a hurry and had so much to do, it was possible she overlooked them.

Miriam would leave the discovery up to her daughter. This just didn't seem like the day to bring it up. She had no idea why she felt this way. Maybe it was because she herself felt so strange and out of sorts, no thanks to her needless worrying about that missing cologne bottle.

Alyssa was bound and determined to get rid of the car she had before this one. It was the same make and model, only it was black, instead of red. With 16,000 miles on its odometer, she couldn't have wanted to trade it in because it was worn out. (Miriam thought of cars, about like she thought of clothes. You used them both until they were threadbare.) Anyway, Michael and Alyssa supposedly had the kind of argument about it, that really put their marriage to the test. Alyssa ended up digging into her own, private funds to buy that new car, all to avoid an ongoing feud with Michael. Luckily she had quite a bit saved, from her career days as a graphic design artist. Short-lived though her life as one, ended up being (comparatively, at least), leave it to her to have made the most of it.

The house was barely out of sight, when Miriam couldn't decide for sure, if she locked the front door. As it was, she was counting on Alyssa to have made sure the guesthouse was locked.

Miriam hated how these little details got her so upset. She never used to be this way. It came down to the fact she couldn't trust herself to remember much of anything, anymore. It had turned into too much bother for her brain, apparently. It was too busy being uselessly absent-minded.

Miriam thought she was doing the right thing by exiting the house, last. It had been a conscious effort on her part, and look what good it did her. She certainly didn't want to ask Alyssa to go back home so Miriam could double-check. She'd made enough of a fool of herself, already today. Besides, Alyssa had one of those determined expressions on her face (as seen from the side, no less), so Miriam hardly felt as if this was any time to inconvenience her. Alyssa had in fact looked like that the second she'd made sure the kids were strapped in, she strapped herself in and glanced to make sure Miriam was safely secured.

And Miriam was glad she never thought twice about a seat belt, not that Alyssa's driving skills were cause for alarm. It was just that you couldn't help feeling like she considered the other vehicles on the road as obstacles, more so than simply other cars.

Still, there was no denying it. Alyssa was one heck of a good driver. While she drove, however, there wasn't any conversing. She did her job and you kept your mouth shut. Actually, the relative peace and quiet was relaxing. All that could be heard was Lasandra and Colin, talking amongst themselves.

Alyssa broke out of her state of deep concentration, at the first light they missed (having gone through three intersections when the light was yellow).

It was a relief to see Alyssa was no longer in that faraway place. And soon they arrived at the Phoenix Funtime Complex. Alyssa parked closest to the entrance they typically used, on the north side, versus the east side. The latter was where the customers parked, who were interested in either the driving range or else the go-carts.

Although the north-side parking lot wasn't exactly crammed, the restaurant was. The room in which they usually dined, was the designated site of some lucky boy or girl's birthday party. Whoever it was, he or she was one heck of a popular person.

The hostess was insistent they not leave. She beckoned them (despite their obvious hesitation) to please follow her. She sincerely regretted the inconvenience, but if they would please sidestep the party, there were plenty of tables, overlooking the driving range. (Sure, because everyone knew better than to show up and stay to eat, when a party was going on.) The flimsy partition, which obviously acted as a divider and nothing more, would not be helping alleviate the noise.

This was one merciless foursome, Miriam thought. She was proud to be part of this little crusade. Alyssa's kids clearly inherited their mother's do-or-die determination.

The affable hostess laid the kiddie menus at places adjacent to one another, facing the party, not the driving range. Maybe it was intentional, Miriam didn't know. Happenstance or not, Lasandra and Colin "typically" (the other two times Miriam was here with them) played musical chairs, before deciding where to sit. On the rare occasions Miriam had also dined with them in the past (it must have been lunch, someplace), they did not end up sitting where the hostess laid the menus, either. It was almost like a responsibility of theirs to reject the hostess' idea of a seating arrangement.

This time? They must have been eager for an eyeful of the party-in-progress because they obediently sat themselves right down. That gave the "adults" a driving range view, not that either one cared. If anything, Miriam enjoyed the usual view of the miniature golf course.

When Miriam did glance up and look straight past Lasandra's curly, brown-haired head, she beheld none other than her son-in-law, on the driving range. He was not alone, and Miriam didn't mean he was the only one out there, hitting balls. A short (like Miriam herself) blond instructor (who, unlike Miriam, was not old, nor looking as if she ever felt inadequate in any way whatsoever) was giving him a lesson—if you could have really called it that. They were getting a lot more done than most golf teachers and their students typically did.

Miriam wondered if Alyssa had any idea Michael's instructor was a female. Well, it was plain as day to his mother-in-law, who nonetheless could hardly believe her eyes. She hoped and prayed Alyssa's eyes never saw them at all. Miriam didn't want there to be a scene, especially for the kids' sake. But then again, Alyssa had yet to fail to keep them in mind, had yet to fail to put their *welfare*, first and foremost. If nothing else, this stood to be the supreme test of her role as the consummate mother. So far, Miriam thought he daughter deserved an "A+."

By the time the large, thick crust, double cheese pizza with sausage and pepperoni arrived, Miriam's anxiety had completely disappeared. She felt better than she had—in years. Also, she was a starved as everyone else at the table claimed to be. In a few months she stood to gain back the 20 pounds she lost since Kenneth died. What a silly, foolish waste, pining for a man who wasn't quite the saint Miriam thought he was, all along. All Alyssa had to do was excuse herself to go to the restroom, while they'd been waiting for dinner to arrive. Upon her return, a confirming look in the direction of the driving range, a subsequent nod, and the remark, "Well, having Colin wasn't so easy, just because I'd already had Lasandra, but believe me, it doesn't mean I won't try anything twice," really said all.

"HEAR NO EVIL?"

You, Bert Hessen, come to the Ocotillo Bar, every night of the week for a few drinks. It's safe to call yourself a "regular." You have quite a number of years on you, versus the rest of the clientele, but it doesn't bother you. You look damned good for your age. A lot of that you owe to your disciplined exercise regimen. You have a lap pool in your back yard and you make daily use of it. In your school days, you swam competitively. (You didn't win much, but you were still as competitive as hell.)

Old age is just a frame of mind, you are the first to say so—and know so, not that you're *that* old. But in today's society, anyone over about age 35, is deemed over the hill.

When you make your entrance, you like to come through the front door and pass all the tables of men and women, having their cliquey little parties, every night. You want the females to take notice of you because you are the epitome of what a middle-aged man ought to look like (and you still have your hair, even though it's turned silvery-gray).

You always leave by the side door, but there's just nothing like passing all those merrymakers, feeling like you're a king and they're all your subjects.

Now, tonight, you can hardly believe the sight you behold, as you approach the otherwise empty bar counter. A burly-looking, broad-shouldered chump is in your seat. You almost stop and rub your eyes, you're so certain they're deceiving you. And your eyesight is fine. It's simply that nearly without fail you have the entire counter to yourself, every night around seven o'clock. Now, not only is there this—this *person*, he is in your *seat*, your *favorite* stool, the one furthest to the right, of all those situated on the left half. (The bar is actually divided right down the middle, so the sexy

34

drink waitresses can pass in between—and the customers can make a pass.)

Seriously, you would never do such a thing. You have pretty damned strict moral standards, even now that you're a widower.

You want to sit in your seat, damn it! And when you draw near to the very person who "stole" your stool, the smell of his aftershave about makes you gag. You wonder if he's trying to attract females or drive them away. Well, you would be more than happy to tell him right now, this isn't a pick-up joint. If you sincerely thought that would get rid of him, you'd be glad to tell him so.

Rather than look obvious about your aversion to him, by sitting at either the far left or far right of the bar, you decide the best thing to do is fight fire with fire, so to speak, and sit to his immediate left. You'll still have plenty of elbowroom because you're left-handed.

As for him, if he's left-handed, you hope he feels mightily crowded and decides to do something about it—like get lost.

You don't understand it. Maybe it's just women, but she had it all. She was still relatively young (her 45 to your 55) and in good mental health—until the moment she decided to overdose on sleeping pills. That was after she'd drunk almost a whole bottle of champagne.

You shirk any sort of blame whatsoever, but you know, deep down inside, it's for the sake of your sanity. Sometimes, things don't turn out quite like you might expect—not that you had an outcome in mind. Damned if you weren't the one caught with the surprise, but luckily not the one without his pants.

Then this happens. Some Yahoo with his broad shoulders and thick neck (and thick head, maybe?) occupies your seat with that fat butt of his. It's an otherwise "dead" Friday night, too. Just the same groups of yuppies are in here, having their private little get-togethers.

You're a pro at this point, on the great art of keeping your cool, despite your blood being past the boiling temperature. The breathing techniques you learned as a swimmer, way back in high school and college, come in handy at a time like this.

With that, you finally take a seat to his left and dare him to give you a dirty look. Are you kidding yourself? He's too damned lazy and lost in thought to bother to acknowledge you at all. Well that really floors you, come to find out. Fight fire with fire? How about the war is on? That's more like it.

You are the epitome of cool. You are living proof that not only the younger generations know how it's done. If/When this guy looks at you, you're going to smile like your life depends on it. There's nothing like a goodwill gesture, even one soaked in sarcasm.

Soaked. Now that's really an appropriate adjective, given the circumstances. Guess who Sharon was messing around with, but the goddamned "pool man"? You still can't believe he had some special something or the other, which you obviously didn't (And you saw him in the buff, from the front and you can attest, he did not have a bigger [or longer] rod, than yours.) Phew, You're relieved about that much.

It was the lovers' fault they actually believed you when you said you'd be gone all weekend, that you would be on your way, at a *precise* time. You had some errands to run before you left Phoenix on your way to your cabin in Flagstaff.

You also forgot something at home and had to stop there. Who could have predicted just how surreptitious that would be. Life's so damned chock-full of surprises, there's absolutely no way a person could become bored.

That, however, was precisely what must have happened to poor, lost Sharon. You don't think in terms of the nameless "pool man" because a guy like that is always game. Someone like *you* is made of much sterner stuff. Small wonder you were the one wronged.

It's been a good three months since the demise of those two, and you frankly have yet to feel any true remorse. You can't help thinking they both got what they deserved. Whenever anyone does, in any situation, sympathy has no place. ("Want this theory tested, pal?" you'd be willing ask anyone.)

You mention to Joe the bartender, on a nightly basis, how "sad" you are about losing your wife. This, ahem, is not a lie. You *are* sad, damn it. Look what she did but leave you high and dry, a lonely widower, you are. Now you have to start all over again. Even though she wasn't so special you'd call her one in a million, or one of a kind, you put a lot of time and affection into making her more of a woman. You made her feel like a princess, even if she wasn't the classiest or prettiest woman in the world.

As soon as you feel up to it, you're going to "look around" for another wife. A man like you deserves to be married, meaning you have the finances to support just such an investment. (Isn't that what wives are? Most of them, anyway.)

But this is not the place to do any wife-hunting, if you didn't make it sufficiently clear, before. It's not because the babes in this joint are too young for you, either. If you marry again, you in fact would like to find a "young" wife, one who at least can still have kids—and wants them. Ever since you lost Sharon, you've come to the conclusion, kids might have helped keep the relationship alive (not to mention her).

Just the two of you together was kind of a sterile combination, in more ways than one. You could have had kids, but she adamantly did not want any. Maybe you have to watch women who say that. They end up being the ones who stray, like she did, but she sure didn't have to look far, did she. You were married for ten long years (not to complain, but it really did seem like a lot of time), and not once did she even joke that she wanted a kid or two. You two didn't joke about much of anything. You call the relationship sterile. How about joyless, you dummy? (At least you know you're not perfect, although you are loath to admit it.)

The house is too big for one person. If worst comes to worst you'll sell it. The only thing is, you had that pool built, especially for you. Most people in the neighborhood have a pool about the size of a Jacuzzi. They obviously aren't serious swimmers, like you. You're a bit of an elitist and proud of it.

One quick glance in the direction of your "companion," and you're already drawing conclusions, about who he must be. He's definitely from out-of-town, but he's not a tourist. He's one of those trend-spotters, paid by some progressive company, to do some "spying." He may even be a local-yokel, but you still think he works for someone. A guy like him, wouldn't even tie his shoes, if he found a good enough reason not to bother.

That's enough speculating. You're only getting carried away, and frankly all that matters to you is that he's occupying your seat (and you hope to God this is the one and only time). You have no idea how you'll react, if he decides to make himself a "regular," like you. This bar is only big enough for one outsider. And in your respective ways, that's exactly what both of you are.

Suddenly you feel this need to befriend this outsider, since you two have something in common. Just because you prefer to sit alone at a specific place, doesn't mean you don't know how to make the best of any situation. Damned if you didn't prove as much when you surprised those two unfortunate adulterers.

However, you would really like to be able to relax a little more, first. You're not in any hurry to be congenial. You'd like to savor a couple sips of your much-anticipated vodka-tonic (with a twist of lime). The only problem is Joe has yet to appear. What's with him? Can't he see you sitting beside this guy? You even joke that perhaps he only waits on whoever is seated in that one stool.

You want to drive home the point you are the hotshot, the regular customer here, so Joe just *better* say, "The usual?" or "The usual, Mister Hessen?" or you will never forgive him. At the very least you'll be glad you've never bothered to tip him. You don't happen to think he *should* get a little extra. The sexy drink waitresses go to more trouble than he does, wearing their micro-minis and stilettos (but this is still *not* a sleazy joint, even if their outfits make it sound like it is).

Finally, he makes his much-awaited appearance, wearing that expression of his, one that makes him look like he spends his time in the back, with a lemon rind in his mouth.

Then, the shock of them all, Joe has the nerve to stop at Yahoo's place, before yours! Worse, Joe does so, so he can light the S.O.B.'s cigar! He also asks him if he wants another beer, to which the chump replies, "No thanks." Any dummy could see he barely touched the beer he has. It's one of those "special-dark" kinds, and anybody who can get through even one of those awful things must have a lead-lined stomach.

Well, now that you have the distinct pleasure of enduring the stink of that ass's cigar, it's what you get for complaining about his annoying aftershave. You can't believe the way Joe is bending over backward for this guy, and you know for a fact he isn't even close to a regular here. You always knew there was something weird about Joe, something that made you unconsciously regard him with contempt. There is absolutely no way in hell you are going to tip him now, not after this elongated wait. You refuse to reward stupidity. And, like always, you will wait until you are finished drinking, to pay him.

Once he has a second to make eye contact, he says, "Evening, Mister Hessen. The usual?" to which you nod and have to exhale. You honest-to-God were holding your breath. But he didn't disappoint, as it all turned out. Now you can take the liberty of looking at the stranger, to make sure he got it. If he *is* impressed at all by your seniority here, he's got it well-hidden behind a mask of nonchalance. You almost wave a hand across his face, to make sure he is really there. That's how saucy you can be, especially when you want to know something for sure. He's still left that beer right there on the counter, and the cigar ended up in the ashtray, to his right. Joe must have done such a lousy job of lighting it, it went back out. Sitting and reflecting seems to be this guy's favorite thing to do. O.K., so you too really are a lot alike, what can you say?

Suddenly he notices you looking at him, and he tries to give you a friendly smile. You say "try" because there's something either pained or else fake about his expression, you don't know which. You feel yourself blush because you didn't want him to catch you looking at him. You make a weak attempt at returning the smile, but it's got to appear fake as hell, if only because you feel like such a dummy.

You try to bolster your confidence, telling yourself this redneck (and it really is, too. He must have gotten too much sun, playing golf today—except, would he play golf?) is in your seat, remember? You logged many an hour in this place, and where was he all that time, but watching half-naked dancers at some scum-bag blue collar bar, one in which if *you* walked in the door, all the heads would turn toward you in reverence, of course. Only in another lifetime would any of those chumps have the opportunity to be you.

Now you realize what gets your goat the most about this guy. (You just stole a glance at him, once he finally looked away.) He didn't even have the common decency to shave before he came here. Is that disrespectful or what? He had better not get laid tonight because he sure as hell doesn't deserve it. Does he need to be verbally reminded, this is not the strip-joint, nor some crappy dive bar?

Maybe you're just too stuck on rituals, but you always shave before you come here. Never mind you know you're going to be sitting alone, carrying on mumbled conversations with yourself. (God only knows what you might have said, especially these past three months since Sharon died.) Still, you don't say much. What the hell would you want to tell him? As it is, you regret the few things you have shared, such as lamenting the loss of your wife. Well he's got to know you weren't *too* madly in love with her, as you came here alone to drink, even while she was still very much alive.

But see, drinking at a bar is all about solitude, as far as you're concerned. It's your quiet time, and if she ever came here with you, she would have talked the whole time. In fact talking and taking showers were her two favorite pastimes (and adulterous sex, of course).

Since drinking is obviously a solitary pursuit for you, you really would be better off staying at home to do it. There's plenty to be said for being able to get as wasted as you wish, since you don't have to worry about driving home. You can just crawl to bed—or hell, pass out on the floor. What a life.

Meanwhile, curiosity is getting the better of you. You admit it. You would like to know this guy's reason for showing up here tonight, out of the blue. And as if to conveniently provide you with the ultimate nerve-stimulus, Joe brings you your drink. To think you were getting kind of comfortable, without it. So much the better, however.

Joe can't seem to depart fast enough, and that's A-O.K. with you. You're still kind of mad at him for ignoring you, although he *did* bring your drink promptly. And there's no less than two lime twists, perched on the glass rim. Now that's more like it, you think.

All you need to do is take one small sip and immediately you feel better. These are the kind of moments that make life worth living. They flutter past, gone before you know it, but still. Luckily you're a sensual man, or you'd be in the same boat as this stranger here.

Hell. You feel kind of sorry for him. Look at him, you tell yourself. Deprived of the powers of perception, he's forced to vegetate. He can't even do any actual reflecting. The least you can do is show some interest. He really is quite a sorry sight. It's almost like he's picking his brain, just to figure out how to use it better.

Before he gets any more despondent with being so out of touch with himself, you kindly ask him, "So what brings you here, tonight?" You also stopped him from picking his cigar back up. He was just going to make another attempt at smoking it. That was a swift move, and you congratulate yourself on your timing.

And what do you know, he can hardly wait to unload his woes: "I had something real ugly happen at my house tonight, and I'm trying to decide if I should go back and see just how much damage was done, or if there's more, or if—I just dunno." He shakes his head as if he's literally trying to loosen all these jumbled thoughts. You pity the guy. That was exactly how you felt the night you caught the two lovers, in bed.

It's impossible (you are certain) he had the same thing happen to him. Still, you feel it's in your place to advise him because if you did it all over again, you wouldn't have left the scene of the crime, so to speak.

With that, you tell him, "You might want to retrace your steps, pal. I can almost guarantee from experience, you won't regret it."

Your comment elicits raised eyebrows from him, like he can't believe you, of all people, would have any idea. What is it? Do you look just too together, too professional, too organized, to ever hit a glitch in your life? Well, then, you'd be glad to tell this guy otherwise. You in fact can hardly keep your mouth shut. The only thing that assures you, you will, is the fact he's about to do the talking and you're much too polite to interrupt.

"My wife Jenny and her lover musta made the mistake of thinking I'd left for my fishing trip, sooner that I did. It wasn't my damn fault I had supplies to buy after work, and then I had to stop home for something I forgot. I can't even damn remember what it was now . . . I get there and the pool man's truck is parked in the driveway. He usually takes care of the pool on Tuesdays and Fridays, but not at dusk, man . . . The garage door is closed, so I don't have me any idea whether Jenny's home. I park my van in the alley, 'cause immediately I'm suspicious. Either this pool schmuck is fucking my wife or he's cleaning out my house—and I don't mean dustin' and moppin'. The latter seems more figurable though, at this point, 'cause I'm not imagining my Jenny, fuckin' around. She's a real neat-freak, who's got a major thing about dirt and germs, and most especially sexually transmitted diseases. I mean, thirty minutes easy, she takes a shower after sex, and here I am, married to her! Anyway, it's kinda possible the guy's robbin' my house, though there isn't much of value, to take, besides the big-screen TV. But he might think I can afford to have him take my possessions, since I can obviously afford to pay him plenty to take care of my lap-pool, which I had 'specially installed when we moved in. The previous owners just had some little three-foot deep, kidney-shaped joke. I'm a man who likes a real swim, or I don't wanna bother myself with getting wet."

Damned if you don't practically shake with emotion, you so completely identify with this guy's attitude—about everything, so far. It's like he's a sort of kindred spirit. This goes to prove they're found in all walks of life, and you can't by any means, judge them by their appearance alone.

For now, so you don't interrupt his train of thought, you only comment, "You're a swimmer, too, eh." You wouldn't know that from looking at him, either. He's not overweight, but he doesn't have a body nearly as sleek as yours. Didn't you call him beefy? Or broad-shouldered, anyway. Yeah. He looks like he works out with weights—in the sun, so he gets his neck burned.

You're not being funny when you make these observations. You're highly attuned to subtle nuances (you think). Your computer analysis career made you this way. You're pretty good at doing things on the fly. Brainstorming is another thing you know about.

Right now, however, you're concentrating on this story. It's so damned eerily parallel/similar to your own, you are tingling nonstop now. You're in fact so surprised, the best thing to do is keep your mouth shut and silently marvel.

Your new friend, the "other outsider," goes on: "Before I go inside the house, I check the back yard, just to make sure I'm not bein' paranoid and freakin' for nothing. I look over the wood gate, and there ain't a pool man in sight. I immediately just start trembling with rage. I still don't know for absolute sure what's up, but I do know my territory—one territory or the other's, bein' invaded."

After taking a quick sip of that awful-looking beer, he continues: "Like I said, I was kinda behind in getting the show on road, but I did have on my jacket, 'cause I wasn't picturing getting back out of my van 'til I reached Flagstaff. Stoppin' here was strictly last minute. Little did I know how that coat was gonna be comin' in handy, for me. I tell ya, stickin' my left hand in the pocket and makin' like I had a gun, looked pretty damned believable to me, and *I* knew the truth . . . So I real quietly unlock the front door and go inside. It's funny, but the second I was inside I knew exactly who was where, doin' what—or just did. Well that eliminated any fear in me, I can tell you that much. I was just real, real mad, but I knew keepin' my cool was gonna save the day. I mean, hell, I was so flipping mad I coulda gone straight in that bedroom—my bedroom—and strangled the two damned adulterers, together, at once. I mean it, man. And I'll betcha, I ain't the only man out there who's felt that way."

He takes another breather, and you can't wait for him to go on. You are completely mesmerized by his story. As it unfolds, it just continues to sound exactly like your own! You doubt he'd believe you, however, if you told him so. Besides, you want to let him finish before you make any all-encompassing statements. Sometimes you're too presumptive, so you're going to temporarily put a lid on it. It's good discipline.

He needs another sip of his beer, if only to wet his throat. As for the cigar, it's definitely out by this time, and he appears entirely oblivious to it. Although when he briefly smoked it he used his right hand, he uses his left one to drink his beer. You wonder if he is indeed left-handed, or perhaps he's ambidextrous? You still don't know his name, yet you'd like to ask him this. The strangest things arouse your curiosity. You certainly have been more interested in his "yarn," than your drink. You finally take another sip, however, a nice long one.

"Then I see 'em," he goes on, "the two, count 'em, *two* champagne bottles—empty, sittin' on the wicker nightstand. Now I know they've not only been fuckin' around, but they're just plain fuckedÊ.Ê.Ê. Oops, excuse my language. Like I said, there just ain't no experience on earth, like seein' a sort of stranger in bed with your womanÊ.Ê.Ê. Anyways, I knew timing was everything, so I needed to wait until one of the dumb drunks made a move, and if my common sense was gonna serve me right, Jenny would be getting up, much sooner than later. She had such a thing about takin' her thirty-minute shower after the deed, I couldn't see her lyin' there for long."

"Sure enough, she gets fixin' to get up. Of course, lover-boy next to her, don't *want* her getting up. He's thinking he's some hot stud, and he's gonna screw her some more. She tells him so lovingly I about croak, she's gonna pee and clean herself up a little bit. I wanted to call to him, he better just take his nap. It'd be a while."

You can't keep your emotions to yourself, any longer. Damned if you can hardly even sit still. Quick, before you say anything, you take another sip of your drink. There's no better remedy. After doing so, you have to tell him, "That is—or was—my wife Sharon to a T. What do you know."

He nods but doesn't seem particularly concerned or impressed. Maybe he knows dozens of women like them. He's probably been around, more than you. You had kind of a late start, thanks to your sheltered upbringing, and you never have been one to make love to just any woman. (To think you ended up marrying a woman who was no better than a—a whore! That floors you to no end.)

This poor guy is just all caught up in his own troubles. If this story keeps unfolding the way you think it will, he doesn't have any idea, all the complications that await him.

Bolstered by another swallow of that repulsive-looking beer, he says, "I don't hang back too far when Jenny gets up and goes in the bathroom. Now I wish I woulda hid more, not 'cause she saw me, but because I had the pleasure of seein' that fuckin' loser ogle her butt-naked body. Damn it. I almost lost it then, for sure. I knew then I had nerves of steel, holding still like I did, in spite of it allÊ.Ê.Ê. Anyways, I knew I had thirty minutes to do something, before she'd be around to witness it. She took a piss and came back out, I was gonna have to take serious action against her, too. In a way I wasn't feeling like I knew her, either, and I was this like vigilante, called in to right some wrongs."

You keep your mouth shut, but damn, how you want to tell him you felt exactly the same, while you were going through your own, similar incident. He didn't need to worry. There wasn't anything the matter with him, at least not according to your take on the situation.

He leans over a little more and speaks slightly more softly (not that he was ever loud): "I cool as a cucumber put my left hand in my jacket pocket and make like it's a gun. I walk straight into that room, the second I hear the shower water's turned on. Lucky I didn't hesitate 'cause old beached-whale, pool man's already about ready to doze off. When he first lays eyes on me, I think *he* thinks he's dreaming. He does this dopey-lookin' double-take, then starts rubbin' his stupid little eyes. I'm already wondering what the hell my wife sees in this loser. I know from his occupation alone, he doesn't make even half as much money as me. I can hardly wait to see what he's got down below. If only for that, I need him to get his ass outta bed. But besides that, I got a mean trick I wanna play on his drunk self, and I intend to get a good belly-ache of a laugh— my sole intention at this point, you understand."

You nod because somehow you do indeed understand. You get a little nervous, anticipating the direction this story is taking. You wonder if you should warn him, there's not time to lose, like you originally had in mind to do? Otherwise he might find himself with some real explaining to do. He might also feel quite guilty. Don't you know all about that, and it's been three months since you experienced your own, private calamity.

Smiling wickedly, he goes on: "I got a hell of a kick, just out of seein' him look like he's having the bejesus scared outta him, yeah, right before my very eyes. He could rub those eyeballs all day and night and I wasn't gonna disappear." He snickers and says, "I tell him to put his hands way above his head and get up. I tell him not to try nothing fancy or clever 'cause my gun's loaded and I won't think twice about using it. That was true, 'cause if I'd really had a gun, I wouldn't have hardly needed an excuse to blow his brains outta his head . . . Anyways, he does what I told him to, though he's awful clumsy about it. Either he's really wacked or else the shit's been scared outta him, I don't know which . . . I open the back door, leading to the pool and tell him to go outside— backwards, please. He ends up tripping so bad on the step, he almost falls on his butt. Meanwhile I get a good look at his you know what, and I can hardly keep a straight face. I know, I know, when it's doin' it's thing, it looks more impressive, but there still wouldn't be enough to brag about. So I eliminate that reason, as to why Jenny wanted him so bad. It had to be something else."

"You can just tell, this guy don't have any idea what I got in mind to do, and truth be told, I didn't have any idea, myself . . . Then I see the pool, the route he's taking and I think, *Perfect*. Make the dope fall backwards, into the pool. It's gonna be a pretty damned cold dip he's gonna have to take. And since he's gonna be fallin' in the deepest part, he's gonna have to do some outright swimmin' to get to the shallow part. This is no baby pool I'm talking about, if I didn't make myself clear before . . . Anyways, after he almost backs into a chaise lounge, he falls in the pool. It happens so fast, neither one has time to really realize it. That's fine for him, of course, saved him from being surprised, but for me, I'd wanted to really savor the moment, ya know what I mean?"

As you nod for all you're worth, he continues his story: "I'd wanted to get a good laugh outta this, like I told you, but instead I found myself staring in horror as he floundered around, either too cold, drunk or scared to swim. If the latter was the case, it would logically mean he *couldn't* swim. But that made even less sense because he worked for his brother's pool company and took care of my pool, this very one."

"I found myself feeling like a real fool. I didn't know what in the hell to do, so I did the only thing that seemed to make any sense . . . I left. And I came here 'cause I just didn't have the gumption to drive all the way to Flag. I'm trying to figure out where I'm gonna rest my head for the night—if I'll be able to sleep, having been done over by those two. *I'm* not worried about no alibi, 'cause I don't think I did anything wrong—not really."

You can hardly wait to advise him on what to do, since all the circumstances are so amazingly similar to those surrounding your very own personal crisis: "Pal, if I was you, I'd go back home as soon as I could. Believe it or not, about three months ago, on this very same day, a Friday, I stopped home from the office on my way to a fishing trip in Flagstaff, too. I caught my wife in bed with *my* pool man, and I pulled the same exact trick on him—and he couldn't swim, either—or at least he was too drunk to try, and the bastard drowned in my pool. I just so happen to have a nice big lap pool, myself, with a diving board and everything. Well, I did *not* go home to save this shit from drowning, but what was worse, my wife Sharon, was so upset, she swallowed a whole entire bottle of sleeping pills, and died that night, too. She must have seen the dead body floating in the pool, once she finally came out of the shower. And since she'd take a twenty-minute shower easy, after we made love, she probably took a thirty or forty-minute one, that night."

That said, you expect this guy to pay Joe, leap up and run for the door. Instead he just looks at you—amusedly, no less. What's his big problem? Doesn't he believe you? Here you've gone through life, having everybody always tell you you look so sincere, and this idiot thinks you're just blowing smoke. You knew all along, there was a reason you initially held him in quiet contempt. You just knew.

But alas, you don't know quite everything, and that is about to have a very heavy (and humiliating) price.

Fortunately, you're not held in suspense for long. Your stranger-friend is all business, once *his* business is about taken care of. He matter-of-factly says, "I'm a police officer, Mister Hessen, and I'm sorry to have to tell you, you're under arrest."

You do not, by any stretch of your limited imagination, believe this. You nervously laugh (it comes out sounding more like a bird squawking, than anything else) and "reassure" him, he's made some sort of mistake. Then you call Joe: "Joe! Hey, Joe! Where are you, my friend? I need you to vouch for me and tell this gentleman, I never leave here, without paying. Honest, I do. I mean I don't. I mean—Joe, where in the fu—where the hell are you?"

Just like a goddamned jack-in-the-box, Joe pops up from beneath the counter, right on the other side of where you and this "deluded" guy, are sitting. His voice shaky with nervousness, Joe nonetheless has enough steadiness in him to declare, "You paid for your drinks, but you talked to yourself enough over the last couple months, for me to piece together, your role in that 'double-death' I'd read about in the paper."

You're speechless. You've completely lost your pluck. You have had it.

In the meantime, the copper throws a ten on the counter, to cover both drinks (and a tip). Then he gets up and nudges you in the shoulder. He says, "Now Mister Hessen, are you gonna come quietly with me, or are you gonna embarrass yourself?"

Well of course he ought to know the answer to that one. He sat here long enough to get to know you pretty well, even if he did most of the talking. God, how you'd like to cry you were framed, but what would be the use? You're just going to have to hope the jury for your case, takes an extremely dim view of adulterers, not ruthless pranksters, like you.

Joe and you don't exchange even one more word before you depart via the side door—with one beefy cop calmly (but firmly) holding onto you. Gee, you scored tonight. You're not leaving, alone. That's a first—and a last. Maybe, just maybe you should have tipped Joe, even a pittance. Just like people are paid to turn a blind eye, he might not have "heard" you. One monkey to another.

"REST INCREDULOUS"

For Valerie Merkel (known to friends and acquaintances as Valerie Hale), being a writer was a do-or-die profession. Unlike some actors deciding to act, writers did not have this option. They were fated to write. Despite the runaway success of her first novel, *Hope and Love and Eternity*, she knew she was by no means a great writer. She didn't even come close.

Nonetheless, she intended to write until her dying day, and if the critics wanted to pan anything of hers, so be it (so she claimed). Writing was an addiction, not unlike the one she had for the caramel cappuccinos at her favorite hang-out, Rudolfo's. Here she was, seated at her usual spot in the corner, where she could watch, without being watched (so she thought).

Valerie had been coming here every day, since returning from her nationwide book tour. She wrote and ruminated in this private little corner, and it felt so refreshing to get away from the lonely confines of her Camelback Mountain-top mansion.

Right now, she happened to be waiting for her third cappuccino, hoping to become wildly inspired. She needed some sort of impetus so she could review this manuscript, one last time. It was a sequel to *Hope and Love and Eternity*. It was not a good omen, she had yet to think of a title.

Her one consuming passion always was to read. It provided her with the finest, most convenient escape possible. Nowadays it came in handy, when she needed the patience to sit and read the same damned thing, over and over.

The only problem was, when it came to life experiences, she didn't have a whole lot. She purposely led a sheltered existence. She knew precisely why one critic lambasted her first novel, for having a "thin" plot and "weak" characters. God, how she hated to be told things she already knew.

Fine, so the critics resented her, and meanwhile she had to endure the sad fact her parents were *almost* impressed by their daughter's accomplishments. She'd tell herself time and again she didn't give a damn what anyone thought of her, but in the back of her mind, her attitude was exactly the opposite.

Her parents were the epitome of the traditional, conservative-minded intellectuals. Her mother Meredith was a retired research pathologist, and her father Saul worked for a pharmaceutical company. She hated to have to say this, but she couldn't stand either one.

Valerie came in handy for her mother, however, when Valerie was growing up. Meredith loved nothing more than to brag to her sister Dana, how intelligent Valerie was. She never had any idea Valerie listened in on these telephone conversations. Valerie couldn't seem to resist, either.

For a time, maybe Valerie even liked to hear her mother brag about her, knowing Meredith would hardly ever deign to compliment her. It was the only way Valerie knew she did anything right. Dana's daughter Kelly wasn't nearly as intelligent as her cousin Valerie. She was forced to rely on athletic prowess to impress her parents. That kind of "talent" didn't even register with someone like Valerie's mother, especially since it involved downhill skiing. Her niece could only prove her worth to society, doing something that required snow, who cared. Meredith would have been more impressed if Kelly made snow sculptures.

It was hardly any wonder Valerie headed east to college. She wasn't about to stick around the north central part of Indiana, any longer than necessary. There were some great schools in the area, so what? That was *her* attitude. And with a perfect grade-point average, she had her choice of schools. She picked the small, private Rosen College, located in Boston.

Physically distanced from her parents, it didn't take Valerie any time at all to realize how much animosity she'd been harboring toward them. She blamed herself for how she felt, and if anyone had an aberration, it was her.

But damn it all, she made something of herself, and she was proud of it, even if she was the only one to feel proud, really proud. (Her mother was welcome to tell the nosy journalists whatever bull crap she wanted, but Valerie was always treated as if her presence could barely be tolerated. It was something Valerie wished was all in her imagination, but it was not.)

Where was her cappuccino? It seemed like she'd been waiting forever for it. The holdup couldn't be due to any fault of Carl, her "regular" waiter. He really hustled for her. Maybe she truly was addicted to them. Oh well, that was still better than being an alcoholic. And yes, for someone like her, it was indeed an either/or kind of situation. Her only regret was today the caffeine was failing to work its magic on her, and she had a manuscript to write. She would end up staring off into space or else having a cigarette. Smoking was obviously some sort of remedy for boredom. It sure as hell didn't inspire her. In fact nicotine gave her a headache. That was a good thing, or she would have been a chain-smoker. As it was, she looked much older than her 25 years.

For more reasons than could ever be mentioned, that book tour did her in. She liked familiar surroundings, and she could only get a decent night's sleep in her own bed, even if she didn't particularly like the house it was currently in. Ever since she settled into her post-bestseller life, she felt as if the mere light of day was too much to endure. It wasn't the sunny Phoenix climate that was doing this to her, either. It was all in her head, and that alone scared the hell out of her. She knew she was quite capable of doing something entirely stupid and impulsive, which she wouldn't even have the relative "luxury," of regretting.

Valerie couldn't imagine a life without writing, and now, without having it be received. For better or worse, she never had to go through the long phase of obscurity, most writers did. That alone made the crappy aspects of fame, worth it (and she refused to go back on her word).

If she didn't present her publisher, Arc Press, with a finished manuscript very soon, she would give them a good reason to doubt her credibility. She'd be doing some serious doubting, herself. And she certainly fully expected herself to endure another book tour, as surely as Arc Press would expect her to go on one. Their high hopes for the success of her sequel went double for Valerie. She put herself up to maintaining a standard, perfectionist that she was.

She was recommended to an agent in New York, via a counselor she had in college. It was a dream come true, at least that's how most writers would have seen the opportunity. Valerie just wished the dream weren't tinged with some very unwanted realities— namely the brief, tumultuous affair with none other than the counselor himself. It was the result of her yielding to those crazy impulses of hers.

The amazing part was it wasn't like she got around—before or since. There were a number of times in her life (like now, for instance) in which she did without any physical contact at all with a man, and she was perfectly content.

That was the one time in her life, she behaved recklessly, but she didn't regret it. She called it her "promiscuous phase" and refused to analyze it any further. She knew that with or without the affair he still would have referred her to her agent, Sherry Cornelle.

Despite all the money *Hope and Love and Eternity* had so far raked in, Valerie had a mortgage to pay on her mansion. That was from spending faster and more furiously than it came in. If the sequel could be even half the success, she'd be in good shape. (Ideally, however, she wanted the sequel to outdo its predecessor— not to pay off the mortgage, but to make her happy.) If not, she'd have to rely on the continued brisk sales of her original novel, to keep her financially afloat.

Valerie made herself a memorable human being, or should she have said her publicist Marty Matthews, made her so? He did one hell of a job of getting her on every TV and radio talk show in the country—or so it seemed. Sometimes, when the camera would be on her, she'd think, *I bet my hair is so frizzed, the viewers think they're looking at two writers.*

She was indeed self-conscious about her "prone" to be flyaway hair, although it had improved drastically, ever since she found, totally by going "eine-meine-miene-moe" in the phone book, a great salon. She picked Maxine's, on Indian School, in the Desert Oasis strip mall. Mallory was the name of Valerie's hairdresser. He literally gave her these neat little packets of conditioner to put on her hair. That eliminated the guesswork, involving how much to use.

No one ever gave Valerie anything for nothing, so that alone was a pleasant surprise. If it was a common business practice at Maxine's, they had the right idea, for winning customers' hearts. And Maxine herself deserved the credit for choosing Mallory as the most suitable hairdresser of hers.

As for Mallory, she'd only been to him like three times so far, but she could just tell, he wanted nothing more than to have her relent and say she was ready to let him really change her hair. Even though this offered the possibility of giving her a much-needed lift, she couldn't quite tell him, "O.K., work your magic on me, Mallory." Indeed, as unruly and unflattering as her hair currently was, she couldn't get the nerve to take a chance.

It also had to do with a reluctance to part with the familiar. And that was why she fled to Rudolfo's. She enjoyed writing and liked the accompanying sounds of people conversing, glasses clinking, plates clattering, although it was pretty quiet there, when she chose to occupy her table.

Valerie loved to be waited on by Carl. He worked every day but Tuesday (and Monday, when the place was closed). He treated her like a friend but also, like a queen. Maybe this perfect balance came from many years of waiting tables, but some of that just had to be natural. He was a natural-born server, if she did say so, herself.

He was a lot like Mallory, who was a natural at cutting hair. You could feel as much, in his every scissor-snip. Not only that, he really turned her on, the way he'd run his fingers through her hair, during the pre-shampoo, consulting time. Then either Gerry or Stella would lead the way to the back, and one of them would shampoo and condition her hair. Valerie always felt a little embarrassed because she'd still be thinking about Mallory. God, the few minutes of consultation time, made her feel like the sexiest, most sensuous woman on earth.

That was way more than her husband ever did for her. Oh, she forgot. She didn't want to mention her impulsive marriage to a "librarian" from the U.K.—so he said. Why would anyone lie about that? It wasn't as if he told her he was a billionaire.

He had a genuine accent (she thought), but she wasn't sure what else about him was the real thing. Valerie got taken, but it was mostly by her confounded impulsiveness.

No, it wasn't as if he decided to divorce her and was trying to get millions out of her. Life was never that simple. He told her he had to return to Wales, and she obviously misinterpreted that to mean he was coming back.

They'd met while he was "on holiday," and she was on her book tour, having made its stop in Phoenix. Flattery got him everywhere, from the second they met. He could really play the charmer. Maybe he didn't believe she'd take him up on his marriage proposal, but he didn't have the nerve to say he was joking, once she accepted. His remedy was to conveniently disappear.

If he wanted to know the truth, she couldn't believe it, herself, she took him up on the offer. As much as she disliked being completely alone, as she was right now, she wasn't what she called the marrying type.

There was no need to worry, some terrible fate might have befallen him. A couple months ago, Valerie received none other than two sets of bath towels from his mother Ina, who lived in British Columbia. They were wonderfully plush, but the shade of green was so awful . . . Valerie really didn't want to say what the color reminded her of. Anyway, the most interesting part was the tag on each towel, which read: "All Cotton. Made in England. Wash Before Use." Valerie was familiar enough with "the English Way," to realize these instructions made perfect sense—for them and only them. Maybe she just wasn't eccentric enough for her man.

So. Valerie had her mother-in-law's address, and she could contact her, yet what was the point? The great unknown was much more fun. The moral of the story? Never marry a man for his accent, alone.

There was a lot to look forward to, if she ever did finish book number two, for Arc Press intended to take the next tour to new heights. No, Valerie wouldn't be asked to entertain her fans in any extravagant way. Rather, the tour would be much longer, covering all of North America and some of Europe. She could hardly wait. While she was in England, she intended to make a surprise visit where her husband was a "librarian" and ask him who in the hell he thought he was, abandoning her. All she had to show for their marriage was a cheap ring she paid for herself and two sets of piss-green bath towels. (Valerie hated to be so crude, but the color really was repulsive.)

She certainly didn't want to divorce the S.O.B. before seeing him again. Besides, at this point, it wasn't as if he cramped her style in any way. She never did change her name to his and in fact on a daily basis called herself by Hale, her mother's maiden name. Her fans only knew her as Valerie Merkel, and if all this name-game playing confused people, so much the better.

Even though the press pretty much left her alone, the same couldn't seem to be said for her parents. For all their pomp and ceremony, however, they enjoyed being hassled for information. Somewhere deep inside their musty old souls, they actually had a sense of humor.

For the most part, Valerie had estranged herself from them. There just didn't seem to be any remaining reason to maintain communication with them, let alone a relationship.

That did it. She wasn't going to even attempt to do any more work, rehashing this manuscript. She put in more than a day's work at this point—or so she felt. And here came Carl, with caramel cappuccino number three. She wasn't going to expect it to inspire her. Once she decided she was finished for the day, she stuck to her guns. Besides, she'd read the damned thing so many times, she could hardly be objective about it anymore.

It was time to let her mind relax—or as close as her mind ever would. That was the reason for this great bulk of reading material she carried around with her. Today her black straw tote was especially weighted down, as she had with her, this morning's *Arizona Republic*. She didn't have time to read it before leaving the house.

She'd slept until almost noon, not atypical of her, especially if she worked all night. And last night, she put in a few hours. Rudolfo's wasn't the one and only place she could get anything done, but she definitely enjoyed herself here, more so than in that museum-sized house of hers.

Anyway, Valerie's Tuesday-to-Friday housekeeper Anna fairly burst in the door, and Valerie could hear her downstairs, going through her list of upon-arrival complaints, never suspecting for a second that between being downstairs and using broken English, (she was fluent in both Spanish and English) that her employer could hear her: "The day come, I know, I see those dirty dishes and madre mia, yo voy a gritar," (she's going to scream). Obviously, even though she was one hell of a good housekeeper, she had a thing about dried macaroni and cheese. She wished Valerie would at least rinse the plates, if she was going to insist upon leaving them in the sink.

Valerie practically subsisted on macaroni and cheese. That and Rudolfo's amazingly delicious cappuccinos and occasionally, one of their chocolate desserts—when she was a good girl and got a lot of work done. (She would not be having any dessert today, and it had in fact been awhile.)

She had heard Anna loudly grumbling and for some reason, it really struck a chord. Valerie leaped out of bed, leaving the sheets in a heap. She couldn't get ready and get out of the house fast enough. So Anna had an especially messy bedroom to scream about, too. Fortunately Valerie was safely out of earshot, having sped down the mountain in her black Jaguar convertible. She felt like she was returning to normalcy, every time.

Valerie could finally read at her leisure. There was something to be said for paying people to take care of you *and* leave you alone. Whoever thought of the idea of a restaurant, was a real genius.

Because it was Friday, she pulled out the section with the entertainment listings, before looking at anything else. It wasn't like she planned or hoped to spend a night on the town, alone or with anyone. It was a natural inclination, perhaps because that portion set the paper apart from the rest of the weekdays.

She proceeded to open it, only to find her very own goddamned mug—in a hazy color close-up. She was so horrified she almost shut the paper, but at the same time she was compelled to stare at it, shocked by the unexpected publicity. It was certainly the last thing she wanted or needed, right now.

Actually, however, it was fortuitous she first saw this godawful photo while she was in a public place. In the privacy of her own home, heaven only knew how she might have impulsively reacted.

The whipped cream in her cappuccino would melt, and the drink itself would be cold before she could even think about putting it to her lips. She was paralyzed by embarrassment and humiliation. She could tell she would never be quite the same, again. She forced herself to breathe deeply and try to keep her mind clear.

God, did she look bad in this picture, not a single complimentary thing to be said about it—undoubtedly the point. Someone was obviously out to slay her. Well, he or she did a miraculous job. Whoever it was knew exactly where her weak spot was—a candid photograph.

The best part? She hadn't even gotten to the schlock written about her, printed below the picture. Valerie well knew the power of the written word.

In the meantime, she was taking her time, savoring the entire experience of being so completely, incredibly humiliated. She was in fact so much so, she almost wasn't at all.

Someone with a zoom lens, snuck this picture, that was all there was to it. It was just another day's work for the photojournalist whose name was—Bruce Brennan.

O.K., Bruce Brennan. Valerie would have liked to shove him into a corner and tell him most succinctly, he had a job to do, and she did, too. And did he know how much harder he made it, by exposing her, at such an inopportune time? Did he? If he didn't, she felt sorry for him. If he did it on purpose, to goad her, well, she was undecided what his fate deserved to be.

Valerie felt totally violated, as harsh and crude as it sounded. Clearly, however, she was caught completely unawares, exactly what this schmuck Bruce Brennan wanted to "capture." Now watch. The jerk would end up receiving some sort of award, for this "real-life" photo.

She was certain no other "celebrity" would feel the way she did, right at this moment. No. Writers, with their life sentences to write, didn't have the great lives, many expected. The harsh reality of the situation was their livelihoods depended upon them to exist, separate from the rest of society. They also had to maintain a certain amount of isolation, or they'd never get any work done. Life itself was one big goddamned distraction, as it was.

Then the minute Valerie had tried to indulge in some "privacy in public" she was taken advantage of. The timing could not have been better, with her furtively lighting a cigarette—looking every bit as if she were hiding her habit from her mother.

The manner in which she lit her cigarettes was the actual "habit" of hers, not smoking itself. Nicotine gave her a headache, but every few days she just couldn't seem to resist, out of boredom. This idiot Brennan obviously caught her on a day when she had the urge to puff. She was pretty sure that was on Tuesday, Carl's day off. She could rest assured of as much, because Carl very simply would not allow such incredible unfairness to take place. He protected her privacy, he really did, and he was extremely careful to leave her alone when she wanted to be. He had some sort of sixth sense about it.

That "college kid" who filled in for him, he probably took a bribe and let Brennan hide in here while he did his thing. *He* sure as hell didn't have any reason to look out for her best intentions. He was smarmy and smug enough to think he was at liberty to do whatever his little heart desired. Oh, did he think he was so good-looking, surefire proof he had no conscience. Just like with her husband, Valerie refused to even mention an alias for the duplicitous little shit.

Ah, to hell with him. Valerie wanted to concentrate on this Brennan a-hole—specifically the details about this photo, every glaring flaw. Her forehead lines were all the more noticeable with her head cocked as such, all her mental energy seemingly on lighting her cigarette. It even appeared as if someone were doing so, for her. That wasn't the case, but that wasn't to say Carl wouldn't have been glad to rush to her side and light it for her. He'd offered so many times, he finally figured out she preferred she do it, herself.

Carl cared about her, he really did—and this wasn't something her wild imagination dreamed up. It was impossible to mistake genuine goodwill—or so she thought. Perhaps he felt sorry for her because she always came here alone. Little did he know she was running from her "screaming maid." The truth never failed to be more interesting than fiction.

It wasn't as if Valerie had anything to hide (besides her marriage). She simply didn't think Carl needed to hear about the daily woes of being a "Successful Writer" (who was really only resting on her laurels, when she called herself that).

Mallory her hairdresser was another person she could say more to than she did. She was obviously accustomed to writing her thoughts, not verbally expressing them. Also, she was ordinarily a private type.

Valerie felt like a goddamned scapegoat—by default. Anna thought she had it so hard, having to clean up after Valerie. Did it ever occur to her, she got paid for the privilege? For crying out loud, it was a totally ludicrous situation.

Anna would never survive, if she had to endure the kind of pressure, Valerie did. She had the inescapable burden of living up to her past success with her first novel. Arc Press would be breathing fire by the time Valerie finished telling them, "Just a few more months, I promise," etc., etc. Luckily, she wasn't committed to an actual deadline, having forfeited her advance to be able to do that. However, she did have a contract with them, and she therefore "owed" them a book.

They could count on Valerie, they really could, to be certain she took her job very seriously. If she had to make 2,000 more trips to Rudolfo's, writing and editing while she was here, so be it. Between that and plenty of all-night writing sessions, she could possibly finish the novel by the new millennium, less that a year away.

With that admission, she could now really go at it and make *this* announcement: The manuscript needed to be thrown in the garbage. Ouch.

There, phew. She got that out of the way. And she was spared having a critic proclaim to the entire free world, that that was what she ought to have done with the damned thing.

Right now, Valerie felt herself to be a parody of a writer, a mere essence of what she was, before. "Before" what? Before she was wildly successful, but of course. That success only made her feel like a total fraud, like she was fooling everyone for the time being, anyway. And once they figured out the truth? This rotten second book would only be further proof. They almost had the last laugh, but thank God she had the foresight to divert the seemingly inevitable.

Fortunately, it didn't take too long for the frantic, almost desperate attention to which she was paid, to die down. Valerie certainly didn't get any writing done, in the initial phase. Her imagination came to a standstill because there was just too much going on. Never mind she knew all along she wanted to write a sequel to *Hope and Love and Eternity*. She soon realized a sequel was not as easy as she thought and actually required more organization than if she'd started with a new set of characters.

Then, to top it off, she just had to marry a man she didn't even know, she certainly did not love, not even while standing at that kitschy Vegas chapel with him. They should have simply gotten married in Phoenix, but it seemed so convenient to go to Las Vegas to tie the knot because that was where Valerie's book tour was headed, next. So yes, it was a marriage of convenience, in the truest sense of the word.

Sometimes Valerie wondered where the hell the time went (not to mention her sanity). It seemed like only yesterday, she was a teenager, all innocence and completely anonymous—what she missed most. During times like these, she really did long for obscurity. Then she could quietly rewrite her novel without any distractions.

It was actually a natural progression for Valerie to aspire to become rich and famous, not only to prove her worth but to give her mother Meredith something to really brag about, to her sister Dana.

So Valerie needed to be philosophical about having this horrible picture of herself, shown to hundreds of thousands, if not millions of readers. Still, she couldn't get over the fact she had absolutely no opportunity whatsoever to do something with herself, to look better.

And the one feature of hers that really needed some help? Her hair. Her goddamned mess of hair. Her hair, that dark brown, flyaway mess (in spite of Mallory's goodwill attempts to straighten it out and settle it down).

Totally out of her character, but desperate for some solace, Valerie was irresistibly compelled to ask Carl a favor. She wanted him to identify the "celebrity" and (hopefully) tell her the woman was alluring or whatever—just some other adjective besides "ugly," the only one stuck in her head, at this point.

Hell, Carl was as good of a friend as any. Together, they could read the article, below—assuming he did not yet read it today. She waved him over, not being at all subtle, like she usually was. He looked concerned, even from a distance. The poor dear probably thought she had a major complaint. Here, at Rudolfo's? This place was the next best thing to heaven for her, at least when *Carl* was working.

Dutiful Carl immediately went to the table of Rudolfo's most famous customer, never hesitating even a split second. Valerie Hale (as he knew her, but was Valerie Merkel to her fans) had yet to exploit her clout in any way, and Carl was most thankful. Today, however, was quite possibly the day when she had some sort of outrageous demand. He wasn't going to jump to any conclusions until he heard what she had to say. He'd been a server his entire adult life, and he knew it was a bad habit to even think hastily. Besides, she tipped him so generously, she deserved to be granted quite a lot of leeway. And so too, she was a writer, and if what "they" said was true, writers craved sympathy and understanding.

Valerie Hale was completely harmless, however. If she did any destroying, it would be to herself. More than a few times he'd looked over at her table and was horrified by the sight. She'd be holding her pen just so, so it would appear she was about to use it to gouge her eyes, in total frustration. Carl had never before witnessed such intensity in a person, especially an otherwise plain-looking one.

Carl genuinely liked Valerie Hale (something that couldn't have been said for all his customers, although giving him large tips, pretty much ensured likeability from him). Anyway, he didn't want to appear to be poking fun at her, but she did look awfully comical, whenever she lit a cigarette. She'd lean over to do so, as if she were doing something illicit. She didn't have to worry. It wasn't a smoke-free restaurant. The owner, Rudy Olaffson (an actual "Rudolfo" didn't exist) wouldn't have had it, any other way.

Having been thus summoned, Carl had the opportunity to do a little evaluating of Ms. Hale. She appeared even more expectant than when she was waiting for her first cappuccino of the afternoon. It made her look childlike, she was so full of anticipation.

He felt sorry for her. He could tell, her fame and fortune hadn't given her quite everything she wanted—or maybe too much of the wrong things. Wasn't that always the way?

She held up what appeared to be the Friday entertainment section of the *Arizona Republic*. He couldn't see it clearly, so he had no idea if she even wanted him to see whatever was there. Maybe it was some sort of clandestine signal, He'd waited tables his whole life, but that didn't mean he knew it all, Customers always liked to set new precedents.

Then he saw a hazy color photo of someone, when she waved it a second time. He instantly perceived it as a "very important person." That was a conclusion drawn from seeing the picture for no more than a couple seconds. It was quite apparent Ms. Hale could barely contain her mental frenzy—which wasn't only caffeine-induced. He noticed she hadn't even touched her third cappuccino, and the whipped cream had long ago melted. That alone was a definite cause for concern. It was safe to say something had her very upset.

She laid the paper on the table and motioned for Carl not to hesitate to come close, really close. She said, "Carl, please, have a seat here, next to me, I would truly appreciate it." He obediently pulled a chair away from the empty table behind hers, as it seemed to be the easiest thing to do.

He got one more glimpse of the photo before she proceeded to lay her arms across it, effectively blocking it out. Something told him the picture supremely irritated her, and she was not intentionally hiding it from him. Nonetheless, he was afraid to ask to see it again when she demanded, "Who do you think that is?" nodding at the face she was suffocating with her forearms. "I *was* going to ask you if you think she's pretty or not, but I don't care. I'm more worried about whether you think she has any dignity."

Carl was ready to panic. He never got over the phobia he had in his youth, of being asked pressing questions from his mother Olivia. Typically, he'd be late for dinner, all because he was literally stuck up in a tree. (He used to love climbing the trees in the woods behind the Akron, Ohio home where he grew up.)

He'd stammer and stutter, knowing he was damned for telling her where he was (she warned him he was going to break his neck) but equally damned if he lied. (She could somehow see it in his eyes.)

Not for the life of him, could Carl ask to see the picture, one more time. If only he knew admitting defeat would end this game, would he pipe up. Until then, he would attempt to fabricate his own picture, from those two quick glimpses, and try to think of who the person resembled (in all her dignity).

With all the confidence he could muster, he answered, "She looks like a former First Lady or maybe someone playing one, like an actress, in a movie. Either way, she looks plenty dignified."

Carl must have uttered one atrocity after another because Ms. Hale commented on his reply with a "Hmmm," a cross between a sigh and an exclamation of disbelief. Things were not going well for him. This was the one morning he didn't get a chance to give the paper even a quick once-over.

She waited a couple seconds for him to retract his remark, and then she impatiently cried, "That's me!" and it was more than apparent she didn't take it as a compliment, being compared to a First Lady. Carl never could understand women. She went on: "Did you happen to see the schmuck take this lousy picture? I know for a damn fact it was taken here. I just know." There was no changing this woman's mind, either. Never mind the picture did *not* rob her of her dignity.

She held the paper close to her face and read, "Bruce Brennan. Do you recognize the name?" not hiding her exasperation (and impatience with the whole situation). Poor woman. She was under too much stress, even before all this.

Carl replied, "No, I don't," and that was the honest-to-God truth. That yob Brennan must have had a field day, hiding somewhere around in here, waiting for the perfect moment to secure his candid shot. It probably happened while that kid Andrew Wisekoff was working. That Brennan guy might have slipped him a fifty—or maybe didn't even have to do that much, to make sure Wisekoff turned a blind eye. Kids these days had no sense of right and wrong.

Carl feared perhaps this would put an end to Ms. Hale's visits. She looked sufficiently upset to be ready to try a new place. Even though this unfortunate incident didn't occur while he was working, he felt entirely responsible.

Ms. Hale moved the paper so he could more easily see the article below what she considered a most unflattering picture. (It *looked* like her. He didn't understand the big deal.) She politely ordered him, "Carl, if you would, please read this with me and tell me what you think. The jerk has me on the spit with the picture, so he's probably roasted me, with what he wrote. If you disagree, please, by all means, let me know. The salvation of my day, if not more, rests on all this."

This was entirely too much of a burden for meek and mild Carl, and he certainly couldn't read as quickly as Ms. Hale. Even his normal heart rate was several beats slower, per minute, than hers was.

Clearly, however, she needed some placating and had no one in whom to confide. So long as she didn't have a problem with him being who he was, then it was all fine and dandy with him.

And so began the article below the picture of Valerie Hale (Merkel). Its title was, "If You Have to Ask, Sometimes You're Better Off—Not?"

> Wherest goes the "new" resident of our resplendent Valley, the authoress of the mega-bestseller, *Hope and Love and Eternity*, a story of love and redemption (and its share of redundancies)? What does a new author *do*, one who finds her first novel such a smashing success, there doesn't seem to be a need for an encore (although there have been rumors aplenty, the author herself promised her publisher, a sequel). She supposedly started on it as soon as she finished her book tour, some fifteen months ago.
>
> It's possible that's just a whole lot of fabrication, just like the one about her impulsively marrying a con artist (keeping creativity in the family). No one has seen "Mr. Merkel", but be on the lookout. Just like his elusive wife, you never know where he might decide to turn up.
>
> It's safe to say our beloved, best-selling author can move at lightning-fast speed, should it strike her fancy. She purchased her opulent Camelback Mountain-top mansion during her book tour, in the Valley. If she wanted to finish the sequel in a hurry, no doubt she could. Like all creative people, however, the need for inspiration must be taken into account.
>
> This particular photo-journalist happens to be one of Ms. Merkel's ardent fans, and he took it upon himself to do the research for this article—i.e. he suffered from simple curiosity and didn't have an actual assignment.
>
> Recalling days of yore, I identified myself as a free-

lancer and tried to open some doors in the publishing industry, that were quite firmly shut. Given how important publicity can be for a writer, this initially came as quite a surprise.

But then, publishers know better than to stick their necks out, too far (they'll only stand to get their heads chopped off). That explains the brusque reply I received when I phoned Ms. Merkel's publisher, Arc Press, one day recently, inquiring if there was any credence to the rumors regarding a sequel to *Hope and Love and Eternity*, a novel thin on plot but fat on hype (equaling a best-seller, a surefire recipe).

The representative at the other end was polite but there could be detected an air of curtness. To her, I was only exploiting my credentials, and she meanwhile failed to see this as free publicity. She essentially decided I was only trying to extract classified information from her. I'd had no idea I was speaking with a receptionist for the CIA (if they exist).

I have only to conclude that somewhere along the way, journalism seamlessly meshed with storytelling, leaving the two, interchangeable. I sincerely do "hope" Ms. Merkel will forgive me, my "nosiness." Like a real journalist, I only sought to ferret out the truth, the real truth. Meanwhile, the picture of her will have to suffice. Forgive those of us who only want the real thing, warts and all. Now, if only I could have gotten to the bottom of this . . . Bruce Brennan

There was no possible way to expect anyone to empathize with how Valerie felt about this article, which went right to the edge of maligning her, yet at the same time was the bare-bones truth. Brucie was right, in his smug little way. She was at a loss as to what to feel, besides incredibly numb. She felt like he knew more than he was telling the world and could blackmail her, if he would so choose. No, worse, like a "good" journalist, he'd simply expose every embarrassing truth about her, make her feel like a real fool.

She'd almost sooner die, than have her hasty marriage revealed—
unless maybe her goddamned husband came back here to live.

Finally, Carl finished reading the article and appeared
uncomfortable. Valerie'd let him go in a minute. She was tired
of complaining to the wall, the tablecloths, aloud to herself (or
silently, to herself, if there were too many people around). She
didn't want to alarm anyone. (She was alarming enough, to
herself.)

Valerie smiled at him as reassuringly as she could, considering
the circumstances. (*She* was the one needing the reassuring.) She
calmly said, "I just wanted one person in the real world, to read
that article with me and pretend for a minute, they were me. A
writer can't conserve his or her energy for writing, in the modern-
day world, because people always want to know what you're up
to." Never mind the picture of herself, of which the chump was so
proud—all thanks to the fact she wasn't "camera-ready." Life was
not fair, and Valerie still didn't even realize the extent of the mental
damage this incident inflicted.

Carl told her, "I'm sorry, Ms. Merkel. If he'd been here when
I was workin', I would have pulled him out by the shirt collar and
stole his film—if you wanted me to, of course."

Valerie was suddenly so sick and tired, she wondered how she
bothered to get out of bed this morning. Oh, that's right. She was
fleeing her 7500 square-foot mansion, getting away from her maid.
Only in the civilized world.

She dismissed Carl, saying, "Thank you, Carl, for lending me
a sympathetic ear and for reading the article, not that you didn't
already read it today?"

He smiled. "As a matter of fact, I didn't have a chance yet."

Not hiding her sarcasm. Valerie exclaimed, "Good! One more
reader of that slanderous article, and two more eyes to see that
unflattering picture of me. I'm just *so* glad."

Carl looked very uneasy. Valerie patted his shoulder. "Don't
worry, Carl. It's not your fault it happened. I've just got to learn to
take the good with the bad, and plenty of writers out there, would
take this publicity as no more than a positive sign. Any publicity

is supposed to be good, even crappy pictures and backhanded compliments."

He nodded, looking somewhat relieved. He obviously thought Valerie was being reasonable about this. Well, she was—for now.

Before leaving, Carl asked her is she would like a warm, fresh cappuccino. "No thanks, Carl. I've had quite enough." She wanted to mourn in peace—mostly the fact she lost it so completely, if momentarily, to do what she just did. She actually *ordered* Carl to sit beside her and commiserate. Clearly she was completely off her rocker. What the hell lay ahead? She hated to even imagine it.

In fact it was high time for the check, and she told Carl so. She needed something stronger than cappuccinos to do the trick, but she wasn't into anything harder than that. Illegal drugs weren't her thing, but that was how much she'd have to up the ante, at this point.

There had to be some way to salvage the day, if it was the last thing she ever did.

With that she pulled her phone from her black straw tote. She knew the number by heart, of the place she had to call—not because she dialed it often. Rather, she had a good memory of the numbers that were most important to her (and there weren't a whole lot of those).

What luck. She called Maxine's and none other than Maxine answered. Not one to lose a valued customer, Valerie could tell, Maxine said, "Of course Mallory could take you now . . . Could you give him twenty minutes? He's finishing a client, right now."

Feeling like a hog (a desperate one, at that) Valerie said, "If it's too much bother—"

"Nonsense. Lila's his last client of the day." (*All the more reason not to wait for Valerie to show up*, Valerie thought.) Mallory undoubtedly liked to end on a positive note.

Maxine said, "We'll look forward to seeing you," before the line went dead, and that pretty much sealed it. Valerie didn't know if she felt important or like just another moocher, taking advantage of her so-called clout, as well as Maxine's goodwill.

Valerie ought to have been happy. She was getting exactly what she wanted and you know what? It made her feel miserable.

Wait a minute. She needed to get a grip on herself (were that possible). She was going to have Mallory fix her hair, do what he'd wanted to do with it, ever since the first time he laid his sexy hands on it.

Valerie had to smile, in spite of herself. She only imagined he was attracted to her, but hey, fantasizing didn't hurt anything. With that kind of name, he was probably gay, but he sure didn't seem like he was—not that she trusted her judgment. She didn't really give a damn what sex he preferred because even if he was straight, she'd never rest convinced he was attracted to her. He just seemed too—too sexual. She was much too bland and boring for a swinger like him. Forget how cozy he'd get with her. He did that with all his clients, the women, anyway. It helped make them feel at ease, even "loved." He certainly loved their hair, and he raised hair cutting and shaping to a high art.

There were no sexual innuendoes, involved in his cute little passes. He was a lot like Carl. Mallory wanted to make you feel at home.

Valerie could have speculated all day, whether Mallory possibly felt something for her, whether he was gay, etc., but she knew she had a crush on him—straight or gay.

With that she was on her way to "see" him and hope he could work some of his magic, on her hair. He truly was the consummate professional.

About halfway there, Valerie had a terrible thought—that he'd seen that picture of her, in the paper, today. Good Lord, what would he think of her now, she wondered, except that she was too homely to even take a decent picture?

She considered calling Maxine's and canceling, but then she'd really feel like a fool, one who absolutely could not make up her mind—an eccentric, creative type who was disorganized, a deplorable fault, as far as she was concerned.

No, plow ahead. She really had no choice. There were several situations in her life that needed rectifying (including an entire novel to rewrite), so it was just as well she got started on the hair issue. Her personal appearance was always something she neglected. And her hair had been plaguing her for long enough. She ought to have been grateful for that stupid picture, as it served as one hell of a wake-up call.

So Valerie was finally admitting defeat on her hair, which was obviously how it had to be. Mallory knew from her initial visit, she was a stubborn broad. Therefore, there would be no reason to do much, if any explaining, once she arrived at her destination.

Where did some of that obstinacy come from, but too many years of obeying her parents and only resenting them, all the more, because of it. At this point in her life it would have been welcome news to hear something outlandish about her past, like she was adopted.

She only seemed too old and detached, to be concerned about these things. All she really wanted was a simple, logical explanation as to why she could never come close to getting along with her parents.

Sitting at the intersection of Indian School road and 56th Street (only a few more blocks westbound and she would be at Maxine's), she realized she was in such a hurry to leave Rudolfo's, she paid the bill but stiffed Carl! She could hardly believe it.

It figured. She'd been considering maybe never going back there, she was so embarrassed by her ridiculous behavior. Now she *had* to go back once more and tip him double (not that she didn't typically tip him generously).

Truthfully, she didn't mind having to show her face there, one last time. That gave her an extra day before she had to start trying new places to hang out unnoticed, work on her novel (she could hardly wait) and drink caramel cappuccinos.

She might have to go through a few places, patronize them once or twice, before having to move on to another. The wait staff might not be to her liking, or the atmosphere would not be conducive to creativity, or it might just be a lousy dive for spending the afternoon, hanging around.

But she wouldn't worry about it. One day at a time. And if

Mallory worked the magic she knew he could, no one would recognize her. She'd have a good laugh over that.

She was glad she would be fixing her hair before someone made a negative comment about it. Ditto her book. Arc Press didn't want some half-baked story, and she didn't want to give them any less than her best effort. Valerie's agent Sherry Cornelle, would have to make them understand the sheer amount of integrity Valerie had. They would just have to be patient and quit being simultaneously so furtive. It made her nervous. As private as Valerie was about her life, she didn't exactly hide. She went to Rudolfo's everyday and brazenly set up shop, didn't she.

The first thing Mallory thought when running his fingers through Valerie Hale's tangled, wiry, brunette rat's nest, was it all might stand up and walk away, yet. It would be doing her a favor. A woman like her had much too much on her mind, to be even remotely concerned with keeping that wild animal on her head, tamed.

If she was giving family and friends trouble, that was the problem. Not even PMS had the effect on a woman, unruly hair did. Mallory took great pride in being cheaper but as able, if not more so than a shrink, to help change a woman's outlook—for good. Obviously if the problem wasn't in the head, it was on top of it.

Mallory heard Ms. Hale was married but separated. This was not a subject he would have ever breached on his own incentive. It was poor business practice. It was up to his clients to talk about their personal lives.

Anyway, that was neither here nor there (although he was undeniably attracted to her). That too was poor business practice, especially should she not be "interested." Valerie Hale's personal life was her own and would stay as such, as long as she wanted it that way. And Mallory wasn't a gossip-hound, so even if she did ever care to become talkative, she could rest assured what she said would go no farther than him.

It just so happened Mallory only had female clients, and he

affectionately referred to them (to himself) as his "girls." He loved every single one of them in a nurturing kind of way. He loved women in general, so it was no stretch at all on his part, to be so demonstrative around them—all of them, except Valerie and a couple who had the most jealous husbands ever to inhabit the planet.

Valerie was one of his newer clients, and she was not easy to figure out. He had a feeling she was no different from any other woman, however. She needed plenty of affection, just to stay alive, yet he was wary of her. He felt like he would be overstepping his bounds if he became "touchy-feely" with her.

She most definitely needed a good hairdresser, one who could do something with that mess of hers, once she gave the final "O.K." It was Mallory's number one priority in life, to make his "girls" love themselves. Everything else was secondary.

So far, Valerie and he had only greeted one another, the only words they exchanged before she sat in his chair. Still, the look in her eyes, said she was ready for a change. Yes. She was ready for him to make her beautiful. Every female had that indelible right. Now, he was doing his hair texture test, running his fingers through it and sort of meditating—almost like conjuring up the creative forces to help him work his magic with the scissors.

Mallory didn't press his "girls" to go for a certain style or color, but when it came to conditioning, he couldn't keep his opinions to himself. He was a fanatic about it. If a woman's hair was dry, it made his job ten million times harder. It was the one time he ran the risk of offending a client, telling her, her hair was in bad shape.

Valerie took the news well, when he first told her she needed to follow a strict conditioning program for her frizzy, dried-out hair. It was a relief she could take some orders. Some women who came in here couldn't be told anything at all.

Today, Mallory hoped to be given the chance to show her what he could do. And the longer he indulged in assessing her hair texture, the more certain he became, it could handle being colored, should she want that, too. A lighter color or some blond streaks would brighten her face and make her look younger. But he wouldn't bring this up, not today, or at least not before he cut and styled her hair—*and* it was a success. She would need to make a special appointment with Maxine's fabulous colorist, Eve Vance. Knowing Valerie Hale what little Mallory did, she would want her hair colored now, tonight. She might try to color it herself, if Mallory put her off. She'd stop at the drugstore on the way home. She'd only end up distraught because someone like her would not have the patience to do a good job. And proper hair coloring was *not* for amateurs.

Mallory didn't mean to sound so sure of himself, concerning Valerie Hale and her attitude toward her hair, but he learned a lot about women, over the years. And like the experts say, there's nothing like learning a subject you also happen to love. You become pretty damned expert, yourself, without even trying.

Mallory married a woman, much like Valerie Hale—dogged in her beliefs, yet prone to occasional bouts of impulsiveness. That impulsiveness would inevitably lead to major regrets, sooner of later—usually sooner. That meant there wasn't even an opportunity to enjoy, if momentarily, the results of the impulsive act.

His wife Zoe in fact ended up leaving him, but they never got divorced. At this point she'd be too ashamed of what she did, to contact him to ask for an annulment.

She didn't even have the common decency to tell him face-to-face, she was leaving him. He instead had the distinct (and alienating) pleasure of reading a note she wrote and left on the kitchen table one morning, close to twelve years ago:

Mallory,

I'm O.K., so don't send the search party for me. I'm missing on purpose. I can *feel* you calling me an impulsive nut. Stop. It only makes you look better. I can't take any more of a man who loves his clients' hair more than he loves his wife. I need sex more often than every bicentennial.

Regards, from a woman who only *seems* like a nymphomaniac,

Zoe

Gracious. She was so sexually frustrated she couldn't even write love and be done with it. She should have been a writer, herself. Instead, last he heard, she worked for an insurance company, in Tampa, Florida. Her strawberry blonde hair, once straight and shoulder-length, had to be giving her absolute hell.

Mallory truly believed she'd return to him someday. Either way, she so completely broke his heart, he could probably never love anyone, again.

Nowadays, his mother Edith came by his apartment and made sure he wasn't starving. For a 46 year-old man, he really couldn't complain about the care and attention he received. She brought him leftovers, and that really helped soothe his soul. Also, he did not feel like cooking, after a long day at Maxine's. He was on his feet nonstop, and that was more tiring than if he walked all day.

It was ten years and running since Maxine opened this salon, and Mallory was the first and only male, ever, hairdresser of hers. In all that time, there had yet to be a "girl" of his, who was dissatisfied with his work. Nary a one. He worked at a couple salons before Maxine's, and between them all, there were a few complaints, but still, nothing worth noting. The complete lack of any complaints whatsoever in the past ten years, proved how much he had perfected his skills.

Mallory was well aware, however, his reputation was at stake, each and every time he "did" a girl of his. That kept him modest and forever on his toes.

Despite having the appearance of a swarthy Don Juan, Mallory was a sappy sentimentalist who took monogamy in any relationship, very seriously. Not all women liked that kind of man, as his wife Zoe could attest. She wanted plenty of hot sex, and that was about it. Handsome as hell though he was, he was clumsy and altogether disappointing in bed. He was clearly made to be a hairdresser, not a gigolo.

Mallory wished to take the liberty of speculating for a minute, a difference between Valerie and Zoe. Valerie wanted to be pampered, even if she didn't realize it. Glancing at her in the mirror as he finished caressing her hair, gently massaging her scalp, and pondering, he was certain he saw emotional neediness in those soulful brown eyes. It put new life in them, and it seemed like she was trying to read *him*, too.

He could hardly keep from breaking his strict rule and telling her it was all right. If her husband hurt her confidence by leaving her or whatever he did, time would heal the wound. It only *seemed* to take forever.

Some men could be such brutes. The determinedly failed to heed the emotional fragility of most women. Mallory felt like he could empathize with women, more easily than men.

His hair assessment finally finished, his attention was completely focused on Valerie. He broke the silence, asking her, "Do you have something in mind? A style you're ready to try? Layers, maybe? Are you ready for those?" (Are you ready to surrender to that tangled mess?)

She replied, "Sure, I'm ready for layers, as long as I don't end up looking dorky, you know."

Mallory laughed adoringly, because of her honesty and humility. He hoped to God she didn't take it the wrong way. Her hair was probably about driving her insane as it was, and he didn't want to send her over the edge, before he even got started.

He told her, "I will give you something that you can blow-dry for a tousled look, or wear more sleek. Either way, I can guarantee, you will feel like a new woman, sexy and beautiful and free." He got himself excited, giving these pep talks. He wasn't trying to overdo the situation, but he got incredibly passionate about his work. And if his "girls" were as psyched up as him, the positive energy was a great facilitator.

Valerie Hale was Mallory's kind of girl to spruce up. Some women who walked in here were so beautiful already, they could wear mops and still look ravishing. God did all the work on them, so there wasn't any encore, yet they still were the ones who fiddled and fussed, more than the rest.

Valerie Hale needed a reason to think more of her appearance than she did. She most likely thought her career didn't depend on her looks, so why bother? But there, she was mistaken. If she didn't feel good about herself, how could she get any writing done? At least that was what *he* thought.

If she didn't mind him saying so, he would make her his "creation." He would make her feel as good about herself as all those petite, pixie-faced women with their long, straight hair that only needed a quick trim every month or so.

Mallory was going to get one, final confirmation from Valerie, before he went ahead and started snipping (only after a trip back to the shampoo bowls, of course). He pulled her hair up, trying to make it the same length as it would be, once he finished. He said, "See, this is what I have in mind, when I have cut it this short. Then we add layers, and it will be fabulous, so easy to take care of."

"That's what you say, because you're the professional," she quipped. "But don't worry. I still want to go through with this. I really need to get rid of this nuisance, on top of my head."

Mallory had to laugh. He told her, "If you get impatient with it, you can always throw some mousse on it and just leave it be. Once you have those gorgeous layers, you will have more options than you have now. So if you're late for your night on the town, don't sweat it. You could even go out with it a little wet and just let it dry on its own. You will look magnificent."

She said, "If I need it styled for a night out, I'll come here and let *you* do it. That's how much of a big deal it would be. I'm not much for partying. I never was, and I'm getting worse with age."

Mallory was positively mortified. Valerie might as well have just told him she lost her firstborn. Quick to rectify matters, he suggested, "Perhaps this new 'do will turn you into a party girl." He wanted to add something about making her husband take her out, but he still believed she was estranged, if not divorced.

Mallory didn't like to do the shampooing chore, although for Valerie, he didn't mind. This is what happened when you had to work overtime. But again, he was so full of anticipation, regarding this latest challenge, he didn't mind missing a couple of his favorite TV programs.

Indeed, the shampoo "girl" Gerry (she was 50, easy) was gone for the day, as was the receptionist Allison. Guess who was hanging around in the back room, presumably counting nail polish bottles, but "that" manicurist, Mona Reilly? She should have been long gone by this time.

Lately, he didn't imagine she spent an awful lot of time checking him out, especially from the waist, below. She had a guitarist/songwriter boyfriend named Dennis, and they lived together. She complained he was so obsessed with "making it" he had no time for her. She seemed one hundred percent like the cheating type, if only occasional dalliances. Her roving little green eyes always looked like they were brimming with perverse thoughts and every kind of sexual mischief.

This was one night in which Mallory wanted nothing more than to be alone with Valerie Hale, but certainly not because he had anything illicit in mind. He just didn't like knowing Mona was in the back room, doing God only knew what, besides eavesdropping and intermittently poking her head out. She was not a book-loving fan in awe of Valerie Hale, either. She herself was a poet, and her uncle was supposedly well-connected to some New York publishers. But she "didn't want" to be a published poet because she wanted to use her creative energies to collaborate with fame and fortune-obsessed Dennis. *(Yeah right,* thought Mallory). She claimed, that way, they would become "evenly" famous, and they wouldn't be jealous of one another.

He just wished she'd kindly gather up her things, put them in her hippie-looking black knapsack, all decorated with beads and colorful patches, and get the hell out—provided she drove her junker here today, and it wasn't in the shop, yet again. If so, she had to wait for Dennis to breeze by on his buzz-saw-sounding yellow Yamaha.

Mallory took his time, shampooing Valerie's hair. He found he was actually a bit nervous about his impending job. Here he thought he was well beyond the work-jitters. He could have cut hair blindfolded if he really had to. He relied mostly on feel. That was so essential for him. There always existed the remote possibility, he stood to disappoint a client (like he did to his wife, in bed). But if he managed to please that one client last week, not a regular one but an out-of-towner, then the chances were good, he was in O.K. shape with Valerie.

The biggest problem with the client last week (he hesitated to call her a "girl") was she couldn't hold still. At the same time, it was imperative she talk—nonstop. And when this woman talked, she really talked. It was quite an experience, fixing her crooked haircut.

The woman was from Dallas and had a regular hairdresser, who was young and inexperienced. Woe to the poor girl, was all he could think. Woe to himself, as well. It was even later that day, a Thursday, his most favorite day for watching TV. But a distress signal was a distress signal, and just like on this occasion, Maxine happened to be here, to take the call.

As for the client, she was right outside the door. She was calling from a cell phone. Her husband and she stopped by, hoping the salon was still open. Even though the blinds were closed, she took a chance.

Muriel Pace was her name, and she called the opportunity to have Mallory fix her hair, one more lucky break. Lately her life had been on a winning streak, and after so many years of misery, loneliness, and desperation, it was a real turnaround. It was no wonder she couldn't sit still and seemed to be on her own little personal crusade, to tell the world about it.

Things really came together when, six months ago, she revealed she married a wonderful philanthropist (giving away the fact she found someone filthy rich). He was such a kind, down-to-earth individual, he once and for all shattered her perception of rich people being stuck-up and selfish.

It was a love at first sight encounter that changed the lives of Muriel and Philip. She wasn't too self-conscious to admit she was the housekeeper at a house where he was invited for dinner. Mutual chemistry ensued, and Philip wasn't above later telling his hosts he liked their employee as much as he enjoyed the meal she helped the cook prepare.

Their story went a long way to proving that love conquered

all, and it renewed Muriel's hope that possibly, God willing, she would someday be reunited with her daughter, who she had to put up for adoption, twenty-some years ago. That was all because she had an abusive husband who blamed her for getting pregnant (after initially saying he wanted a child). He was a psychopath, it was safe to say. Muriel ended up running for her life, even though she had no place to go.

She found work as a housekeeper, however. The one stipulation was she would have to give her child up for adoption. Her employers happened to be close friends with a couple, younger than them, who wanted to adopt. Muriel had to surrender all ties to her child, and she would never be told any details of the adoption. That still seemed preferable to starving in the streets because she was unemployed. Then, for sure, she wouldn't even be able to carry the baby to term. This way she was guaranteed of medical help and a job, both before and after she gave birth.

Now, today, with both her former employers deceased (she was actually working for someone else when Phil and she met), there was absolutely no way for her to find her daughter. She had no idea what her daughter's name might be, and her daughter probably didn't know Muriel's—if she even knew she was adopted.

Phil said he would be glad to give Muriel as much money as she needed, to help her track down her daughter, but money in this case was entirely useless. Money obviously not only couldn't buy love, it couldn't change reality.

Indeed, after hearing that heartfelt story, Mallory had to agree, she had made a point, one that he never considered. It made him thoughtful and helped to see that even those who seemingly had it all, didn't. Probably no one in this world, had it totally made. It was all part of the plan, so to speak. Otherwise there wouldn't be a need for heaven (let alone women who needed *him*, to make them beautiful, as they were heaven-sent).

Mallory liked Mrs. Pace, even if she was a bit of a nervous Nellie. Darned if Valerie Hale and she, weren't a lot alike. (And that was as far as his thoughts went, on the matter. He unfortunately wasn't much for deep thinking.)

When it came time to settle up, he found he couldn't take any money. What was that supposed to mean? He had no idea, himself. Mrs. Pace made it more than clear, she was no longer hurting for money (and she certainly was not exactly a joy to work on, with all her head-shaking and body-moving).

Well, Mrs. Pace was adamant he at least accept a tip, especially since Mallory "saved her life." If she felt that strongly, then he supposed he would take the twenty she thrust in his hand. He could order a pizza when he got home, kick back and relax. It looked like it wasn't going to be nearly as late as he'd expected.

Maxine wouldn't mind at all, he wouldn't take any money for his work (but he would not mention his tip to either her or the IRS). Maxine had stayed late to collect the receipts and would rather the slate was clean, until morning. Also, she knew the positive aspects of offering various "freebies" to customers.

Sure enough, Mrs. Pace's parting words were, "I'm going to be telling all my friends about you, Mallory. I hope you don't mind. I have two who spend every winter here and have been trying desperately to find the right hairdresser. And if Phil and I are ever back in town for another fundraiser and *I* need a hairdresser, I plan on calling you. You are a *godsend*."

Mallory thought that last compliment was a bit extreme, but he loved the flattery, nonetheless. It was one of the reasons he so thoroughly enjoyed what he did. He almost felt like a real "somebody," after a day like that.

So too, if he pulled off making Valerie Hale fall in love with herself, he will have scored another major victory. And his ego would be extremely satisfied (until tomorrow, when he had to start, all over again).

He made sure not to go too far overboard with the blow-drying and styling, or poor Valerie would be overwhelmed. He also made sure that she paid close attention to the techniques he used with the dryer and the styling brush.

The closer he got to the "finished product," the less possible it was for her to keep a huge smile from appearing on her face. That made Mallory so excited and thrilled, he certainly couldn't (and didn't) suppress his own urge to smile.

Damned if Mona almost ruined this special moment, sticking her head out of the back room, yet again. He thought for sure she'd slipped out the delivery door by this time. She could well see Valerie's new 'do. The least she could have done was compliment her. But Mona wasn't the type. She in fact didn't seem to like Valerie Hale and was apparently not a little jealous of her. That was a bit unsettling to know, considering Valerie had her own troubles, just like anyone else. Not even the stunners who Mallory "did," made Mona Reilly jealous. It was evidently something besides looks that set her off.

Well, Valerie had Mallory's approval, and she positively glowed once he was finished (and it wasn't just from the heat of the blow dryer). Her new style truly worked the miracle he hoped it would. She could do without the color change, so he decided to wait to mention it. He could bring it up when she wanted to do some more changing.

He gave her a hand mirror, so she could do the final look-over. A gorgeous smile appeared on her face, and no longer could she even attempt to stop it. Mallory couldn't help beaming just as much as she was. He pictured Mona rolling her beady green eyes at the sappy sight.

Valerie couldn't seem to get enough of admiring his work. Wow, was he flattered. She said, "I love it, Mallory. I feel like a new person. I almost *look* like a new person. I wish I would have done this, a long time ago."

He told her, "I'm glad you like it. Otherwise I wouldn't sleep a wink, tonight."

She handed him the mirror, saying, "Oh, don't lose any sleep over me," and Mallory imagined Mona getting in another eye-roll or maybe even sticking out her tongue, in Valerie's direction—and his own, for that matter.

Valerie went way above and beyond the call of duty and gave Mallory an embarrassing $20-dollar tip. Then he recalled that was how much Mrs. Pace tipped him for her fix-up job, but she didn't also have to pay for the work, itself.

He saw Valerie to the door, unlocked it for her, and locked it again, once he said good night. In the meantime, Mona had taken it upon herself to sweep up Valerie's hair. What was this sudden desire of hers, to be so helpful? She typically could hardly keep her manicure station neat and orderly. Everyone who worked here, agreed Mona Reilly was the designated "slob." (And Mallory had her privately tagged as the resident slut.) And she was about to prove him good on his word. For some reason, maybe because Mallory felt entirely defenseless, knowing he loved Valerie Hale but could never have her, he let Mona treat him to her sexual favor, right in his very own chair. God, not even Zoe ever did these kinds of things for him. Forty-six and he didn't ever have any idea, what he was missing. He supposed he ought to have been grateful to Mona, but he wasn't about to say it to her face. He was still as alone in life as ever. He was just a sorry soul who could only take sex seriously if it involved love, not lust.

Mona returned to the back room, not out of shame, of course, but to freshen up before Dennis came to pick her up.

Zipping his pants, Mallory happened to turn slightly and he could have sworn there was some movement, outside one of the windows. The blinds were all completely drawn—he thought. Ah, who cared. He was so tired and care-worn, nothing seemed to matter, not right now. If Mona called that a favor, then she was the only one who got something out of it. Ecstasy was just too damned short-lived, it never failed.

Almost. Al-most. Valerie *almost* stuck her neck out for Mallory, and now she was *so* relieved she didn't. She might have known, he was only flirting with her, with his eyes. By no stretch of the imagination was he dropping sex-related hints. The manicurist had the pleasure of making his day—or his evening, actually. She might have known, her instincts were kaput. That meant one and only one thing. There was no possible way she could write another book, not one worthy of public scrutiny.

Nonetheless, it was all worth it. In the meanwhile, she was checking out. In the morning—or on Tuesday, actually—Anna would have a sight (and smell) to *really* scream about.

"B.P., B.O.D.
(BEAUTIFUL PEOPLE,
BETTER OFF DEAD)"

I awoke one October morning and decided my husband Tom, a former model, was going to die. Hearing him gargle in the bathroom filled me with resolve. It wasn't necessary to glance at the clock to know the time was 7:45, when he chugged Listerine and made the accompanying noises.

Tom's extraordinary handsomeness was no longer enough to keep me from feeling a certain malaise, whenever I laid eyes on him. Obviously, the reverse was true.

What I hated most about him were his unvarying rituals, from the 7:30 A.M. *toilet*, all the way to the 10:30 P.M. "jammie time." (That was *his own* term.)

With the remote control in his slightly greasy mitt (at 9:45 he ate a handful of corn or potato chips, not that he needed to, but he was human, after all), he hopped in bed to watch some more TV, having spent the whole evening doing so, in the living room.

Those grubby hands indicated his true regard to cleanliness, if not his obsession with television.

Lounging there in bed, I considered how remorseless I would feel, blowing the brains out of such an exquisitely-shaped skull. The only problem was I didn't have a gun.

How to knock him off would be my priority. I certainly couldn't rest until the deed was done. The world would be unburdened of a Beautiful Person. All they did was strut like peacocks, making all us short, fat, comparatively unattractive people feel like s—.

If I'm supposedly no great thing, how did I snag this god? We both must have thought we were getting bargains. He correctly guessed a girl like me didn't require as much maintenance as those *other* females, his counterparts.

We first met on a shoot in Maui. Needless to say, he had the good old job of "making love to the camera," while I made sure he looked his absolute best, pulling it off. I'm going to take the liberty of stating my job was the more stressful of the two. Inevitably as well, if the photographer was at all famous, he or she wasn't about to take the blame for crappy pictures.

Tom didn't even take a bad picture, but in the fashion business, perfect is almost good enough. That meant I had plenty of poking, primping, and adjusting to do. All the while I played the mediator for the photographer and his "muses," so to speak. Not for the life of me was I trying to impress this model named Tom.

The entire trip I only saw him when we were working. If he'd turned up in the hotel bar or lobby with one the female models on his arm it would have been the most natural sight in the world—two Beautiful People, together. There was no doubt in my mind he was straight, despite his slightly effeminate air.

There wasn't any chance of dumpy, dowdy me, making a pass at a man like him. One thing I'm not is *dumb*.

As for *his* intelligence level, it was open to debate, and as much as I wanted "to get to know him," I feared there wasn't a lot.

A weekend in September, I was off. The last thing I expected was a phone call from Tom, but that's precisely what I got. He invited me to dinner, at a bistro about halfway between our respective one-bedroom walk-ups. I can't reveal the name of the place because I don't want any Beautiful People descending upon it.

We'd had an early frost and it was quite chilly that night. I vividly remember because it naturally decided Tom's outfit—a camel-colored fisherman's sweater, a black turtleneck and baggy brown cords. Magnificent. He unintentionally fashioned it for me when he stood to greet me. I breezed in about five minutes late, having underestimated the time it would take me to walk from my place.

After helping me remove my black leather trench coat, he signaled to the waiter, to open the champagne. It was only then I noticed he'd order it.

My, but this was starting out with a bang, and it even felt kind of romantic. I'd been completely uninspired by each and every exotic destination of mine. I almost gave up on romance because of it.

And at 30, I wasn't getting any younger. Tom was 26 or 27, himself.

Right now he was flushed and nervous, with something important to tell me. I was 19, the last time I saw a man looking like this. Studying ancient history at Cornell, I planned on doing God only knew what. Mid-term sophomore year, I got bored and eloped with a Literature major/amateur photographer. *I* wasn't in love, but once we arrived in New York, I fell in love with this great, big city.

It was fine with me, Eric never did finish proposing and in fact had to move back to his parents' farm in southwestern Pennsylvania. I stayed, hooked on the nonstop thrills of the city, a world onto itself.

On this night, I was beginning to believe Tom was about to pick up where Eric left off.

Sure enough, he did, and in a touching way, getting down on one knee, ignoring the olive oil and bread crumbs on the cocoa-colored tile floor. Restaurants here simply aren't the cleanest. Even the ones in the five-star hotels feel grimy, no matter *how* spic and span they might appear. It only makes me love New York, even more.

The point is I know what love is, accepting the good with the bad, recognizing that faults add charm to places, as well as people— or they *should*.

As for Tom, the prominent cheekbones, the square jaw, the straight nose, the deeply set brown eyes and the thick black hair, not to mention the perfectly-proportioned, six foot-two inch frame, were no longer enough to keep me from hating him for being such a slave to the clock.

Almost as if he knew what I'd had in mind this morning, this *evening* he had the gall to say, "Let's think about going back to Maui at Christmas. You know, we never really took a honeymoon. What would be better than going where you and me first worked together?"

Over my dead body if yours isn't, buddy, I thought. Luckily he didn't take any heed of my frustration. He was too busy watching television, seated in his recliner. Meanwhile, I was rearranging the sofa cushions for the umpteenth time. Since he got off work a good two hours before me, it was plain to see he took a nice nap. I wasn't about to accuse him of being a lazy slob, nor was he going to admit it.

That was fine with me. It fueled my anger, and I kept my death wish in mind for another week. If he made reservations for Hawaii, he didn't mention anything. How quaint. We both had a surprise.

In all seriousness, what did he think? I quit the place I originally worked because I was sick of traveling. Nowadays I reported to the Dolce Studio, located on the 32nd floor of a recently renovated building, a mere 10 minutes' walk. I loved the trip home because I'd stop at the corner market and pick up some groceries. Dinner that night depended on whatever had looked enticing.

I had it down to a science, how much to buy without it being a burden. (Easier to get mugged that way.) At the same time it was important to give my arms a workout. Even non-Beautiful People can't afford to go to rack and ruin.

On this morning, I was so excited about the plan I had, it was impossible to eat breakfast. When Adonis himself came home from work (the modeling world said bye to him about four years ago, and he worked in the payroll department of a publishing firm. I don't even know the name. Shows you what I thought of it. A friend of a friend got him the job.), I intended to strangle him with one of my Hermes scarves while he sat in his recliner. Actually he'd be waiting for me, which was even better. It was in fact "too perfect," as my friend Izzie the makeup artist would say.

If I wanted to marry a model, it was a shame her brother Allen didn't propose. He was only five feet-seven inches, a more reasonable height for a five-three-me.

Allen was admirably determined, too. There was no other way he would have made it in this mad world of fashion and modeling. Everybody says when he goes to Hollywood, he'll be the "Next Big Thing."

In the meantime, Tom will have gotten fat, although it was taking forever. Finally he had a paunch, but you could hardly see it when he was seated, not at all when he tilted the damned recliner.

You'd think if he was overweight I'd make peace, but no. Those moneymaking cheekbones would still protrude. Besides, my body wasn't getting any younger or thinner, and it just so happened I was *five* years older than him. Strangulation was the only way to end his life, so I could stop feeling the *unfairness* of it all.

With the utmost patience I endured his 8:45 kiss on the cheek good-bye, followed by the sickeningly trite farewell: "Toodles, darling."

Ever so dutifully I handed him a meager sack lunch. Poor thing. He didn't want much at noontime, so he could lose all control in between without having to feel guilty.

It took all *my* control, to keep from laughing in his face and slamming the door on him as he departed.

Feeling like a little dervish, the last thing I wanted to do was sit around for an hour before it was time for me to leave for work. Instead, I puttered around.

At precisely 9:50, I was on my way out the door and the phone rang. If it was Izzie, who should have been doing up a model, I'd tell her, "Later." If it was my mother, I'd tell her, "*Much* later." (She and I did not get along. I never forgave her for letting my father run off with a woman no younger than herself, not a penny to her name, yet was entirely remade by a plastic surgeon. My father fell in love with this synthetic wonder and paid all the long-overdue doctor's bills.)

A woman's voice said, "Hello Madeleine. This is Therese." The only Therese I knew was the receptionist at Dolce Studio. After I returned the greeting she told me, "Gina Winter's using all her own people, so you don't need to come in, lucky duck, you."

I was nearly frantic about missing even one day of work, so I had to ask, "It's O.K. with Vito?" just to be sure. It amazed me he agreed to this arrangement, since he was a stickler for having things *his* way.

Therese lowered her voice to say, "Gina's usually three to four hours late, but she showed up early with all her assistants in tow, stipulating they work. He couldn't very well tell them to spend the day at the museum."

"Have they started?" I had to know.

"Gina's still getting made up, but it's a go, Madeleine, don't wait for the phone to ring," she assured me.

I had a day to kill, when all I wanted was to stay busy until it was time to kill my husband. The last thing I could do was stay cooped up in the apartment, awaiting his return.

Therese signed off but not before recommending I take advantage of the Indian summer weather and go to the beach. There was no use in explaining I could do without seeing a beach, for the rest of my life.

For two cents I would have showed up at the studio anyway, just to hang out. Vito liked me so much, he wouldn't have minded. I'd in fact looked forward to meeting Gina Winters. She was, after all, being touted as one of the hottest new actresses. The picture of her would be on the cover of an entertainment magazine. Even while the shoot was going on, it would be party time in the studio. The fashion mags were the ones who turned shoots into chores.

It was just as well I was off, since I worked better under stress. I went ahead and "executed" my plans for the day: I took a long walk, I had lunch at a place Izzie and I occasionally met, and I saw a romantic comedy at a theater Tom used to take me to, before he got cable TV. Not surprisingly, the movie didn't do a thing for me.

Tired from the walk earlier, I took a cab back to the apartment. Later I'd muster the strength to pay a visit to the corner market.

Barely was the cabbie paid, including being rather generously tipped, he sped away as if fleeing the scene of a crime. He must have assumed I made a mistake and wanted him to return a couple bills. Sometimes New Yorkers really are ridiculously suspicious.

Two seconds later a shot rang out, followed by a woman shrieking. Having turned away from the curb, I looked to my left and not more than thirty yards from me, laid Tom. There was blood all over the sidewalk, and the assailant already disappeared.

Crouched beside him was the source of the ear-splitting shrieks—a blonde-haired beauty, all legs, you could tell, even in her position. I didn't recognize her, but she was probably a model. Only I'd be stupid enough to pass up the opportunity to exploit my looks.

As for Tom, he had one ritual too many, didn't he. At least now I knew why the sofa cushions were always a mess.

"ONE LONER TO ANOTHER"

Marvin Corseglia had enough of those goddarned kids and their motor-scooters. He'd lived in the Camelview neighborhood of Phoenix for close to twenty-five years and never had a complaint about noise—until this. A veritable posse of them passed his house about every night of the week (although Friday nights were the favorite). They were just as happy (if not more so) to use the sidewalk as the street, for their antics.

And it wasn't even a reasonable hour when they initiated their merrymaking. Try 10:00, 10:30, even 11:00 P.M.

What was the matter with kids these days? Marvin wanted to know. As much as they emulated athletes, they themselves were a bunch of lazy good-for-nothings. Standing on those scooters did *not* constitute exercise.

It wasn't as if Marvin Corseglia didn't like kids. Just because he was a bachelor/loner, didn't mean he hadn't any feelings. Hey, he was a kid once, although his mother Agnes was so strict with both his sister Thalia and himself, it could have hardly been called a truly "happy" childhood.

But that was neither here nor there. He lived alone by choice, never married—by choice, all that crap. Nobody *forced* him into this situation. His mother wasn't *so* strict she warped his sensibilities. No. He was smart enough to have avoided that kind of thing.

Anyway, thanks to a generous inheritance from his parents when they passed away, his father Ralph in particular, Marvin was able to retire at age 50 and sell his carpet-cleaning business. Close to ten years now he'd been retired, and taking it easy never felt so good. He didn't miss those working days, one bit.

Marvin got the cash, his sister inherited their parents' house in Omaha. She lived there still, with her husband Roy. He was a carpenter—when he got together the gumption to get up and *do* something.

They had one daughter, Yolanda. Marvin didn't know her very well, since she too lived in Omaha, where she had a pretty decent career, something involving computers. Marvin couldn't say for sure what exactly she did for the company she worked for, but if what she wrote in her occasional letters to him were any indication, she was one smart girl.

Marvin liked her and felt a strange sort of rapport with her, even though this was something he'd never admit to her. Maybe it had to do with the fact she was pushing 30 and had yet to marry, still rather unusual for women. If the complaints from her mother were any indication, Yolanda wouldn't be marrying anytime soon, either. She was too devoted to her career to care about much else.

Being that one good turn deserved another, Marvin had willed his house to his niece. He really had no one else to give it to when he passed away. Thalia didn't want for anything. She had her bum of a husband. The only thing she could have maybe been wishing for was a husband for her daughter. Well, if Yolanda had her own house, she'd be closer to the "ideal situation," wouldn't she. Right now she lived in an apartment. Given the fact it was in Omaha, Marvin didn't know how she couldn't have gone insane by this time. As for himself, he wouldn't have lasted five minutes, having a carpet-cleaning business there. He didn't go outside much, but he sure liked knowing the chances of it snowing, were practically nil.

Up until the time this group of kids got hold of these motor-scooters, it was a peaceful street. In fact, the residents of Buena Vista Lane were all old enough to be grandparents, so any kids seen playing outside were just visiting.

The rabble-rousers came from a street or two over, probably Pueblo Way or Adobe Circle. Funny thing, the names of most of these streets reminded you of the desert Southwest, so you'd never guess most of the houses were traditional, ranch-style structures. It was why he liked it as well as he did, the irony of it all.

He was kind of ironic, himself. To those trouble-making kids, he probably didn't look like he'd raise a stink about their disruptive behavior. The truth of the matter was he'd complained about them many a time, to the police, yielding absolutely no assistance in ending the madness.

Marvin Corseglia was to the point where he had no choice (he felt) but to take matters into his own hands. It was Thursday night and even if he didn't hear a peep from the buggers tonight, you could rest assured they'd be out in force, the following night. He would be ready, starting now.

The first stop was his garage, to assess what he did and didn't have, so he could drive to the hardware store, in the morning. It was only a few blocks away, at 56th Street and Thomas. Everything around here was conveniently located, which went a long way in explaining why his 10 year-old Buick Century only had 45,000 miles. That and the fact he was an armchair traveler, didn't feel the need to get out much and see things. He preferred reading about it all, in a book.

Besides, these motor-scooter demons proved the direction the world was headed in. Why go any further than your front doorstep (or living room window, for that matter) to see (and hear) all you needed, to draw the necessary conclusions?

Yes, he would have to make that trip to the hardware store, there wasn't much choice. There were no odds and ends he could make use of, for what he had in mind to do.

He hoped they *did* terrorize the neighborhood tonight, too. The noise would give him that last bit of resolve to go through with his vengeful plan because he wasn't by nature, a vindictive person. He was just like any animal that preferred flight to fight. When backed against the proverbial wall, there was nothing left for him to do. The police just kept on maintaining they couldn't catch someone they couldn't see, not that they doubted the existence of the seemingly elusive motor-scooter brats. They would have to instigate some sort of stake-out, which they evidently weren't inclined to do.

Their casual attitude toward the whole situation, positively floored Marvin. To him, these kids needed to be reprimanded now, not in a couple of years, when they'd have their drivers' licenses and would be terrorizing the neighborhood in their hot-rods, instead. And next thing you knew, they'd be into booze and drugs, and one night some innocent bystander would get killed.

On way or another, however, the guilty party would get off, scot-free. Daddy would know a good lawyer, who could get his well-intentioned son, off the hook. And thank God for that because he had a scholarship to some hotshot Ivy League school, coming to him. Yes sir, he was still a good kid, he really didn't *mean* to hit that woman walking her dog. (Gee, that sounded like Mrs. Siever, a neighbor of Marvin's, who lived four doors down, in the direction of Monterosa Street.) She was the most devoted dog-walker there ever was. She'd been through a few dogs now, over the years, but all of them got their nightly walk, like it or not. Right now she had a scruffy-looking black and white thing that looked like a cross between a Cocker Spaniel and a Cairn terrier. She must have had her fill of pure-breds because that was all she *used* to have.

Just knowing how loud a barking dog *could* be, kept Marvin from liking them. He really wasn't particularly fond of animals in general, so he certainly didn't want a cat, since *they* were quiet. He liked peace and quiet, but he didn't need an animal around him that might as well not even be there, it made so entirely little noise.

Studies proved that noise caused anxiety, hypertension, shortened tempers, frazzled nerves, and in this day and age, people didn't need it. They were all at the breaking point, as it was.

Too many people. That was what it came down to. There was only so much room for everyone, and it didn't seem like anyone was getting more respectful on one another's space—exactly the opposite.

Marvin's sister Thalia only had Yolanda because she said the whole "child-birth thing" was something she only intended to endure, once in a lifetime.

Marvin was glad. It eliminated a lot of confusion when it came to willing sizable assets—such as a house. He'd heard enough tales of otherwise loving siblings, ready to kill one another, all over the contents of a will. Luckily his parents knew to split everything down the middle when it came to money and material possessions.

If Yolanda didn't have a use for the house, she could always sell it. This was a prime piece of real estate, in all actuality, unassuming though it looked.

He kind of let the back yard go to hell, not for any lack of pride. He happened to prefer an empty swimming pool to a full one and by allowing the grapefruit trees to grow every which way, he had more privacy (as if he didn't have enough, with the concrete wall around it). This way, he could pretend he didn't have any neighbors at all.

The noise-making culprits had to be boys. Marvin couldn't imagine girls getting a kick out of disrupting the neighborhood— unless he just didn't know girls very well, these days. He supposed on determination alone, to be as masculine as possible, there might be one or two in the bunch, however.

Thalia, growing up, wasn't ultra-girlish, but she sure didn't care to play with boys, no games whatsoever. Heck, Marvin didn't like playing with any of them, either. He found them all to be immature and boring. It was no wonder his parents could tell their son was introverted. They weren't exactly the smartest two people and needed a glaring sign. The only thing was, they never could have guessed he was also sociopathic. For people like them, that was harder to figure out.

Marvin could have been a genius if he'd had more intellect. Yolanda must have inherited some of it, what little his family had.

His father Ralph really was a pretty pathetic individual. It wasn't his stupidity that got to Marvin, but rather the fact the man didn't do a darned thing about it. He was perfectly content, being ignorant. He in fact didn't like to do *anything*. Getting up from the couch was an activity, in and of itself. Funny thing, Thalia married the same kind of man their father was. It was darned good *he*, Marvin, never married. Most likely he would have picked a wife that was like his mother Agnes. By this time all her ragging would have driven him to hang himself.

It wasn't so much Marvin enjoyed his own company, as he just never found anyone with whom he cared to spend much time. He could completely identify with his niece's preference for solitary pursuits. It was her *nagging* mother who had the hang-up. Time and again, Thalia complained she "couldn't for the life of her, understand" how her daughter could "waste" so much time, especially Friday and Saturday nights, when she could be out having *fun*. Instead she was *fiddling* with her computer.

As for Marvin, he couldn't say he was ever best friends with his steam cleaner, back in his illustrious carpet-cleaning days, but he would have just as soon stared at that, along with someone's floor, as the face of some woman, seated across from him, in some dimly-lit restaurant that supposedly had ambiance. (If it did, he felt too awkward to be able to appreciate it.)

It came down to false pretenses. Marvin could never even think about ulterior motives (such as the hope of some *sex*, after dinner) let alone be even remotely romantic. If anything, he was secretly a down and dirty kind of guy (but too inhibited to even realize it).

None of that was here nor there, at this point of his life. He went through the closest thing to a "sexual phase," he would ever have to endure, long ago. Thank goodness those days were over. Finished. Done.

It was highly likely, if not entirely true, Yolanda was making some pretenses of her own these days but not happy at all about it. Meanwhile her mother didn't have a clue, the hell her daughter was putting herself through, all to please society.

Thalia made a great mother, actually. She was so naturally maternal, she didn't know when to lay off.

Marvin really was a reasonable person, himself. And in relation to the motor-scooter situation, he would have been glad to issue some sort of fair warning to those kids, but he had no idea where they lived. They were just upright bodies, whizzing by on their noise-makers. They really didn't allow for him to be rational about this.

Milton and Shirley Matterling used to have a bloodhound— or some such breed of baying hunting dog. Marvin was surprised he knew as many breeds of dogs as he did, considering the low opinion he held for "man's best friend."

Anyway, that thing used to bark and bray (you thought only donkeys did that?) at anything and everything and nothing at all, any time of the day and night. Marvin held out quite a long time before crossing the street, to complain. He kept waiting for someone who lived behind or on either side of them, to raise hell. (It didn't help, Frank and Glenda Malcolm were both deaf.)

One day he had enough. Marvin could not get through Chapter Three of the ancient Egyptian history book he was reading. The wording (and the words themselves) were bogging him down as it was. He didn't need to hear that blasted dog. What was worse, just when you thought it had finally shut up, it started again.

It was seven in the evening and even if no one else was distracted from their brainless television-watching, Marvin Corseglia could no longer tolerate being disrupted from his never-ending quest for self-teaching.

He sure as heck surprised Shirley with his sudden "visit," and when he told her what was wrong, she claimed not to have "any idea" her dog had been causing such a ruckus. It was pitiful, how evidently ignorant she was of the noise her dog was making.

He gave her a stern ultimatum: "Don't ever let me hear that dog bark, again, or I'll shut it up, myself."

And he didn't. He had no idea what they ended up doing with the animal, but he heard (not literally, of course) they now had two cats.

Rather than be proud of himself, Marvin never quite felt the same. The look in Shirley Matterling's eyes was what did him in. He hurt her. Truthfully, he didn't know he had it in him to be so mean.

It was just as well he couldn't try to *reason* with the motor-scooter delinquents. They, as well as their parents, would most likely be indignant.

You could just about bet, *all* parents weren't like them, however. The world wasn't *completely* ruined, not yet. The ones who came to mind were the mothers who were with their daughters, selling

Girl Scout cookies outside ABCO's entrance. *Those* mothers would not be condoning their daughters' decisions to do things like ride motor-scooters at 10:30 at night (not that those girls would want to, anyway).

Realistically, girls were smarter than boys anyway, and they didn't even have any interest in mindless pastimes. They didn't care to treat their adolescent years like it was a rite of passage. (And for boys, it seemed to take forever to end.)

Marvin had to admit, he fell asleep last night before he heard a peep from the motor-scooter renegades. It was possible he slept through their racket because if he fell asleep in time, before they made their rounds, he could sleep through just about anything.

But this was *no* time to lay down his guard, not when he knew they weren't finished making noise. Unlike Shirley Matterling and her loud-mouth dog, those little cretins were perfectly aware of the ruckus they made, and that alone constituted most of their fun.

After one more cup of coffee to make sure he was energized (this was no small project, just thinking about it. Didn't he already say he was an otherwise reasonable person?) Marvin was off to the hardware store.

Once there, a clerk couldn't seem to *wait*, to be of some use to Marvin, asking him, "Need some help, sir?" And Marvin had to smile at that, thinking, *Yeah. I've been alone my whole life, but now I've got me an accomplice.*

"I'm looking for some heavy wire," Marvin told him, with a definite nod. "Oh. And some wire cutters. I'm not sure I got a pair sturdy enough for cutting the kind of wire I have in mind."

"Yes, sir, right this way," the clerk beckoned him. His deference made Marvin think this guy knew his customer here was up to something devious. Either way, it sure made Marvin feel like a criminal, and here he hadn't done a darned thing wrong—not yet, anyway.

Walking to his trusty old Buick, purchases in one of those

heavy paper bags you don't see much of anymore, his spirit was renewed. He'd set up his little booby trap only if he really couldn't help but go through with it. He would not make it a requirement. It'd be well and fine with him, if that cloud of anger and vengeance didn't suddenly appear and hover right over his head. As he made it clear already, he was *not* an inherently vindictive person.

Still, that clerk in there, sure made Marvin feel like a deranged person. It was almost as if he had psychic powers, only Marvin didn't really believe in any of that silliness. (He had to say, however, he did *not* imagine he felt something between Yolanda and himself.)

Sometimes Marvin didn't especially look forward to nightfall, but on this day, when he had a plan to put into action, evening couldn't come soon enough. He was actually looking forward to the chain-saw buzz of the motor-scooters.

One thing he had to make sure to do was wait until Mrs. Siever walked her dog past his house, before he did any wire-stringing.

See? Just like a real, live criminal, timing was everything. That one thought alone, kept him from being able to concentrate. He would *not* be getting much reading done this afternoon. That really bothered him because reading was usually his favorite pastime.

To make absolutely sure he didn't fail to see Mrs. Siever and her mutt—er, dog pass the window, by 7:00 P.M., Marvin's main activity involved sitting in his reading chair and staring out the living room window.

About 8:20 P.M., Mrs. Siever and that loathsome dog of hers (sorry, Marvin couldn't help himself) passed the window. As critical as he was of her pet, Marvin had to say, he *wasn't* that way toward Mrs. Siever. In fact, she seemed like kind of a nice lady. It was hard to tell, but she must have had quite a lot of patience, to put up with that obnoxious drunkard of a husband of hers.

At just about precisely 10:30 P.M., Marvin could hear the distant but familiar buzz of the motor-scooter gang.

They were starting kind of late tonight, and anticipation alone had instilled Marvin with all the nerve (and anger) he needed, to go through with the deed. He just so happened to have left the door open and only the screen door was closed. It was something strictly last-second he thought of to do, realizing he'd never have time to finish setting up his booby trap if he waited until they were already coming down the street. And if he had to wait for them to make a second pass, he'd go insane.

In the meantime he'd wrapped the wire around the mesquite tree and only had to attach it to the telephone pole, and he'd be all set. The proper length was already cut, the excess wire (there was lots of it) safely stored where no one would suspect it might be.

His whole body felt tense and incredibly nerve-wracked as he made his way outside. He had his flashlight but he didn't really need it for anything. Thanks to the streetlight, he could see plenty well enough. The rest he could do by feel.

Damned if his hands weren't so shaky he couldn't complete the deed, finish setting up his trap!

The buzzing grew louder. Time was of essence, and there was not one second to lose. Not only were they gaining on him, they were growing in number, he was certain of it. It was now or never. Could he pull it off? Could he give these punks their just reward?

Doris Siever finally (after a week's worth of wondering and debating) reported to the police what she suspected—that Marvin Corseglia was unwell. She knew because *usually* he could be seen sitting in his living room window, reading (and looking terribly lonely).

Anyway, he seemed to be a creature of habit, so something *had* to be wrong.

And she was right. Marvin Corseglia indeed was not well. He was in fact quite dead. Since he wasn't in constant, everyday communication with anyone, it came as no surprise a frequent (nightly) passerby would be the first one to realize something was amiss.

It just so happened Doris Siever paid closer attention to Marvin Corseglia than he was ever aware. And all the neighborhood on

Buena Vista Lane respected him for his partiality to being reclusive. Not a one of them derided him for being "different," in this respect. Part of this respect was borne of the fact he'd been living on this street longer than anyone else. Unless Mrs. Siever was mistaken, her husband Mack and she were in second place. They'd been here quite a long while, too, by the bye. She chronicled her life by the dogs Mack and she had. They had a black Cocker Spaniel named Chester when they first moved here from Pennsylvania. Then they had a miniature Schnauzer named Mopy and now their present dog, Rascal, a Cocker Spaniel-Scottish terrier mix. He was a present from their daughter Cheryl and her husband Larry. Their Cocker Spaniel accidentally got the neighbor's dog pregnant. Those things happened when you lived in Pennsylvania and didn't have a concrete wall around your yard, like you typically did here in central Arizona.

If nothing else, Marvin Corseglia earned all his neighbors' respect for having the staying power he did. And now, come to find out, he had suicidal tendencies his entire life. Nobody would ever know what drove him over the edge. He didn't leave any sort of note, behind. Poor man. Mrs. Siever felt sorry for him all along because be must have been miserable, living alone in that rather big house. Her husband Mack was drunk, in a stupor every night, but at least there was another human being in the house. If worst came to worst, she could get by with just her Rascal for company.

Rascal was actually the one who deserved most of the credit for having alerted Doris Siever to the very real possibility, something was the matter with Marvin Corseglia—not that she couldn't see in his window with her own two eyes. It was just that she'd become so used to seeing him there over the years, she couldn't really "see" when he was indeed no longer there.

But anyway, darned if that perceptive little Rascal didn't take to slowing his pace when they'd pass Marvin Corseglia's house. Now supposedly he hung himself on a Friday night, and that would be about right. She thought she remembered seeing Marvin seated there that evening, when she took Rascal on his walk, later than usual. (She'd made lamb riblets for dinner and had a heck of a time cleaning up afterward.)

What struck her as odd that night was the fact he was staring out the window, he wasn't reading. She probably wouldn't have even noticed him there (which was *usually* the case), except that she involuntarily looked in that direction because she felt as if someone were staring at her.

He was staring at her, all right, but it seemed as if he were actually looking past her. At first she thought there was someone in the street, about to come up behind her, but there wasn't a soul to be seen. That look of his gave her the chills. She would never forget it, for as long as she lived.

The next night she couldn't say whether he was sitting there or not because she made a point of turning her head so she absolutely couldn't see a thing, not even out of the corner of her eye. Obviously he must not have been there, and if Rascal slowed his pace on that night, she didn't pay him any heed.

The following night, however, he noticeably did slow down, and for a second she thought he was going to relieve himself. What a horrible scene *that* would have been. Shirley Matterling had a run-in with Marvin once, about her dog's annoying barking. She was at a loss as to what to do to stop him. Just like some people liked to talk, that dog liked to bark. This occurred mostly when he was outside, but outside was where he lived. The night of the day when Marvin Corseglia complained, Rufus spent it in the utility room.

During the night, the dog died. He was only four years old. It was later diagnosed he had a stroke. Shirley Matterling was devastated. Owning another dog was out of the question. She loved Rufus too much. She got two cats, instead.

Word spread soon enough, that Marvin Corseglia had hung himself with electrical wire. As awful as it was, everyone silently agreed it was better he took his own life, than somebody having murdered him. Then there'd have to be an investigation, and worse, a killer would be on the loose.

Doris Siever spoke up to her husband, something she didn't typically do: "I knew Marvin Corseglia was a lonely, troubled man. I should have at least taken him a loaf of my zucchini bread every once in awhile, just to let him know we cared about him."

From the comfort of the family room sofa, Mack Siever looked at his wife like, *Speak for yourself, woman.* Besides, he had his own theory about the demise of Marvin Corseglia, and who would know better than another man, close to his age? Hang women and their supposed ability to empathize. But he wasn't going to waste his time telling his dog-loving wife. Let her crow all she wanted, about what she mistakenly thought she knew about a man who lived way the hell down the street.

Marvin Corseglia wasn't sick, at least not until the very end. *Something* happened that broke the "camel's back," and he saw hanging himself as the most appealing escape. Who could blame him? He never drank, for God's sake.

When Yolanda first found out she'd been willed her Uncle Marvin's house, she was like, "I don't believe it. It's a joke—right?" as in she didn't know him *that* well, she deserved a house valued at three hundred and some thousand dollars. How could she even leave the Omaha area, when she had a great job? For that reason alone, moving was completely out of the question. Getting away sure sounded nice, however, even *she* had to admit. She would be thirteen or fourteen hundred miles away from her mother, the one who seemed to think advising her daughter was her number one, ongoing priority in life. If this was the price of being an only child, parents ought to be required to have a minimum of two kids, at least in Yolanda's opinion.

Her mother couldn't seem to get over the fact her only daughter stood a good chance (voluntarily) of failing to make her a grandmother, anytime in the future—near or far. At this point she probably wouldn't even care if Yolanda had the kids out of wedlock. She wanted them and that was that.

Yolanda wasn't about to explain to her mother, just how important her career was. It was *all* she cared to have time for right now, and she couldn't guarantee she might not always be this way. Her mother deemed this attitude "selfish," while Yolanda considered nothing to be more selfish than having kids you didn't really want.

And she really didn't want to keep that house Uncle Marvin willed her, so she had it put on the market. She was beginning to think it was some kind of cruel joke he played on her, leaving that, like she needed the responsibility. One look at all the old clothes and personal items he left for her to box and give away, she was more than certain he had some sort of morbid sense of humor of which she was never even remotely aware. Her mother probably didn't have any idea, herself.

Flying to Phoenix to meet with the realtor and look the place over, to make absolutely certain she didn't want it, Yolanda felt like the two-day trip put a serious crimp in her busy work schedule. Her supervisor had been telling her for weeks, she was due for some time off. Ever heedless of such recommendations (she was a completely devoted workaholic, after all) she felt bad, requesting two days off, which turned out to be Thursday and Friday, giving her a four-day weekend. She feared she might never be the same. If she lost even one bit of her enthusiasm for her work, she knew who to blame, and she'd never forgive Uncle Marvin, even though he was dead.

Yolanda didn't have the house appraised but instead decided on a price, based on what other ones in the Camelview neighborhood were selling for. She made the price actually quite low, lower than what the realtor advised. Yolanda simply wanted it sold quickly, so she didn't have to spend seemingly forever, paying the utilities.

Her mother was neither jealous, nor bitter, nor especially happy for Yolanda's relative windfall, following the reading of Uncle Marvin's will. Her mother received a paltry inheritance—a couple thousand dollars in cash and his ten-year old car. Yolanda was beginning to think her mother was glad her brother died.

He requested to be buried in Omaha, so that was certainly easier on Thalia than if he'd made some other sort of request. He was "obviously unbalanced," as far as she was concerned, so any last requests could have been as wild and outrageous as only a sick mind could conjure up.

The house didn't sell and didn't sell. Yolanda wondered what in heaven's name was holding things up. (She thought houses sold like produce in a supermarket, at least when it came to a popular place to live, such as Phoenix.)

Finally it was time to decide what to do—slash the price, rent it—or live in it. The last choice was still anything but enticing because what about her job?

Then, while discussing matters with Amanda Peters, the real estate agent, the truth came out: no one wanted it because Yolanda's uncle "expired" in there.

Yolanda was supremely appalled. Were people superstitious? Was there some sort of strange "vibe" they picked up? Well, Yolanda didn't believe in any of that supernatural mish-mash, so she found it *very* hard to sympathize.

It wasn't even like there was a lingering odor in the house, like maybe you could *smell* a dead body was once in the shower of the master-bathroom. He'd locked the door, so that must have done the trick. (It also helped he had the air-conditioner on, set to about 55 degrees Fahrenheit. For someone who was declared insane, Uncle Marvin had a tidy, no-mess death.) He must have been trying not to inconvenience anyone, including Yolanda. Just maybe he *did* will her the house as a favor to her, *not* to make life more difficult.

Yolanda told the real estate agent to take the house off the market for a couple of months while she decided what to do. If nothing else, people would learn to forget about what happened in the house. Yes, they would. Yolanda would use the typical person's logic (or illogic) to her advantage. She always *knew* her intelligence was good for something besides creating innovative programs for the company that employed her. Darned if she wasn't amazing even herself, with some of her ideas.

Out of the blue (or so it seemed), Yolanda had a once-in-a-lifetime career offer that she knew she'd be a fool to pass up. It involved accepting a transfer to none other than Phoenix, Arizona. If she passed up this opportunity, it would be only out of stubbornness, regarding her refusal to go along with what was "fated" to happen. (Even she admitted there was a point at which a person could be a little *too* practical-minded.)

In her long-term range of goals, what she eventually wanted to do was work independently of any company and only be available on a limited-contract basis. (This was *not* something her boss ever needed to know.)

The most amazing part of her acceptance of the transfer to Phoenix? Her mother was all for it, as it turned out. She may have seemed ambivalent before, but she wasn't anymore.

Then Yolanda realized a possible reason for her mother's sudden shift toward approval of Yolanda moving away—a change of environment just might help jump-start her libido. Another possibility was good old fate would come into play, and Yolanda would meet the man of her dreams in the sunny Southwest. (Even her practical-minded mother fell for this?)

In case her mother cared to know (which she didn't. She never liked the real truth), Yolanda's libido was doing just fine. All the egotistical morons out there, were the ones who tried to kill it, time and again.

If it weren't for that unmistakable male essence, what it did for her, Yolanda would have suspected she might be asexual. (No, contrary to the accusation of one former boyfriend, she was not gay.)

Yolanda wasn't about to string a bunch of comparisons together between Uncle Marvin and herself, but she believed that this was how he felt, toward women. Her mother never spoke of him in anything but a tone of derision—in varying degrees, depending on what she was mentioning about him. Growing up, it was clear she considered herself the younger but wiser one. She was welcome to kid herself all she wanted, but Yolanda seriously doubted that was actually the situation.

That brought Yolanda to something important she wanted to admit right now. (She was kind of ashamed of it, although she should not have been the one to feel as such.) She had a very hard time respecting her parents because they were both so dumb. They were lucky she was such an obedient child, or she could have made life for them, sheer hell.

But now that those days were long gone, they might as well have never occurred. Her impeccable behavior was taken for granted, and that was the end of that.

There was one piece of Uncle Marvin's furniture Yolanda couldn't part with, and that was his favorite chair. It was almost embarrassing that what had sentimental value for him, also did for her.

It was already Friday. She couldn't believe it. She'd had the whole week off and made good use of it, moving in and getting settled. She hardly had a chance to work on her computer the whole time, but she intended to put in an hour or two, this evening. After that, she wouldn't have any trouble sleeping, she would be so exhausted.

Falling asleep was a real issue with her. Once she did, she was pretty much out of it, but until then, one noise heard a single time, would keep her awake the whole night.

On this street, it couldn't be said there was such a thing as traffic. Occasionally a car would pass the house, on its way to Monterosa Street, but there were more convenient streets to use, for going north and south.

Then about 10:30, Yolanda first heard it and she was petrified. She couldn't even place what the collective noise reminded her of. Once she identified them as chain-saws, she really got scared. A gang of chain-saw wielding murderers, that was who it was! She figured Los Angeles wasn't too far away, and just maybe this gang decided to set up camp, right here.

As it became louder, she actually became less afraid, probably because she could tell she was mistaken. No one could move on foot that fast, carrying a chain-saw.

Fortunately, before her imagination conjured up an even more ridiculous scenario, such as aliens had landed from outer space, she caught a glimpse of the source. There were half a dozen, maybe more, motor-scooter riders, using both the street and the sidewalk as their thoroughfare.

They quickly passed but they'd be back again. Yolanda was as certain of that as she could ever hope to be. She also knew that if she couldn't get to sleep tonight, she would be very upset about it in the morning. She didn't give a damn it would be Saturday and she could sleep in. She never slept in, even if she *was* tired.

Besides, tomorrow, she had someplace to visit, bright and early—the same hardware store she stopped in today, for some picture hanging supplies. The clerk bent over backward, to be helpful

She'd need some wire, some cutters—and heck, that clerk was kind of cute. If she still liked the look of him tomorrow, she might ask him to join her for a casual dinner. She wouldn't be able to stay out late, however. She needed to get home and prepare her booby trap.

"TOO GOOD TO BE TRUE"

Mara saw all the food laid out on tables in the banquet room of the Sagebrush Inn, where she worked as a housekeeper, and she wasn't able to resist.

The sign outside the door read "Keep Closed." Indeed, that was precisely what she would do.

Mara never even *read* the bulletins posted on the employee's bulletin board. Why should she obey some lousy sign? You didn't need to be up on the latest (so she thought) to know this feast was in *someone's* honor, and certainly *not* her own.

All this food, just to lay her eyes upon it, was too good to be true. For an old woman who'd subsisted on a diet of beans and rice ever since she didn't know when, it was high time she received her due. She never stole a thing in her whole life, yet she felt her honesty had been taken for granted, by both her employer and the guests at this hotel. (You ought to see some of the valuables people leave laying around. Do they think a woman like her is blind?)

So now there was no time to lose. Any minute *someone* would come along and ruin everything.

But gosh, Mara hardly knew where to begin. Just like "anyone else" (all of the partygoers being rich, she could hardly believe this was an opportunity to group herself with them) she would start with some hors d'oeuvres—or appetizers. She liked the second word, better. It was *plenty* fancy enough.

She stared in wonderment at all the elaborate artwork, displayed upon the table. They call this food? It was a table brimming with masterpieces. If she wasn't so hungry, she'd be content to stand and stare at all of it. She never knew you could fit such visual extravagance, atop a fat square of rye bread.

She hesitated a moment, having second thoughts about treading where she had absolutely *no* business. Then she reminded herself she'd worked at this place for over 25 years and didn't have a fringe benefit to her name.

Still, rather than dirty any of the white china plates sitting next to the trays of finger foods, she would be satisfied using one of the cocktail napkins.

She picked a couple of the most eye-appealing appetizers and carefully placed them on a napkin before putting one then the other, in her mouth and swallowing them. She didn't even bother to savor them yet she already knew they were the most delicious things that ever touched her palate.

She looked back at the table. Goodness, she didn't make even a dent in the inventory. No one would ever know what she'd been up to. Now it finally came in handy, she taught herself not to be a glutton. (It happens to run in the family. Her sister Anita's a real pig.)

Mara had manners, too. She *could* have just picked those appetizers right off the table and plopped them in her mouth. Her family was poor but she'd had a strict upbringing and was taught proper etiquette.

She licked her fingers as a gesture of contentment and as a final nod to how good those appetizers tasted. And now she *really* understood why they were called appetizers. She was more famished than ever. She didn't eat since supper last night (cold beans, leftover from the batch of beans and rice she'd made, two days prior to that). The best part was she ate it while watching TV. That was her favorite thing to do—eat and watch TV. If there was a TV in here, she'd sit down and really enjoy herself.

Mara turned and looked at the tables set up, and the beautiful flower arrangement on one, caught her eye. It looked so delicate— unlike herself. She always was clumsy, and age only made her more so.

Anyway, these partygoers, wherever they were, had it made. Not only did they have a feast for their stomachs, but for their eyes. Mara could imagine the atmosphere, once everyone arrived, and it would be more pleasant than watching TV. If someone put a bouquet in the center of her dingy kitchen table, she'd stare at that, instead of the television screen.

Growing up in Milltown, a small, north-central Arizona town, she once had the opportunity to step right outside her family's house in the late spring and summer, and pick all the flowers she wanted. Ever since she moved to this now smog-ridden city called Phoenix (all to find work and a husband), she'd missed out on many of the simple pleasures she once enjoyed.

Just for that, Mara decided to grab a plate and fill it with appetizers. It was as large as a dinner-sized plate, but it would still be impossible to tell she filched some snacks.

Where is everyone? she wondered as she nonetheless shamelessly piled the plate with appetizers. She couldn't dwell on the question because she was too busy concentrating on food.

She did realize, however, that the plate she took was different from the one at each place setting—and she didn't mean in regard to size.

No, the china used at the table had a most distinctive, ochre-colored pattern, while the plates for the appetizers were plain.

Suddenly, it mattered to Mara, to only dine upon the best. And while gazing at the crystal water and wine glasses, her throat started to feel dry. She sure would like something to drink, tap water if nothing else (but white wine would be nice).

The appetizer plate emptied, she exchanged it for one of the shiny, clean dinner plates. She determined she would fill this up with as many goodies as would fit, really pile it on. Whatever she didn't finish, she would give to one of the stray cats she'd seen around the back door of the kitchen. (Mara always was a fanatic about not wasting *anything*, not even leftovers.)

As she heaped food upon food, the individual entrees soon became indistinguishable messes. She momentarily worried she wouldn't be able to taste any food, with all the juices, sauces and spices, mixing together. But then, the bright side was she was kind of actually making a whole new dish, wasn't she.

If she *did* manage to eat all this, she was going to become *very* sick—that she already knew. At the same time, she wanted nothing more then to stuff herself, like she was a Thanksgiving turkey. Clearly it was a sort of mission of hers, to see this out, overeating and all. She liked the idea of indulging at someone else's expense. That made some potential discomfort, worth it. She also liked the idea of being under the gun, so to speak.

Maybe that last enticement was a result of a little jealousy? O.K., here comes the explanation. Mara's sister, Anita, had *her* day in the sun, three years back, and Mara never got over it.

Anita'd won a five-minute shopping spree at Herrera's Cash'n'Carry discount store in downtown Milltown, where she lived with her two grown daughters (neither of whom ever left home and made anything of herself). All these years, Anita was perfectly content to play the queen bee, with her two grown daughters catering to her every whim.

Then, to top it off, she won that shopping spree. Do you know just how many times she must have entered the contest, to win that prize? It shouldn't have even been a surprise, when she found out she won.

Anyway, the shopping spree (with Anita in action, a sight to behold, in and of itself) was videotaped, and Mara had the distinct *pleasure* of watching it—twice—while sitting on the sofa, in Anita's double-wide, at Milltown's Desert Sunshine Trailer Park. If you asked Mara what Anita really needed, she'd say a new sofa, not all the damned bric-a-brac she heisted during that shopping spree. (Among other things, she got a purple afghan for the sofa, when what it needed was new stuffing, at the least, if she couldn't *bear* to part with it.)

Mara, *she* would have hustled her behind over to the jewelry locked behind the cases, which would have been okee-dokee with her. What she would have been after were the more reasonably priced trinkets, found on the carousels, both free-standing and on the glass cases.

Are you surprised, someone like *her*, unused to fine dining and even just the finer things in life could *know* about adornments of any kind? Well, she was sorry to have to pawn her wedding band after her husband passed away, but she needed to pay the hospital bill. (And he generated quite a tab, before taking his final breath. Mara wasn't surprised at all, he was a pain in the neck, right up to the bitter end).

Bric-a-brac and food—the extent of what Anita lifted off the shelves of Herrera's Cash'n'Carry. Hostess' stock would go up, if just a few more people ate Twinkies and cupcakes in the vast quantities Anita did.

Anita always was the glutton, the Miss Piggy of the two of them. Just by looking at them both, however, you couldn't really tell which one was the most fond of food. Genetics blessed the two with short, wide bodies and *slow* metabolisms.

And Anita's daughters, Dolanda and Yvonne? The same way. But they still had youth on their side, so they weren't as fat as their mother, who really ballooned since Christmas. She even started complaining, she might have to go to Herrera's Cash'n'Carry just to buy new clothes, in a bigger size.

What really galled Anita was Herrera's had their drawing again this year, and *she* didn't win. She'd entered more times than ever, even waited the required three years (since she won) to be in the running. She was lucky she squeaked in when she did, in the three-year wait because the owner of the Cash'n'Carry was considering changing the wait to five years.

Mara kind of wished this little spree of *hers*, were on videotape. She'd like Anita to see it someday. She was such a pig, you could bet she would be *very* jealous.

All through their lives, it was the other way around. Mara was the younger sister, always jealous of everything about her older sister. The crowning blow came when Anita married an intelligent, sincere, hardworking man, the kind Mara needed more so than Anita did (if only because Mara was the kind of woman better off being provided for, rather than *doing* the providing).

Life wasn't fair, it was a simple as that. That was one of the many hard lessons Mara had to learn on this journey. All these lessons were merely ways for God to show her *who* had the final say.

But someone like Anita? Impervious. Completely so. She didn't care about a thing, except herself. If Mara could only be jealous of her sister for one single thing, it would be her sister's nerve, her aptitude for ignoring *everything* but what went on within the confines of her double-wide. (Might as well have just described her, she was getting so fat.) Even so, she still wasn't as clumsy as Mara. It only figured, the sister with the conscience would be the one cursed with being a clodhopper. If you didn't believe Anita could *possibly* be so selfish as to *only* think of herself, then Mara would offer that her sister also spent her days concerned with what was going on, on TV, and what was (simultaneously) going into her mouth.

And yes, Mara had to admit, her fondness for eating and watching TV probably equaled her sister's. It was about the only point the two could agree upon, without getting into an argument.

An emotionally and physically abusive bum-drunk. That was the kind of man Mara married. The saddest part? She *loved* the sonofabitch, up to the very (and very bitter) end. Even though they couldn't "seem" to have kids (and God knew, Mara wanted them) she took care of him, still.

She felt in essence, she seriously failed in life because she never became a mother. But believe it or not, the fact Mara didn't have kids but Anita did, was *not* a source of bitterness. Mara never *did* hold that one against her sister, not at all, if only because Anita's two daughters were such lazy, slatternly things. (And Anita married a decent man). Mara hated to think what her husband and herself would have made.

Mara concluded there was a reason behind her urgency to enjoy herself. A decent break in life, never came her way, and she finally knew to take advantage of this situation. (When she referred to "breaks," she meant the kind of ones most people take for granted, such as a real house to call your own (not an apartment), kids, financial security, and someone to look after you in your old age.

Like Mara, Anita lost her husband to a prolonged ailment, but Anita has those two daughters to take care of her. See? Anita always did have it made and nothing's changed.

With that, Mara sat down. She looked at her overloaded plate, realizing she didn't have a chance to grab a roll. What would a meal be, without some bread? Goodness sakes, after all.

Only reluctantly did she get back up in search of some bread. In the process, she clumsily caught her foot on the chair leg, causing her to topple to the floor. On the way down, she hit her head just so, on the side of the table. Her skull proceeded to crack, and then again, when it hit the tile floor. She died instantly.

"My God! You know what, Dane? This is the surprise ending we've been looking for!" writer/director Mitch Mellon tells executive producer Dane Dawson of Hollowhead Productions, as he stares at Mara's prostrate body. "You're an absolute genius!"

Dane Dawson thinks, *I only wish*, and wonders what he can dream up to tell this guy, so he can somehow take the credit. It's the only way *he'll* ever get writing credit for anything. (He has nary a creative bone in his body.) This is why he'll never really "make it" in life. He has this golden opportunity to take advantage of an extra (or someone's body double) passed out on the floor, and he doesn't have a clue what to say or do. God, is he jealous of this fucking writer/director Mitch Mellon. He's going to pass Dane up, real soon. When he wins his Oscar, is the eccentric son of a bitch going to remember to thank Dane Dawson? Probably not. Just like everybody else, he'll forget. What the hell is it about success, that numbs a person's brain?

Dane turns to walk the other way, the direction he assumes Mitch Mellonhead went. Ha! Good one. Get the joke? That can be the guy's name, once he buys out Dane's Hollowhead Production Company. Fine with Dane. He can move to Europe, where they still appreciate film as art.

The next thing he knows, he's tripping on something. It feels like someone stuck a roll of carpet, under his feet. Wasn't this damned floor, tile?

A second later he feels a hand take a confident (strong) hold of his left arm, soundly saving him from a nasty (and very embarrassing) fall. That would have been right in front of all his employees, for God's sake. Forget keeping up appearances for the lucky-duck writer, for a second. Once big-time gets Mitch Mellon, Dane is certain he himself will still be stuck, ordering around all these minions.

Saving Dane Dawson, Mitch cries, "Whoa there, pardner. I verily believe you were going to take a nose-dive. We don't want to lose you, man, especially not before this thing wraps. We shoot this scene with your extra lying there, and we're home free. Tell her to hang in there another hour, hour and a half and we'll have it."

Bolstered by dimwit Mitch Mellon's determination this was all Dane's idea, Dane says, "I'll do my best, but I can't guarantee anything. You know how it is, with these non-union actors." Then he looks down at Mara's inert body, marveling it hasn't moved. This really *is* too good to be true. A little smile creeps across his face. He'll have his day, yet. This is only the beginning.

"HIS PERFECT LIFE"

Randall Schubert in his yellow shorts, walking his two Golden Retrievers, Shannon and Brandy, is quite the sight. He's taking them on their morning jaunt down Desert Jewel, the ritzy Scottsdale street on which they live.

He's been married eight months now. He hasn't changed his dorky dressing habits, one bit. He figures, "No one will see me," meaning no one who lives on this street. But how about the passersby, the commuters in their cars, headed south, using this as a back road?

There aren't too many of those, he retorts. Besides, they're all strangers. (He happens to have a certain arrogance that transcends logic.)

In a minute the cars will be soaring through here because he seems to have forgotten, it's later than usual. Last night he and his beautiful, blue-eyed, blonde newlywed wife Crystal attended a sumptuous gala. It was a fete he hopes is never again held on a Wednesday night. He's already looking forward to next year's bash but can't stand the thought of getting up for work the following day.

Hopefully he didn't make too much of a fool of himself, last night. He was having so much fun, drinking and dancing, he was heedless of everything else. Clearly he's not accustomed to enjoying himself.

Randall is rich, successful, and now married to the most beautiful, conscientious woman in the world. He considers himself extremely lucky, but as they say, "Once a bachelor, always a bachelor."

Of all the people who most wholeheartedly believe this? His mother, Hilda. That's the kind of approval he gets, having found the right woman, with whom he fell madly in love, at first sight.

He has friends (Brad Fennel comes to mind, and he's really his best friend) who are working on their second and third marriages. Randall meanwhile had been patient and discerning, yet still realistic he might never find the right girl.

Poor Brad. He married a woman who's not into diamonds and furs but horses, the most expensive obsession a woman can have.

The last thing Randall counted on was finding a woman who's perfect in every way, and he means perfect, as in compatible. He's not one to fall into that trap of excluding reality. He knows absolute perfection doesn't even exist, but if it did, it would be in the form of his wife.

His mother did not meet her future daughter-in-law until the wedding and when she did, took an instant dislike to her. The image is stuck in his mind, and he can't help feeling uncomfortable because of it.

To this day (via long-distance, as she lives in Dallas), Randall cannot get an answer out of her, as to why she doesn't like Crystal. She won't deny it, however.

Randall feels he's been given no choice but to put the whole issue on hold, in his mind. When he does talk to her, he's limited to discussing the weather, her rheumatism, and how much money his younger brother Michael needs, to extricate himself from the latest slew of debts.

Michael's not married, need that be mentioned? What Michael needs is a keeper.

Probably *some* woman would love him, for his charming personality, his rakish good looks, even the fact he *is* a rake. What he survives on is Hilda's weakness of character—i.e. she can't resist his continual pleas for financial help.

Through it all, Michael is the one she most adores—or simply the one she adores. He was always the troublemaker, and she loved him all the more for that.

Randall and Michael grew up in a modest suburb of Boston, where conservatism was the norm. Even so, with Michael's hippie-ways, he came closer to fitting in than Randall, who always felt like the nerd.

Sometimes Randall wonders if he never really escaped that image of himself, so he's *compelled* to wear yellow shorts.

As the president of his own computer consulting firm, he's climbed the ladder of success through determination and hard work. Despite it all, he feels as if he lost his mother's regard, having committed himself to marriage.

He kind of has an idea, what it comes down to. She thinks, after all Randall has done (including being in the army, from which he was honorably discharged, after critically injuring his right leg), he *still* lacks the discipline and compunction to hold a marriage together.

Randall maintains he has what it takes and he's even been known to make enemies of his friends, by offering unsolicited advice on marriage "ground rules." He believes because he's been single for so long, he knows everything about being married, as observed from the outside.

There's no doubt, his mother's ill-fortune in married life has a major influence on her regard (or lack thereof) for Crystal.

It was rumored (a subtle way of saying it's a fact) Randall's father Calvin (known as Vinny by his close friends), at the age of fifty-some, ran off with his twenty-something secretary. She proceeded to rob him clean, leaving him penniless and entirely humiliated, in a dingy, Miami Beach hotel. There he hung himself, out of what must have been pure shame.

The only good that came out of it was Hilda received a large inheritance. To this day, she lords over it (except of course when Michael wants some).

Just about every time she talks to Randall, she reassures him, Michael and he will each get half. It's hardly any reassurance to Randall, however. What Michael needs is for Randall to watch over his share. Randall hates having money go to waste, and that's exactly what will happen.

It's not to say Randall is frugal, but his father worked very hard to make what he did. He was in fact somewhat of a workaholic, and overwork stressed him out.

The age discrepancy between Randall and Crystal, bothers

Hilda, as well. She knows what a "younger woman" can do to an "older man." She obviously believes her son is as prone as anyone, to fall prey.

Proof of Crystal's youth is the fact she can get by with exercising but twice a week and still stay in shape.

Luckily she only likes to exercise indoors, on her stationary bike. She's much too alluring to be seen exerting herself, especially not in those skimpy outfits of hers.

Randall maintains he's not the jealous type, something he vehemently believes. He's quick to make that point as clear as the clearest day possible, here in the Phoenix Valley. Given the pollution index here some days—well, so what. Randall is proud to say he's his own person, knows the irresponsibility of letting negative emotions get the better of him.

If money was a factor in helping Crystal say yes to Randall's marriage proposal, so be it. At least that is what he *claims*.

To backtrack a little, as he thinks about all this some more, he admits he actually can't *afford* to get jealous because he can't trust himself not to retaliate in a stupid, thoughtless way. And what he'd do would be *so* dumb, he'd be better off not living afterward. Why is that? Because he will have totally lost all respect for himself.

Randall must confess, there *is* some risk to marrying a man like himself, if only because he's set in his ways. His yellow shorts are the ultimate proof.

Still, he loves Crystal all the more because she *doesn't* make a comment as he bounds out the door, his two dogs leading the way, straining at their leashes. He's dressed like a dweeb and *should* be told so.

On a morning like this one, however, her eyes were still closed when Randall left the bedroom. She too had a late night, although she spent most of it waiting for him to finish drinking and dancing.

Usually she's already up, fixing his breakfast, French toast and bacon or else an omelet and link sausage, are his two favorite meals. A "simple" breakfast is scrambled eggs and toast.

She claims she rarely cooked before knowing Randall. She worked at the front desk of the posh, intimate Sienna Resort. That was the very place he first laid eyes on her. Randall was there to speak at a convention, as a last-minute substitute. Talk about coincidences.

In the past eight months she's become quite the gourmande. She must have some sort of natural affinity for it. And now that the courting days have passed, the two of them stay home for dinner, most evenings.

That's fine with Randall because he gets sick and tired of the approving gazes, even from goddamned waiters.

Randall has found he prefers restaurants with waitresses, and the clientele is predominantly past the age of 50. (He'd say 45, but damned if he's about to categorize himself with an "older crowd," not when his wife's 29. He intends to hang on to 45, until he's 70.)

He's purposely forgotten his birthday, not that he's ever been fond of keeping track of such trivialities. There was no celebrating them in his youth, so he certainly doesn't want to now, not when the last thing he wants to do is grow old.

Randall's father didn't make his fortune until the family had become accustomed to living very modestly. Now that his mother has the power of money, it's gone to her head. She really does believe she has something over Randall, with her "reassurance" he stands to inherit half her fortune.

If she *were* to disinherit either one of her sons, it would be Randall. Michael is quite simply beyond reproach. He has no expectations to live up to, either.

It all comes down to Randall having married Crystal. He made a grave enough error by marrying at all, let alone her. As much as Randall trusts his own judgment of people, over his mother's, she makes him have niggling doubts. And he's going to let those doubts get to him.

His mother must suspect Crystal of being the same kind of woman who preyed upon her husband Vinny. If she'd like to know, Crystal didn't marry for financial security (but it sure helps). At Randall's recommendation and subsequent urging, she quit her job, to devote herself full-time to the household. She even eliminated the need for a maid because she *likes* housework.

Randall wants to be pardoned if he's incorrect, but that hardly seems like a gold digger to him. It sounds to him like she's a woman who is devoted in the truest sense of the word (not to mention more than willing to run all those errands he would fit in, on his way to or from the office).

Come to think of it, Randall kind of misses some of the places he used to go. One of them was the drycleaners. An absolutely adorable Asian-American girl worked there and was always so friendly to him, in that subtle but sincere way that's indigenous to them.

Another place he used to frequent was the Boston Harbor Restaurant and Caterers. Never would he surprise Crystal with dinner because she'd feel like she cooked something for nothing. He'd have to call her first, and that would ruin the spontaneity. That is the price to pay for having someone in his life.

Randall has told Crystal, countless times, how much he likes that restaurant. They don't go there more often because the atmosphere is a bit too casual for his taste. It makes a better lunch-stop.

A car *flies* past. The goddamned driver about took Shannon to work on the hood of his car. Randall *thinks* it was a man. He gives women the benefit of the doubt, not to drive so recklessly. If one did, he bets she'd be in a sports car, not a big, silver Mercedes sedan.

This is the first time he's had a close call, walking his two prized pooches. For the sake of safety he's always walked them into the traffic, Brandy on his left, Shannon on his right. Until today, he never thought he stood to witness a calamity, involving none other than his favorite of the two.

Since he feels so strongly, he should have trained Brandy to walk on the right. Randall quite honestly didn't intend to get two dogs. He simply couldn't decide between the two.

Damned if he doesn't love them both. He never thought he could love anything but a woman.

Neither did he expect two dogs to have such entirely separate personalities, and Shannon's is what makes her his favorite. She's more quiet, not as frisky as Brandy. She seems more thoughtful than her sister, if that's possible.

"Damn it!" Randall seethes as another car whizzes past, not bothering to allow much room. He really *can* tell it's later, and he resents the fact he's been diverted from his schedule, even this little bit. And there was no mistaking it, a woman was driving that black BMW station wagon.

By now the trio is almost to the corner, and the majority of the traffic flow (which it has come to be) *seems* to be going in the opposite direction—or soon will be. Randall is adamant about not turning around before reaching the corner.

Shannon and Brandy fortunately have a big yard in which to play, or they wouldn't get enough exercise, not just from their daily walk. Still, it's a good mile and a half in distance. Dogs like them really need a jogger, to put them through their paces. In Randall's mind's eye, he sees a rock-solid, twenty-something guy, six-pack abdomen, black hair wet with sweat. *He's* wearing shorts that are shorter than Randall's, but guess what? They're *red*, a much more masculine color to cover those sinewy thighs.

Randall can't jog, thanks to that old army injury. He stresses his right leg in any way and immediately he's in pain. If he wants a washboard stomach he'll have to get it by lifting weights (and eating less).

Staying in shape *is* hard work. It requires the kind of religious devotion he saves for his job. Plus, he really likes to eat, and he's not one to deprive himself of fattening foods. The only thing he's ever deprived himself of is his sexual indulgences. God knows, Randall could have any woman he wants.

And since he's happily married, that really should be in the past tense. Hey, it's not *his* fault that money has a certain allure, especially for women who are none too bright.

Crystal, however, is intelligent, not that it makes her completely immune. Having money to freely spend is something new to her.

But Randall never dated any women who had money. Or maybe it should be said he didn't ever *want* to.

And now, there's newly-divorced Mrs. Freida Stevens, with

her Mediterranean-style mansion, perched on the corner of Desert Jewel and Arroyo. She has the option of saying she lives on either one of those streets but chooses Desert Jewel, the same address as Randall.

It's too late to have any regrets, but sometimes he wonders, *What if?* because he always was attracted to her.

Randall and his dogs pass her house and he tells himself everything happens for a reason. He simply wasn't meant to be with her. God must get a real kick out of putting powerful, successful men like Randall, in their places, is what Randall concludes.

Meanwhile a good dose of reality appears seemingly out of nowhere, in the form of a dozen or more male cyclists. A collective sense of camaraderie is in the air, and Randall finds himself resenting every goddamned one of them, their taut, muscular bodies clad in colorful spandex. He finds himself hardly able to keep from making a rude comment, as they can barely seem to give Randall and his dogs, any room

He squelches the urge, however, just like his mother "taught" him, and he was never even the one who needed reminding.

Suddenly Randall's compelled to start jogging. He's tired of having Shannon and Brandy tugging at their leashes, ignoring his commands to heel. They usually listen to their master, too. It's as if they're purposely getting on Randall's nerves, having sensed he's a little uptight this morning.

The late start has got to be what has made Randall so anxious and frustrated. He's always been a slave to his schedule and all his various rituals. He also knows he won't have s much time as usual, to linger over a second (or third) cup of coffee.

He could certainly *afford* to be late to the office, but since he's the boss he feels obligated to set an ongoing example.

Roaring around the turn and whizzing past Randall and his two dogs is a red Alfa Romeo Spyder. The car's moving so fast, it's impossible to see the driver. Once again, it takes all of Randall's control not to give him/her/it, a piece of his mind.

He's almost positive it was a woman. These days, they are hell-bent on proving they can be as aggressive as men, and they're doing a damned good job.

The next thing he knows, his knee goes out on him and he about falls down.

"Hold up, girls," he beseeches Shannon and Brandy, as they remain oblivious to what's happened and continue pulling on their leashes.

The bicycle gang ought to see Randall now, looking more pathetic than ever.

And he's more than willing to describe himself as such. Of all the "successful businessmen" who gather at Desert Verde Country Club (to bullshit. This is not about anything else.), he's pretty awfully goddamned sure he's the only one who did not have his wife sign a pre-nuptial agreement.

Somehow, his mother knows this. She also holds it against him. Not only that, it's Crystal's fault she said yes to Randall's marriage proposal.

There are tears in Randall's eyes. The pain in his leg must be getting the better of him.

Finally he arrives home. The dogs aren't even breathing hard, while Randall's about ready to pass out. He feels completely outdone.

Randall would give anything to be young again but wouldn't trade the wisdom that comes from experience. He's one of those who must learn everything by first making plenty of mistakes.

Shannon and Brandy are in their prime. Randall got them right after he bought this four thousand square-foot, two-story, Spanish-style house, complete with a pool and a large back yard. He wasn't lonely, he just wanted some company. In fact, at the time he was seeing a woman by the name of Lydia Gephardt. She was saying, "I do," to herself, when the last thing Randall had on mind, was to propose.

It's interesting to note, how Randall's mother doesn't think he was sufficiently discerning when he chose a wife. She must know he followed his heart, just like she did.

With that, Randall realizes the reason for her partiality to

Michael. And that is what the basis of contention is, between Randall and herself.

Also, his mother probably did something hokey, like checked out Crystal's astrology chart and concluded her sign and Randall's (whatever it is) are incompatible.

Offhand, he can't think of when Crystal's birthday is, but it'll come to him. He wants to buy her something special (expensive) when it comes around.

It'll be the big three-oh. He wonders what she'd think if he threw her a surprise party. Randall's only problem with that is the probability of it not turning out to be much of a surprise, for whatever reason. Not just anybody can pull it off.

Now that he finally stopped breathing hard, he figures he'd better go in the house. As it is, he used up what few leisure minutes he had. At least Crystal didn't see him suffering and wonder how she could have married a man who's on his last legs.

What's with this sudden self-consciousness about how Crystal regards himself? Randall wants to know. She doesn't even *think* that way.

He limps into the house, trying not to imagine what he must look like. If he can make it upstairs, he's going to look for the business card a masseuse by the name of Vicki Vixen, pressed into his hand last night, at the party.

She must have seen Randall gyrating, from across the room and *knew* he'd be hurting this morning. It just didn't end up being for the reason she might have anticipated. Randall can hold up just fine, when it comes to having fun. Sometimes looks don't belie the truth.

In the case of Vicki Vixen, that last name is probably an alias, but it certainly seems appropriate. Short, petite and exuding sexuality, she's a likely antithesis of Crystal. All they seem to have in common is their naturally golden-blonde locks, although Vicki's are cut into a sporty bob, while Crystal wears hers long.

Randall hopes she makes office calls, not just house calls. He doesn't want Crystal to have to witness a masseuse (an attractive one, no less) showing up at their home. As for himself, he already knows he couldn't tolerate her, having a masseur.

Randall realizes he hasn't had a massage, a *real* massage, in heaven only knows how long. There was one place he used to go, where clients had the option of more than just a body massage. Straight-as-an-arrow Randall never even had the nerve to inquire what the various "services" were.

Having left Shannon and Brandy in the utility room, Randall goes upstairs. As soon as he reaches the master bedroom, there's the sound of the shower water running. He wonders *why* Crystal isn't in the kitchen, getting his breakfast ready. She's got the whole damned day to take a shower. (He didn't bother to check and see she already prepared most of it.)

Needlessly infuriated, he stomps into the walk-in closet. While he's *waiting* to use the shower, he can look for Vicki Vixen's business card. If he remembers correctly, he placed it in his lower left suit coat pocket.

As he's groping for it, the shower water is turned off. Then voila, he finds the card. He feels slightly appeased, but nonetheless he *is* awfully edgy today.

It'll be a few minutes before she even has on her robe. She's even more methodical than Randall, when she dresses and undresses.

"Randall? Are you in the house?" Crystal calls loudly enough to be heard downstairs.

"I'm right here!" Randall tells her, as if he *was* downstairs.

"Oh! I'm sorry," she says, clearly surprised he's so close by. The bathroom door still closed, she tells him, "Your breakfast's about ready. I did that first because I didn't know what time you'd left for your walk."

Randall tried to take her willingness to please into account, yet he *still* can't seem to help but get exasperated. Even if she's making him an omelet, he can't appreciate the gesture, not today.

Moments later, she heads downstairs. Randall stays hidden in the shadows, in the closet. He watches her like an animal being preyed upon. In her snow white terrycloth robe and matching terrycloth slippers, hair piled atop her head, she looks positively marvelous. The sight of her is enough to make him spring forth, become the one who's doing the hunting, yet he hangs back.

Sometimes Randall is almost sorry eating is one of his favorite pastimes. When he finds himself suffering like this, he takes it as a personal affront.

Crystal's omelet did it. Either that or else the sausage patties. He wants to blame the omelet because more of the blame can rest on her.

He wonders how he even got to work, but then his stomach wasn't hurting, not like it is now. Seated at his expensive granite-top desk, at least he can say his knee and ankle don't hurt. He has every intention of calling Vicki Vixen, as soon as it's a little later. He's not sure what time you call a masseuse for an appointment, but he'd like to make sure she can come at six P.M. (After much careful calculation, Randall decided that would be the best time.)

And when he *does* call her, he's going to use his private line. He sure as hell doesn't need his gossip-monger secretary Dorothy Ratzel listening in on his conversations.

She *usually* leaves the office by 5:30, allowing plenty of time for Vicki to arrive, minus having the two collide. (Randall really does believe he can cover all the variables.)

But Dorothy means well, Randall doesn't want to sound like he doesn't appreciate her dedication and loyalty.

She arrives before Randall, every morning, and that says a lot, right there. So what if she uses the extra time to fiddle around on the computer?

Still, Randall knows that spreading rumors is one of her favorite pastimes. Fortunately he has yet to have one, come back to him. (He's aware not even the boss is immune to the possibility.)

Dorothy can't be blamed for enjoying gossiping as a hobby. She's divorced, lives alone and only has a cat to keep her company. She had two but one died not long ago. That's the one time Randall saw her upset. She even failed to greet him that day.

And her morning pleasantries are no trifle. She does so with genuine enthusiasm, as if she wants you to be as happy as she is.

Yes, she did notice Randall limping into his office earlier, and she demanded to know what was wrong, in that polite but firm way of hers.

Randall fudged his reply, saying he tried taking up jogging again. (He wasn't about to admit exasperation was what got him to lift his legs, higher than usual.)

Dorothy's been with Randall through the times when he had a couple of rather rocky relationships. She never outrightly offered any advice on how to deal with certain situations, but she always did one hell of a job, commiserating with him.

So far, she's been mum about Crystal, hasn't really mentioned anything, good or bad.

Dorothy first met her at the office Christmas party. Randall wasn't married to her yet. If Dorothy had known what was destined to transpire, she undoubtedly wouldn't have been so nice to her.

The coincidental way Randall and she met, is what makes Dorothy scornful of her. Women obviously can't be happy for other women who are lucky in love.

Randall remembers the day he first laid eyes on Crystal, as if it happened only yesterday. (And really, it wasn't *that* long ago.)

He spied on her from across the lobby of the Sienna, indulging in the fact she had no idea she was being watched.

Even once she *did* know, Randall didn't care. That was how he knew he was in love.

Later he would find out she was there to fill in for a sick co-worker, just like he himself was filling in for a speaker who was ill.

Randall did some business-card leaving of his own, but she did not end up calling him. He ended up getting ahold of her, barely a week later, and he was already lovesick as hell. He had called the hotel and ended up speaking to Ronald, the co-worker who'd been sick. Randall identified himself and Ronald obviously took him for legitimate because he told Randall the days when Crystal worked.

She was surprised to hear from Randall when he called. She must not have been forewarned, he wanted to get ahold of her.

Randall's stomach starts making gurgling sounds. He knows his nervousness isn't helping matters. Today he has a lunch date with a bigwig potential-client. It's *not* the kind of day he wants to have to deal with a case of food poisoning or whatever the hell he's got.

Right now the mere *words* "food and drink," make him nauseous. Having to skip lunch would be bad enough. To think he couldn't hack a power lunch, complete with double martinis, is a mortifying possibility because he'd feel like he missed out.

Before Randall gets down to work, he gives Vicki Vixen a call. *Now*, of all times, he realizes he failed to kiss Crystal good-bye. It's bad enough he didn't kiss her good morning. He was entirely too distracted to think straight (and doesn't feel any better, now). He can tell it's going to be a *long* day.

But he doesn't *need* to feel bad. As far as he's concerned, it's *her* fault he's sick this morning. What he'd like to do is call *her* and let her know as much. He doesn't want her to spend the day having *too* much fun, oblivious to his pain and misery.

Vicki answers the phone, sounding chipper. If she too had a late night last night, she does a good job of hiding it. (And by the way, who invited her to the party, or did she invite herself?) Maybe she's a self-promotion wizard.

Randall tells her who he is and where they met. She sounds positively thrilled, and in response to his proposal, she says yes, she can come to his office at 6:00 P.M.

One last thing, before Randall hangs up. She'd like a phone number where she can reach him. He's in such anticipation he's going to get exactly what he wants, he rattles it off, neglecting to keep his guard up. *No one* has the number, except Crystal.

He did it now. He feels like a smarmy, careless fool. And that makes him the most upset of all is the fact he didn't really *do* anything wrong. God, how he sometimes wishes he could be free and easy, like his brother, Michael.

His stomach really feels topsy-turvy, thanks to all this anxiety.

If it's possible to have a mid-life crisis hit you all at once, then this is what Randall determines he's being forced to endure.

He gets up to use the lavatory—one all his own, private use. He's *so* glad he doesn't have to face Dorothy. It's not typical for him to stir from his office before 11:00 A.M. He'll only raise her concerns.

As it is, Dorothy's been looking at Randall differently ever since he became a married man. She seems worried about his welfare. And right now, Randall is so disgusted with Crystal, he'd be all too tempted to tell Dorothy *all* about it.

This very minute, Randall is willing to bet Crystal is out buying yet another pair of shoes.

Oh, that's right. It might be too early. Neiman-Marcus isn't open yet.

He calls home and there's no answer. She's probably standing by the store entrance, waiting for the magic hour when the doors are unlocked.

Rather than listen to his own voice reeling off a boring message ("You have reached the Schubert residence, etc. . . .") he hangs up.

She'd just better *not* be home but didn't pick up the phone, knowing it was him.

No, that couldn't be. She didn't get him sick on purpose—he doesn't *think*.

Oh, hell. It doesn't even matter. He's never been so angry with her, and that's the important part. He's going to try calling her again, later. If she still isn't home, he'll leave a message.

Three o'clock. Randall decides to give her until then. She'd better be home and if she's not, she will be getting one hell of a rude message.

Then he has an image of her driving the white Jaguar convertible he bought her as a wedding gift. He pictures her being tailed by so many men, it's impossible to tell she's being followed.

It's amazing it hasn't bothered him long before. Maybe he just knows it will only drive him insane to be worried about what his beautiful wife is doing whenever she's out of his sight.

Jonathan Lamping is the name of the lawyer who handles all of Randall's personal affairs. Randall'd like to give him a call and find out what kind of pre-nuptial agreement it might be possible to have written up, now that it would no longer be pre—but rather post-nuptial.

Randall isn't personal friends with Jonathan, unlike some men he knows. That's because they need to make relatively frequent use of their lawyers' services ('a la having pre-nuptial agreements written up, is second nature).

Jonathan himself has only married once and has stayed with his wife for a number of years. Randall finds that most admirable because hardly any of his friends have pulled that one off.

"Lamping and Associates, Judy speaking," the secretary answers when he calls Jonathan's office.

Randall identifies himself and Judy proceeds to make him feel important, saying, "Oh, hello, Mister Schubert," in that certain tone of voice. But then she adds, "Mister Lamping just left for Maui," as if Randall must have been apprised of as much, but he forgot. (Hey, he shouldn't feel bad. It's not like they're good buddies. He just said so, himself.)

Still, Jonathan *did* tell him he was going away with his wife Cheri and no one else. The kids were staying home. Grandma was coming to keep them company.

But Randall forgot, just like he seems to forget everything, these days. And this morning in particular, it seems like the whole world is trying to make Randall Schubert crack.

"Would you like me to have Jonathan call you?" Judy offers.

"No, that's all right," Randall is quick to say. He wants to analyze his situation some more, before he actually talks to Jonathan. This might just be a blessing in disguise.

Randall has a ridiculous fantasy of moving Crystal's hand across the page of the *post*-nuptial agreement Jonathan Lamping just drew up for him. (She just so happens to sleep like the dead.)

Before the employee meeting, Randall needs a breath of fresh air. He braces himself for Dorothy's display of concern, when he limps past her desk.

He escapes her notice until he's reached the frosted glass door, leading to the corridor. She tells him, "Mister Schubert, I have a memo for you. I completely forgot." (That's unusual for her. No, *unheard of*, for her.)

He goes to her desk to retrieve it, only to read his potential client, the bigwig, has canceled on him. This is just the kind of thing Randall hates, especially on a day like today. He now has the opportunity to speculate to the high heavens, the reason why.

Randall takes the elevator down, glad to have it to himself. He feels he must look as out of sorts as he feels.

The second he reaches the ground floor, he's ready to go back up. His stomach is giving him a hard time. Good old Dorothy will be so concerned she'll probably leap out of her chair and assist him back into his office. Now he really does believe he is losing his mind, to senility, if nothing else. He's not kidding himself, he's no longer young.

Luckily (and he thought he had none left), Dorothy isn't even at her desk. He sneaks back in and breathes a sigh of relief.

After a couple minutes, he feels sufficiently organized to face his employees at "their" meeting. When he comes out of his office, he about gives Dorothy a heart attack. "Oh, my," she says. "I hadn't any idea you were back."

Randall can't seem to help getting a kick out of having surprised her. It's all in fun, however.

But so what if he *did* get a sort of perverse pleasure from it? The meeting finishes early and all his employees will be free to go to lunch. He's found over the years, extra-long lunch breaks are the surest way to please.

As for his favorite place to have lunch, it's the Elexir, just down the street. No reservations are necessary for Randall. He's one of the elite few who has his "own" table.

Randall willingly will spare the world the details of the employee meeting. No one had any major grievances to air, not that he was expecting as much.

It would have taken a whole hell of a lot to bend him out of shape, as it is. Crystal and pre-nuptial agreements are all he can think about.

He was the first one to arrive in the conference room and proceeded to watch the employees (mostly females, strictly coincidence) make their entrances.

Randall never would have guessed just how short women like to wear their skirts and dresses. Age differences sure aren't at odds, when it comes to showing some leg. Dorothy sauntered in last, and although she's the most elderly of his employees, she had the second shortest hemline.

Actually, it was the third shortest, if you counted the twin Jacobi sisters as one and two, with their lavender twill mini-skirts.

Crystal has a great pair of legs, even better than either Gwendolyn or Jennifer Jacobi, but she doesn't like to flaunt the fact. She doesn't *need* to.

So to lunch did they all go—the employees, of course. Randall intends to stay in his office and get some work done. Now that his stomach *finally* feels better, he'd rather not push his luck.

And he really does believe he has some. The hotshot potential client canceled and that is just perfectly fine.

Randall proceeds to place his feet on the desk, puts his hands behind his head and nods off.

He can't say how long he's been out of it, but the red light is blinking on his phone. Not only that, he's since acquired one hell of a crick in his neck.

Dorothy's been trying to get ahold of him and he's been asleep. It's utterly inexcusable but there isn't a damned thing he can do about it.

Once he feels sufficiently awake, he calls her and says, "Yes, Dorothy? What is it?"

She replies, "I just wanted to tell you I was back from lunch, Mister Schubert. You said you had a couple dictations for me, when I returned."

"I did? I did," he says, unable to believe he actually forgot.

As if eager to shove it down his throat, Dorothy tells him, "You pulled me aside after the meeting, specifically to say that."

Randall needs five minutes to organize himself, so he tells her to come in his office, then. (He's going to think of a couple people, besides Jonathan Lamping, to whom he wants to send a letter.)

What time is it? he wonders. It's 1:45. Dorothy's only had to sit on pins and needles for the past 30-40 minutes, waiting for him to answer, trying not to be worried about him.

He decides to call Crystal. He'd rather she *not* be home at this point, so he can leave a sarcastic message.

And he gets just what he wants because she's not home.

She doesn't answer the phone. She can't be in the shower because she already took one. She can't be swimming because she doesn't like to swim. She can't be napping because she doesn't like to.

Well, Randall is completely awake after *his* nap and he is most incensed. Patiently he waits for the beep before saying, "Crystal, I don't know if you're there or not, but I want to tell you, I will not be home in time for dinner. I want to stay late. I'll pick up something close by and be working until I'm not sure when."

That'll show her, he smugly thinks. (And he hates it when Dorothy's smug, doesn't he.)

It's definitely the most rudely he's ever spoken to anyone, let alone his wife. Let alone? Does that mean he should be on his best behavior with his spouse? Well, then he's proving that's not the way *he* does things.

Crystal might have to get used to being a little lonely at night because there's always mountains of work for Randall to stay late and do, making good on his word he's putting in overtime. So he lied a little. One measly time won't hurt anything (he mistakenly thinks).

It's funny. Before Randall was a married man, he made it a rule, not to overdo it. How ironic he now thinks maybe he should become a workaholic.

There's a knocking at the door (or thumping, actually, given how sound-proof and heavy the door is).

"Come in, Dorothy," Randall tells her and here she appears. She looks hesitant, however, not her usual, efficient self.

"Are you ready, Mister Schubert, or should I wait a few?" she wants to know.

"No, Dorothy. Please, come right in," he tells her. "I'd rather get these dictations out of the way now, before I get too involved with something else." (Yeah, and on a day like today, he's not getting a thing done.)

Two o'clock is drawing near and with six o'clock but four hours away, he will never be able to concentrate on any work.

Meanwhile, Dorothy doesn't seem to want to sit down and get started. Randall's obligated to ask her, "Dorothy, is something the matter?"

She keeps looking at Randall, wearing an expression of such dramatic concern, he commands her: "Please, have a seat," but he's thinking, *Sit down, for crying out loud!*

She does as she's told but continues to clutch her stenographer's pad and pen, as if holding onto them for dear life. She tells Randall, "I went to the Boston Harbor for lunch today . . ." and Randall can't wait for her to finish. He just has to reassure her, "That's understandable, since you had some extra time for lunch and they have great, great food."

She looks positively horrified that Randall thinks that's the extent of the story. Dorothy finds it imperative to clarify herself, even if she only mucks things up, even more: "I don't mean to meddle in your personal life, but when I was there, I happened to see your wife with——."

"Another man," Randall states, as if he'd been waiting for the chance since the day he married her, the little sneak. Who likes to *show* her love, rather than say, "I love you." He might have known. He just might have known.

Randall feels the bile, rising in his throat, as it sinks in, the fact that this is *his* life they're talking about. It's a shame it's so easy for him to jump to conclusions.

Dorothy commits to this much (all she *has* to, thanks to Randall) and any more, she'd be speculating, not telling the truth: "I saw her there with I *think* your friend Brad Fennel."

Randall could die, hearing her utter his best friend's name. No, not quite. First, he wants to kill a couple people.

He *must* be strong. Dorothy absolutely *cannot* see him fall apart.

Neither is it necessary for Randall to inquire further as to what exactly the man looked like. Dorothy saw Brad at the wedding. And unless she wasn't in the room at the time, she saw Brad dance one number with Crystal.

Randall is much too upset to discern if Dorothy might be secretly delighted his marriage is already on the skids. She's too polite to say, "I told you so," but the look is in her eyes.

Despite the myriad of distractions, Randall manages to give the two dictations to Dorothy. When that's over, he says he'll call her if he needs anything. In other words, he wants to be left alone.

Six o'clock finally draws near. Randall spent the entire afternoon in his office and now he feels the effects. (He wants to go outside again.) At the same time, he's hesitant to get up, open the door and find Dorothy hasn't left yet.

But he does and he finds that yes, Dorothy has left for the evening. And Vicki's not yet here, so it's unlikely they collided in the ground floor lobby or in the elevator itself.

Then he reaches the outer door and wonders why it's unlocked. She couldn't be intending to return. She must have forgotten, Randall thinks. She was awfully absentminded the whole day, so he will overlook the error. (He refuses to entertain the notion she might somehow know about his massage appointment and rightfully so.)

Just as he turns away from the door, he can hear the elevator, across the corridor, come to a stop. He opens the door again, in order to greet Vicki Vixen. His first reaction is she's much prettier that he remembered. It must be because she looks better with less make-up.

She's dressed in what appears to be an off-white cotton tunic, something you'd wear over a bikini, if you were going to the beach. It comes complete with a see-everything cowl neck and gold lame, braided belt.

Her taut, compact little frame has Randall on fire. None of that lanky, long-leggedness, like Crystal.

Despite her hands being full of this and that, she insists upon lingering and introducing herself again, accompanied by her shiny white teeth and enthusiasm. Self-promotion is her middle name.

Greetings out of the way, she says, "I'm so pleased I have this opportunity to give you one of my massages," and Randall is so mindlessly flattered he doesn't reply. He simply shows the way to his office.

Vicki doesn't hesitate to tell Randall, "You're limping," and he's impressed by this astute observation because he thought he'd covered it up.

The second she sees his office she asks, "Could we do you out here?" meaning in Dorothy's office. "There's a bit more room."

Randall agrees, trying not to appear flustered. His office is his sanctuary, and he really wanted to have his massage in there. Otherwise, he probably wouldn't have requested this office call.

She sets to work, preparing her table and politely orders Randall to take the white terrycloth robe she laid out for him, into his office. There, would he please take off all his clothes.

Before he shuts the door she lets him know, any portion of his body, not being massaged, will be covered by a sheet.

Randall has to laugh at her reassurance because she obviously (mistakenly) thinks he's overly-modest.

The door shut, he slowly undresses, folding each item of clothing. Looking down he sees his black silk socks and realizes those must go, too. Since Vicki supplies a robe, she ought to provide a pair of slippers, too. She gives a good massage, and he'll offer her that recommendation. (Fortunately, however, new carpet was installed, a couple of years ago.)

"Knock-knock," Vicki says as she also does so, on Randall's door. "I'm just letting you know, Mister Schubert, I'm ready, whenever you are."

"All right. I'll be right there," he says, scurrying to finish undressing. He might have known he was moving too slowly. He delegates the careless ripping-off of clothes, to all the muscle-bound studs she massages. They're undoubtedly her favorite ones to do. Every once in awhile she likes to have a client like Randall, to keep her grounded in reality.

When flabby Randall does finally appear before her, donned in that white robe that's *almost* as white as Crystal's, he feels terribly self-conscious. She *did* correctly speculate about his modesty.

Meanwhile, she's busy apologizing: "I wasn't trying to hurry, you, Mister Schubert. I just wanted to let you know I was ready. Sometimes my clients wait for me. I had one who started working on his report, thinking I wasn't prepared to start."

By this time, Vicki's gesticulating every which way, anxious to explain herself. She looks so entirely human (and self-conscious) Randall can hardly keep from kissing her.

She guides him to the table she set up. It looks soft and inviting, nothing like he would have expected from what she carted in here.

He lays his head where she shows him to, untying his robe as he goes down upon the table, face first. She removes the robe and in its place she covers Randall's body and legs with a sheet.

She explains the ingredients in the oil she intends to use for her massage, which will start with his head, neck and scalp, the "nerve center." She will then massage his arms and hands, going on to his legs and feet and finally his torso, before having him turn over. (He hopes to be too relaxed to worry he'll be looking like a beached whale.)

Then the whole process will be repeated. Thankfully she's very professional, and he doesn't doubt she'll have the stamina to give him a worthwhile massage.

Before he knows it, the scent of lavender oil gets to him and he feels intoxicated.

It isn't until she politely tells him to turn over that he's aware of what kind of situation he's in—one in which he is completely unable to hide the effect of this extraordinary massage. He has the single-mindedness of his lower to extremity to thank.

Randall decides the best way to avoid embarrassment is to pretend he's asleep. Unintentionally that's exactly what he proceeds to do.

He isn't out of it for long, but the amazing part is what awakens him, as he is being manually stimulated (to heights of ecstasy he never dreamed possible).

Vicki goes any further (such putting her lips or tongue on him), and he will be at her mercy, once and for all.

There would be no use in crying rape because he's certainly not being held against his will. Indeed, rhyme and reason have deserted Randall by this point in time.

Besides, Crystal already beat him to the punch line called adultery, so there's no possible harm being done with this foray.

Vicki takes him to the top, licking, sucking, and rubbing his member, with infinite skill.

There's a loud commotion outside the door. The last thing Randall needs is visitors, but guess what? It's his birthday! He should have remembered.

"Surprise! Happy Birthday, Randall!" all his friends (and Crystal) cry in unison.

His 46th. He must be truly loved, despite all of his doubts. His best friend Brad Fennel teamed up with Crystal, to pull this off, making a last-minute change, by bringing the party to his office. She *was* going to have Boston Harbor Restaurant cater it to their home, but she picked up the order herself, along with Brad.

What could Randall possibly have to say to that?

"THE OPPORTUNISTS"

Rachel only works at the Scottsdale Pack 'n' Save because she has to make a living. She certainly doesn't work there because she's always aspired to be a cashier for the rest of her days. She's only 29, but sometimes she feels like she's 39.

Being a checker isn't as easy as some people think. Or maybe they don't think anything at all, and that's why they blame *her* for how expensive grocery shopping is.

Given how rich most of these customers are, they shouldn't care.

Besides, even if she *owned* the damned store, there wouldn't be much she could (or would) do, to lower the prices. Everybody's got to make a living and those in the retail food business are no exception.

Supposedly, the store only makes one or two cents per item, which isn't much.

She considers herself a wage-earner in this particular industry, not as reliant on the whims of the customers, as those above her. Therefore, her salary is lower but her headaches are fewer. And as she already mentioned, she won't be doing this forever.

Rachel is an aspirant to "a better life," as she calls that elusive something that can't be named. Her ticket to that place is her boyfriend of five years, Zachary Harris.

She's been referring to herself in her mind as Rachel Harris (versus Dunbar, a name she hates) for so long, she sometimes forgets that is *not* her new name.

Just the fact that Dunbar is her "maiden" name, makes her want to scream. She absolutely *cannot* wait to get rid of it.

But the best she can do for now is try not to think about the situation too much or she will go insane. (It's the same philosophy she follows when dealing with some of these Pack 'n' Save customers.)

Still, there are some days, especially as of late, when she doesn't think she can take another minute of this.

And the best part? It's a predominant job requirement, she put on a happy face.

It's that or get fired. How's *that* for options?

Yet some of these customers can really test your mettle. This store may cater to the rich but it also caters to more curmudgeonly customers than any other supermarket in the Phoenix area. You can bet they're *all* filthy rich, so there's only *so* much sympathy Rachel can have toward them as they complain about all their aches and pains (in addition to bitching and moaning about grocery-related issues).

Still, there's one thing that's a greater test of Rachel's patience than all that complaining and carrying on—waiting (and waiting) for her boyfriend Zachary to propose.

But don't misunderstand, Rachel loves him to death (or, 'til death do they part), but as she said, he *is* her ticket to a better life, "the good life," a life free of having to *work*, the life of luxury.

Boy does it seem like *so* long ago, when he gave her that ring. No, it wasn't an engagement ring. It was just a ring (Use your imagination. The guy's *loaded*), but it was only the third date. At the time, Rachel worried things might be moving too fast, and there wouldn't be a opportunity to catch her breath.

Now? Talk about *breath*. She's been waiting with baited breath for at least two years, for him to at *least* say, "Let's move in together. Your place or mine?" (like there'd be any real question). His "place" is much more spacious and newer, and it's a condo that's entirely paid for. It doesn't even seem like a "bachelor pad," as it's clean, it's well-decorated, and the fridge is always well-stocked.

Meanwhile, Rachel rents her cheap studio by the month, having decided not to renew the lease this last time. She *must* be holding out on some kind of sub-conscious hope that any day Zachary's going to say "Honey, that's enough of us being apart. It's sheer torture for me, too. I just couldn't admit it sooner."

On some level, he has *got* to realize he is torturing her. Never mind for a minute, what it might or might *not* be doing to him, as he seems perfectly content to meet for dinner a couple of times a week, throwing in some sex here and there, for good measure.

But she's told him, 10,000 times easily, she *loves* him. (And she *means* it.) Oh, he's said it too, only not as often, and she wouldn't expect him to. He's a man, after all.

But he *is* a true romantic, only maybe not so sappy and sentimental as some. (Those are called hopeless romantics, aren't they.)

Zachary doesn't waste time, going overboard. After all, he has to make a living, himself. That leaves only so much time for frivolity.

Rachel considers herself one lucky woman, even though she wasn't born rich, and her boyfriend won't get more committal with her. The most he'll do is maybe take her to brunch on Sunday, after taking her to dinner, Friday and Saturday. He still won't leave any of his stuff at her apartment, however.

Actually, the most often they *can* go to brunch at this point is every other Sunday because for the remainder, Rachel has to work. That gives her a couple weekends a month to *really* be his girlfriend, which will have to suffice.

Still, when they go out, it's so easy for Rachel to become jealous of any woman who makes eyes at Zachary. Not only is he extraordinarily handsome, he exudes that aura of wealth.

Rachel knows she's pretty enough not to look out of place with Zachary, but there's plenty of women out there, much more attractive than herself. That's *all* there is to it.

The worst part is seeing those annoying little lines on her face, and it seems like she's getting more and more, by the day. Aside from making herself endure this job, she takes good care of herself. It could only be genetics (and Zachary's obstinacy) that's bringing her down.

One good thing about working where there's so many elderly customers, is there isn't *too* much beauty competition passing through the check stands.

When a real hot babe *does* appear, Rachel takes great pleasure in making small talk, as she discreetly analyzes what exactly makes the woman seem so much more beautiful than herself.

Nine times out of ten, it isn't that the woman has "better" or "prettier" features, but that she exudes a certain aura that spellbinds. Some even have their crows' feet and laugh lines firmly etched in their faces, and they *still* have Rachel beaten in the looks department.

When Rachel is tired and/or plain sick of waiting to become Mrs. Zachary Harris, *her* lines seem deeper than ever. It can be *so* depressing. God, if her face starts to sag, she'll *really* look the part of the unmarried hag. Not even her hair will save her, in all its healthy, natural blondness.

Clearly, Rachel will *need* the diamonds, the expensive clothes, and the fine Italian shoes, to help keep her looking her best. (The facelift will come later. She doesn't want to get one *too* soon.) Zachary isn't one to shower her with gifts, not that she has an actual "wish list." He's big on flowers and chocolates, things that he can give her again and again, as they constantly need to be replenished.

Whenever he proposes (and he will, he *has* to), Rachel won't hesitate for even a second, before saying yes. She could care less if she comes off looking like the eager beaver. She's as liberated a woman as any other. Damned if she's lived alone since she finished a two-year stint at Sonora Community College.

There is *nothing* un-liberated about a woman who willingly goes after a man, wanting to be a part of his life, wanting to have his children . . .

Rachel can state this with supreme confidence because no one's pulling her arms off, to *pull* this off.

All this says nothing of the daily anxiety she must endure, thinking about when her relationship with Zachary will finally advance to that one certain level, the one "that changes everything."

The problem (so to speak) is there's never a waking moment she isn't thinking about Zachary. (And she probably dreams about him, too.)

It's nonstop, just like the groceries the customers throw on the conveyor belt, for her to weigh and scan or just scan. It really *is* amazing, just how much some people manage to buy, yet by the looks of them, they *must* be living alone. (Her observations aren't ever particularly accurate.)

But then, judging by the lines on her face, she *ought* to be the mother of two or three by this time, so sometimes you really can't tell.

Rachel just can't help that she feels *so* far behind in the game of procreation. To hell with Mother Nature and the "biological clock" and all that. Just the clock itself is ticking, and *time* is slipping away. What does Zachary think? That she enjoys this job, that she'd *really* rather do this full-time, holding off homemaking and motherhood, indefinitely?

Sure. And while she's on the subject of bullshit, in case she didn't already mention it, Rachel positively *loves* big orders like the one she's doing right now. She especially likes to see it unloaded by the most beautiful woman she's ever laid eyes on.

If the customer has shopped here before, Rachel would have remembered.

Admittedly, however, some people really do have forgettable faces.

The woman might have been in here on one of those rare occasions when Rachel has off. (She's starting to feel like she works here every day.) And during the day is the only time this goddess would shop here. In the evenings, she's busy attending (or throwing) dinner parties.

Rachel is glad she didn't see this Vogue-fashion model before today because it would have been impossible to gaze upon her objectively. She might have even been *mean* to her, telling her this check stand wasn't really open yet, it's still too early. With Rachel's luck, however, her boss Rick Severson would be watching.

Fine with her, if he is. She's not doing anything wrong. She's worked here almost as long as he has (and *she* has the lines to prove it).

Actually, it's only appropriate to have this blonde (not as light but natural, nonetheless) vixen be Rachel's first customer of her 8:30 A.M. to 5:00 P.M. shift. Rachel can spend the rest of the day congratulating herself on her courtesy and self-control. (What does she have in mind to do, have a jealousy tantrum?)

Rachel has an aside, for Zachary dear: Any beautiful, classy women around here, are taken, so he doesn't have to bother searching one out. He also needs to realize that some rich, fabulous-looking women (Rachel just *knows* she'd look great in a chinchilla fur coat) are made, and not *all* are born heiresses.

Well, there might be a *few* who are self-made, but that's still largely uncharted territory. It comes down to being so much smarter than men. Why work yourself to death, to make your millions, when you can marry them?

And Rachel is certain that's how this foxy lady "made her fortune." How else could she look so well-preserved? (Rachel thinks she's 35, easily, but could pass for 27 or 28).

She's dying to see that rock of a ring the woman's bound to have, but so far she's kept her hands pretty well hidden. Either that or else she doesn't deign to wear such a museum piece *just* to the grocery shop. (It's one of the most lowly forms of shopping, isn't it.)

Rachel hopes she pays with a credit card or a check. She's feeling uncommonly nosy, wanting to know the woman's name. A little curiosity never hurts (so she thinks).

Truthfully, Rachel really does believe she's completely immune to any major problems/upheavals in her life, all because Zachary won't make her Mrs. Harris. (That's a sufficient burden right there, feeling like she's on-call or something.)

Besides, it's important for Rachel to thank the customers by name, if she does know it. It's all part of the kind of customer service this store prides itself on providing.

Finally, Rachel makes eye contact with the woman long enough to squeeze in a greeting: "Hello, how are you," to which there's hardly any reply. The woman's too intent upon unloading her cart.

Even if she *wasn't* nice, so what? *She's* rich (and the customer). She's under no obligation to be even remotely friendly.

Rachel would almost bet this woman's husband is the one

who owns that house on the south face of Camelback Mountain, that's higher than any of the others. Rachel can't help but see the damned thing every day, driving to work. Inevitably she misses the light at Camelback Road and 56th Street. She turns her head to the left and there it is.

God, sometimes Rachel wishes she could tell Zachary exactly how she feels. She could be like the customers and not be under any obligation to be "nice," because she'd have her "good life."

But she doesn't *blame* any of them for being the way they are, especially the older ones. They have so many aches and pains, all the friendliness has been sucked out of them.

See? That proves (once again) you really do need to get going and do what you want to do in life, because you're not, by any means, young forever. (And she bristles just thinking about this.) She might even find herself getting mad, before the day is through—mad at Zachary, believe it or not. She sure can't afford to get mad at any of the customers (even though every day, there's at least one that about sends her over the edge.) After all, she's only human. She'd probably even get mad at her own kids, once in awhile. It's only natural. It wouldn't be healthy to be *too* nice to them. (But she knows she'd be *so* grateful to have them, it would be a daily struggle *not* to spoil them positively rotten).

But she could never have too many, could she? How does anyone decide when enough is enough?

She's never even been able to decide which orders she prefers checking—the smaller ones or the monstrous ones. *This* one isn't the largest she's had come through, but it's a good size.

So too, this gives Rachel the option of more time with each customer, to make small talk. Either way, it's better when it's busy because then *she's* busy and the clock moves faster.

Rachel's number one, all-time favorite customer is Mrs. Donaldson. She could have *ten* carts of groceries, and Rachel would be perfectly content. And it just so happens Mrs.Donaldson will only use *Rachel's* check-stand. That is the most sincere form of flattery you could ever bestow on Rachel.

And Mrs. Donaldson needn't ever worry, the line might get

too long at Rachel's check stand. Not only is she a whiz of a cashier, this store is well-managed, so Rick Severson the manager will make sure plenty more check stands are opened, if necessary.

Rachel could never be as frank with her mother as she is with Mrs. Donaldson.

And Rachel's only option with her mother is to converse via long-distance, as she lives in Florida.

Admittedly, Rachel finds it amazing she's so eager to talk to Mrs. Donaldson, about plenty of rather *personal* issues (all directly or indirectly related to Zachary).

It must be Mrs. Donaldson's ready smile, those gorgeous hats she wears, that always match her designer outfits, and did Rachel fail to mention—Mrs. Donaldson has *lots* of money? (Therefore, Rachel can say she has "made friends" with someone rich and can listen to some of the laments of the rich.) She can also pretend Mrs. Donaldson is her mother-in-law (because Rachel has yet to spend as much time with Zachary's mother Adrienne as she spends in total with Mrs. Donaldson, just checking out her groceries). And what *is* Mrs. Donaldson's first name, by the way, besides Mrs. Thomas Donaldson? She's always paid in cash, so Rachel's never seen her name on a receipt, only a check, once.

Two boxes of cornstarch appear for Rachel to scan. (Up until now, there's just been produce, soda pop and bottled water.)

Cornstarch doesn't sound like typical fare for a million-heiress— or the wife of a millionaire, whatever. If she's going to do any baking, wouldn't she have the housekeeper buy something like that? (Rachel loves to bake, if only she had more time.)

She can't wait until *her* kids are big enough to help make Christmas cookies. No more years of buying ready-made dough and feeling like she's missing out on the true spirit of the holiday season.

There's more to come here, that would indicate this woman's going to do some serious baking/creating. It isn't even Thanksgiving yet. No, there's not a cookie sprinkle to be seen, but there's plenty of other goodies.

It's high time for Rachel to make a comment. (She's definitely one cashier who can't help herself. And her boss Rick Severson doesn't call her on it because it's a contribution to the *friendly* atmosphere (at the expense of having her *almost* appear nosy).

In orientation, however, cashiers are reminded not to comment excessively, especially about a customer's purchases. It can make them "uncomfortable."

All Rachel is really guilty of is she likes to hear herself talk. She can be especially loquacious if she had an especially memorable date with Zachary. (And she feels as if some progress is being made in their relationship.) She's smiling at the whole world, then.

But damned if it hasn't been a long time since she got *that* feeling. However, it can't be said things are falling apart, so she has to be grateful for *that* much.

O.K., their relationship is holding steady. Still, she thinks it just might need some sort of spark, a change of one kind or another. She needs to do *something* differently, that much is for certain.

Realistically, she should have thought of all of this sooner, but she was wasting time, feeling sorry for herself and totally failing to be even a little objective about the situation. Had she made a plan, by now she could have been executing it.

But today *is* a new day and there's no better time than during her working hours, to do some *real* thinking. This job can bore her silly, sometimes.

Hopefully Mrs. Donaldson will be here before five. Early morning is *usually* when she shows up, but every once in a awhile she doesn't come until Rachel's shift is almost over. That's when she only has a small order, so Rachel has less time to talk to her.

Getting along as well as she does with Mrs. Donaldson, proves Rachel is destined for great things. She's been unfortunate in that she wasn't *born* into riches. It must have been her due, to keep her in her place. Otherwise, she just *knows* she would be terribly vain.

Look at this customer, curling her luscious upper lip, as if pretending to be busy, concentrating on unloading her cart. Too bad if she hates small talk because Rachel is in just the right mood for it. She's going out tonight, and she has a feeling something big is going to happen. Zachary might just have a special surprise for her.

"Oh, these look tasty," Rachel comments about some blueberry muffins the woman must have picked up from the bakery table by the lobby. (She can't be expected to make *everything* from scratch, can she.) Even "a woman of leisure" has only *so* much time on her hands.

Rachel goes on: "They have the best apple strudel pies, if you're ever in the mood for pie," (that, courtesy of Zachary, who's told her as much).

Oops, Mrs. So-and-So here, might not be into pie. It's kind of a down-to-earth type of dessert, and there's nothing down-to-earth about *her*. Rachel feels a tingle of pride, reflecting how Zachary somehow strikes that balance between highfaluting and genuinely sincere. (See? How can she help but love him?)

Well, Rachel is *not* especially trying to make friends with this woman. (Right. And she'd never admit she'd like to do lunch with her.) She would listen most attentively to whatever the woman had to say.

For now, it would be most appreciated if the woman would simply reply, not just nod or shake her head, or do strange things with her collagen-enhanced upper lip.

Rachel reluctantly supposes she'll have to be content with the smallest of favors, such as the bagger at the other end, doesn't stick the pork roast on top of the muffin container.

Here it comes, on the conveyor belt, proof positive this customer has kids—three gallons of milk, two white, one chocolate. Evidently she doesn't realize these see-through plastic containers quickly allow the milk's nutrients to escape. Otherwise she would reject buying them. (Rachel read this tidbit of information in, she thinks, *Parents* magazine. No, she didn't buy it because she was fantasizing. She happened to be on aisle two during her break, picked it up on a whim and started reading. *She* doesn't go outside and have a smoke during her time off. (She's aware of the unhealthiness of that habit, even if you're not carrying a fetus.)

Doubting the dumb, lazy bagger will ask, Rachel takes it upon herself to say, "Would you like the milk in bags?" to which the customer quickly responds, "You know, what I'd like is some of the groceries in paper bags, but no, you don't have to bag the milk at all."

She's a typical rich person, isn't she, getting bored easily. She even needs variety with her bags.

And that decides her housing arrangement, as far as Rachel is concerned. Her husband, her three kids, and herself, have a home not only at the top of Camelback Mountain, but they have a condo in Aspen, a beach-house in Malibu, and a thoroughbred farm in Kentucky. There.

"Do you need ice or stamps today?" Rachel asks by way of her thoroughness. (She's not under any *real* obligation to pose the question.) The initial greeting suffices, yet she's bending over backward to be nice, and she has no idea why.

This annoys her because she's one who needs a reason for *everything*. And that itself is why it so completely aggravates her, Zachary has yet to propose. What *is* the reason, why not?

The woman dismissively tells Rachel, "No thanks. I'm all set," and Rachel thinks, *Well, sor-ry.* (Something good has *got* to happen when Zachary takes her out tonight.)

It's more than time for him to present her with an engagement *nugget* (the size she expects the diamond to be). That would be the best way to describe what she envisions, as she's not much of one for describing diamonds, in terms of carats.

The only *carrots* she knows about are the ones she checks for Pack 'n' Save customers. Mrs. Richesse here, just bought a five-pound bag. Rachel speculates they're for the lamb riblets she's going to prepare, except she bought that particular meat, someplace else, perhaps a specialty shop.

The woman *might* use some of the carrots when she prepares the roast she bought, but Rachel doubts it. If so, wouldn't she probably also want potatoes? As far as Rachel can see, she didn't buy any of them (unless she got them on another day).

Rachel would like to ask her if she remembered potatoes, but she doesn't want to seem like she's trying too hard, to be helpful. Plus, this woman appears to be completely organized. They're the ones who most resent (logically) being reminded of items they *do not* need. She wasn't too happy about the stamps and ice question, was she.

Rachel must face it, she tries to be too many people. She's simply not intelligent enough to keep all the roles straight. No wonder Zachary Harris hasn't proposed. (And no wonder he never dares to come in here while Rachel's working. He doesn't want to "surprise" his girlfriend, so he claims.) Quick, rescue the customers from Rachel, not vice versa. If he doesn't give her that rock of an engagement ring tonight, heaven only knows what Rachel could be compelled to do.

Once she does lay eyes on just such a ring, she will never be the same. Not even Rachel realizes the significance of timing. She sure won't be able to concentrate, when an eye's always on "the rock," so to speak. (No longer will she just be staring hopefully at the *clock*.) The reflection of that ring will cause most of the old fogies to have no recourse but to turn away.

Even the young, *rich* women will be jealous. And that will mark Rachel's first, major leap toward evenness with them. (Still, she's doing better than most women her age, especially her friends from school. None of *them* have a mega-rich boyfriend.)

So relative to the situation, she's accomplished a lot. In regard to her life, however, she's back to where she started, and she wants to *marry* the sonofabitch.

She declares that she cannot take much more. (Mrs. Donaldson would reassure Rachel, by saying, "Just when you don't think you can take another breath, you *do*, darling.")

Somehow, Rachel manages not to make a running commentary as she finishes the order, and that's a good thing because it looks as if suddenly it's going to be very busy.

Rich Severson will not see in time to call a third cashier to the front. (There's also a cashier working at check stand number eleven, which may as well be miles away from Rachel on number three.) On a morning such as this, there's but two reasons you end up having her be "your" cashier and that is: you want her to "check you out"; or you just happened to finish shopping at this end.

The latter is the case with Ms. Peterson. *She*, of all people, has no particular preference. This is the first time she's shopped here, but she'll be back because this place has Capitano cocoa mix. *That* is hard to find as she happens to be addicted to the stuff. (Everybody has *something*, don't they.) It's most definitely the greatest creation, second only to rich young men. They both make life worth living, even when a nosy, gabby cashier tries to ruin everything.

She's given Miranda the creeps, the way she's not only checked but checked-out every single goddamned item. She must think she's getting to know her, through her purchases. Miranda would *love* to tell the chick the truth (except it's none of her goddamned business). And that is, that she shops for other people, for a living. This is *not* her stuff. (Thank God. *She* wouldn't want to have to put it all away.)

Miranda is not sure how long she can keep her red-lipped smile glued on her face.

This cashier-chick whose nametag reads "Rachel," is really testing her to her limit.

Miranda would have traipsed to the other end of the check stands, if only she'd known. This cashier-chick's long blonde hair up in a bun, she only *seems* like the picture of efficiency. True, she's not exactly slow (the total charge will be announced any second now), but there's something about her gabbiness that makes it seem like Miranda's been waiting forever. Maybe it has to do with this *lull*, while Rachel helps the inept bagger, finish with the groceries. He's having a hell of a time with the paper bags, which she's sorry she requested he use, as well as the plastic ones.

Admittedly, being a cashier at a supermarket isn't the easiest, most fun job on earth. (At least it doesn't *look* like it.) And you'd have to put up with customers constantly complaining about this and that, including taking the blame for how expensive groceries are (as if the cashier's responsible for the actual price of everything. *How dumb can people be*? Miranda wants to know).

Fighting boredom, that's Miranda's thing. (It sounds vaguely familiar because all women like her are hard to keep satisfied.) And that's why she's so thankful for this job.

It doesn't *allow* her to get bored because no two days are exactly the same. Also, there's plenty of perks.

Looking most expectantly at Miranda, Rachel tells her the total is $112.24.

"All right," Miranda says but is unprepared with her money. She was too busy spacing out.

Actually, it's her *client's* money, and it's kept in a separate compartment of her wallet. The few dollars she carries with her, aren't allowed to mix. She's *all* business in *that* respect. (At the same time, if it weren't for receipts, she'd tip herself an extra dollar here and there.) Miranda calls herself an opportunist and she's proud of it (proving just how much of one, she really is). But hey, *she* doesn't wait for things to go her way. She *makes sure* they do.

Rachel is disappointed to be presented with 120 dollars (all twenties) in cash. She can't *believe* this woman is going to get past her, and she will still not know her name.

What are the chances of her coming through here again, in the near future? Meanwhile Rachel will be going crazy, wondering who she is.

When she *does* come back, Rachel will either be having that seemingly rare day off, or else she'll be on break. (You can find her in the magazine aisle. This time she'll be flipping the pages of *Modern Bride*.)

Rachel hands Miranda her change, telling her the amount, seven-something. Then, "Thank you. Have a nice day. Would you like any help out?"

For a second Miranda doesn't know quite what to think, whether or not to accept the carry-out service. She's not worried about having to part with the buck tip she'd feel like she should give the kid (because she'd stiff him). No, she doesn't want to draw undue attention to herself, and right now she feels like that's what she's doing.

She decides to tell Rachel, "No, I can take it, myself," and the bagger-kid takes that as his cue to disappear. Fine with Miranda. The last thing she *ever* needs in *her* life, is an audience.

Still, it's not like there isn't another customer. In fact, there's a short, fat lady who's just finished unloading about twenty items from her cart. She's patiently waiting for her turn. And behind her there's a woman wearing a dark purple fedora. If she weren't attractive (and feminine-looking) she'd look like a man, how some women of a certain age tend to look, wearing that kind of hat.

And the next thing Miranda knows, there's none other than a man standing before her, ready to reach out and grab her if she tries to make an escape. She already knows what he's after, those two Capitano cocoa boxes she hid in her purse. Once a kleptomaniac, always a kleptomaniac. It's the reason she had to leave the store where she formerly did all her personal shopping. The owner decided not to prosecute because she was otherwise such a good customer (and she didn't look like she could *possibly* be a criminal).

Meanwhile Rachel's still trying to figure out what's going on. (Being bound and determined she *knows* this woman, has her figured out, has its price.)

Miranda isn't quite as calm and cool and collected as she might appear. And she made the mistake of wasting too much time, fumbling with the change. Not only hasn't she gotten her wallet closed, her purse isn't as tightly shut as it could be. If the plainclothes officer wants to call her on her crime right then and there, he can see the evidence, to do so.

Then, Rachel looks up and sees Mrs. Donaldson in the background. There's the one customer with a small order and then it's Rachel's confidante's turn. God, where to begin, with all her laments. (She's all but put *this* customer out of her mind, already. Who cares if she's about to be apprehended for something?)

But not so fast, Rachel. As Miranda gets flustered (she thought for *sure* no one saw her steal that cocoa mix) out of her open wallet, falls a snapshot. And it's not just *any* snapshot. It's one of a bathing suit-clad Zachary on a beach somewhere, looking tanned and happy, better than Rachel's ever seen him.

Two-timing (or more) Zachary Harris has a personal-shopper/shoplifter for a girlfriend, in addition to a cashier. It shouldn't be too much of a surprise that their paths would someday cross.

"LUCKY NUMBER SEVEN"

Ena Kruper was one happy widow. Because it was so easy to misunderstand reclusive people like her, some folks in Bricktown said she was a witch. That was their way of explaining the fact she was antisocial yet perfectly content.

And she had seven cats, by the bye, they'd add with a wink and a smirk. Well, what of it? Did people think only a witch could have so many?

The simple truth of the matter was it took that many to make up for the absence of Harry, her dear, beloved, deceased husband. Eleven years passed and she missed him as much as the day he died—"in his sleep," so the doctor said.

Ena knew better. She knew Harry wasn't ever fond of cats, but he tolerated the two they'd had, Boris and Lowry, because he loved her.

And he died because those two cats did something to him. She never bothered relating a word of this to anyone. Instead she calmly waited for something to come up on the coroner's inquest. Nothing did.

For the longest time she wanted to tell someone one of the cats scratched Harry and poisoned him. It just didn't show up on the autopsy, was all. That was the proof those pragmatic medical authorities needed. Not even the red marks on his neck, by his jugular vein, convinced them something was awry. They claimed those marks were the result of him being careless with the razor. But he died on Sunday, and he hadn't shaved since Friday!

As much as Ena loved Boris and Lowry, she just knew they were guilty. She didn't dare accuse them, no sir. She knew better than *that*. Put a hex on a cat, he'll put a hex on you. You didn't need to be a witch, to figure that one out.

To keep the "cat-presence" at a minimum, one tom was let outside to roam while the other kept Ena company. The house the four of them shared was on a huge lot, but the house itself was very small. There was one bedroom and the "TV room," with a daybed, which doubled as a spare bedroom. It wasn't as if any family members would be coming to visit Ena and Harry in their little house on the Kankakee River.

As much as Ena wanted kids (Harry didn't appear to care, one way or another) she didn't have any. Nonetheless, sure as Boris' orange and white fluff or Lowry's orange, white and touch of black fluff, *they* weren't out cavorting and fornicating. They were fixed all right, and had their shots kept up-to-date.

Ena doted on them, caring for them just like they were kids. She even worried about them, every time they went out. If the house had a basement, maybe they could have lived there. Harry never did get used to having cats around. He said they were too quiet and sneaky for him.

He didn't really complain, not like he could have. He'd go in the TV room and shut the door if he didn't want to see a cat. Meanwhile she'd sit in the living room, gazing out the bay window, a cat in her lap.

Boris and Lowry knew to stay away from Harry, even at night—especially at night. The living room led directly to Harry and Ena's bedroom and there wasn't a door. Still, whichever cat was inside for the night, knew to keep out.

No matter how much sitting around Harry did, he had a thing about getting a good night's sleep. Years of hard labor at various physically demanding but low-paying jobs, made him this way.

Yes sir. They knew, and that night, the night he died, she'd made both cats stay inside because it was storming like the dickens. So there was an exception to the rule, and Harry complied. He was compassionate enough to know, even if he were a cat, he wouldn't want to prowl around in the rain and sleet. And Boris and Lowry were from the same litter, so it wasn't as if they couldn't stand one another.

Not long after Harry died, both cats disappeared. Since they were both 13 years old, she figured they went off to die, themselves. *Good riddance*, her subconscious startled her by stating.

Unbeknownst to Ena, Harry had provided for her, bless his heart. The house was not only paid for, she had a sufficient allowance to support herself and two new companions—or more actually.

She didn't want to make any hurried decisions, so she let herself be lonely for a few months. This time perhaps she'd get two tabbies and keep them inside.

Even before doing that, maybe this was her opportunity to take a trip—a long one. She'd not seen much of the world in all her 67 years. The last time she'd gone someplace faraway was with Harry, a couple years before he died. They visited his infirmary sister Phyllis in Duluth. She passed away soon after they made the trip, and Harry didn't want to go to the funeral so they didn't. All the burial arrangements had already been taken care of anyway, by the convalescent home. One of the nurses who took care of Phyllis was the recipient of her life savings—$750.00.

Harry got a big kick out of that. He said he didn't get anything because Phyllis never forgave him for acting like a "typical brother," when they were young.

Having decided to take a vacation, Ena got in her white Chevrolet Impala and drove to the travel agency in Bricktown. There, she told the pretty, bright-eyed travel agent she needed to go someplace but wasn't sure where to go. The woman proceeded to fill a white folder with colorful brochures. There were enticing photographs of everything from castles in Europe, to beaches in the Mediterranean, to ports of call in the Caribbean.

When Ena got home, she spread them out on the kitchen table and made herself some tea. She wanted to add milk but it had gone sour, thanks to no cats being here to help drink it.

Worse, she only ended up completely confused. She concluded she'd diddled around long enough. There was no reason to waste any more time sitting under a palm tree, staring at an ocean in which she had no intention of immersing even her big toe. Her toes were rather big, too. Harry was a sizable man, and Ena had had no trouble taking up much of his shadow.

After throwing away all the brochures, she went back out, this time to the Bricktown Humane Society. Suffice to mention when she went there that day eleven years ago, she ended up bringing home two litters' worth of cats. She even gave the humane society an extra donation every year around the first of December.

In return she would receive a Christmas card. Even though the signature, "Bricktown Humane Society," was embossed, not written by anyone, she was most grateful it was sent to her. It was the only card she received, all year long.

All this time, she only had those cards to sustain her, as well as plenty of reminiscing. She also counted on catching glimpses of the paperboy, Joey, who took over the paper route for his older brother Michael. She also looked forward to seeing the mailwoman, whose name was Anne. She took over for Mr. Kensington, who retired a couple years ago.

Ena missed having physical contact with other people, more than she ever realized. That would explain why she felt so lonely. Not even watching television or taking a trip to the supermarket would shake this feeling.

She wished she'd kept all those colorful brochures for the vacation destinations. Looking at them would have been better than nothing. When she last tooled her by now rusted Impala past the building where the travel agency was, there was a hair salon in its place. She'd have to go to a travel agency in Kankakee. Unfortunately, her car couldn't be trusted to make the thirty-minute trip, not in the wintertime.

Worst of all, she was sick of these cats. Not one of them appeared interested in dying soon, either. This was what she deserved for keeping them in the house. They'd live forever because they couldn't go off and die.

If she had six instead of seven, she wouldn't have quite as much of a burden. She certainly wouldn't find herself lonely with six, not now that she felt so completely helpless and alone.

It was not a little surprising to Ena, she didn't feel this way, long ago. This was definitely a case of too many of a good thing. She should have stuck to two cats.

Before letting these regrets get to her, she would find something to do. She decided to knit an afghan. She hadn't knitted since making pullovers and cardigans for Harry.

Yes, she'd knit herself a warm, cheery-looking afghan with which to cuddle. No more cats would be able to sit on her lap while she watched TV or she looked out the bay window in the living room. This way they wouldn't have any idea just how weary she'd suddenly become of them.

She'd also been letting the brother-sister duo of Mimi and Christopher, both with long white hair and patches of black, sleep on the bed at night. Even though there still wasn't a door for the bedroom, she'd make it clear she wanted privacy.

Those two were obedient—for cats. Ena would only have to make her point one time and they'd understand.

Charles was the type who didn't mind her. Not surprisingly he wasn't from the same litter. He wouldn't be caught dead lying close to Ena at night.

He was stubby-legged little tom with short, smooth, light gray fur and pale green eyes. His favorite place to lounge was the kitchen counter, right next to the stove. That happened to be one place where cats were completely forbidden, as well as the kitchen table. It took her appetite away to see him up there, never mind the fact he had his shots and she kept him brushed. (He was the only one who whined in protest, too.)

Since Charles was getting up there in the years, it was no longer so easy for him to leap anywhere. He still did from time to time, however, if only to irritate her.

It galled her he *knew* enough to get down when she appeared. Even so, he'd wait for her to do it. She would, while firmly ordering him, "No, Charles." She decided next time she'd give the old coot a good swat.

Charles was in fact the worst offender for languishing on every piece of furniture save the bed—while *she* was in it. He was the only one who wouldn't be sorry she was too busy knitting her afghan to have lap company.

Given the opportunity, Charles was also the one most likely to vamoose.

It was hard to believe she always made doubly sure no cats, including him, were ever by the front or back doors when she opened either one.

If Charles weren't the runt of the group, between no less than *both* litters, he'd undoubtedly boss them all around. He was also by far the ugliest one. He was actually demented-looking, if not demonic-looking.

The January days passed, and it was thankfully an unseasonably "warm" winter. Still, it was cloudy, damp, and windy. Meanwhile Ena was sure Charles was keeping a close watch over her with those strangely colored eyes. She'd look up from her knitting or the TV screen and there he'd be in the doorway, staring. Or she'd be sitting in the living room, upon the brown velour sofa, waiting for the mailwoman to appear. She'd look down, to her right, and there he'd be, in the coffee table shadow.

An intense hatred for Charles was overtaking Ena's very soul. She didn't even care if he knew. The rest of the cats, even Mimi and Christopher, who lost a comfortable place to sleep at night, were as loving as ever, rubbing against her stout legs and making soft purring noises.

Not Charles. He was getting too crotchety for his own good. Should she turn him outside? No, it wouldn't be fair. It was too cold, Plus all of them including him, were de-clawed. He deserved the chance to defend himself and at his age (just like herself, come to think of it), it couldn't be expected of him.

Throwing him out in the middle of winter was too cruel to do, Ena concluded, no matter how vindictive the looks were in those eyes of his. He was *just a cat.*

One morning Ena couldn't find Charles. She looked everywhere for him, despite having arthritis in her knees and being a bit overweight, both making it difficult to get down and up again. He couldn't have been in the TV room or the bathroom, one adjacent to the other, because lately she'd kept those doors closed. As it was, unless he hid behind the daybed, he couldn't escape her notice. It was impossible for him to slide beneath it, no matter how slinky a cat could be, not even a runt like him.

Only after she peered beneath everything, lifting the skirts of the two stuffed chairs in the living room, checking under the sofa, even looking inside the oven, was she finally stumped. Did she inadvertently leave the door open today when she stepped outside to see if she got any mail? No, she didn't think so.

If she did, he'd only go as far as the shrubs under the bay window or else the bedroom window. No matter how demonic he tried to look he was a coward. He'd sit there and bawl, letting the whole neighborhood know he was there.

Ena would not get rid of Charles until he keeled over and died. With her luck he'd outlast his brother and two sisters, as well as the three in the other litter.

She told herself to face it. She really didn't have a whole lot of luck and at 78, things weren't going to make an abrupt turnaround. She'd married Harry when she was a slim, shy, rather pretty girl of 20. Lordy, she was but a girl back then, too. She wanted to be a good wife for him, hoping in turn he could help make her a mother, what she dreamed of ever since she was little, herself.

There was no doubt Harry was the one who held up the parade, but "back then," there was no such thing as blaming him—not outrightly. That was possibly why he tolerated any cats at all. It really wasn't such a secret he hated them with a vengeance, but since he was no use in enabling her to bear children . . .

The cats, Boris and Lowry, knew all along. They knew what was going on in Harry J. Kruper's head better than herself, Ena Kruper, his wife of 47 years.

With that she waddled (she felt she was moving at the speed of light) into her—or what *was* Harry's and her room. Grunting, accompanied by a number of creaks and cracks from various joints, she got down on her elbows this time, roly-poly stomach on the worn, pale blue carpet. She lifted the dusty pink bedspread, gasping, "Yah!" when she saw Charles' eyes shining back at her, unblinking.

A low rumble could be heard from deep inside him, coming up through his throat, ever so slowly. It was the most hideous sound she'd ever heard in her life, from anyone or thing. From another place and time it came, and it touched a chord inside her, made her afraid to make him move. He must have already known she was going to get the broom, from behind the back door, in the kitchen. This was his subtle warning to save herself the effort.

In turn she had a sudden, irrational thought—to set fire to the bed and flee, letting the house burn down with all the cats inside.

All for Harry, was the only reason she didn't. He labored his whole life to pay the mortgage on this itty-bitty house.

She calmly heaved-ho and got up (with only a minimum of noises this time) to get the broom. She'd harass his companions and decide if she would *choose* to heed his warning.

Since these clever *kitties* knew so much, she'd just have to think ahead of them. On her way to retrieving her weapon, she glanced around the living room, tallying up who was where. They were all present, save of course for dear Charles.

The broom stiffly held under her right arm, she returned, aiming specifically for Charles's sister Lolly, ensconced on the back of the stuffed chair closest to the front door. She hoped to scare the daylights out of every single one of them, including comparatively innocuous Mimi.

If they made a racket as they scattered, Ena didn't hear them, not even Lolly, who got her butt hit. Their cries might have been drowned by the loud crashing sound of the cherry red heirloom hurricane lamp that she inadvertently knocked over after hitting the cat.

Drat it, she thought. Now there was a mess to clean up. And she never even gave Charles the what-for. She went back to the kitchen to get the wastepaper basket and a dustpan. It bought her some time before she went after Charles. She'd have to think about this.

Yes, Ena was afraid of that cat. Scared to death. And that made her hate him, even more. Either Charles or she would not leave this house alive. She was sure of it, just like she was sure Boris and Lowry were responsible for Harry's death.

Ena left the broom in her bedroom. That was its new, rightful place, beside her maple dresser, whose finish had dulled with time.

Charles did not leave his hiding place before nightfall. What happened in the living room earlier must have proved to him, Ena meant business. Now at least he knew what it was like, to be afraid, to feel it in your bones.

She sat alone in the TV room, the door closed. Her afghan was almost completed yet she couldn't bring herself to work on it. As still as a statue she watched television. No matter how funny some of the jokes were on her favorite sitcoms, she couldn't laugh, not when Charles was having the biggest laugh of everyone.

Ena fell asleep with the TV on. She awoke as the "Late Show" was rolling its closing credits. Well, she had a right to sleep in her *own bed*, she told herself. Maybe that little bugger finally moved. He had to come out by morning, to use the litter box and have breakfast with his cohorts, provided he could *deign* to join them. Or was he on his own now?

Sure as could be, she was *not* about to give him the satisfactions of looking under the bed before getting in it, herself. All she'd do was give herself another good scare, exactly what Charles wanted. He hoped she'd die that way.

She went to sleep, imagining the medical examiner, seated in his plush office, writing down her cause of death as "heart failure." It sounded perfectly logical, for an old woman like herself.

In the early morning Ena awoke midway through a dream. Harry was in it and she was telling him something about Mildred Duchovsky, a friend from school days. Mildred died even before Harry but there she was, at the grocery store. She was buying a huge bag of cat food even though she didn't have a cat. "But you just never knew," she claimed.

"I'll say," Ena muttered as she sat up and tried to recall the strange dream.

When she couldn't, she decided it was just as well. Charles was probably in it too, someplace.

She got dressed and made the bed before giving any thought to looking underneath it.

No, she would not. Charles was more than welcome to come out and eat breakfast with the rest of the group. She included herself in that. They were still a family, even if they didn't get along so great these days. It wasn't the first family like that, was it?

In the kitchen she looked out the picture window. It snowed last night, a good three inches. She could shovel the sidewalk leading to the front stoop. She'd leave the driveway. It was too long for an old lady to shovel. She wasn't going anyplace for a few days. Not only that, the daytime highs for the next few days were supposed to be above freezing, so most likely the snow would melt.

If it got too bad, Mr. Clarkson, who lived next door, would come over with his snow blower, after doing his own driveway. She told him once, to only do hers when there were six or more inches. That saved him some trouble since he did it for nothing, taking pity on an old widow. He was a science teacher at either the Bricktown junior or senior high school, she couldn't recall. His wife taught art class at an elementary school over the state line, in Indiana—*that* much Ena knew. With a good forty-minute commute each way, the woman'd undoubtedly rather stay home on a day like today, although the Clarksons didn't have any cats. They had a dog, a Doberman pinscher. With the nice, big fenced yard, he could romp to his heart's content.

While Ena was outside she was not about to leave any food in a bowl for Charles, who had yet to make an appearance. She would, however, leave the water bowl. That was plenty generous, given the fact he scared the bejabbers out of her yesterday. Not only that, he knew she hated him and neither one had a thing to lose at this point, aside from their lives. *He* had nine of them, didn't he. She only had one. Even if she *was* a witch, she only had one.

A week passed. The snow melted, then it snowed again and

got colder so the snow didn't melt. There were no cat tracks outside but sure as heck Charles was not in the house. He very simply was not anywhere to be seen, heard, or *smelled*. Ena couldn't decide if she was relieved or frightened. She was on her guard, that much was for certain.

Countless times she looked under the bed and he was never there. If he *ever* was, it wasn't when she checked. She kept the broom by the dresser, just in case.

While cleaning, she took to sniffing around every hidden place, expecting to smell something fetid—a rotting body or cat crap. Nothing. Lifting chair and sofa skirts became second nature.

Harry would have argued she didn't have much of a sense of smell. More than a few times he good-humoredly complained of the "cat odor," and Ena couldn't detect it.

She went back to her knitting and by the end of another week the afghan was finished. It was perfect timing. The temperature was supposed to plummet. She could use an extra bit of warmth for her old bones. The threadbare gray wool blanket on the bed wasn't doing it for her. In fact she woke up one night shivering. She didn't need to turn up the thermostat, just more warmth around her body, without wearing all her clothes. She might have to do that, if absolutely necessary. Harry never liked it very warm, and she never did quite get used to sleeping without him by her side.

Under no circumstances at this point would she invite a cat to join her, not even Mimi and Christopher. Ena was adamant about that.

They could thank Charles. He was playing a trick on her, determined to have the last laugh. She'd show him. She might just sleep in the TV room, the door locked, until he reappeared.

Joey Martlin told his mother he didn't think he should deliver any more newspapers to Mrs. Kruper's house. She must have gone away but forgot to tell him. Or maybe she just didn't want the papers delivered anymore.

Mrs. Martlin said we can't be too sure of that, and as soon as Joey was off to school, she phoned the Bricktown police. She herself didn't know Mrs. Kruper, but she was aware the woman lived alone, was old and had seven cats. The poor thing might have tripped and fallen! She wished Joey would have mentioned this sooner. There was at least a week's worth of papers, she imagined, scattered about, some covered with snow. She intended to give her son a talking-to when he got home from school, although she wasn't sure quite what to get after him for. Both Joey and his older brother Mike were pretty darned good kids.

Mrs. Martlin identified herself for the lady who took her call. She proceeded to explain her suspicions and why they were raised. After giving a couple more details she was told a squad car would be dispatched to 110 Shady Lane.

Officer Beress knew the area. It was the best part of town if you liked seclusion or had kids and dogs, with those spacious yards.

The Kruper house was the only one on the long, tree-lined street, that was never remodeled or had any additions. He and Officer Stryker agreed their kids would go crazy here, thinking they had playgrounds of their own.

It was as quiet and still as could be when the two patrolmen stepped out of the squad car. Officer Beress told his partner to radio for an ambulance. Some things you just knew. That snow-covered car of the old widow's was indication enough, not to mention all the papers left on the stoop.

Officer Beress would ring the doorbell, not that he expected anyone to answer. Hell, he'd be surprised if someone did.

"Meow," said a cat, leaping out from the bushes beneath the living room window, whose drapes were drawn.

"Yow!" Officer Beress exclaimed when he saw the scrawny little gray cat with the strange-looking green eyes.

From inside there began a chorus of expectant meows. Recovered somewhat (but there was plenty of eeriness in the air), Officer Beress sing-songed, "Hey, kitty, kitty. That your buddies locked inside the house? How come you're out here?" Then he called to Officer Stryker, to send for animal control while he was at it.

There were a number of questions that would forever remain unanswered. The medical examiner couldn't find anything unusual, performing the autopsy of Ena Kruper. She died peacefully in her sleep, dressed, the television on. Even though it was a week before her body was discovered, decomposition was minimal because she kept the house quite cold, presumably to save money. After all, she had a number of cats to keep fed.

Supposedly she had seven in all, six of which were locked inside the house, hungry and dehydrated but in quite good health. They'd managed to push open the bathroom door and drink the toilet bowl water as well as the drinking water that dripped from the shower and sink faucets. They were unable to reach Ena's body because the door leading to where it lay, was locked.

Curiously, about the seventh cat. He was the first one of the group to be found, as he was outside. When the officers pried the door open and entered the premises, the cat led the way. They both testified that to be so, yet the animal control officers never found him.

Also, Ena Kruper's body had some strange red marks on the neck, near the jugular vein. A veterinarian called in to examine the marks agreed with the medical examiner, no cat could have made them, whether or not he had claws, let alone access to the room.

"R.I.P. (ROCK IN PEACE)"

Every little town needs a rock star. Tampeka, Illinois had Gillie Charmand, former (but the group still sold quite a number of albums) lead guitarist of the Backstabbers.

Gillie Charmand spent nearly fifteen years touring, recording hit albums, and spending time with other musical celebrities, some of whom were living legends.

Once the Backstabbers broke up, Gillie returned to his hometown of Tampeka, where he bought an old farmhouse and restored it. He had wanted to continue with the band but the lead singer, George Janusky, was the one who effectively put a stop to things. He threatened to sue if any of the members used the name.

Gillie told himself it was just as well. At this rate he'd never be an icon anyway, not even if he started a new band. Having realized fame and fortune, he'd accomplished more than most people.

His remodeled farmhouse was situated a couple hundred yards from an unpaved county road. The surrounding pine trees provided plenty of privacy and shelter from the winter wind. He also owned 30 acres of adjoining land. The Wittings brothers 5,000-acre farm encompassed it, so there wasn't a neighbor in sight.

Gillie Charmand had himself one hell of a fast car—a black Porsche 928S-4. The "S-4" supposedly meant it had all-wheel drive, although it was doubtful the tires hardly ever touched the pavement, the way he drove.

Fortunately Gillie didn't go out much. As it was, Sheriff Wilton Detrimer didn't want to have to catch him speeding. He heard enough stories about how indignant celebrities could be, when reprimanded.

The last thing on earth he wished to do was upset Tampeka's one and only. There was a tacit agreement with the two part-time deputies, to turn a blind eye if they saw a black Porsche going "a little too fast."

Gillie Charmand was the only person for miles around to even own that kind of car. He had to take it up to Chicago to have it serviced. It wasn't really that far, not if you drove like he did.

There were plenty of mechanics around but none who had the finesse or know-how to deal with a Porsche (or its owner).

Gillie Charmand probably wouldn't have let just anyone touch it, to begin with. That car was like a family member. Folks even claimed when he talked about it, there was an unmistakable look in his eyes. With his parents having moved to St. Augustine, Florida, he really didn't have an immediate family. That rock group he was in, was like a family too, squabbles and all.

He even supposedly tried marriage, no less than two times. In both cases it was said he neglected to make the ex's sign pre-nuptial agreements. Either he believed in true love or else was too lazy to bother with understanding legalese.

Still and all you'd see him around town and he was as nice and polite as could be. He just drove too fast. Backstabbers fans passed through Tampeka from time to time, so maybe he just wanted to avoid them. Chip's Amoco at the corner of Main and Chester got the most business from these "tourists." The rest of the merchants got a few nibbles, and a scattered few fans ate at the one restaurant in town, the Cozy Corner Diner on Dixon Avenue.

There were no fast food joints here. To find one of those you had to take Route 26 back toward the interstate. That was way out of Sheriff Detrimer's jurisdiction. All he knew was there had yet to be a Gillie Charmand sighting at the Cozy Corner Diner. His Porsche was undoubtedly sighted speeding past it plenty of times, however.

Yesterday it finally happened. In came one of the Wittings brothers to tell Sheriff Detrimer what Gillie Charmand had been up to.

Lomis Wittings happened to be on his tractor at the time, disking his property on the northwest side of Route 26. Gillie Charmand was not only speeding northbound on Paulson Street, he ran the stop sign. This wasn't the first time, either. Lomis would have let the whole thing slide except just now, coming to town to pick up supplies at the Grant Street Grain Elevator, Lomis' blue Chevy pickup about got run off the road by a speeding Porsche.

Lomis said that singer-fella had better stay home if he couldn't obey the rules of the road. An innocent bystander was going to get killed. He and his brother Carl sure wouldn't have sold him the old house, if they thought he'd turn into a nuisance. Soybean prices bottomed out that year, and they made a pretty penny selling him a house they were fixing to tear down.

What Sheriff Detrimer had to do was talk to Gillie Charmand. Even though he was old enough to be the musician's father, the notion of having a one-on-one with him, made the sheriff nervous.

It was imperative he make Gillie Charmand understand the townsfolk were concerned for his welfare, aware as they were that his parents lived far away, and he didn't have any close friends.

Logic told Sheriff Detrimer that inside that recluse Gillie Charmand there still lived the ego-driven rock star. The last thing Sheriff Detrimer wanted to do was rile up that part of the man.

A couple weeks passed and Sheriff Detrimer thought about what he would say to Gillie Charmand. Things were quiet. (There were no more complaints.)

It was the middle of April, the first really warm, sunny day since spring officially began.

Sheriff Detrimer felt like he had ants in his pants. Maybe he was suffering from that phenomenon known as spring fever. He was hungry, too. His wife Dorothea promised him his favorite meal for dinner tonight—lamb riblets. He was imagining the taste of that succulent meat, when into the station stormed Alicia Carver.

On any other day, Sheriff Detrimer would have described her as withered, old and frail. Period. Appearing so extraordinarily incensed, infused new life into those brittle little bones supporting that four-foot, eleven inch frame. Hell if she didn't look six feet tall, telling him, "I just came out the door of Betty's Hair Boutique 'n' somethin' blew by so fast, I about had my perm straightened. Lucky thing I wasn't wearin' a wig. I gotta be thankful for that much."

The old lady wasn't joking, but still, Sheriff Detrimer had to smile. It was that or else burst into laughter. She didn't give a hoot about offending Gillie Charmand. She was rabid about the matter, even spit on his desk.

Rightfully getting angry with the sheriff too, she leaned toward him, placidly seated at the spit-upon desk. She said, "Actually, before I came here to lodge my complaint about you know who, I went back into Betty's. She 'n' I agreed 'n' Libby Heckel 'n' Mary Schiller too, both getting their hair done, that *we* have to take it upon ourselves to stop this nonsense. It ain't a generation problem, neither. That little gal Betty's got workin' for her now, I can't remember her name, but she agreed. That fella's a problem. And by the way this isn't the first time I seen 'im hotroddin' it . . . You don't tell 'im to slow down, a couple carloads of us proud Tampeka citizens are goin' right up to his doorstep with the petition we're gonna have everyone sign, tellin' 'im to move away, if he can't be a law-abiding citizen."

Sheriff Detrimer cringed at the prospect. Gillie Charmand didn't have a gun, he was pretty sure. If the guy did, there'd be plenty of perms losing their curls. All he'd have to do was fire a shot in the air and the folks would want him thrown out on the double.

Gillie Charmand was most likely using Forest Lane, where Betty's shop was, to avoid the light at Dixon and First Avenues. It was mostly a residential street, and Betty Muldoon in fact had her salon in a portion of her remodeled A-frame house.

Sheriff Detrimer was left with an obligation at this point. Now all he had to do was get Gillie Charmand to agree.

When Gillie Charmand heard the phone ring, he was startled. It'd been a couple months easy, since it last rang. Buddy Germaine, the former bass player of the Backstabbers, contacted him. He was one of the few celebrity-musicians on the planet who could speak for himself, didn't d—k around with assistants or handlers. Gillie always did have a soft spot for bass players. Along with drummers, those two were the most down-to-earth and easygoing. As for the effin' lead singers, he had yet to meet one whose head wasn't stuck in the clouds. Hell would be as frozen as Antarctica before the Backstabbers' former lead singer George Janusky came off his flipping high-horse.

It was a cry-your-eyes-out shame George didn't O.D. and their drummer Craig Biltz did, about three years ago, already.

Instead Georgie-Porgie (don't say it to his face) was still out there, making the world take notice of him with a third solo album (or solo-flop, your choice).

He had plenty of nerve, thinking anyone gave a rat's ass what some 45 year-old has-been did with his mediocre voice. It was even less than that when he was belting out lame-ass songs. Gillie'd never waste his money buying one of the damned CDs, only to hear how stupid it was. He hoped it sunk into oblivion like the other two the pompous a-hole made since the Backstabbers broke up, almost ten years ago.

Georgie-Porgie even managed to get an "explicit lyrics" warning, slapped on the cover. The old bastard was either desperate to impress or trying to deny the fact he was too old to play the rock-and-roll game. He deserved to be the latest laughingstock of the record industry. The Backstabbers never had to resort to shock tactics. All Georgie did was prove he was the biggest idiot of the four of them.

It was his fault the band broke up. Gillie was as infuriated as the day the egotistical peroxide-head announced he wanted out.

Gillie might have predicted the demise of the group if he'd used his own noggin a little. The name for the band was thought of by none other than the one who turned on everybody.

On some days it seemed like Gillie just laid eyes on the nitwit's face and on others it seemed like he dreamed the whole experience, twelve years' worth. Plus, for four years prior to that, Gillie lived hand-to-mouth, having practically run away from home at 17.

It was amazing he could live such a quiet life back in the town where he grew up, considering how accustomed he became to nonstop activity, as well as constantly socializing with a coterie of famous pals. It was possible he was bored out of his skull and not even aware.

All he asked from the citizens of Tampeka was they'd treat him like everybody else. Over the years, they'd done just that and he was most grateful. He imagined they were a little wary of him, which was O.K., too. It was something that would never change, just like as long as there were class rock stations, you could hear the Backstabbers' music. And Gillie Charmand was proud to say he contributed no less than three number one hits to the band.

There. The phone finally stopped. If he didn't feel inclined to answer it, he could simply turn it off. Hopefully an obsessed fan didn't somehow get his number. It happened from time to time, but none of them had yet to find his house. A few of them cruised around town once in awhile, checking out the house he grew up in, that kind of thing.

The phone started ringing again. He wished this was a hallucination, for more reasons than one. These days he avoided drugs and relationships because neither one was worth the accompanying hassles.

Twice he married for love and both times he got sucked dry. Thank God for royalty payments or he'd be sober, alone, *and* broke.

If he felt like he needed to cut loose, he'd go for a drive in his Porsche 928. With four-wheel drive it was like an exotic-looking, all-terrain vehicle. He bet it could even be a boat. When he visited his parents in Florida at Christmas, he'd been tempted a few times, to drive it into the ocean, just to see.

Around here was perfect for speeding. The roads were flat and deserted, save for an occasional pickup truck moving about two miles an hour. If you didn't see a cop, there wasn't one. And some of these roads were patrolled by county police, not the Tampeka ones. The former were undoubtedly much less forgiving to someone like him.

The phone stopped again. One more time and he'd answer it. He really ought to, anyway. His parents might be trying to get ahold of him. It was worth every one of his 42 years to have the opportunity to say that. Gillie was indebted to none other than the fortune and fame brought on by the Backstabbers' success.

Speaking of that, he never finished the story about Buddy Germaine. He'd called, said he'd be passing through and wanted to stop in for a visit. Gillie gave him directions and eagerly awaited his arrival. He hadn't seen the dude in a long time.

He made sure to pick up plenty of beer, the best drink for reminiscing. They couldn't do too much partying because Buddy's wife Carol was with him and she was straight as an arrow. She was even into herbs and meditation, all that crap.

Carol was his third wife and Buddy really did love her. It just took musicians longer than most other people, to find "a mate." (Gillie always did find the human condition rather peculiar.)

Buddy kidded him a little, said the third time's a charm, all those stupid sayings. He didn't keep on, however, not with Carol sitting right there. Gillie didn't get a chance to ask him if he made her sign a pre-nuptial. He probably did. It was a shame women didn't leave you with any choice on the matter.

Gillie didn't believe in that kind of impersonal prevention measure. If he couldn't trust a female to share and share alike, he'd gladly stay single. He'd also had his fill of slatternly girlfriends. So it came down to the lesser of the evils, was all.

Self-sufficiency was good for the soul, too. Not even one of Carol Germaine's herbs provided the ultimate answer. So tomorrow he had to pick up his jacket at the cleaners. Little things he did, to while away the day. He could shoot down Forest Lane to get there, avoiding the godawfully long light at Dixon and First. On thing he *didn't* like to do was kill time sitting at intersections. He sat at that light so long one day he started pulling gray hairs out of his head. That turned into quite a project. He decided to let it go gray if it wanted, making it harder for Backstabber fans to recognize him.

Anyway, about the reconciliation that took place with his father, it actually came about because of his father Clive's boss' son, Billie Crampton.

Clive worked at the Crampton Bearing Company in Decatur,

and one day in '79, he was called into his boss Edward Crampton's office. This was an unprecedented situation, given Clive's place on the corporate totem pole. There had to be a reason he was summoned, and for the sake of friendly chit-chat was not one of them.

While Clive tried to decide if his boss was smiling or snarling, Mr. Crampton said, "My boy Billie's a huge fan of that group the Backstabbers. Correct me if I'm wrong Clive, but isn't your son in that group? He plays lead guitar or some such. Now this is all hearsay from a starstruck fourteen year-old . . ."

Clive was determined he was neck-deep in trouble, all because of his "famous son," who'd essentially run away from home several years ago. He himself had been attempting to ignore the publicity his son's band was getting, all because he was ashamed of their success. Now Mr. Crampton had taken offense to it and most likely wanted him to leave his conservatively-minded company.

Clive somehow managed to acknowledge his boss and confirm the speculation. For all intents and purposes, however, he sat as still as a statue.

Meanwhile Mr. Crampton said, "Well, well. My boy Billie *was* right. Now Clive, if your son *ever* comes to visit, *please*, if his schedule isn't too hectic, it would mean the world to my son and me as well, if Billie could shake your son's hand. The boy in all honesty, Clive, worships that group and your son Gillie, in particular. Calls him the baddest axeman there is, as a compliment, I presume, blah, blah, blah . . ."

With that, Clive received a crash course in what celebrity status did to people. It took even his stoical, superior boss and turned him into a driveling, ass-kissing fool.

Clive himself felt like a fool and a half (this related with all humility). Post haste it was necessary to contact Gillie. He began by placing a call to the record company, whose name he had the good fortune of knowing because Gillie's mother Abigail owned all the Backstabbers' albums. It was the only way of having up-to-date photos of her son. If she actually listened to their music, she didn't offer any opinions.

Gillie in the meanwhile lost track of just how long it had been since he talked to his parents, partly because he wanted to forget the past and partly to ease the accompanying pain he nonetheless felt. He and his father had never been close, so a reconciliation offered them an opportunity to be closer than ever before.

Yeah, despite success Gillie had felt bad, even bitter. It hurt not having an immediate family with whom to enjoy the material gains. Nine times out of ten too much partying was the result of feeling sorry for himself, not because he was happy.

Suddenly bygones were bygones, *and* Billie Crampton got the chance to meet his guitar hero when Gillie returned to Tampeka for the first time in years. Everyone's life changed for the better that day, and Billie even got a couple free guitar picks. The kid's eyes about bugged out of his head, and that alone was worth the trip.

It was such a relief for Gillie to reunite with his parents he felt almost let down. He attributed it to the fact he was on the defensive for so long.

All that good feeling might have been what induced him to move back to the area. Having rented a house in the L.A. area and purchased one on separate occasions (only to lose it to an ex-wife), he never did really feel like he was "home." He missed the seasons and had his fill of predictions when the "Big One" would arrive.

Plus in comparative terms you couldn't beat the housing prices here.

He could hardly believe it. The #$@! phone again. Someone was most certainly trying to get ahold of him.

"Hello," he gruffly said into the receiver.

"Hello. Mr. Charmand?" a man asked. Gillie couldn't *begin* to imagine who it might be. He hadn't been addressed as such since he didn't know when.

"Yes," he answered, letting some suspicion seep into his voice.

"This is Sheriff Detrimer, down at the Tampeka Police Station. How are you today?"

"Fine," Gillie replied. Now he *was* suspicious. Cops did not call to ask your state of health.

There must have been a lull because the copper wanted to know, "Are you still there, Mr. Charmand?"

Gillie reassured him yes he was, and then had to bite the side of his mouth—hard—to keep from making a wisecrack or two, to the tune of, "No. I'm . . ." He happened to have a couple of doozies in mind.

Then he had *this* humbling, horrible thought. Some chick, a thousand miles away, got pregnant through osmosis and expected him to pay the hospital bills. Or, even better, she was listening to one of the Backstabbers' hits he himself penned and spontaneously got pregnant.

Sheriff Detrimer said, sounding *much* more pleasant than Gillie bet he usually did, "I wondered if you weren't too busy to . . ."

In the meantime Gillie was ready to slam the receiver back in its cradle, his impatience was so great. He'd break the cop's eardrum, and to think the guy didn't even need to attend a good old rock-and-roll concert, not even one of the Backstabber's.

" . . . make an appointment, to—"

"Sure, Chief—er Sheriff Detrimer, sir," Gillie cut in to say. He was just trying to make it easy on the guy. It was more than a little plain he was uptight. Plus, Gillie was dying to find out what was up—or not. "Want me to come down there right now?"

"That'd be most considerate of you, Mister Charmand, if you're not too busy," Sheriff Detrimer said.

"No, I'm not at all," Gillie told him, while thinking, *You know I don't have a damned thing going on in my life!* He added, "I'll be right there," to which the sheriff hastened to say, "Take you time, Mister Charmand."

Before leaving, Gillie grabbed a couple guitar picks, wishful thinking on his part. He had a feeling this was something more involved than making someone's day.

Sheriff Wilton Detrimer watched *Mr.* Gillie Charmand (Wilton couldn't resist the mister part, although Gillie did insist he please call him by his first name) walk to his black Porsche, most deservedly the man's pride and joy.

As for their "friendly meeting," Sheriff Detrimer concluded it was a complete success. There wasn't another law enforcement official around these parts who could have handled the situation any better. He wasn't trying to undermine Gillie, because of course, he helped. The guy was genuinely real nice. Never mind the fact he was looking a little frayed around the edges. He'd done a lot and been through a lot.

Gillie was most humble, saying the last thing on earth he ever wanted to do was scare or intimidate anyone and he profusely apologized. Being that polite was due to his Midwestern upbringing.

Sheriff Detrimer was proud of Gillie Charmand and he was proud of himself. He was quite the diplomat. He always did have a hunch that was inside him. He just never had much opportunity to put it to use.

Even though he just stood to shake hands with Gillie and say good-bye, he got up again, this time to stretch. His stomach growled. Boy was he hungry now. He'd gotten so needlessly worried about the meeting with Gillie, he forgot about his appetite—and that savory meal.

Sheriff Detrimer felt almost let down because everything *did* run so smoothly. Perhaps he should follow up with a note of appreciation, letting Gillie know the Tampeka residents were happy to have him for their "celebrity citizen." That sounded most complimentary, he was certain.

He'd ask his wife Dorothea's opinion, while they were having that delicious lamb riblet dinner. She herself was rather adept at diplomacy, raising three sons who were only a year apart in their ages.

This morning she'd been apprised of the talk Sheriff Detrimer hoped to have with Gillie Charmand, which happened much sooner than expected.

Reflecting on all this, Sheriff Detrimer decided he was one of the luckiest men in the world. He loved what he did for a living and his wife was a great cook.

Blazes, *what in blazes next*, Gillie thought, as he drove (he was not speeding) home from the police station. In another mile or two he was going to really let it rip.

He liked his story better, about the girl getting pregnant through osmosis. Right now he felt more duped than ever. He was essentially *summoned* to the police station, plain and simple. He wouldn't have gotten even half as much courtesy and respect if he wasn't "who" he was. Oh well. He'd just better be thankful that celebrity-status crap came in handy.

Reaching a deserted, flat stretch of Paulson Street, he sped the rest of the way to the stop sign at Route 26. No one was coming from either direction for as far as he could see. It was tempting to run the damned thing. A couple weeks ago he did and it felt so good. Sheriff Detrimer could tell him to slow down, but Gillie would continue to run stop signs, specifically this one. A man needed a *few* freedoms.

He did stop this time, however. He didn't want to get killed before dinner. Chicken gumbo was on the menu tonight and he made a mean batch. If he ever wanted to open a restaurant, the residents of Tampeka would wait in line to dine there. He could educate their palates about what constituted tasty food, besides salt and grease.

Having eaten in restaurants around the world, he knew a little about "fine cuisine," and he could put that effin' Cozy Corner Diner out of business. Admittedly he had never set foot in the place. However, he sure as hell sped past it plenty of times.

Before adding the finishing touches to the gumbo, he was going to pour himself a stiff drink. It'd been awhile since he got plastered. There hadn't been an occasion to drown his frustrations.

He'd toast himself, for knowing better than to drink and drive. How could he, when he liked to speed? As far as he was concerned he didn't do anything wrong.

The following day found Gillie driving back toward town. He was also enduring the most acute hangover of his entire life. Reverberating in his eardrums was the "talk" he had the day before with Sheriff Detrimer.

There was no doubt about it. Last night he drank way too much. Worst of all, he was no longer used to tolerating the aftermath.

Too #*@! bad. He had things to do and by hook or by crook he would do them and get back home again, all without getting a speeding ticket. That didn't mean he wouldn't exercise his "freedom to speed." Good one. It made him chuckle, despite this throbbing head.

He reached the corner of 500 south and Route 12, where he turned left. Finally he was on paved road. From this point it was a straight shot for about two miles, until he reached Paulson Street. He quickly shifted into fifth gear, feeling the motor purr along. Going 90 m.p.h. he felt better already.

He should have eaten more of that gumbo he raved about. The problem was he got drunk before he ate anything and of course that killed his appetite. Maybe one of these days he would quit punishing himself.

Sheriff Detrimer cleverly alluded to the same thing, concerning speeding. He claimed the residents were worried about Gillie's welfare.

If Gillie wasn't feeling so completely humiliated, he would have laughed in that copper's fat face. Should Gillie ever be summoned to the police station again, he'd take the sheriff a pot of his chicken gumbo, appealing to the guy's appetite. He'd forget about why he summoned Gillie in the first place.

Yup, Gillie too could play the game. That cop thought he was *so* smart, kissing up to Gillie's rock-star persona, wrongfully assuming he was selfish. Self-loathing maybe, but not selfish. *Sorry, Sheriff Detrimer,* Gillie sarcastically thought.

All Gillie ever wanted was to be a legend in his own time. No thanks to George Janusky, it wasn't meant to be, not while they were know as the Backstabbers.

A comeback. It was never to late for one of those. Every muscle in his flabby but not fat (not yet, anyway) body twitched at the mere mention.

Gillie had in fact penned a few tunes in the interim, although it was hard to write when he lacked inspiration. That was how it was for him, anyway.

For whatever reason, perhaps because he'd been depressed (and more bored than he was aware), these songs were wholly different from the ones that made the Backstabbers famous.

They were also polar opposites to the cock-rock crap Georgie-Porgie had on *his* latest album. Those songs only showed how the idiot had regressed.

Gillie got sick of criticizing the guy, even if he deserved it. Unlike some people he was sick of mentioning, Gillie himself didn't feel any particular need to live up to the name "Backstabber."

By this time the intersection of Paulson and Route 26 was about 150 yards ahead. He looked to the left, to the right, and to the left again, debating if he should run the stop sign. There wasn't a car in sight.

Suddenly he felt so good he could hardly contain himself. It was all thanks to his idea about a comeback. Luckily he didn't think of it sooner, or he would have dismissed it as a joke.

Glancing to the left one more time, he still couldn't see any cars. He downshifted, just to hear the engine revving. Then he shifted back to fifth and feeling like a kid again, he exclaimed, "Yahoo!"

The westbound 18-wheeler was exceeding the posted 55 m.p.h. speed limit when he barreled into a black Porsche, sending it flying. The tires on that car really never did touch the pavement. Meanwhile the truck jackknifed. Although the driver was shaken, he was miraculously uninjured.

Gillie's parents, Clive and Abigail, were devastated by the news of their son's tragic and sudden death.

Attending the funeral was an impressive number of friends and fans. Gillie would not have been disappointed by the size of the turnout.

With his body laid to rest in the Tampeka Memorial Cemetery, the town would become an important stopping point for both die-hard Backstabber fans as well as new recruits.

The lyrics to eight songs Gillie had written, were found in one of his guitar cases. Clive Charmand contacted the record company and explained the situation, just like what he did when he needed to get in touch with his estranged son, all those years ago.

Three of the songs made a talented young bandleader by the name of Georgia Heinz, into a superstar. She dedicated her debut album on a major label, to "Gillie Charmand and his spirit." He was in turn recognized as the "driving force" of the Backstabbers' success.

Owing to his untimely death, he became a legend.

"BEAUTIFUL GIRL"

Moyra Williams woke up the Tuesday after Memorial Day, with the decision to murder her year-old son Nathan.

She never could recall what she dreamed and last night was no exception. When she awoke, however, she'd made this resounding decision. Whatever she dreamed allowed her to make this clean break from a mental impasse she'd lived with, ever since giving birth to the little monster.

Before you conclude that worse than deluded, she was one of those bitch-women who hates her child, you have to understand her situation. Moyra had been estranged from Nathan's father Shep for six months prior to giving birth (or about three months after he was conceived, whichever you prefer), and only one time did she have intercourse with the man. It was most certainly a dalliance, and Nathan was the result of utter carelessness.

The day Moyra and Nathan were brought home from the hospital by Moyra's mother, CeCe, and everyday since then, Shep had tried (to no avail) to see his son.

Moyra refused to marry Shep and at one point if she at least felt indifferent toward him, she now hated his guts. Not only that, he cut grass for a living, and what kind of job was that? *She* was a *career woman.*

She'd gladly whack him off, except it was more logical to kill a helpless infant, living under the same roof. People were also much less likely to be suspicious of a baby's sudden disappearance, provided the reason sounded valid. By this time the whole neighborhood was used to Shep's daily visits, and the subsequent tantrums she threw in the doorway. She might have even threatened to kill him.

Someday she'd find herself a real man and have another child, simple as that. If Shep's stupidity and laziness were passed on to their son (she shuddered to write the word "their"), there was no hope, and she was doing the kid a favor—not that it was necessary for her to justify what she intended to do, not her. Moyra was fully her *own* person.

By the bye, she was also intelligent and ambitious, but the child was in the way of her plans, all the big ones she had. She wanted to move to New York someday and edit a fashion magazine. Right now she wrote a self-help column for a few dinky local papers. Sure the column was "syndicated" but here again, she hated to use the word. She wasn't deluded by the fact her readership only included one measly county in north central Indiana. At this rate it would take forever to be ready for the big time. She was constantly distracted by the smell of talcum powder and the sound of Nathan gurgling or gargling, whatever the hell he did. It seemed like just about everything but swallow his tongue. That would be too good to be true.

Seated at her computer terminal, in her home office that overlooked Lake Talbot, was at one time her place of refuge. Now that she knew there was constant companionship in the other room, she lost her haven.

Argh. She could smell poop just recalling the little mite. Fortunately her mother came by this morning and took him shopping with her. Can you *imagine*?

When Moyra needed to go to the store she made her mother come here and sit with him, or else she called Della, the girl next door. Pretty, not quite 14, oh how Moyra wished she herself were young and innocent again. The wiles of boys got the better of her, the day she turned 16. If teenaged girls obsessed about boys, Moyra practically died, thinking about them.

She had to smile at that. It was so ironic her unfettered one-night stand with a charming, handsome nobody, would lead to her desire to kill the result.

Nowadays editing her column was impossible to do without getting up every few minutes, to peer out the window. It was as if she needed to confirm the lake was still there.

At least she got something useful out of this nervous habit she didn't have before Nathan was born. It gave her the idea to drown him, as the way of finishing him off.

She'd carry him to the pier, stick him underneath it, and let him gurgle to his little heart's content. Afterward she would incinerate the body, right along with a ton of old newspaper clippings she'd kept as research material for a novel she had yet to write. At this rate it would never get written, not when she could no longer properly relax, not even at her terminal.

She would tell her nosey ex-boyfriend "their" son died of SIDS. It sounded plausible. She herself was rather sickly as a child, and it wasn't until blossoming as an adult, all the ailments and maladies had run their course.

The only one who might be suspicious was her mother. Also, unlike stupid, lunkheaded Shep, she might try to get some information from the hospital, and of course there wouldn't *be* any information to give.

The mere fact Moyra called her mother for anything and everything that was even remotely amiss, especially when it came to Nathan, stood to throw a monkey wrench in her plan.

Her mother was patience and understanding themselves. In back of her mind she must have wished it was her. *Loathsome*, was all Moyra could think. She just wanted her freedom.

The boy was much too young to resemble his father, which could have explained some of this incessant unease. Maybe it just galled her, Shep too could have tried to prevent this.

Waxing and waning, she was letting the month of June pass by without going through with her plan. She finally told herself the Fourth of July would be the day—midnight, marking the end of the holiday. Even though the whole neighborhood would celebrate, everyone would be in bed by then. Lake Talbot was such a staid, predictable little town. She liked it. If she neglected to lock a door at night, it was O.K. In fact sometimes she enjoyed "pushing her luck," just to see if a robber would

come in the house. Her dachshund Donnie was guaranteed to
bark at any total strangers.

She like him so much, she kept his wicker bed by hers. She
had to be careful when she got up every morning, not to trip on
the bed. Usually he went downstairs early and waited to be let
outside.

She could have put his bed somewhere else in the room, but it
just wouldn't have been the same. If she couldn't sleep (Many
nights she suffered from insomnia, about the only problem she
had *before* her pregnancy), she'd lop her hand over the side of the
bed and stroke his short, smooth fur.

Tomorrow was the Fourth. She was glad she didn't have to do
the deed tonight because she could hardly stay awake to get ready
for bed (scrub her milky-white complexion and apply three separate
moisturizers to her entire body) and put on one of her long, lacey
nightgowns.

The evening of the necessary task, she would stay up until it
was time. She counted on being full of anticipation. Knowing what
lay ahead, her mind and body were evidently gearing up, which
explained this exhausted feeling.

The last thing she remembered before drifting into a deep
sleep was the silky smooth texture of her golden blonde hair upon
her cheek.

She was a beautiful creature who deserved much better than
Shep, and she wouldn't give herself away again, until this special
man came along.

Moyra awoke to the alarm clock, buzzing in her ear. "Turn
that off," she muttered, still half-asleep. She was hardly used to
awakening to it, for she would turn it off before it "got her," as she
called it.

Sitting up, she felt different. *Now* what did she dream that she
couldn't remember? Then she glanced at Donnie's bed and saw it
was empty. If she didn't feel well-rested, she would have been
jealous of that dog, how easy it was for him to get up early.

This was in fact the best she felt since having Nathan. Thanks to him, she'd been feeling eternally sapped of her youthful vigor, and at 27, that simply wasn't fair.

She was aware of the hormonal changes that accompanied a pregnancy, but she'd insisted to her doctor, her whole brain was scrambled, as a result. She even went so far as to use an example, saying it was like she'd been on one of those carnival rides in which you're turned every which way, standing up.

He'd given her his most patronizing smile and assured her, "These things take time, Ms. Williams."

Things? What things, Dr. Mollton?" She'd wanted to scream but kept her teeth clenched.

The next time she needed a check-up, she'd go to Chicago. She didn't even trust Indianapolis, which was actually much closer, to have a sufficiently knowledgeable doctor.

No sooner did she get up, making sure to sidestep Donnie's bed, than a clap of thunder made her jump. She was so silly. For a second she thought it was an earlybird, setting off some fireworks. She grinned, picturing poor Donnie, scurrying to the relative safety of the recliner in the den. He was undoubtedly sorry he left the bedroom but was too lazy to ascend the stairs with that sausage body of his. He was in fact a bit overweight. She couldn't resist feeding him table scraps, he was just so cute.

Looking out the window, it was impossible for Moyra to see the lake, not only because it was still dark but because the branches of the maple tree, taller than the colonial-style house, blocked the view.

Come to think of it, there was a chance of rain this morning, but the weatherman assured everyone it would clear up "in plenty of time for the barbecue or picnic you got planned."

"Who the hell says?" she'd yelled at the TV, pointing the remote control at his pale, cherubic face. What was his name? Rick or Dick Chortle, something stupid like that. It was beyond her, how he got a job doing the weather on the six o'clock news. At the very least, if she didn't move to New York, she needed to seriously consider moving back to the Chicagoland area.

After putting on her slippers, which took a couple extra seconds to find because it really was awfully dark (yet she refused to turn on a light, since it was supposed to *be* light), she went downstairs to let Donnie outside.

She never hurried to check on Nathan and luckily for him, he knew to be quiet. Had she ever heard even a peep from the other end of the hallway, where his room was, she would have made a point of ignoring him. Besides, he was still peeing and crapping in his diapers, while *Donnie* was housebroken.

If the dog was understandably scared, however, he might relieve himself on the floor. This past spring she had new carpet installed in the den and her office, as well as having the linoleum in the kitchen replaced with Saltillo tile.

Upon reaching that very room she stopped short at a puddle of blood. She was immediately certain of whose it was, so she was not at all surprised to see Donnie's inert body, by the door. Before kneeling to see if he really was dead, out of the corner of her eye she saw a note on the table. In the same instant she pressed the dimmer switch, there was a crack of thunder and a flash of lightning, and the electricity went off.

She held the piece of paper close to her face and read the following, relying on the lightning flashes to see:

> Nathan is with me, where he belongs.
> Don't try to find us. We'll be long gone, with new I.D.'s,
>   before you can figure out how to explain this to your
>   mother.
> We all spoiled you. Killing your dog was the only way to
>   show you. Beautiful girls can only love themselves.
> Even a guy like me who cuts grass figured that much out.

"HOME FREE"

Grace Wittender became more demanding as she aged and her health deteriorated. Michelle Wittender's mother Cloris was so accustomed to catering to her 85 year-old aunt, this change went unnoticed. Michelle, however, could tell the old woman was having a great time, taking advantage of her mother.

Michelle and her mother didn't have a car. They lived above the family seamstress shop, located on the Lessing town square. Lessing was a quaint little Indiana town, 60 miles southeast of Chicago. Because the surrounding area was no longer all that rural, the two Timmers drugstores did a steady business.

Michelle's mother would bicycle to Aunt Grace's house on route 212, also know as Bitteroot Road, nearly everyday. Whenever necessary she would take the old woman (she was actually Michelle's *great*-aunt) her prescription of painkillers, procured from Timmers, due south of the square.

With the other Timmers located at the junction of Main Street and Bitteroot Road, it was more convenient to patronize that one. Aunt Grace's house was a good seven miles away, as it was. Going to the drugstore farthest from it, added at least two miles to the entire trip. It was bad enough Bitteroot Road was narrow, winding, and lacked a posted speed limit.

It was impossible for Michelle to point out the logic of using the store that was closer to Aunt Grace's, without upsetting her ultra-sensitive mother. Not only that, her mother, in a fit of anger, might relegate the responsibility to Michelle.

Something about the old woman, not just the way she ordered her niece Cloris around, made Michelle dislike and distrust her. If at all avoidable she didn't want to do her great-aunt any favors.

Michelle could understand the reasons for her mother's loyalty, but she took it to the extreme. Aunt Grace essentially raised Cloris because Angela, Michelle's grandmother (Cloris' mother) was a real floozie.

Supposedly, however, the Wittender family had British ancestors who contributed knowledge to science and medicine. Michelle felt a moral duty to show the world this family was still capable of accomplishing something, so she wanted to be a molecular biologist.

Her mother was on her way to an achievement when she was accepted to Felding College in Boston. It was known for having graduated a number of famous writers and philosophers. During the first semester of freshman year she accidentally got pregnant. The janitor's son Clarence Dowager was the father, and he was not only unemployed but illiterate.

At Christmas Cloris returned to Indiana, to become a mother. Her holiday gift was a swift blow to the head, courtesy of the steel-toed boot of her pig-farmer father Darryl. Why he didn't kick her stomach was anybody's guess. Anyway, Michelle's life was spared, to be raised by a mother with brain damage. Menial work was all she could do to support her illegitimate child and herself.

Perhaps her father did her favor. Effectively numbed, she could live in relative peace, not obsess over the sin she committed.

Once Michelle was old enough to assist her mother with the seamstress duties, she did so. She was also a housecleaner and babysitter for some of her mother's customers. Comparatively well-to-do, many of them lived in the Federal and Italianate-style houses on Main Street, within walking distance of the town square.

Now that school was underway again (Michelle was a high school freshman), there wasn't enough time to clean house and baby-sit for more than two families. Even so, she was kept very busy, leaving Saturday the only day she had to visit with Aunt Grace.

Monday night Michelle found she couldn't go to sleep, yet she was exhausted. The pancake-thin mattress and pillow weren't to blame. The dingy, little windowless room wasn't, either. It was Aunt Grace. Even though the old woman and Cloris didn't say much in Michelle's presence, she knew it wasn't usually the case. Her mother wasn't a talkative type, and her dementedness added to her placidity. She therefore made the perfect audience for one of her aunt's diatribes.

Aunt Grace never did approve of Michelle receiving a public school education, and she once stated "the influences" were going to get Michelle.

If "the influence" included boys, Michelle could have assured her, there wasn't any reason to worry. None of them even noticed her. The one she might have gotten along with was Henry McAllister, but his face was always buried in a book. It would be sophomore year before he and Michelle made eye contact.

Over the summer, Michelle figured out what Aunt Grace wanted her to do—quit school by age 16 and work full-time in the seamstress shop. She didn't think Michelle should even do any more babysitting or housecleaning.

Her mother was proud of the amount of cash Michelle raked in over the summer. It was safe to say, comparing what each one left in the bank account they shared (an old, chipped ceramic cookie jar), that Michelle had made more money than her mother. Hopefully her mother hadn't gone so completely bonkers, she forgot the value of a good education.

Heaven forbid Michelle ended up stuck in the middle of this family feud, spending the rest of her life cleaning houses, babysitting, mending clothes and watching her mother make gaudy beaded necklaces. That was what she did in the evenings.

This was a possible fate, should Aunt Grace succeed in poisoning her mother's already addled brain. Aunt Grace either didn't *want* Michelle to make something of herself or else didn't *believe* she could. What difference did it make to her? She had a house of her own and a car, although she never drove it. Maybe it didn't work. It certainly wasn't in good shape. She needn't be concerned, not when she had an able-bodied niece to run errands, the boy next door to cut her grass and a clerk from the grocery store to deliver her list of items. That service cost her only four dollars more than the groceries themselves.

That was four dollars Michelle could have put to good use, not that *she* wanted to do Aunt Grace's grocery-shopping. Cruel as it sounded, she'd be tempted to lace all the food with arsenic.

Michelle liked to think her interest in science kept her from taking this notion seriously. Only characters in novels did outlandish things like that.

Thankfully her mother was resourceful. She used Aunt Grace's empty pill containers to store the various beads for her necklaces. The hobby shop on the east side of the square (versus the west side, where they lived) sold the beads in those cheap little bags. Once you tore them open, beads spilled everywhere.

So as if it wasn't enough Aunt Grace wasted money (and obviously had more than them), she was running (and ruining) both their lives with her demands and criticisms (from across town, besides). An added touch was those empty pill containers, dozens in all, prominently displayed on the buffet table in the sitting room.

Michelle finally fell asleep. She dreamed of choking Aunt Grace with one of her mother's necklaces. It was amazing her mother continued dutifully making them, although they did generate some extra income, because Aunt Grace hated them. She never wore any jewelry, as it was. Her standard outfit all year long, consisted of a knee-length, blue gingham housedress, either a cream-colored or a black wool cardigan, and coffee-colored, terrycloth booties.

Aunt Grace in fact once told Cloris (and she didn't know Michelle heard), "I can get somethin' prettier at the five 'n' dime, 'n' if I do ever want a necklace from there, I'll make *you use* your money to get it."

Tuesday was an especially busy day at Michelle's mother's shop. It seemed all the women in Lessing, young and old, had a garment that needed mending. A day such as this dictated Michelle would cook dinner (the meager evening repast), provided she returned from babysitting before her mother finished work.

Her mother usually visited Aunt Grace before it was time to open the shop, at ten o'clock. It was open until 6:00 P.M. on weekdays except Fridays, when she stayed until 7:00 or 8:00. Other days too, such as this one, she would remain open past six, catching up on her work. Saturdays she was only available by appointment.

Michelle got back from Mrs. Pollack's at 7:15, only to see her mother's red, upright bicycle was missing from the foyer (a patch of white tile in front of the stairs). Michelle kept her similarly designed blue bicycle, which was missing its kickstand, in her room.

Evidently her mother didn't visit Aunt Grace earlier today. Soon it would be getting dark in the evening, and she wouldn't have any choice.

No time would be wasted, deciding what to prepare. That was good because Michelle was starved. There were only two boxes of macaroni and cheese in the cabinet and a bag of carrots in the refrigerator. It didn't get much more imaginative, either. Michelle was grateful Mrs. Pollack and Mrs. Jarvis, the other lady she was continuing to work for during the school year, didn't make her cook. Michelle was so unused to blending a number ingredients, she doubted she could pull it off. She pictured Mrs. Pollack's seven year-old son Andy, making faces and innocently complaining, like only little kids can do. Meanwhile Michelle would be as embarrassed as heck.

Sometimes it was hard to believe she was already fourteen. As if it wasn't bad enough she couldn't cook, she had yet to be kissed by a boy.

Aunt Grace's unfounded worries came to mind again. At this rate no boy would *ever* taint Michelle—ugly duckling Michelle. Once in awhile she dared to look in the mirror. There was a semblance of her pretty, slim, brunette-haired mother, who had an ivory complexion, angular features and sea-green eyes (with a faraway look in them). Still, she herself had a long way to go.

All Michelle wanted was to accomplish something worthwhile on her own merit. It was irrelevant if she happened to be attractive. Aunt Grace must have been completely incredulous someone from her family could have this disregard.

One good thing about tonight was Michelle finished all her homework, waiting for Mrs. Pollack to return. During the week,

Andy didn't have a father, either. He worked for a big company in Chicago, so he stayed there to avoid commuting. Supposedly he came home on the weekends. Michelle wished she could meet him sometime, rather than spending yet another Saturday with Aunt Grace.

Michelle's mother returned at 7:45. Michelle was already anxiously wondering if she was O.K. Bitteroot Road had an awful lot of twists and turns, with many drivers taking them way too fast.

Her mother let the kickstand down on her bicycle and approached the alcove where the kitchen was situated. Michelle caught a glimpse of her face, and it appeared more flushed than usual. She even seemed to be a bit out of breath.

There was nothing peculiar about her mother failing to say hello to Michelle, yet something was undeniably different. Whatever it was made Michelle feel incredibly self-conscious all of a sudden.

They sat in silence at the wood veneer dining table, just like always. Neither one watched much television, and this was definitely not when and where either one cared to try to make something out of fuzz on their portable TV's little screen.

Curling her lip, eyes on her helping of macaroni and cheese, Michelle's mother said, "Aunt Grace wants *you* to take her her pills from now on. She's concluded you're not working hard enough, in spite of the money you've made. *I'm* no judge, so she must be right . . . She says a little chit like you *needs* to do more, maybe you'll stop being so precocious. She thinks there's gonna be trouble."

In this moment, Michelle so thoroughly detested Aunt Grace she could have strangled her scrawny, wrinkled neck with her bare hands. The war was on. Fight fire with fire, something like that. Michelle was pleasantness itself when she agreed, saying, "I'd be happy to do anything Aunt Grace needs done."

Even her mother was taken aback by the slick reply, aware that Aunt Grace and Michelle weren't exactly bosom buddies.

Wednesday evening, Michelle noticed quite a lot of cash had disappeared from the cookie jar. The only way her mother could have used so much was to buy groceries, yet all there was in the cabinet was the remaining box of macaroni and cheese. Michelle would have to walk down to Baker's supermarket. She definitely didn't want macaroni and cheese again. Truth be told she never wanted it again in her life—not carrot sticks, either. They reminded her of Monday night and how she felt, being given the what-for from Aunt Grace, via her mother, the mouthpiece. The kill of it all was she didn't do anything wrong.

And her mother was there right this minute, listening to some more of Aunt Grace's needless complaints. There was no way she was busy grocery shopping because if she wasn't here in the evening, she was at her aunt's.

Provided her mother made it home in one piece, wasn't the victim of a reckless driver, she would not be confronted about the money. Instead Michelle would put her hard-earned cash someplace else, such as beneath her ratty old mattress. Her mother wouldn't "think" to snoop.

Thursday was Michelle's favorite day of the week even though the requisite visit with Aunt Grace was just around the corner. Only one day of school would remain before the weekend, when she had more time to complete her homework assignments.

She should have had her mind on biology class, her favorite. Mr. Palmer called on her, wanting to know the difference between protoplasm and cytoplasm.

Immediately he looked exasperated. Here it was only the second week of school and she didn't like him. Nothing was worse than having a teacher you disliked, for a subject you did.

At the same instant the answer popped into her head, he could hardly wait to tell her, "You have got to read the text, Michelle. It's not all gonna just be absorbed into your brain." A few giggles were heard, which only encouraged the S.O.B.: "Isn't that correct? I mean, come on, folks."

By this time Michelle's face was burning up. She hoped he didn't lay into her, even more. Yesterday he got after a dark-haired girl named Char. Although he picked on a couple of the boys, he most assuredly did not like girls—except for Elise Simmskell, a real brain. She also had the nerve to shout answers from time to time. Only she could get by with it.

Michelle was a straight-A student too, but she didn't flaunt it. Well, she'd show Mr. Palmer on test day, when she got an A-plus.

That night at dinner, Michelle was informed she had to deliver Aunt Grace's pills the following day.

Michelle could hardly wait. She wouldn't have to, either. Friday was one day she didn't have to baby-sit. Neither would it be necessary to pick up any groceries because she'd bought enough to last them through Saturday or even Sunday.

Picking up Aunt Grace's prescription of course entailed a trip to the Timmers located in the opposite direction of her house. How could Michelle subtly bring up that part of the errand without giving her mother fits? Her mother proceeded to remind her to go to that store, to pick up the prescription. It would be ready, any time after three o'clock. She called the store and explained the situation. The clerk was very understanding.

They were undoubtedly just as willing to oblige at the Main and Bitteroot store. Michelle hoped before she had to do this again, she'd have the O.K. to go there, instead. She'd make the switch on her own, except the address of each store was most likely on the bottle, above where the prescription information was typed. Her mother wouldn't notice that but eagle-eyed Aunt Grace would.

Then Mrs. Pollack called. It was kind of last-minute, but could Michelle baby-sit Andrew tomorrow, from three-thirty to five-thirty?

Michelle pretended she couldn't fit in babysitting and errand-running before nightfall, so she told Mrs. Pollack to hang on a second. She had to ask her mother, silently praying this potential "conflict" would get her out of going Aunt Grace's.

Her mother didn't even interrupt her bead-stringing to state, "The sun doesn't set before eight, Michelle, and the sky will be clear all day."

At the very least, maybe her mother would have dinner started, even though she worked extra late on Fridays.

Fortunately Mrs. Pollack was true to her word, and at exactly 5:30, her big black Cadillac appeared in the driveway and was put in the garage. Too late, Michelle had an idea. She could ask Mrs. Pollack to drive her to the drugstore and Aunt Grace's.

On second thought, that wouldn't work. Aunt Grace would tell on her, and Cloris would be infuriated. She would demand to know what happened to Michelle's self-sufficiency and sense of pride. Plus, Mrs. Pollack needed to get dinner ready. Later on Mr. Pollack would be home. A globetrotter like him required being served dishes far more time-consuming than macaroni and cheese.

Leaving the Pollack's, Michelle bicycled southbound, the drugstore only a mile and a half away. With the dreaded task finally underway, she felt relieved.

Upon arrival, she wished she had a lock for her bike. If this was going to be a permanent duty, she'd purchase one. Her mother not surprisingly relied on blind faith.

She passed through the cosmetics section of the store, on her way to the pharmacy. She wouldn't dare wear any makeup. Thanks to Aunt Grace, her mother would be keeping close tabs on her daughter's appearance.

Michelle never before considered the fact that this pill-delivery responsibility gave Aunt Grace another opportunity to scrutinize (and criticize) Michelle.

Strangely, no one was behind the counter and no one was waiting for a prescription, yet within arm's reach were two white paper bags containing medication. She turned them both to read one was "Mr. Craven's" and the other was her aunt's.

With a harebrained scheme in mind, she took Mr. Craven's bag and left the other.

She walked briskly back out the door, making it the first time she ever passed the cosmetics section without even a glance. She would have run but she didn't want to attract any attention.

Her mother would still be busy working in the shop, enabling Michelle to go through with her plan. She intended to transfer Mr. Craven's pills to one of Aunt Grace's used containers, sitting on the buffet table. Whatever Mr. Craven took *had* to be different enough to make Aunt Grace sick, if not kill the old biddy. She just hoped his appeared the same-looking as her great-aunt's. Meanwhile her mother would never know. Just to be safe, however, Michelle would take a bottle containing beads her mother rarely used.

She left her bicycle behind the building and took the steps two at a time, careful to be quiet. She didn't need her mother poking her head out the back door of the shop, wondering what the noise was.

Sure enough her mother wasn't upstairs. Michelle peered out the front window and saw two parallel-parked cars. Her mother would be occupied for quite awhile.

She didn't even stop to read what kind of pills Mr. Craven took. It wouldn't do her any good to know because she had no idea what Aunt Grace's painkillers looked like.

Quickly she poured some shiny purple beads from one of the pill containers, into the white paper bag. Then she put Mr. Craven's pills in the old bottle, set it in the back of the buffet table, where the other one had been, and threw the bag in the trash can, beneath the kitchen sink. She also placed the remainder of the day's mail on top, just to be sure.

She put the bottle for Aunt Grace in her pants pocket and flew out the door. If Aunt Grace wondered where the bag was, she'd say she didn't get one. What difference did a lie or two make at this point?

As she neared Aunt Grace's she became more and more in doubt, concerning her scheme. By the time she reached the driveway, it was completely outrageous.

She walked the bicycle up to the front door, only to have it swing open before she was even close. There stood Aunt Grace, in her housedress and black sweater, not a favorable-looking thing about her. She added to her charm by loudly clearing some phlegm from her throat before saying, "Stupid girl, the drugstore people jus'called, 'n' you walked off with the wrong prescription. Lordy me, your mother's getting by on half her brain, 'n' she kin do better 'n you." With that the door was slammed.

Michelle burned with humiliation. She was a real imbecile. The best part was she thought she could make something of herself. Aunt Grace was absolutely right for being so incredulous.

Michelle was so mad, it enabled her to pedal her bicycle as if she were training for a race. Even so, it would be dark long before she was home for the evening. To think she had to stop there right now and undo her dirty work! Only afterward could she return to the drugstore.

She didn't give a care if her mother *was* upstairs. Maybe hearing the whole story would be a shock treatment, and her brain would miraculously recover.

But no. She was still downstairs. In fact a car was parked behind the shop, this time around. It looked kind of like Mrs. Pollack's, except it had an Illinois license plate. If Michelle had to guess whose it was, she'd say a wealthy businessman.

Should someone be wooing her mother, it wouldn't be the worst thing. She was certainly still attractive enough to have a suitor. All he had to do was tolerate the fact she wasn't quite right in the head, and he'd have himself the most devoted wife in the world. Her mother would have the pleasure of telling Aunt Grace to go to hell.

Michelle couldn't help smiling at that one, even while she was busy undoing her deed, including fishing the bag out of the wastepaper basket. Luckily nothing was in there to soil it.

She didn't fear being too harshly reprimanded by anyone from Timmers, but Mr. Craven might not be so forgiving. Full of trepidation she walked straight back to the pharmacy.

Fortunately he was nowhere to be seen. The jolly clerk was full of apologies, as if she was at fault for causing some sort of mix-up. Michelle felt as guilty as could be.

Bag in hand, she pedaled to Aunt Grace's. Many of the drivers had by this time turned on their headlights. She was so busy tallying up who thought it was dark and who didn't, she narrowly avoided hitting a large rock. It would have given her a good jolt and knocked the bag out of her hand, if not caused a flat tire.

This time, Michelle had to ring the bell before Aunt Grace opened the door. The first thing Michelle noticed was the pearl necklace.

It was plain Aunt Grace knew precisely what Michelle was staring at and hardened though she was, it undid her. Hand shaking, she snatched the bag from Michelle and complained, "'Bout time, girl. I had my fill of waitin'." Then she snarled. Wearing her dentures, she could really make a show of it. She looked just like Michelle's mother—or vice versa.

She waved Michelle off, saying, "Git on home, where ya belong. Ya look like a dang rat who's just come outta the cellar, blinkin' like that. Ya better eat more carrots."

The door was slammed with finality. If Michelle was humiliated before, she was so much so now, it was unlike anything she'd ever felt. Bending to pick up her bicycle, she almost fell. Then the tears came. She let them flow as she pedaled toward home. Aunt Grace would never see her cry. Michelle was too strong. Her discipline would be her salvation.

There was a screech of tires and then another and another as if coming from all directions. Michelle suddenly felt a powerful whoosh from behind, lifting her from her bicycle.

She was sailing, free.

"JUMPING TO CONCLUSIONS"

You're a member of Edlemein Country Club, the most exclusive club in the Phoenix Valley, if not the entire Southwest. Only those in the know, would have any idea of the exclusivity of the membership. (And you're known to be elitist and to exaggerate like hell.)

You're not only a member, but you and your wife Marcy live in one of the expensive homes that overlook the golf course. Specifically, you have a perfect view of number 13, a three-par, but a challenging hole nonetheless.

Golf fanatic that you are, this is most definitely as close to heaven on earth as you'll ever hope to get.

Your father Ralph mistook your zeal, for a desire to make golf a career and become a professional on the PGA circuit. It was an aspiration he had to forfeit because he didn't have any moral support nor financial security.

For you, however, he was able and willing to provide everything you needed, all so he could realize his own dream, if only vicariously.

Meanwhile, you could have cared less about making a living at golf, even if it might have made you rich and famous. A job that didn't require you to wear a suit and tie, and you couldn't expect anyone to ever take you seriously.

You kind of ended up following the same path as him, only you make lots more money. Oh, and you lucked out and found a woman who doesn't want kids, just like you. A wife has enough to do, just running a household. And damned if you're going to pay a nanny or two. It's bad enough having Ursula the maid, come twice a week.

Marcy could clean house, but you know, she simply never has. She lived and worked in New York before you swept her off her feet. And during that time, she had the stress-inducing job (for her) of being the clothing buyer for one of the major department store chains. The last thing she had time to care about was keeping her tiny studio apartment clean. So housecleaning never really figured in her life.

She's not lazy, by any means, but it was understood right away that any wife of yours, would not have any sort of job. You support the two of you, and she takes care of household duties Ursula doesn't get around to doing. (That encompasses enough to keep her occupied.)

Christ. How bad would it look if your wife worked? That would certainly leave you with no alternative but to conclude you utterly failed in obtaining the Great American Dream, even if she contributed about two cents (what you'd be left with, after taxes).

You're glad she doesn't have any specific desire to be busy, that she seems to like her life of relative leisure, just fine. If you had to argue with her over a job—whether a piddly or more serious-paying one, you would go insane. (Sometimes you think you're already insane, what with all the hours you've logged over the years, trying to get ahead.) It'll still be five years before your house is paid for. At least the cars are yours (a later model, but not old, silver Mercedes sedan for you and a newer burgundy Jaguar sedan for Marcy).

Your relatively well-paying occupation as a financial strategy planner (your own definition) keeps your head above the good old water—barely. Fortunately, you happen to thrive on lots of overtime. You also know all about handling stress, all the while taking some pretty major gambles with other people's money.

Poor Marcy never was at home, taking advantage of someone else's "investment." You wouldn't have ever guessed she wasn't happy with her job, if you only looked at her success rate. Her boss was damned sorry to see her leave. If nothing else, she has an open recommendation, should she (heaven forbid) want to work again.

As you said before, however, she's first and foremost your wife, and that is a full-time job. You'll make sure of it. She starts getting independent on you, and you'll have a nervous breakdown. It's annoying enough her sister, Melinda's, one of those ultra-liberated types, "happily unmarried" and all that crap.

Much as you hate to admit it (but what the hell), a big reason you never wanted kids (especially a son) is "he" would trivialize your success. You are positive of it. You simply don't have it in you to be encouraging in any way whatsoever. (Small wonder you couldn't appreciate your father's efforts to make you into a golf prodigy. It had nothing to do with the fact you were only ten years old.)

Fine. Why hide anything? So you're one-step shy of a loser. Maybe if you could finish paying off your house, you'd feel better. (Too bad you spend it as fast as you make it.)

The thing is, you could have bought something more modest on less of a golf course, but it just wouldn't have been the same. You suffer from a never-ending urge to live in a house that tells the world you've made it. (Never mind it's more like "barely.")

Worst of all, you could never be anything but jealous of a son, one who most likely would be more intelligent and precocious than you ever were. Essentially, he'd probably be the son your father Ralph should have had.

At the time, Marcy seemed to be glad she was leaving New York with you, to start a new life. Sometimes you think maybe you only saw what you wanted to see. She did in fact claim she would be "temporarily lost," without a so-called axe hanging over her head. Nonetheless, she looked forward to the dilemma of how to stay busy all day. You didn't think about it because females are able to acclimate themselves to new situations more easily than men.

But you two didn't leave New York before her parents, Ashley and Mortimer McKellips, had the distinct pleasure of throwing a wedding (about how it was, too) that was storybook lavish. They weren't especially rich, either. You thought they really did go overboard.

But see, it goes to show, no expense is spared when it comes to celebrating the union of a much-loved daughter with a respectable (read: ambitious), young (thirty, at the time) man. Yes, their 28 year-old, younger-by-three-years daughter was finally tying the knot.

Meanwhile, Melinda was showing no signs of settling down. That must have been awfully disquieting for the elder McKellips. Traditional as they were in their thinking, they probably went to their graves assuming they did something wrong in raising their two daughters. The best they did was marry one off, and she doesn't even have the common sense to want to be a mother.

One thing Marcy never learned to take, was criticism. She'd rather be/do everything right, than be told she's done something incorrectly, etc., in any way. All topics are hot ones with her, and that's all there is to it.

Incidentally, she's put on a lot of weight over the years. You're only now realizing it, really taking notice of how she's slowly changed from the slim, pretty young woman, to the more "substantial," mature one. For five feet-five, she looks taller than she is, and that's what keeps her from looking overweight.

You'd prefer to be shot and left for dead, than to tell her, "Honey, you've really packed on the pounds, these past few years."

The woman's happy, is that such a crime? You don't begrudge her a thing, and certainly not all the happiness she can take. Personally, you couldn't stand yourself if you were too happy, not that she's that way. Between the two of you, however, she's definitely the more upbeat one.

O.K., so you're the moodier one of you two. You can sometimes be quite crabby, truth be told. It's these little things that help you push your dinner plate away before you're finished. Simultaneously, nothing kills her appetite and she looks it.

And you know, it's not like she doesn't exercise. And it's certainly not as if she eats all day. She plays tennis once a week, sometimes twice, inevitably doubles. Logically then, she doesn't burn as many calories as she could. But the thing is, she plays for the social aspect as much (or more so) than the exercise.

She loves having as many different groups of friends as possible—i.e.—her tennis friends, her dinner party friends, her church friends, etc.

As for you, from day one, you've consumed your every waking moment, wondering how long you can continue to fool everyone that you are the embodiment of the Great American Dream.

Maybe it's all coming back to you, how you originally exaggerated to Marcy, that your new job in Phoenix, would earn you double what you were making back in New York. (The distinction you failed to make was you had to start at about the same place, but there was more potential for unlimited advancement. Back in New York you didn't stand a chance in hell of making something of yourself.)

And you not only proved your mettle, you ended up branching out on your own. That of course came with its own price, something you always fail to take into account. (Climbing the ladder of success isn't without its periodic regressions.)

A good example of your hell-bent belief, appearances are indeed everything, was the very first house you owned. Yes, you actually owned it, free and clear.

It was three-bedroom, ranch-style, made of tan brick, in a decent part of town. You got an unbelievable deal because the inside needed to be gutted. Well, you didn't have the money for that, and you were working way too many hours to also make yourself a handyman (lack of inclination, aside).

Who the hell cared? By all appearances you were young and already making it. As long as Marcy didn't invite any friends over, you were all right. (Small wonder Marcy has an affinity for restaurant dinner-parties, versus entertaining at home.)

Speaking of testing mettle, you tested your wife's those first few years of your marriage, not to mention trying your own patience, with yours truly.

This was when you became addicted to working because simple math told you the more your worked, the more money you'd earn. Proof of hard work is this beautiful house of yours, that's almost paid for.

The only thing that kind of gets you, is knowing some (if not plenty) of your neighbors have complete and total ownership of their homes. And there's a couple smart, young upstarts in the group. Damned if you're going to be making friends with them, in this lifetime.

As for Marcy, however, the more people she's in contact with, the better. But she doesn't want to be close friends, not with everyone. You're glad of that much, that casual acquaintances suffice.

She happens to have a way of getting people to divulge all kinds of things, and she doesn't have to say a word. She got the wife across the street to tell her about all the plastic surgery she recently had done, and Marcy was completely embarrassed for the woman.

Marcy's innately a damned good listener and maybe people pick up on that. At the same time, you make a lousy listener. You ought to take some lessons from her. She tells you the same thing ten thousand times and you still don't really hear it.

As intently as she listens to these tales of women perfecting themselves, you'd think she'd take the hint, maybe have some liposuction done. Sure it's an expense you can ill-afford, but she doesn't know that. Besides, you'd sooner see some money go toward getting some cellulite removed, something off that tummy, those buttocks, than have to pay for yet another manicure/pedicure, trim, facial, massage, etc. Her maintenance schedule must be exhausting. Not only that, it's entirely superfluous after awhile. It could be she's obsessed with all her appointments, but it's too easy to assume that's a problem of hers.

No, what it is, is she feels like the consummate rich woman when she pays her visits to all these highfaluting places, and everyone calls her by her first name (because she said it was O.K. to, of course).

Times like these, you pick Marcy apart in such a way, you seem to forget not only is she your wife but you *love* one another. And you've been so goddamned unaffectionate toward her these past few years, what do you think you've done to her psyche? Instead of feeling sorry, you're indignant, and you determine that you're the one stuck with the chubby, middle-aged wife. Therefore you're the one who's fucked, not her.

And just like your obsession with being able to play the 13th hole everyday (if not twice, as well one other hole), you will not let this issue drop. You will not stop and give thanks you have a woman to love. The problem is it seems so long ago since you felt that initial feeling overtake you. It would help you, on days like these, to be able to re-live all the emotions you had as a young man.

But no one can say you don't know how to make the best of just about any situation. You are the only one of your neighbors who plays "free" golf everyday. (And a good thing, too. Think what a mess there would otherwise be.)

It's not like you never play an actual round of golf. But you're really just a piddler at heart because truth be told, what makes you happiest is playing those extra holes everyday, around 6:30, 6:45, later in the summer. You make sure the majority of the players have finished. You have never cut in on anyone, nor have you held anyone up. You're as heedful as they come, when it concerns proper golf course etiquette.

Since number 13 is a hole requiring expertise when hitting the tee shot, you typically use a 7-iron. It's one of only about four clubs you keep in a little tan canvas bag.

Your father Ralph ought to see you out there, sometimes not even properly attired, at least not your shoes. Spikes are a major pain unless you're going to play a whole round.

The morning newspapers, your "free" holes, an occasional round (no more than once a week) and plenty of overtime in your home office, these are the things that make up an ideal life.

In all seriousness, do you think you would have made a good golf pro? Are they obsessive-compulsive in nature? To pursue any goal, you have to be somewhat obsessed. If you have to change your schedule even a tiny bit, you're ready to have a nervous fit. Even you realize that isn't quite right.

And today, doesn't it just figure. Mother Nature's playing havoc with your brain. It's raining. (God, it'd be hell on you, if you lived in Florida.) Only out of habit did you come home from work at the same time as usual. Admittedly, however, you unconsciously got a little too hopeful. Well, the forecasters said it was going to do this. It might even rain tomorrow. Just think, it keeps this up, and the course'll be too soggy to play on, even piddling.

You love it when Marcy has dinner plans. You scurry outside like all hell, playing two holes, tops, and she's inside getting exasperated like you'd never believe. Little does she know, how antsy you'd otherwise be during a seven-course meal, knowing you missed playing your coveted holes. You also can't forget about all those long (and long-winded) conversations you have to endure. To hell with overtime on those days, even you must admit.

When all is said and done, you work your tail-end off for one reason—to make MONEY. That is your impetus. You certainly don't work because you get off on it, like some men. Call you a lazy bum at heart, you don't really care. That doesn't mean you're stupid. (And not to have your level of intelligence doubted is of the utmost importance to you.) It's right in par with you wanting the whole world to think you're rich—not filthy rich, but comfortably well off. You doubt you've got everyone entirely fooled, and that really bothers you, come to think of it.

Who's the least fooled, besides you? You're dying to know. And no, it's not your wife. Pardon you, but she doesn't count. She happens to be the least fooled of anyone.

Given this golden opportunity to ruminate (damned if you're going to squeeze in some overtime while you sit in this kitchen chair, watching the rain drops hit the patio), you are about to confess to your greatest compulsion of all, once and for all—playing your 6:30 golf holes. There. It's good as written in stone. You would literally rather be dead than miss a day. (*O.K.*, You tell the sky. *You can stop now. Please?*) You really are holding out a huge hope you can play even just one hole before darkness falls.

If you wait until tomorrow and it does stop and it isn't too wet, you'll still look like a disrespectful fool. The entire Edlemein Country Club probably thinks you're a lunatic, as it is. That's why they leave you alone and let you play your couple of holes. (This is the crowning proof of your obsessive-compulsive disorder, how little you care what people think, when it comes to satisfying your uncontrollable urges.)

You have to hand it to Marcy. She's never outrightly made fun of your condition, she's never gotten impatient (aside from her exasperation, as you already mentioned, when she's made dinner plans), but you have yet to quit a hole. That's the epitome of poor etiquette, as far as you're concerned. And if you have a positively stellar tee shot, you are not going to neglect to finish playing the hole. That's all there is to it. You don't give a damn if she's got the shower water running for you.

You like having a house that overlooks a short hole. It gives you a view of the whole thing, start to finish. You don't feel gypped. The size of your house, more than makes up for it.

As you continue gazing out the sliding glass door in the kitchen, you realize that yes, indeed, it is stopping. Your prayers just may have been answered.

The truth of the matter is you'd play in a downpour if you didn't look like a real nut-case. Only your wife would understand and she's not even home.

Last night she made a point of taking the time to explain to you where she would be today—not that she isn't sufficiently a creature of habit, herself. It's Tuesday and that's tennis day. Not even a little rain puts a stop to her friends' and her plans because one of them made arrangements at Cambridge Tennis Club. That was formerly the place known as Desert Foothills Tennis Complex, the premier (and only) facility around that has 24 indoor courts.

Marcy and her doubles friends typically meet at Angie Dreyfuss' Paradise Valley home. This time Reggie Cornwall had the opportunity to play hostess. She happens to not only be a member of Cambridge Tennis Club, but her husband Carl is one of the investors who saved the place from being demolished when Desert Foothills went bankrupt.

See? Even Carl could envision the potential in catering to tennis players who had to play no matter the weather—and that yes, it does rain in Arizona, from time to time.

The only possible glitch would be a last-minute cancellation by the very one who made that hard-to-get-at-the-last-minute reservation. It's not exactly an impossibility because Reggie Cornwall is just that way, as Marcy would say.

In fact, Marcy doesn't even like to be at the mercy of another person's conditional provision. You would almost bet she made a back-up plan for today, in case the tennis got shelved for whatever reason, except she didn't tell you—you don't think.

You really have got to make a habit of listening to what she says, all the time, not just when it's convenient, or when you've momentarily run out of things to do. For all the great qualities you possess, you also have quite a few faults.

Now you just stated that with all due humility, but it also just so happens that your sister-in-law Melinda, happily unmarried Melinda, once confessed to Marcy, she got herself one hell of a gem of a man (and better hold onto him).

To have a woman like her pay you that kind of compliment, even if she'd never say it to your face, is no small accomplishment.

Luckily you don't see much of her because truthfully you've always been kind of afraid of her. She's a much more intense character than her sister, and she also happens to be quite intelligent—not that Marcy's any dummy.

You need to catch yourself before you go any further, and you know precisely what it is, you're doing wrong—taking your wife for granted. (Men are naturals at that, aren't they.)

It's just that sometimes you've felt stifled by her utter devotion to being accommodating and infinitely understanding to the point you don't even deserve it. It's almost as if her never-ending desire to please you, works against her.

The ideal woman would be a cross between the two McKellips sisters. She would in fact be such a fantasy woman, you're not sure you could take it. You know yourself, you don't even deserve that kind of woman.

You can vividly recall the one and only time Melinda came to your house and actually stayed for more than five minutes. She in fact spent the night. Looking back, you wonder what induced her to even take advantage of her younger sister's "hospitality." (The two of them never have gotten along.)

Anyway, you're such an egomaniac, you determined she stayed over, in the midst of moving from the West coast back East, all so she could somehow seduce you. You got the hives and a terrific nosebleed, all from working yourself into an utter frenzy, wondering how in God's name you could resist a little vixen like her. (Needless to say you worried for absolutely no good reason.)

It just so happens Melinda loves to play golf. She also happens to be an X-ray technician, and you always think about her having affairs with M.D.s, being able to golf with them and fuck them. (There's no grounds whatsoever, behind this speculation of yours.)

Guess what Marcy hates most about golf? The smells—of cut grass, club grips, moldy old gloves, you name it. Hell if you're about to "make" her play. Besides, your most meaningful games are the ones you play alone, not in a twosome, a threesome, whatever. You just like "puttering around," by yourself.

And damn it all, Mother Nature is definitely trying to mess with your head this evening. SHE obviously has the final say on your plans for the remainder of the day, and that really gets to you.

Then you take a good long look outside and realize that it is actually not hardly raining anymore, although the sky is quite dark. It will in fact be dark, shortly, so it's now or never.

It's imperative you salvage the day, show the goddamned weather that you don't have to take "No" for an answer. You play even just the 13th hole one time, and you'll be satisfied. You worked hard today, you have more work to look forward to later, and if you don't take this opportunity to go relax, you probably won't be able to sleep tonight.

Truthfully, you know what? You don't really have it so good. You really don't. THE GREAT AMERICAN DREAM has a noose around your neck. And like some of your friends (but not all of them because plenty of them have it made) you, fella, are a poor-rich man. And you feel like a stupid idiot, because of that. (And you lauded yourself for your intelligence?)

Somehow, all your pals can live in relative bliss, while you let yourself go to rack and ruin (and worrying really is a waste of time and energy). You know some of them have humongous mortgages to pay, yet they're realistic and don't bother losing sleep over it.

Goddamn the nerve of every one of them, only working five, maybe six days a week. No, you take that back. You're the only one who, without fail, works six days a week, and puts in overtime, at home. You don't know anybody who works as many hours as you. Admittedly, sitting around and doing nothing isn't your thing, but you haven't even allowed yourself to be contemplative—until today, of course, because you've been waiting to see if you can proceed with your schedule.

While you're at it, you need to be grateful for how much crap your wife has tolerated from you, over the years. All that time you two lived in that house that deserved to be gutted, not once did she complain. She was a real trooper. Christ. Some men's wives make a hobby out of harassing the hell out of them. They pick on them about trivial things that shouldn't even upset them (such as leaving dirty laundry behind doors, underneath the bed, etc.). These complaints come out of the mouths of wives who have the luxury of part, if not full-time domestic help. Personally, you'd tell any wife of yours who ragged about your habits, sloppy and otherwise, to plan on saying good-bye to the maid.

It'll be freezing in hell before you tell Marcy, "No more Ursula," and she's welcome to complain all she wants. It's the principle of the matter. Worse, it would be like giving in to the very distinct possibility, The Great American Dream has slipped through your fingers. (Never mind a little housework would help Marcy get into shape.)

Yes, indeed. You'll be telling Marcy that, on the same day you star in your very own, really bad "B" movie. You'll play the eager, ambitious, young upstart who's so worried about climbing the ladder of success he misses a rung, falls on his butt and is no more— THE END.

Ha! You can hardly believe you actually had a sense of humor just now, if only for a second or two. (You never were blessed with being reflective, let alone funny.) But high-minded business people don't need to be that way. There never is a point at which they can be too practical—is there?

One other reason you knew it wasn't in you to be a golf pro, is you don't have much of a philosophical/spiritual side (nor do you care to do any nurturing of it). You'd rather spend the extra time working.

Considering how hard your father Ralph worked, he had his spiritual side figured out better than you. Maybe you're just too intelligent to be spiritual. (You always were good at making excuses.) You're almost as good at that as you are with exaggerating, being obsessed with strange things, not to mention jumping to conclusions.

Aside from everything, you resented him living vicariously, through you. You found it completely distracting and quite annoying. It's a wonder you like the game as much as you do, when you think about how he tried to turn it into drudgery.

It all comes down to the fact that no matter how seriously you take life (and you do, too), you couldn't be that way, not about golf. He worshipped it like a goddamned religion. His zeal was comical (although it sure as hell wasn't, at the time). He made you practice hours upon hours and you resented every minute of it. Only now can you look back on your youth and not feel bitter.

Little bits at a time, people have tried to wear you away, but they haven't succeeded. They haven't because you are much stronger than they anticipate.

Take Marcy, for instance. Sure you have voluntarily taken it upon yourself to support her, but do you think she really wants it any other way, at this point of her life? If something happens to you, you hate to say this, but she might conceivably have no choice but to go back to work. You seriously doubt this would be welcome news. She'd be rid of you, and that would be the extent of the advantages. But it isn't really such an advantage because she loves you—you think.

Where the hell is she, by the way? You know you just asked this question, but it only takes so long to play a game of doubles tennis. It's not like they go into a long, drawn-out, sudden death play-off. There isn't a woman in the group who could endure it. There'd be a sudden death, all right, Reggie Cornwall's, most likely.

By looks alone she's the most feeble of the four of them, Marcy's the one you'd bet money on, to have the most stamina.

Marcy and her tennis-gal pals. You picture them spending 80% percent of their time gabbing, even while the game is going on and maybe 20% percent actually playing tennis. There's never any arguing about points because they have enough to talk about that keeps their blood-pressures up, starting with their good-for-nothing husbands.

The four of them must have decided to spend even longer than usual afterward, sipping alcoholic beverages and sharing sob stories. Marcy's the only one of the group who doesn't have kids, but that wouldn't stop her from picking up the slack. She can simply bear down harder on yours truly.

What are you waiting for, for the last time? It really has stopped raining, now.

You climb the stairs, two at a time, you're so full of sudden anticipation. And what's the first thing you see in the walk-in closet but Marcy's tennis bag. It's almost like the stupid thing tried to get your attention. You don't see her racket, but then you never have figured out where she keeps that thing.

She did not take her tennis bag with her, to go play tennis. It makes absolutely no sense, of course—unless she didn't play tennis, like she went out of her way to tell you she was going to do. It sounds suspiciously to you like she tried to cover her tracks, but failed—all because she doubted your observational skills.

She's got another thing coming to her if she thinks she can get by with having an affair.

Does she think she can do this to you and you'll forgive her? Can you? Why should you? That's the question you'd like to ask. Christ. You've never even been tempted to cheat on her, and you've certainly had your share of opportunities.

Possibly, this is a sort of cry for help, on her part. Yes, you've been neglecting her, and she finally succumbed to the effects. They say women really do wilt, just like flowers, if they're denied love and affection.

You decide to rest convinced (just like that) she was no longer content to complain about you to her friends. It no longer did the trick. She needed someone to whisper sweet nothings in her ear, make her feel like a woman again.

Meanwhile, you must have changed from your suit into something more appropriate for golf because you're ready to go outside and do your thing, the moment you've been anxiously awaiting and of which you were certain had been denied of you. God may be on your side, yet.

She's lucky she isn't home, as it turns out. You have a few minutes to consider your options and plan your initial attack. One thing she can count on getting, the second she walks in the door, is a stern talking to. You intend to tell her outrightly, what you suspect she's up to.

Since she is, by all rights, Melinda McKellips' sister, there really is no telling just how potentially devious she might be. She's your own wife, and you suddenly feel like you don't even know her.

Most assuredly, your number one obligation as a husband is to confront her without delay. You've already put off paying her any attention. You don't want to lose what you think is a pretty special relationship (if nothing else, due to its endurance).

At the expense of blowing it, however, you're going ahead with playing your hole(s). You'll watch for your dearly beloved. You always leave the lights off, but the second she gets home, the whole place lights up like a goddamned X-mas tree. She has most definitely perfected the art of scampering about, turning on every light in the house.

What you actually count on, is to do your thing and come back inside at the same time as she returns. You may even already be comfortably nestled in your recliner, sipping something cool and refreshing. (You're not much of one for alcohol. A lemonade will do.)

You slip into your office long enough to grab your trusty little canvas bag. You head out the door, wearing what else but a pair of white canvas tennis shoes. They suit the purpose on a day like today. You allow yourself to scrimp on etiquette.

You pass the pool and go out the black wrought-iron gate, separating your property from the golf course. You're one of the few people who has a wrought-iron fence around your entire yard, rather than a concrete wall. You wouldn't want to miss even a smidgen of the view.

Also, this means you have a perfect view of your house, from the 13th tee, and that's where you're standing right now, taking stock of the situation. You feel positively euphoric, and you're very thankful, Mother Nature relented. Still, it looks as if it might start raining again, any minute, and there's some loud rumbling, coming from the sky. You feel like you're being warned, not to take this little outing, for granted.

There's no time to lose, that much is plain. Luckily you don't need to spend any of it, debating what club to use. You never have been one to make a big deal out of that.

You tee up a ball and then remove your trusty 7-iron from your bag. Before taking a practice swing, you look over at your house and try to see if Marcy has returned. No lights have yet been turned on. Good. This'll be over before you know it.

A sudden, ear-splitting clap of thunder makes you jump. You barely finished your swing. "Goddamn it," you mutter to yourself.

This may just force you to have to call on using a level of concentration that you rarely have occasion to tap into, no thanks to Mother Nature.

As you swing at the ball, out of the corner of your eyes (or from somewhere above) there's a flash, and instantly you think Marcy's home and she just turned on a light.

She's home, all right, except she's outside, by the gate. She has on a sky blue silk dress. Now you remember, this morning she had to change her plans, because of Reggie Cornwall canceling on her tennis pals. Marcy put plan number two into action and took a day-trip to Sedona with her church friends.

Yes, indeed, she's come outside to plead with you not to play in this electrical storm. Her concern, unfortunately, isn't enough to keep the next bolt from splitting you in two. Too bad. You had one hell of a tee shot.

"A GRAND PRIX RIDER'S
HAPPY ENDING"

Riding down the last line, you feel like you're burning rubber—only thing is, you're on a horse, not a crotch rocket (but same difference sometimes, or so it would seem).

Concentration-wise, you're giving it all you've got and you're damned thankful your horse is, too. There's nothing like having the both of you, being on the money. Usually it's one or the other, or at best, one more than the other. But today, Bingo! You got it baby, and if you weren't thus occupied, putting 110 percent (maybe more) into this, hands steady, legs gripping tightly your steed's barrel, urging him with all your mental mighty might, you'd take a look around at the myriad group of spectators (shows attract all types of people) and yell, "Ya-hoo! I've been waiting my whole career to do this!"

And what exactly, pray tell, is that (besides yelling running commentaries to rapt audiences)?

Why, win a grand prix, of course. You've had more than your fill of second and third-place finishes, losing by tenths of hundredths of seconds.

You're galloping your trusty mount down to the last line, and there is just no way you can lose. No one else has gone clean in this jump-off, and no one's been as blazing fast as you.

Two more fences and you happen to be sitting on one of the cleanest, most reliable grand prix jumpers to come through the ranks, in a long time.

And he doesn't disappoint, clearing this five foot, three-inch vertical, by seemingly a mile. It's a pretty darned spooky-looking fence, too, what with the maze of poles painted orange and black, and the black-cat plywood cut-outs, on the standards.

This horse is just too rock-solidly confident at this point of his career, to let a scary jump get to him. And like his master, he's for the most part void of fear. But that's not to say he's unsafe in any way, oh no. You, the rider, are in complete control of his every footfall, even though right now it's a veritable thundering of hooves.

When your trusty steed performs, some see the athlete, others see the pure majesty, notice his gorgeous white mane flying, the afternoon sunlight hitting his glossy dapple coat, just so. (Yes, there's a shine on him, pretty unusual for a coat of his color.)

This horse is such a charmer and has such a great personality, his 19 year-old Irish groom, Lucy Carron, is in love with him. All you can mirthfully think is, *That's what a girl's down to huh*. No men were good enough for her in her homeland, she's been here in the States over a year and hasn't fared any better, finding a boyfriend.

But it's often the way of the horse-world, is it not. Those outside of it, can't fathom how all of you can be perfectly content with the companionship of your four-legged friends and no one else.

And that's indeed the crux of the matter, the essential reason why you get along with your horses. You all but live in a stall, right next to theirs.

You drive them to the shows all over the country (and sometimes the world, if you're lucky enough); you make sure they're bedded down for the night, long before you can even hope to have some time to tend to your own needs; you nurse them back to health, the rare times they're sick (knock on wood, if you keep things simple but thorough, the problems are few); and you make sure they're ready for the task, before you take them in the ring. *Nothing's* more potentially embarrassing (not to mention disappointing and even dangerous) than riding a horse who's unprepared, whether mentally or physically.

And keeping everything in balance, is no easy job, better believe it. It's why it consumes your entire life, your every waking moment.

Meanwhile it's imperative you too stay in peak physical fitness—

not that your legs are doing the galloping right this minute. But still, it's not easy holding this ton and a third, together. It takes plenty of stamina. And sometimes you're so out of breath after a first round, you're pretty damn sure you haven't taken a single breath, the entire 75-85 seconds, you just spent in the ring.

Yeah. Supposedly a human being can live something like 13 minutes without oxygen, but that would be if you were at rest, not stressing yourself to the maximum. Not breathing at all, in this case, is almost like hyper-ventilating. And if you weren't so damned excited afterward, hyped up, you're certain a couple times by now, you would have fainted dead away—*dead* sure. Maybe even that. You would have passed out, never to return. You can't think of a better way to go, actually.

"Well, at least we can't say he wasn't happy, the last couple minutes of his life," your mother says, after the funeral.

What a way to go. Four faults at the last fence. Witnesses contend you, not the horse, had the heart attack. (If it happens at all, it's usually the other way around, isn't it.) But the medical examiner agreed, that's what took place.

He survived O.K., just kind of banged-up and dazed. In the meantime, you must have been halfway to death, even before your head hit the ground—straight-on. The impact was so blasted hard, you didn't stand a chance.

Now you're in jumper-rider heaven, where all you have to do all day is ride in grand prix classes.

"LIVE A LITTLE"

Bill Motley was proud of the fact he stayed busy, and he kept his nose out of other people's affairs. In this hamlet called Lake Driscoll, these were not meager feats.

There was a "pathological liar" in town, by the name of Joe McCabe. The hopelessly fat waitress at the Lakeside Diner, told Joe he was one. She wasn't especially kidding around, either. Bill had overheard them talking, even though he was supposedly reading his *Chicago Tribune*, which he had a habit of holding close to his face. It was not because he needed glasses.

"Old" Joe was forced into retirement by the steel company. It seemed he was on his way to or already was a hazard to himself and his co-workers. Bill didn't know any of the details (because he minded his own business). He just naturally overheard bits and pieces of everyone's conversations and drew this conclusion.

Joe had frequented this coffee shop for at least as long as Bill had. Bill couldn't even remember the first time he himself came. He liked the red vinyl booth closest to the door, while Joe would sit at the counter, upon a red-cushioned stool, his back to Bill, just about even with him. Bill kept his nose in the paper the whole time, stopping only long enough to shovel down his breakfast— two scrambled eggs, hash browns, and three sausage links.

There was no reason on earth Joe should ever turn around, see Bill, and start a tall tale about him, but you never knew what went on in people's heads. That was especially true in the case of Joe, who had the counter to himself during the week.

As far a Bill could tell, he'd been slipping in and out of the restaurant, unnoticed by Joe, ever since the first time he came— *whenever* that was.

Whatever Joe had for breakfast he either ate before Bill's arrival or was in anticipation of having, later on. Perhaps he liked to linger over coffee, *prior* to eating. To each his own, Bill supposed. The hour he himself spent here every morning was the highlight of the day.

If Joe had nothing better to do than hang out at the coffee shop (and apparently, he didn't), it was entirely understandable he was bored and making up stories. That's all lies really were. They were innocuous, unless you ticked someone off and *he* took offense. (Bill was content with bachelorhood, but he determined a woman would never seek revenge and not in the form of violence).

Why, Joe McCabe could get himself killed. Maybe that explained the reason he spent so much time here. He was staying out of trouble.

Bill had no idea how Joe got here everyday, whether he walked or he drove.

Bill looked over his paper to see the waitress refill his coffee cup. Funny, he wasn't sure if she was the one who usually served him. However, he did recognize the short, overweight brunette who waited on Joe and who served all the tables in the middle of the room—albeit he didn't know her name.

He returned to the article from which he'd been interrupted then looked back up because he'd lost his place. He saw the waitress standing by a booth further down, taking a customer's order.

For a second, the fact Bill didn't know whether or not she was his regular waitress, made him reel. The fiery red hair of hers, coiffed to resemble flames, was completely unforgettable. She had to be close to his age and even with her matching red lipstick she appeared anything but tacky or garish.

She was in fact remarkably attractive and almost looked as if she didn't belong in this little town.

Ever so faintly there was a stirring inside himself but he ignored it. At nearly 60, he was far too set in his ways to have a woman in his life. Heck, even trying one of the other coffee shops on the southwest side of 300-acre Lake Driscoll, would be an undesirable break in his routine.

He lived in Canterbury Estates on Pine Street, just north of the lake itself. It was a small subdivision with modest single story and tri-level homes. Most of the residents of Lake Driscoll lived in the older houses that were along the perimeter of the shore.

The Lakeside Diner was on Lakeside Drive, right on his way to work. He had an income-tax service in Selmer, about a 10-mile commute each way, past corn and soybean fields.

It was perfect for Bill, far enough he was "going someplace," yet not *too* far. The amount of work he had, as well as how much it "taxed" his brain, was just right too. He was also plenty busy yet not overworked or stressed. He tried as hard, if not harder, to avoid the latter of those two, as he did avoiding boredom.

Still, Sunday was his favorite day of the week, even though the diner got kind of crowded. The *Tribune* would be so chock-full of articles it was impossible to read them all in the hour he allotted himself. He wanted to stay longer than he did the other days, but it just didn't seem right. Maybe sometime he'd treat himself to an extra hour. He got excited about that as he drove to his office.

His good feeling didn't last long because he got upset again, trying to think if he recognized "that waitress." Whoever *did* wait on him these past few years (How long *was* it?), did an impeccable job of keeping his coffee cup filled without that annoying "More coffee?" question.

Coffee, a hearty (and artery-hardening) breakfast, and the *Tribune*, all went together. No waitress worth her two cents (not that he was a chintzy tipper) even asked, not ever.

One thing he could recall, it wasn't more than three years ago, he made two stops on the way to his office, the first one to pick up the newspaper at Patrick's Pharmacy. It was formerly located at the junction of Pine Street, where it met Lakeside Drive and essentially dead-ended. (If you kept driving you'd be in the lake.)

Why the pharmacy suddenly closed, he didn't know. He *would* have been quite disturbed, except at the same time, *Chicago Tribune* home delivery service became available. Otherwise he would have had to drive the "long way" around the lake, to pick up a paper at Haven's Drugs. While he was over there he could dine at one of two coffee shops, whose names he didn't know.

Nowadays his drugstore needs could be met at Selmer. In fact his office was at the far east end of a large (huge by Lake Driscoll standards) strip mall. The main draw was a Leeder's Supermarket, almost twice the size of the one in Lake Driscoll. There was also a Price Saver Pharmacy-Superstore, which appeared to carry much the same merchandise as Leeder's, except for produce.

Bill liked to browse through the Price Saver store, like other men liked to do, in hardware stores. He wasn't much of a handyman-type, nor was he particularly fond of the outdoors. He read a lot and especially enjoyed travel books.

The morning whizzed right by and what do you know it was time for lunch. Luckily the mall had an exceptional deli shop by the name of Constanza's. There certainly wasn't one of *these* in Lake Driscoll. He could munch on a thin-sliced roast beef on seedless rye and debate what else he'd done with his free time, all these years.

He stepped outside and got a harsh reminder on his sagging jowls that winter was coming. He went back in to get his unlined, double-breasted raincoat, which was all he had with him.

Even so, the deli suddenly seemed too far away, at the west end. He'd have to pass the supermarket and inevitably a harried mother would burst forth, cart overflowing with groceries and one or two bawling toddlers. You'd think people living a good ninety miles from a major city (Chicago) would be laid-back. Evidently their lives were just too muddled, but that was their business. He just hated when a stranger's problems became his own, if only for a few seconds.

In defense of these women, at least they were too busy to be *pathological liars*. Bill had to smile at that, if only because it was such a big, fancy term to come from such a frump of a woman. (But she did thankfully look familiar.)

A white-haired old lady exited Price Saver, and he felt a welcome blast of warm air. He ducked inside to have a look around. It had been awhile since he afforded himself the luxury of browsing, as he didn't need anything. He wasn't particularly hungry after all, and it wouldn't hurt him to skip a meal.

He soon by golly stumbled upon the women's hair color. By golly again, he never realized the infinite variety. He didn't see a brand that carried a color red, quite as outrageous as "his waitress'," or *that* waitress, except he hated to sound as if he didn't respect her. He did, in a way he couldn't explain. It was safe to call it reverence, and she had him intrigued, that was for sure.

It didn't hurt a thing to feel like this. He'd just keep minding his own business.

He even ventured to guess she had her hair done at a salon, and it cost her a pretty penny, too. From now on, he was going to pay closer attention to how much he tipped her, maybe add a little more. He admired the fact she had the pride to keep herself up, when most women her age would let themselves go to hell. He bet she had a good ten to twelve years on the fat co-worker of hers.

As a waitress she was peerless. Here he hogged the table for an hour, and she long ago (if she was the same one) quit asking him if he wanted anything else, besides coffee, of course. She'd leave the bill on the table, although he wasn't sure when she did so. It was most likely between his fifth and sixth (and final) cup of coffee.

Leaving the drugstore, he should have been watching where he was going. He proceeded to barely avoid knocking heads with a nattily-dressed, handsome young man in a three-piece charcoal gray suit.

"Excuse me," the man was quick to say, although there was no attempt at all to hide his irritation.

Bill felt more than a little tardy with his "Excuse me," since he said it after the man. As if to compensate Bill held out his hand to steady him.

The man hardly needed any help standing and in fact pretended he didn't see or feel Bill's goodwill gesture, all in an effort to continue moving in a forward direction.

Oops. He'd better get back to his office. It was entirely possible the man was on his way to see *him*. It was the only place he could be going. He clearly didn't get in a car and drive away.

Bill didn't have an "Out to Lunch" sign for his door because it wouldn't look professional. He merely locked the door, saving the "Closed" side of his "Open/Closed" sign, for when he left for the night, at five o'clock.

No, the man was not waiting for him. Interestingly, he was nowhere to be seen. He must have walked around to the back of the buildings. Maybe he was an inspector of some sort—not a private detective, just a building or safety inspector.

That sounded so impressive it gave Bill more energy than he usually felt around this time of day. He worked straight through to quitting time and was almost sorry it came around so soon. Good. He could stay enthused for the drive home. He missed the long daylight hours of the summer and early fall. Around this time of the year, it was already dark.

In fact he got tired of the winter weather, and it wasn't even here yet, not for another month would it officially be winter. Selmer had something like two travel agencies. (There weren't any in Lake Driscoll.) Since he had no living relations, no close friends to visit, he could plan a trip to someplace warm, over Christmas and New Year's.

The only problem was he might have to go to a different coffee shop, upon his return. Due to Bill's absence, Joe's curiosity would finally be roused.

He congratulated himself on this foresight, only to turn around and decide he was just being ridiculously suspicious. That could be a by-product of boredom, couldn't it?

Going away sounded so enticing, he might simply have to run the risk of losing his place at the Lakeside Diner.

Bill went ahead and made the necessary plans for a vacation. The travel agent said he was lucky to get reservations so late. "You know, the holidays," she told him. No, he didn't, but he agreed anyway. She wished she could go too—without her kids. By the day after Christmas they were already climbing the walls with boredom. She couldn't wait until school resumed. Bill chuckled, considering himself fortunate he could just up and leave. It felt good.

Until his much-anticipated departure for Miami Beach, Bill kept an eye on Joe McCabe and an ear pricked, but the guy seemingly wasn't talking or moving. *He might be dead*, Bill joked to himself. *Somebody's got him propped there.* He actually wished Joe *would* turn around.

Also in the meantime, Bill kept his paper lowered long enough to faintly catch a glimpse of *his* waitress' nametag. She called herself Clara. He felt kind of sad because he could have known it, long ago. At least now he could describe her consistent service, with some real *authority*, and there was nothing boring about that. Her hair never wavered in color, either—or wildness. She had a good, reliable colorist, probably one at a salon in Selmer, and she herself knew how to tease it just so.

One thing that *was* different, however (and he determined this was definitely a change, not just due to the fact he was being more observant), was she'd acquired some lines around her mouth. It would appear they were due to the way she recently took to keeping her red lips pursed.

He went back to reading about the earthquake that just occurred in Italy, but he couldn't concentrate. It was Clara. He was concerned for her. She was having domestic problems. Her husband (assuming she was married) was jealous of her getting so gussied up, just to wait on tables. Because he himself knew the situation, it was impossible to sympathize. As far as Bill was concerned, the man was just a nut case.

Bill spent ten glorious days, basking in the sun on Miami Beach. He remembered to stop mail delivery, but he neglected to stop the newspaper delivery. He jokingly told himself he ought to go back to Miami Beach. It was amazing he passed such an enjoyable time, away from his regular routine. Not once did he get bored sitting on the beach, watching young, tanned, leggy waitresses serve him all kinds of exotically-named alcoholic and non-alcoholic drinks, complete with colorful little paper parasols. He didn't even *have* a taste for coffee while he was down there.

He never even gave any thought to the coffee shop dilemma—whether or not he should return to the Lakeside Diner. Tomorrow was the start of another work week. Admittedly, he did look forward to getting back to the office. If he lived in Miami Beach, he'd need some sort of employment.

To think he could have this tan, all year-long. He looked quite dapper like this. He'd go to the diner. Hopefully Joe wouldn't notice him, but maybe if he remembered to keep the paper away from his face, Clara would.

He took his place in the first booth and was more than a little startled to see Joe was not seated at the counter. No one was.

After opening the paper, he proceeded to raise it just as high as ever.

"Morning. Coffee?" an unfamiliar woman's voice said. Hell, it was unheard of at this point to have that "coffee" question asked, not by Clara. She simply greeted him and poured.

He said, "Good morning. Yes I'll have coffee, please," and lowered the paper to see a tough-looking, rather tall brunette, and no, Clara didn't add some more worry lines to her face or "get rid of" her red hair.

Like a driveling little kid he said, "Is Clara O.K.?"

The tough-as-nails hussy finished scowling at his coffee cup as she finished filling it and turned her threatening stare on him. Bill got the resounding impression he should have known all about this turn of events.

Had he not gone anyplace, he still would have been in the dark. Thank goodness he had a viable excuse: "I went away for the holidays."

All was immediately forgiven in the broad's darting brown eyes and she explained, "I'm Mike the cook's wife, fillin' in for Clara. She ain't sure jus' when she's comin' back to work. Poor thing. Christmas Day Joe McCabe, a fella she brought to work with her 'cause he sold his car, got his brains blown out with her husband Seth's twelve-gauge. Joe got his just de-sserts if ya ask me, living two doors down from Clara 'n' Seth 'n' makin' a pest of himself. Came right to their door that mornin' and told Seth, Clara was havin' an affair with some young lawyer in Selmer. Sounded jus' like a guy he made up, not somebody you'd see anywheres but on TV. A gal can't get no respect 'round these parts. Clara'd never fool around, knowin' how impulsive that rubberneck husband of hers can be."

This waitress—"Mike the cook's wife," left for a second then asked Bill if he was ready to order. He almost replied no, got up and left.

Instead he ordered dry toast. Anything else he might have thrown up. He wasn't even sure what exactly sickened him, perhaps his staggering ignorance. One thing was certain. If he felt sorry for anyone it was Seth.

Bill found another restaurant to patronize, "The Voyager." It was kind of out of the way, located on the southwest side of the lake, but he could still take the same route home.

He was sure he passed the street where Clara lived (and where Joe and her husband Seth *once* did). He wondered if there was early parole (if any, depending on the conviction) for a crime of passion. Probably not.

This restaurant's atmosphere wasn't nearly as pleasant as the Lakeside Diner's, but not because it wasn't as close to the lake. It was larger and had four waitresses hurrying around. They made him nervous. He didn't dare stay an entire hour, not when the waitress stopped giving him refills after four cups and ignored him.

The portions were quite generous, but not so much more to justify the noticeably higher prices. It wasn't as if he couldn't afford it. He just didn't want to have to tip the waitress more than he ever did Clara. After all, despite the fact her personal life was a shambles, she did an impeccable job.

He continued to frequent "The Voyager." It was that or else try the other coffee shop, also on this side of the lake—"Melvin's."

It looked awfully shabby, however. His stomach was sensitive sometimes, and some of those dives couldn't be trusted. He was having a hard enough time, tolerating how greasy The Voyager's food was.

He could have eaten breakfast in Selmer, but it just wouldn't have been the same. Having breakfast at home was unthinkable. Eating alone was the surest way to ruin a meal, and he preferred saving that for the dinner hour.

Finally one day, around the tenth of March, there was a hint of springtime warmth in the air. Leaving The Voyager he was suddenly so sick he doubled over in pain.

He got to his office, however, and he felt better when he put his mind on his work. He skipped lunch because the last thing he wanted to do was eat and get sick again.

This was the most vulnerable he'd ever felt in his life. He never realized he took his health for granted. He didn't even have anyone to complain to, when he got home.

At five o'clock he locked up and headed for Price Saver Pharmacy, to buy some antacid tablets. He wasn't quite recovered and if he had something for dinner, even just chicken broth, he didn't want to get sick again.

He hadn't been in here in ages. Between that and the fact he had a reason, he felt fortified.

Waiting to have the cashier ring up the tablets, he noticed the stack of this evening's *Peters County Ledger*. He should have bought one of those right after "Mike the cook's wife" told him what happened. Even the *Tribune* might have mentioned it. All those papers buried in the snow he simply unfolded and stacked to be recycled, never reading a single one. This was no time to be down on himself, not when he was feeling under the weather, as it was.

He pulled his wallet from his pants pocket, only to bump elbows with the well-dressed man next in line, to Bill's right. It was in fact the same one he bumped into last fall and who was none other than the hotshot young lawyer, reputedly Clara's lover.

He smiled at Bill, showing his pearly whites. He got Bill's goat because the smile wasn't one of recognizance but pure happiness. Bill was so incensed he couldn't stand it. He couldn't wait to be handed his change and the bag containing his antacid tablets. Unfortunately he didn't make his escape before witnessing the smart-aleck young man plunk a box of condoms on the counter. Bill was embarrassed for how unself-conscious the little jerk was.

Bill couldn't recall walking the fifty yards to his car, but he got there somehow. Clutching the bag, he felt arthritic, old, senile . . . This was how it felt to age all at once. His graying hair probably just turned white. Good God, he felt as if he might die.

Seated in his familiar, trustworthy, ten year-old brown Pontiac Bonneville, he watched the virile young man emerge from the drugstore and get in his shiny, new silver Mercury Marquis. It was still light enough this time of the year, there was no mistaking the fiery red hair of the woman in the passenger's seat. Even if it had been pitch dark, the silhouette of that head, would have given her away.

"FEMININE ENVY"

You go through the sale racks in the "Better Sportswear" department at Alt's, *the* store to visit when you stop in Hickory Hill Mall. If it weren't for this one place, you'd just about give up on this area. It's like a no-man's land, with Chicago way too far east to go *there* to shop. For someone like you, who has such impeccable taste, it's hard, but you persevere and eke out a living here.

You can't complain the rent is exorbitant because it's not. Your one-bedroom apartment in the little town of Shelbyville, suits you just fine and Midwesterners are good at minding their own business. After all, your privacy means a lot to you. You in fact have almost a celebrity-kind of mindset.

But just like plenty of women, oh, how you love to shop. You wish you could afford to do more of it. At the same time, you enjoy the challenge of finding the best clothes for the least money, and you don't really come alive until everything's clearance-priced. Just seeing the red slash-mark through a price excites you.

You have a day off, so you're treating yourself to this shopping spree. You can buy this summery stuff now, a couple weeks before Labor Day, or hold your peace until next year at this time.

From the looks of what's on the sale racks, plenty of women out there don't have the knock-out figure you do. Either that or else they know better than to accentuate major flaws.

But you, oh my, those long, shapely legs of yours are something to behold. They're easily your most flattering physical attribute, so of course *you* don't have a problem scooping up three pairs of cotton-spandex pedal-pushers. You certainly like the price—$16.99, marked down from $39.99. (Were they worth $39.99, to begin with? Well, no matter.) They'll soon be yours, size medium.

You wonder if you should purchase a *fourth* pair. So far you have a pair of the lime-green ones with white flowers, a pair of the navy ones with white flowers, and red ones with white flowers.

If you decided to buy a fourth pair, they'd be lime-green. Truthfully you're not terribly fond of that color. Red happens to be your favorite color, but there isn't another pair of those, in medium.

The best part of sale-shopping is you don't try anything on. You hope it all fits. You don't worry about not looking spectacular in whatever you buy. You'd look like a million, wearing a gunnysack.

But you work at it. Don't let anyone with a sinewy body let you think he or she sits around all day.

Anyway, the sexy pants aren't the only items you must have. There's no passing up purchasing a couple above-the-knee, slip-on cotton skirts, two pastel-colored midriff cotton sweaters, a black shirtdress and two T-shirts, with scooped necks and capped sleeves. God, won't you look dynamite.

When you make quite a sizable purchase, as this one is, it's only natural you want to put something on, as soon as you arrive home at your apartment. First, however, you use a pair of scissors to snip all the tags off your bargains. Now they're yours.

For some odd reason, although you positively adore the red with white flowers, pedal-pusher pants (the identical color as your '67 Mustang) you feel a certain affinity for the lime-green ones. Never mind the skirts and the dress for now. You can wear those to work. Plus, you have on a blouse that kind of matches—a lavender and green thing, nothing special. It might clash a little, but it never hurt to take a "fashion chance." Hell, you could write a whole book on beauty and fashion tips.

You stand in your room, the clothes on the bed. A free-standing, full-length mirror faces you. Although it would be simple to do, you never watch yourself get dressed. This is important to note because when you put on the green pedal-pushers, your attention is completely on doing that and nothing else. Even so, they rip right across the right thigh, about splitting the leg in two.

You can only guess how many fat-thighed, tree-trunk-legged

women tried these pants on before you. You should have been given a discount on top of the discount. But then, if you had tried them on at Alt's and they ripped, you would have probably been forced to buy them, for $16.99. That is, if you'd been found out.

Even though it's a 30-minute drive each way, you decide to go back, hoping to get another pair of pants—for free, of course.

Luckily, most of the drive is clear-sailing—empty, flat, two-lane roads. You could take the interstate, except you have to go kind of far out of the way to pick it up.

Before actually leaving, you put on the red pants. (You look smashing.) You remembered to change your top. You now have on a short-sleeved white silk shirt.

You blast the radio like always, and you can't help speeding a short distance. It just feels so good. You have to be careful because squad cars have a way of appearing out of nowhere, around here. You're pretty damned lucky you've never been caught.

In fact, since you're one who likes to tempt fate, it's amazing you don't do more things to tempt it. You certainly don't think "Someone" is looking out for you. You don't feel you deserve it, since you have everything you need.

And you only paid about two hundred bucks total for all the clothes. You're proud of yourself, for the money you saved. It occurs to you, maybe you ought to consider the ripped pants, the price of such a great bargain and leave well enough alone.

Turn around and go home? Are you serious? you ask yourself, incredulous. Work and home are about the only two places you ever go. This is your day off, to spend how you want.

Socializing never was your thing, or you'd go out just to be seen. You need a reason and a damned good one, or you'd sooner stay home. Plus you're kind of obsessed with looking "just so," and you spend a lot of time achieving it.

A glance in the rearview mirror and you feel a sense of total reassurance. You still look great, yet you neglected to touch up your make-up, before hurrying out the door.

Really, it only makes sense to go back to Alt's and see about another pair of pants. You're not rich and if you don't watch your money, no one will. And you've been known to be impulsive, wasting moolah on some trinket you can ill-afford. And one art you have yet to master is the one called investing. Face it, practicality isn't your thing and you have a phobia about putting much money in the bank.

Now's your chance to dream up the perfect sob-story to tell the saleswoman at Alt's, so you can have another pair of pants for free. The odds might be more in your favor if the one who'd waited on you, were off work for the day. The looks she gave you were most unsettling, as if she were giving you an unspoken message: *Leave!*

You didn't recognize her from someplace else, so it's nothing personal. She's just one of those hot babes (she was at least as gorgeous as you), who feels threatened by any sort of competition whatsoever.

You arrive and park in about the same place as before, quite close to the door. It's apparently a slow afternoon and you're glad for it. Crowds always make you nervous. You have a thing about wanting your space.

And when you go inside and wend your way to the "Better Sportswear" department, you keep on hoping "that" saleslady is at least taking a break. You're terrible with names and hers you can't recall worth a damn.

Whatever her name is, she's waiting on a customer. That's just great. The place is empty, except for this department. Well, you can kill some time by going to the other side of the dressing rooms and picking up another pair of lime-green pants.

Instantaneously you get this—this idea. You'd describe it as harebrained, but it makes perfect sense—that is, provided you get *no* cooperation from Ms. Austere, (*your* pet moniker) and she won't let you have another pair of pants, for free. Your mind's in fact already three-quarter's of the way made up.

You intend to steal them, even though you've never stolen a thing in your life. You don't count what you did the summer you worked at the Dairy Delight in downtown Shelbyville, across from the Laundromat.

The Dairy Delight always was the major draw in town, small wonder, given the piddly size of the "business district."

Even though these days you live but five miles to the west of town, versus on the east side, you've never gone to the Dairy Delight for an ice cream.

Anyway, the extent of the thievery was to filch a mouthful of chopped nuts or some other sundae topping (including hot fudge sauce). You always did like finger food. You haven't changed a bit. No long, drawn-out, sit-down meals for you. This way you don't have to worry as much about your waistline going to hell.

The owner/proprietor Mr. Keller was an old guy, even then, so you wonder how he's getting along these days.

You snuck a total of probably twenty bucks'-worth of toppings, maybe that in nuts alone. At the time, you felt you were getting even, not that he treated you poorly. Sure, the pay was lousy, but you didn't exactly kill yourself, doing any sort of back-breaking labor. He was pretty much indifferent to you, almost like he wished you weren't there.

It wasn't like he was some sort of psycho. He supposedly had a wife and a daughter who was close to the same age as you. She didn't go to the same school as you, of that you were certain. Other than that, you didn't know a thing about her and you didn't care. One thing you were always adept at, was minding your own business.

So you pluck those green pants from the rack and triumphantly take them to the counter. One way or another, they'll be yours, for free.

What's *this*? (You have a close-up of the customer ahead of you, and she's one who looks better up close than far away. That's totally unfair.) Her hair is more blonde (and more natural-looking) than yours, and her skimpy skirt reveals one hot pair of legs. Her face had better be homely.

Worst of all, she's holding you up. You're not about to blame the saleslady, not yet. You want her on your side, if only in your mind. Besides, she certainly wasn't slow, ringing *you* up. You might have otherwise had time to read her nametag.

Finally, blondie leaves and you have your golden opportunity to see if you can persuade—Tanya, that's her name—to give you these pants.

Pulling the ripped pants and the receipt from the bag, you lay them on the counter and tell her, "I was in here earlier today" (don't you recognize me?) "and bought these, and when I put them on at home, they tore apart." You show her the new pants, on the hanger, and say, "I'd like these, but only if I can get an added discount." (You waffling, indecisive fool. You *know* you only want them for free.)

Tanya looks at you, really looks at you, and you finally realize she must have some sort of instinctive hatred of you. Considering you're strangers to one another, she's doing a good job of wishing you'd disappear off the face of the earth.

Meanwhile you hold onto those new, unmangled pants like you life depends on it—appropriately enough.

Does she possibly know you intend to steal them if you don't have your way? And you're sure you can pull of the heist because there's no plastic sensor on the pants.

She gives you this much. She picks up the phone and presses a button: "Geena. This is Tanya in Better Sportswear. Could you tell Gladys to come here? Thanks."

In the interim Tanya stands with her back to you, busying herself with whatever mundane tasks that need to be done. You oh-so patiently stand there, waiting for Gladys to appear.

Gladys ends up coming up from behind, scaring the bejesus out of you. Haughtiness emanates from her every pore, and she's one big, fat woman, old enough to be your mother—or Tanya's.

They both confer, their backs to you the entire time. You can hardly hold in the urge to crack up, laughing. You're caught off-guard whenever something tickles your funny bone, and the sight of those two, one skinny, one obese, does you in. Your control is amazing, but you always knew you could handle any situation—or *almost* any.

Fatty Gladys finally faces you and smiles, looking as jovial as the circus fat lady, herself. You're far too suspicious at this point to believe she might actually *like* you.

But what comes out of her mouth certainly doesn't tell as much. Quite the opposite: "I'm sorry but we can't do anything for merchandise that's been marked down, and the pants you bought were a final sale."

Well la-de-da, thank you very much. Tell me something I don't know, fatso. For all that, you can just *barely* contain your indignation.

But you have one important reassurance—this is the moment for justice and you will make sure you get it. Filching the toppings at the Dairy Delight was preparation for this day. You haven't really lived until you've stolen something.

You stuff the torn pants back into the bag, along with the receipt and pull the pants you intend to steal, off the counter. Your back to the two store-policy-abiding employees, you say, "All right. Thanks anyway." No one can say you *ever* stop being polite, even immediately prior to becoming a thief.

You can't help marveling how coolly you walk past all the racks of clothes, pass the dressing rooms and find yourself "on the other side," with no one to see you.

So utterly smoothly, like you're a pro, you stand by the rack where the pants belong. Instead of putting them back you stick them in the bag, hanger and all. You feel a heady rush of such vindication, you fear for a second, you may faint. You feel more guilty about that than the crime you just committed.

Illicitness really does suit you, and not a soul is around to witness your departure, not even a customer. The place really is dead today. It's a blessing in disguise, and when you pass the sensors, go through the glass doorway and head for your car, you're so happy you could cry.

You don't hurry, but you don't dawdle, either. For once, you wish your car wasn't fire-engine red. It really is awfully noticeable, especially since it's a '67, and the year's '97. Good thing you're not a real criminal, or you'd have to trade it for a more discreet-looking make and model.

Off you go, taking your time as you leave, to avoid any suspicion. You're glad to miss the light at the intersection where the mall's entrance road meets Highway 64. It gives you an opportunity to study the goings on, in your rearview mirror. Nothing's happening and damn do you look good. You're flushed with exhilaration.

You make sure not to speed, driving home, but the closer you get, the more anxious you become.

Soon you arrive and there's no one at the apartment door to escort you inside, not that you expected as much. No. You're just as free as those as those pants inside your bag. You can hardly wait to put them on. You just hope they don't rip.

They don't and boy, are you proud of yourself now. Just call you the dilettante-thief, thank you, very much.

Sure it's your day off but you like to *do* things then, not sleep. Well, that's exactly what you just did, right on the living room sofa. You missed the six o'clock news, you missed dinner. Hell if stealing a pair of pants wasn't exhausting.

You're starving but cooking isn't your style. That means it's time to go get something to eat. How about going to the Dairy Delight? Memories of working there have given you a taste for custard, maybe even a hot fudge sundae. If you spill some on your new pants, you'll just have to wash them (versus mending them).

When you arrive, you park your red car in the far corner of the lot, not giving it a second thought. So you want to remain inconspicuous. You taunt yourself, saying you should have stayed home, if you're so afraid.

Well, you didn't put on fresh lipstick for nothing and you're positively famished by this time. Anyway, you're kind of curious to see Mr. Keller again. Although people as stable and unassuming as him annoy you, they do provide a sort of comfort to bohemian types like you.

You stroll up to the front of the building, narrowly avoiding tripping over a couple bicycles. Then the culprits—er, the *owners*, come into view. They're standing off to the side, each one busily licking a big chocolate custard cone.

None other than by-now-octogenarian Mr. Keller is at his post. He's lost most of his white hair and all that remains are a few wisps.

You tell him you want a hot fudge sundae. (It only seems fitting.) You have crushed nuts on your mind, although you maintain the ones you snacked on while working here, don't qualify as stolen. (And if nothing else you prove conclusively how stubborn you are, in your line of thinking.)

No matter just how stubborn you may be, it doesn't keep you from feeling very distracted by those two boys. They just started staring at you, you can see out of the corner of your right eye. They're too young to be undressing you (wishful thinking). *Anything* but that. You could care less how many faults they find with your features. You're one of those who looks better as the whole package.

They ought to hurry over to the other side of the building, where they left their bikes. You never know just who might come up and steal them.

But no. They stay put and continue to find you as mouth-watering as their chocolate custards. Mr. Keller meanwhile moves at a snail's pace, preparing your sundae.

Finally (time really does stand still) he places his latest masterpiece on the counter. It even comes complete with a maraschino cherry. He didn't have *those* when you worked for him, or you would have filched those, too.

He opens the window and takes the five-dollar bill you hand him. You're feeling so generous, that's generous, *not* guilty, you *almost* tell him to keep the change.

But of course you don't and when he gives you the change, he really looks at you, for the first time, ever (including when you worked for him). So deeply does he see into your baby blues, you're certain he's looking right through you.

You're intrigued, of all things, wondering what he's thinking. It's impossible he recognizes you (so *you* maintain). You've changed so much since high school.

The spoon's jutting out of the side of the sundae and you can hardly wait to grab hold of the handle, filled with tasty custard and hot fudge. Sugary food isn't typically your thing, but you are positively famished.

The wait *was* worth it because it seems the two boys have since magically disappeared. You start walking back to your car, keeping your eyes on that spoon, lest it jiggle loose.

You completely forget their bicycles might still be laying around, so you proceed to trip right over them.

It really *is* your lucky day, you sarcastically think before you start to actually fall. As you do, you mutter every blasphemy you can think of. (And you have one hell of an imagination.)

Your hot fudge sundae is now airborne, and you expect any second to hear the raucous laughter of those two boys. It would be too good to be true they both disappeared off the face of the earth.

Yes sir, you took the closest thing to a nose-dive without actually falling on your nose. You get up as quickly as you can, but you're not on your feet before Mr. Keller's whiny voice asks, "You O.K.?"

"I'll be fine," you reply, meaning you'll give yourself about thirty seconds to get your bearings, and get the hell out of here before you're so humiliated you literally burst.

Then you notice the huge hole on the left knee of your pants. Funny, there's no blood, just that gaping hole and a whole lot of gooey black grease on both the right pants let near the ankle and the skin on your ankle. It's safe to say the pants are trashed.

So when Mr. Keller offers to make you another sundae, you tell him O.K. He can even charge you for it, and you won't hold it against him. You're feeling like "Someone Up There" is teaching you a lesson, maybe even more than one. So if He isn't actually looking out for you, He's got an eye on you. Same thing? Perhaps, perhaps not.

You spy the two boys, across the street, harassing the pop machine outside the Laundromat. They must have been inside there, while you were putting your life in jeopardy—thanks to them. You're so grateful they missed you fall, however, you don't mind. You don't even mind you ruined two pairs of pants in one day.

With as much diligence this time, if not more, Mr. Keller makes you a second hot fudge sundae. You can hardly wait for him to finish, and when he does, it's plain he doesn't expect to be paid.

Not only that, he tells you, "I'll clean up that mess, don't worry about it. I wish them kids wouldn't leave their bikes layin' in the way. They need to learn some responsibility."

"I agree," you say, but your mind is on your pains, reviewing what hurts the most. Amazingly your knee doesn't hurt at all. The pants took the brunt of the fall.

Mr. Keller tells you, "It's all got to do with the public school system. Kids need the discipline they're guaranteed to get at private schools, especially the parochial ones. That's where me and my wife's daughter went."

Well, you're not sure of the soundness of his comment, but he's supposedly the authority, at least compared to you. Plus, he has the never-ending chance to observe all these twelve year-old customers.

You feel kind of sorry for Mr. Keller, when all is said and done. The least you can do is listen to him talk, although you don't pay attention to what he gabs about. You have your hot fudge sundae to savor and it's absolutely delicious. As soon as Mr. Keller takes a breather, you intend to tell him just how good it tastes.

Then from behind you, making your neck stubble stand on end, you hear a man say, "Thanks Mister Keller, for stalling 'im. Sandy Fine, a.k.a. Alexander Finnitski, Shelbyville's one and only transvestite. Yeah, Sandy, you really are quite the poser, getting yourself videotaped, stealin' a pair of them exercise pants. Mister Keller's daughter Tanya had her eye on you, from the start, 'n' word spreads fast 'round here. Now Mister Keller can tell *her*, the rest of the story."

And it's *the end* for you, isn't it. If only you'd been born a female, maybe, just maybe your life would have been different.

"IMPATIENCE"

My one-time friend Joanne was voted the "Most Impatient Student" of our graduating class, an award made specifically for her. When I heard she'd gotten pregnant, I immediately concluded it was either untrue or else she'd made a mistake. I could not imagine her tolerating the time it took to make a baby.

Well, if the conception was mistake number one, things would snowball from that point on.

Actually, her initial error was quitting her job at Synthetic Tool Prod. (Everyone seemed to like calling it that, as if leaving the remainder of the name, to the imagination.) The boss himself, Shorty Callanan, even called it that. He wanted to prove he could shorten words, since his name was Shorty. He certainly wasn't short, unless of course you thought a man just shy of six feet tall, was.

Anyway, Joanne quit her job there at the end of October, for no better reason than she was extremely bored. So she said. Then voila, right after that, she found she was pregnant.

Here it was, the beginning of June. She had two more months to carry this baby around, and she was feeling fatter than the fattest person on earth. To top it off a heat wave had struck the Chicagoland area. With the record-breaking temperatures, she was part of history being made, yet she was too completely miserable and cranky to care.

This was the very life she'd been pining for, all those long, hot, boring hours in the factory! There was nothing to look at in the hot, stuffy place, save the black rubber conveyor belt that chugged along, bringing her the next thingamajig to help assemble. For years she worked there, yet she was never certain what her labors helped create.

These days she did some needlepoint, watched lots of television, and took plenty of naps. She'd sleep even more than she did, except it got so boring. If she was feeling anxious she'd find herself looking out the front window, *hours* before her husband Jerry was due home from work.

Ever since early spring, he'd been coming home later. Overtime meant his paychecks were bigger. In his own way he really did try. She knew he wasn't at some bar, drinking with his buddies, because that kind of thing didn't interest him, not on a regular basis. He wouldn't even have to tell her where he'd been, as her nose was good at picking up all sorts of aromas, especially the bar-related ones.

Joanne initially took the job at Synthetic Tool Prod. to help support Jerry and herself while he finished his Master's at the University of Chicago. They also lived off a small inheritance from his father Harold. "Meager" was really a better word to describe the amount of money, but she hated to seem disrespectful, especially of the deceased. Among the four Brewster siblings, Jerry, the eldest, received by far the least. Blatant favoritism if there ever was.

His mother Elaine got the most and no one seemed to mind, until she told everyone she intended to will it all to Jerry. He always was mama's favorite, and keeping that in mind was the only thing that enabled Joanne tolerate the nosy old biddy (along with knowing she was worth plenty of cash).

Unfortunately the tides turned, sometime between this past Thanksgiving and Christmas. There was a heated telephone exchange between Jerry and his mother, and it was the first time since marrying, Joanne and he didn't visit Elaine at her townhouse in Ft. Myers.

Jerry succeeded in estranging himself from every member of his immediate family. Were his father still alive, Jerry would have been estranged from him, too.

Elaine was the only one Joanne cared about, for the reasons just stated. As for Jerry's siblings, his sister Wanda was nothing but trouble. In fact the night of that fateful phone conversation, Joanne was almost certain Wanda was at the townhouse, visiting her mother. She played referee as she listened in, and you could bet she wasn't about to root for her brother. It wasn't personal. She liked to "beat" her younger brothers Chris and Tom, not to mention her older brother Jerry, at celebrating Christmas with Mother. Everything was a game, and Wanda wanted to win.

There was a time when Jerry and his mother were so lovey-dovey, it was disgusting. Elaine would get so cute with him she'd even pet him like he was a dog.

There were a couple instances in public places, Joanne pretended not to be associated with them.

In essence, Jerry did not discuss family matters, and Joanne wasn't one to pry.

However, since they didn't go to Florida at Christmas, Joanne had been climbing the walls. It wasn't cabin fever but an intense curiosity about Jerry's "inheritance status," as she called it. Possibly it was strictly coincidence he worked longer hours these days to earn more money, but if you were smart like Joanne was, you learned to decipher subtle clues.

It was impossible to deny, any longer. Joanne was disgusted. She used to daydream to no end, what Jerry and she could do with a substantial inheritance, not the piddly amount his senile, old coot of a father left behind. Jerry would never reveal the exact worth of his mother, but he did once joke she was "loaded." There were only two times Jerry used that adjective—to describe someone either extraordinarily drunk or else extraordinarily rich.

But of course right before the bottom fell out of their nest egg, how appropriate in more ways than one, Joanne was going to make a baby. Because she was inherently impatient, perfect timing would never be her forte. Accuse her of being a little too spontaneous, she didn't care. All she knew was life wasn't fair.

Getting pregnant was a cinch, too. What was all the fuss about, for other couples? God must have blessed her, since she was forced to do without the material blessing of her mother-in-law's money.

Wasn't there some Greek myth in which the mother, who once loved her son turns on him, only to be struck by lightning and killed? Elaine needed to brush up on her mythology.

It was possible Joanne spent the night dreaming her mother-in-law met a fiery death of some sort. She herself kept sweating like crazy, but she didn't dare rip the cover sheet and the blanket off the bed, not when Jerry had them both pulled up past his head. He was *always* cold. Damned if she hadn't hoped to start looking for property or maybe just a condominium, in a warmer climate, using some of their inheritance. Elaine wasn't in ill-health (as far as Joanne was aware) or about to die, but never hurt to hope.

Well, one thing Joanne's mother-in-law couldn't make Joanne do in vain, was speculate about what to name the baby (which Joanne prayed would be a girl).

Jerry wanted a boy and that was that. Joanne and her doctor agreed to keep it all a secret. At least she was open-minded enough to say she'd love either one, and truthfully she was tickled to death, knowing in barely two months, the suspense would be over. She had a thing about surprises, big or small, and this one definitely ranked at the top.

Her love of surprises went back to her elementary and junior high school years, when on Friday afternoons, her mother Isabelle would bake an after-school treat.

Joanne would come through the kitchen doorway and deeply inhale, trying to guess in less than ten seconds, what her mother had made.

Joanne always guessed correctly, within the time allowed, and the smell of gingerbread never failed to put her in an extra-good mood.

Gingerbread men reminded her of Christmas, what *used* to be her favorite holiday. Now she detested it, thanks to Elaine Brewster. How was Joanne expected to explain to her child, a boy *or* a girl, Mommy hated Christmas? That sounded awfully disturbing, didn't it. She'd have to "cross that bridge," pardon the cliché, when she reached it. She wasn't in any hurry, whenever she considered all the labor pains she'd have to endure. She happened to be highly intolerant of any pain whatsoever.

The night she lost her virginity she was fifteen and hardly prepared to accommodate her well-endowed boyfriend who was twice her age. The whole world heard Joanne Cosecki scream that night, and it wasn't a cry of pleasure.

Before you start assuming Joanne's been around, she only dated one other man besides Mr. Macho, who had no business messing around with a 15 year-old. When she met Jerry, she knew the search was over.

By the time Jerry and she started a serious relationship, she had learned how to be much more objective about men, not so stupidly emotional.

Titus. That was most likely what she'd name the baby, if it was a boy. She never mentioned that name to Jerry because he'd crinkle his nose or roll his eyes. He had yet to reveal any of his choices, but you could count on them being unimaginative ones.

If it was a girl, there was absolutely no doubt—Tiffany. Joanne loved that name because it reminded her of Tiffany jewelry or Tiffany lamps. So what if she liked connecting the name to something classy? That way she'd never get tired of telling the little girl to eat her Brussels sprouts or clean her room, or *go* to her room and leave Mommy the hell alone.

In the meanwhile, Jerry would continue his ridiculously inane rituals, such as talking to her belly: "Yoo-hoo in there. You'd better be a boy!"

Joanne would smile down at Jerry's blond, tight-fisted curls (as bound and determined as the man himself), and she'd say to herself, "It has to be a girl. I *cannot* be suffering through this, for a boy." And at times like those, when Jerry was acting so dumb, she meant it. She even felt capable of killing the baby, were she to give birth to a boy. These barely controllable feelings frightened her.

Later she would reflect on them and prayed to God she wasn't truly so wicked.

To inwardly threaten was one thing, but to act upon manic impulses was an entirely different matter.

Right now there was an excuse. Her vengeful feelings were delirium—induced. Here it was, the first of June, and it was blazing hot. It was the last thing she needed with two months' *gestation period* remaining.

Joanne never did have much use for summer, once she was finished with school, not that she didn't like it. She was pretty and sociable, the two best attributes to have. Being intelligent wasn't so important, although she was that, too.

Enough was enough of getting up early and lugging books and notebooks to a place where adults treated you like you landed here on earth (on your head), from another planet.

Working at Synthetic Tool Prod., all she ever did was daydream about exactly what she was doing at this moment—lazing around in a pair of shorts and a braless tank top. She never took into account being pregnant, so now she needed a damned bra.

The shirt didn't cover the straps and whenever she'd see one out of the corner of her eye, she was ready to scream.

It was against company policy at the assembly plant, to bare so much skin, bra or no bra. She didn't think that was fair because it got unbearably hot in there, even when the weather was mild.

Dress code-wise, it wasn't as if her boss, Shorty Callanan, didn't set a good example. She had yet to see him in anything but a suit, and although by noontime he might remove the coat, he didn't loosen his tie or roll up his white shirt sleeves. She found this kind of discipline an incredible turn-on. He also happened to be very handsome, but in a cute, more boyish way than Jerry.

Shorty spent the majority of his time in his office, overlooking the workplace.

He could watch his employees anytime he wanted. Instead he was always busy at his desk.

Joanne had her back to that window, the whole time she was working. "And it's better this way," she'd tell herself. She simply couldn't afford to be attracted to him. She'd felt that special, certain something for him, the first time they'd met, when she was interviewed (all too briefly) for her job.

She didn't know what made her think he wasn't married then, but he had to be, by this point in time. Most men simply did not get out of bed on their own volition five mornings a week and dress themselves in exquisitely-tailored and immaculately pressed suits.

Oh, well, what difference did it make? Joanne was taken, and an affair behind Jerry's back was out of the question. She just hated to think she could have somehow more thoroughly investigated. (To have done so without making him raise his own doubts about the kind of wife she'd be, would have been impossible.)

Plus, he could be so incredibly defensive. You'd think he had something lurid to hide. But if she hadn't snagged him, another woman would have, and Joanne never would have forgiven herself.

She wasn't unhappy with their union, not by any means. Boredom, as of late, had given her more than ample time to do some soul-searching, was all.

Jerry had his good points, Joanne wasn't about to deny it. As already mentioned, he didn't stay out late. Neither did he get drunk, nor abuse her, nor waste anything, nor was he neglectful of their possessions.

He didn't cheat on her, but the more she thought about it, she couldn't make the claim with as much conviction as she did, the other points. There was really no way of knowing for sure. And supposedly the best time for two lovers to rendezvous was during the lunch hour.

If Jerry wasn't at a luncheon meeting, he had lunch at his desk. Or did he? Or was that new secretary of his, lunch? Sure. He *did indeed* eat at his desk. Joanne didn't even know the woman's name. Oh, Jerry told her, but to Joanne, the woman was just a voice at the other end of the line, when she called his office.

The secretary just started a couple months ago. Joanne was terrible with names, unless it was something catchy or unusual (like Shorty Callanan). The woman's name *did* have a "Mrs." before it, *that* much she recalled. However, she was divorced. However again, she had three kids, ages 14, 12, and 11. It was safe to say the woman'd lost the bloom of youth, something Joanne was mortified would happen to her, after having only *one* kid.

Joanne decided to play a clever little mind game. She'd tell herself one million times, starting right now, during the commercial break between soaps, she was *happy!* She had on the shorts and tank top she'd fantasized about wearing, whenever she'd no longer work at Synthetic Tool Prod. Never mind her bulging belly. She could rest assured it was nothing permanent.

She chanted she was happy about fifty times before she was sick of the stupid game. It wasn't helping, she wasn't fooled, and damn it all, she was tired of lying on her back, on this woolly old couch. They wouldn't be buying a new one, not for a long time. The baby boy or girl would be a major investment that paid *no* dividends.

Joanne didn't think that was a cold-hearted complaint, just the truth.

Cold-heartedness itself was her mother-in-law Elaine Brewster, who obviously couldn't be relied upon to pull through with a few bucks.

Luckily Joanne was quite a thrifty woman, even though she did also happen to enjoy the finer things in life, from time to time. Her wardrobe primarily consisted of baggy jeans, shorts and oversized shirts and blouses. Sure as hell, she wasn't about to waste precious money on maternity clothes. And neither did she intend to experience this a second time.

Maybe she just didn't dream big enough, meaning all she aspired to was doing nothing and dressing like a slob. One thing making a baby *did* accomplish, was boosting her mother Isabelle's regard for Joanne. Joanne in fact felt as if she'd been given a second chance at winning her mother's unconditional respect.

Joanne didn't go to college, and she didn't marry the right man (as far as her mother was concerned). Isabelle maintained Joanne was only "asking for trouble," marrying a man with droopy eyelids. Joanne couldn't take such an idiotic remark seriously, hence she didn't heed it.

Oh, and he had green eyes, hidden somewhere behind those half-closed lids. "You know what kind of men have *that* color of eyes," Isabelle said, batting the lids of her own baby blues.

Joanne told her to keep her mouth shut. It sounds like an audacious thing to tell your mother, but Isabelle was used to it, not just from her sassy daughter.

See, Isabelle was prone to drinking too much and when she

did, she became loquacious and a bit lascivious. Joanne found her mother's behavior pathetic, especially since she herself exercised such patent control.

It was time to get up and refill her lemonade glass. The pitcher was by the kitchen sink. While she was at it, she needed to use the restroom. There was a half-bath by the back door.

No flip-flops to bother finding, to put back on her feet. She usually wore those with her favorite outfit, but when you spent most of your time lying down, you were better off barefoot. That explained the out-of-season footwear—pink wool booties her mother knitted for her, last Christmas. There was hope yet, of spending the winter holidays in Florida. Isabelle was thinking about moving to Tampa.

She'd been a widow for a number of years, even before Joanne married. The house of hers in Crystal Lake was too big and lonely these days.

See? Joanne figured a member of *her* side of the family would rectify the situation somewhat. You couldn't count on the Brewsters, not in the long run. And you know, just maybe Jerry wasn't being true to her, not anymore.

Suddenly she got a strange, nauseating feeling, not especially pregnancy-related. She felt like she was teetering, about to fall off a cliff. She wanted to stop walking but it seemed like her legs insisted upon moving without her. This was a completely surreal experience. Even though she'd never taken acid she knew some people in high school, who did. What she was experiencing was exactly one of the kinds of things they described happening to them.

In the next instant Joanne was slipping backward and only by grabbing onto the closest ladder-back chair, could she save herself from a serious fall. The left corner of the seat, caught on the underside of the table, so it turned precariously but held fast.

"Goddamn these shoes!" she seethed. She knew better than to wear them when she felt like a whale on two legs. Oh well. They gave her another excuse to hate Christmas.

She went down pretty hard on her butt, but she wasn't hurt,

just a little shaken. Thanks to the extra fat back there, the landing was easy.

Never mind the baby. He/she was *fine*. It really irked her to think "it" remained totally oblivious to all the harsh realities of the world.

Here she went again, with this needless vengefulness. It was disturbing and it made her worry what kind of parent she would be. As much as she wanted to raise her child unlike *she* was raised, it seemed as if she would end up being just like her mother—at times indulgent but for the most part distant and unaffectionate.

Admittedly, however, her mother was totally devoted to the task of raising a child and never, ever physically deprived Joanne of anything.

It felt good to sit on the cool, lime-green linoleum and take her sweet time, getting up. One thing this pregnancy taught her was the necessity of taking her time.

Her doctor couldn't stress that enough, especially for a "high-strung" woman like herself.

She liked being described as such, but she could do without most of the rest of the rhetoric, such as his recommendation she take one of those Lamaze classes.

She was her own woman and *no one* would tell her what to do. When it came time to have the baby, everyone in the delivery room would think she'd already been through it once or twice.

Still, she couldn't fight the fact she wanted a girl. And Jerry, with all his heart and soul (the spineless creep), wanted a boy. Wasn't that so cute. What in heaven's name was the matter with him? Didn't he know how much more trouble boys were? That all they did was get dirty, get into fights, and get all the neighbors wishing you'd move away, thanks to their assorted pranks?

Of course Jerry knew, she quipped to herself. He was a man and what was that but an amplification of a boy's most endearing attributes—endearing if you unconditionally loved that person. As for Jerry, she couldn't commit to that notion until she did some more soul-searching. Married to him, she was aware she shouldn't be thinking like that.

She used the bathroom but skipped having some more lemonade, even though it was initially why she got up. What she needed was a nap, so before lying back down on the sofa she turned down the volume on the TV. Oh, and she'd gone into the bedroom and traded those hazardous booties for her perennial favorites after all, her flip-flops, even though by the time she awoke they'd both most likely be on the floor.

This pregnancy broke Joanne's habit of sleeping on her stomach, and she was secretly immensely grateful. Ever since reading in a fashion magazine, sleeping on your back helped stave off under-the-eye bags, she'd wanted to change positions.

Easier said than done. And not to find something for which to blame Jerry, but he used to encourage her to sleep on her stomach. He did, himself (yet looked none the worse for it, unlike herself), and he'd lop his left arm across her back. He didn't *want* to rest his arm on the pillow, around her head.

However, ever since she had to sleep on her back, he'd resigned himself, in a big way. Not only did he keep his arms and hands to himself, he slept as far away as possible. In a king-sized bed that translated to a hint. The next step would be him voluntarily sleeping on the sofa, the one where she was ensconced.

With that not-so-soothing thought she drifted off to sleep.

Joanne thought (mistakenly?) she was in the house. Still, she wondered why a breeze was blowing on her face. She also felt something tingling her tummy, as if perhaps a parade of centipedes was slowly making its way across it.

She awakened enough to realize no bug in the world belonged anywhere on her, let alone a troop of them. And never mind the baby for once. *Wherever* something crawled was off-limits.

Before opening her eyes, so she wouldn't be tempted to scream, she gave her stomach a light but firm slap, saving the boy/girl inside, any undue stress but effectively nailing the bugs.

"Aargh!" she said, aware it was going to take more than one slap, after all, to chase away the pesky things.

"Ouch!" a voice exclaimed. It was rather high-pitched, making her think for an instant that it came from her *own* mouth.

Finally Joanne opened one eye, then the other, only to see Jerry kneeling beside her, smiling—a sappy-looking smile at that. To top it off he leaned over and pressed his lips to her bare stomach, afterward saying, "A kiss for good luck. A boy we can name Billy."

Billy? When in the hell did he come up with that one? This was the first time he actually mentioned a name, and that was the best he could do? This only renewed her desire for a girl, unless he also intended to call *her* Billie.

He stood, his knees cracking. "I brought dinner," he told her. Well, at least he forgave her, her slovenliness. He was also understanding of the fact it wasn't easy, not only making a baby but carrying it everywhere, with you.

Nonetheless, Joanne didn't say a word. She was ambivalent about the whole thing. Lately she'd been sloughing off *way* too much, and she feared this was the beginning of a new habit she'd need to break. Therefore, Jerry was only encouraging her downfall, good intentions aside.

"I'll cook tomorrow night," she promised, mostly to herself, to keep from getting needlessly angry.

He patted her head and departed, loosening his tie on the way to their bedroom. "If you decide you want to go out, I'll be glad to take you, baby doll." He knew she loved to go out to dinner, at least before she became a recluse, thanks to her big stomach.

Joanne watched his back and curly head of blond hair as he disappeared down the hallway. Only when her forehead started to pound was she aware she was scowling.

Alcohol in Jerry's bloodstream was the only possible explanation for his placidity. She sat up and tried to read her watch, which was askew. The leather band must have stretched because there was no way in hell her *wrist*, of all things, had shrunk.

It was almost six-thirty. He was quite a bit later than usual, but she had to take into account he waited for carry-out. O.K., so he had a couple of drinks while he was waiting, probably at Bistro Italia. That was no crime, provided he drank alone. It was hard to imagine Jerry doing *anything* alone, but she'd have to, for the sake of her peace of mind. The thing that bothered her most, ironically enough, was she couldn't smell liquor on his breath. She happened to have a good sense of smell, too.

Well, this was no time to heap stress upon stress, just like the doctor warned her. In that case, did he have something to recommend for a pregnant woman who suspected her husband of adultery?

Ever since Joanne was pregnant she'd had no interest whatsoever in sex, for a number of reasons. It had created a mild but ongoing tension between Jerry and herself.

She could be quite temperamental anyway, so that aspect was nothing new.

Perhaps then he was simply sick and tired of her, pregnant or not. Now *that* was an entirely different matter.

Luckily for Jerry she *wasn't* cooking dinner tonight. She'd be all too tempted to put rat poison in the rat's meal. Seriously, he must have felt guilty about something illicit he did today, so he was trying to make up for it, in his mind, by bringing dinner. She hoped it wasn't sex-related. She'd sooner he killed someone or robbed a bank. Hey, they could use the money.

She looked around, expecting to see her right flip-flop. The left one miraculously was still on her foot. The right one wasn't anywhere in plain sight, so she'd have to find it some other time. Once she stood, that was it, no leaning, bending or kneeling for her.

Emitting a grunt and two long groans, she got up. She couldn't resist looking around, hoping to see the errant flip-flop. What the hell did it do? Walk away without her, it was so disgusted by how tubby she was? Asking herself these stupid questions only made her feel more tired and crabby and ineffectual than ever. Not even sarcasm could rescue her when this thing called life was completely out of her hands. Yes indeed, she was at the mercy of fate, and she hated every damned second of it.

She did manage to find the remote control and put it to use on the talking head who was making her last, trite little comments before the end of the newscast. It was a bleached blonde who was much more homely than pretty and way the hell past her prime.

Joanne had to wonder who the old hag slept with to land that job of hers. Damned if life wasn't plain unfair. You had to be crooked to get anywhere.

For some strange reason they didn't have cable television, probably because Jerry liked to spend *his* evenings playing with his computer. However, he wasn't the devotee you might think, of the "chat rooms." He was a one-on-one, in-person kind of guy. With his perfect face and body and charming personality (when he wanted) he could find the women he desired, *all* himself.

If Joanne did a little pleading, she hoped maybe he'd run down to the Video Depot and pick up a couple movies. The Video Depot was in a new strip mall on Lancaster Street, near the corner of Mehrer Boulevard, not more than five or six miles away. That was still within the Breckenridge town limits.

Voila, tonight Jerry was out to earn as many gold stars as he could. He said, "Sure honey. I'll go get you a couple movies. What'll it be?"

Joanne couldn't stop the tingle of sheer happiness, all due to hearing him sound so sincerely willing to please. She'd never given it any thought, but a cooperative man was a major turn-on. Men themselves didn't buy that one because they dismissed just such a guy as pussy-whipped.

She moved to give him a hug and a kiss good-bye, but he was already on his way. She didn't dare stop his forward motion, although it didn't seem like anything could slow him down, tonight. She wished *she* could eat as little as he just did for dinner and still have not only plenty of energy but a sense of humor. She polished off all her lasagna *and* half of his spaghetti dinner. She couldn't wait until dessert, which she'd have in another hour or two. If she ate it now, she'd be up all night, pigging out.

Joanne had let Jerry hurry along, so *now* where was he? It seemed like he'd been gone for hours. Maybe he was in one of his thoughtful moods and was taking his time, deciding what two movies to pick for her. Tonight she'd made the mistake of telling him to surprise her. On any other night, it wouldn't have had such a detrimental effect.

As it was, Jerry could be the consummate dawdler. A five-minute repair around the house never failed to require three trips to the hardware store and six coffee breaks.

The errand itself was time-consuming because it was imperative he flirt with the salesgirl, no matter who she was. It was as if he was doing penance for causing yet another minor earthquake in a female's life. Yes, he was *that* handsome. He was also ridiculously, *needlessly* friendly to men. He stopped short of ever appearing condescending, but possibly it was in the back of his mind. There was no way he didn't have at least a smidgen of vanity in his blood.

Joanne was never in a situation with him, that made her become jealous, but she did lose her patience plenty of times. She didn't have a whole lot to begin with. Still, it irritated her to recall that Jerry would carry on, oblivious to her arms crossed over her heaving chest, her toes tapping the floor, or her face becoming more red and shiny by the second.

Patience and a lack thereof was a big reason why this pregnancy-ordeal didn't suit a woman like herself. (She loved the sound of that. It was *almost* as if she were too good for slaving through the trials and tribulations of the human race.)

The worst part was she felt like a wizened old biddy, and there were still two months to go! Feeling asexual could only be some sort of preparation for menopause.

Peace of mind—or better yet, peace of *body* and mind was apparently not to be found here on earth, save for in rare moments. Maybe you had to be born male. So, should she too wish for a baby boy?

When Jerry finally returned, he fairly *floated* through the doorway, bringing with him the unmistakable stench of cigarette smoke. And *he* didn't smoke. There was only one way he could reek like that, anyway. He took the Video Depot clerk two doors down, to Herschel's Cafe and Wine Bar. They had a couple drinks and a bite to eat. Hell, he was gone long enough, they probably fucked while they were at it.

Joanne was so intensely angry she was utterly at ease. She even thought maybe her heart stopped beating. There was but one, single thing she wanted to do and all her thought processes were focused on it—kill her husband.

While Jerry excitedly waved the two video choices, Joanne had to choke back the urge to tell him the perfect slot for them both, at once.

The two movie titles were *Mom's Day Off* and *Ms. Mom*. He and the salesgirl put their heads together and decided this was *the* subject matter to drive Joanne insane.

"I'm going to bed," Joanne announced, at the expense of hurting Jerry's feelings. That, however, seemed quite impossible when he was wearing yet another one of those sappy grins.

"What?" he asked, and for a second, surprisingly enough, he did look hurt. Even more surprisingly *he* tried to embrace *her* as she started making her way to the bedroom. Realizing she felt like crap (in the physical sense. Of the resentment—induced kind, he hadn't a clue), he didn't try to stop her.

Joanne wanted nothing more than to go to sleep on her stomach and when she awoke in the morning, she'd no longer be pregnant nor married to Jerry. He'd be long gone, leaving behind a farewell note. She'd resume working at Synthetic Tool Prod.

Out of the goodness of his heart, Shorty Callanan would take her back. Even working part-time would be better than sitting around here. It would also be easier to return there than start someplace else.

While she was at it, she would find out Shorty's marital status. If he *was* married, she couldn't imagine a man like him even *considering* a divorce, no matter the kind of convincing Joanne was willing to try.

It would just be her luck if he married only recently. In the meantime she'd been loafing around, letting her philandering husband show his true colors.

If there was anything resembling a bright side to the whole debacle, Jerry was very private about the affair(s). Joanne could rest assured a mistress would never turn up in their bed. He knew this wife of his, meticulous though she was about keeping the house clean, wouldn't have any qualms about getting the sheets and carpet bloodied.

Finally Joanne realized she was standing in the doorway of none other than their bedroom. She needed to get in bed, fast, before Jerry was aware she was thinking, fast.

First thing was getting away from the two-timing S.O.B. She'd find herself a devoted man to help raise her child. This was the ultimate way to teach a ne'er-do—well like Jerry, his much-deserved lesson.

Isabelle Cosecki felt like the luckiest woman alive. It was Christmas, she'd just moved to Tampa, Florida, and her daughter Joanne was here for a visit, along with her new, five-month old baby boy Titus and her almost equally new husband Shorty. It sounded like the names should be reversed, but if a grown man called himself that, it wasn't for Isabelle to decide. She was from a generation in which the man's word was a good as God's.

But times changed and she was so proud of her daughter's innate ability to keep right up with these changes, if not be slightly avant-garde. Yes, to be a real woman of the '90's, it was imperative you make snap decisions. And that was precisely what Joanne did, divorcing her husband Jerry, Titus' biological father, going through a rapid-fire divorce, and marrying the man she should have married the *first* time. But that was the whole idea of second chances, wasn't it.

From the words holy matrimony on, that Jerry Brewster fellow just wasn't Joanne's type. So intent was she, upon making him hers, she failed to consider just what kind of man she was latching onto. And if Isabelle did say so herself, her one-in-a-million daughter deserved much better than a man who needed a leash— a short one. In Isabelle's book, adultery was as horrific a crime as murder. They both required the guilty party to be 100% oblivious to the hapless victim. In this case, dear, sweet, one-of-a-kind Joanne just so happened to be pregnant with Titus when she first became aware of her then-husband's evil ways. It was no small accomplishment she carried the baby to term, inundated though she was, by so much stress.

Isabelle wasn't about to question her daughter's decision to divorce Jerry, but she *was* awfully hasty about it. "Go, Go, Go," were the watchwords of these young women of the '90's. Isabelle wasn't certain a two-letter credo, repeated twice, was such a good thing.

Well anyway, Joanne and her husband Shorty didn't drive twelve-hundred miles, from the far western suburbs of Chicago, to be judged on their merits. Most importantly, Joanne was her own person, and Isabelle was extremely proud of her.

If Joanne *did* have a fault (and goodness knows this was pushing it, to even call it a "fault"), she could be impatient and was prone to jumping to conclusions.

It was part of her make up, not something that could be changed one iota. You just had to hope you didn't get in her way.

Thank heavens Isabelle wasn't. And she would make sure to let Joanne know, she was willing her this lovely two-bedroom condominium. She still had plenty of years to enjoy it, however. Unlike her unfortunate husband Williston, Joanne's father, she didn't have any dreadful, hereditary illnesses to possibly face.

So in awhile (hopefully a *long* while), Joanne and Shorty would have a pleasant home away from home.

"But please, Joanne," Isabelle wanted to say, "Don't hurry your mother along. Let her enjoy a few years of peace and tranquility. Please?"

"JEALOUSY"

Another day of having her drive you insane with her displaced affection—as you call it. How many more goddamned mornings does she expect you to lie in bed while she leaves the coffee maker to do its thing, while she goes to do hers, behind the honeysuckle bushes you so strategically planted? It'll be five or six more years before they've grown enough to be of any use. Too bad you didn't think of planting them, sooner.

You are no longer fooled. There *was* a time, however, when you thought you could win her love, make her feel something *real* in her heart, toward you. Then you figured out she'd always be looking over her shoulder, even while supposedly "loving" you.

She's essentially incapable of open, unfettered, honest affection with you. The few times she's come oh-so close to baring her soul, she withdraws, going even further back into her shell.

Time might heal some wounds, but this one of yours has obviously festered and oozed pus until healing is a total impossibility. Major surgery will be required to remove it, and in respect to your beloved wife Nadia, it means you must put a stop to her shenanigans. If nothing else, she *must* be confronted.

How to do so? Talking about it at this point would be like jumping into the well of insanity, but at the same time, it's not as if you two don't communicate. You communicate quite well, in fact, for a married couple.

And yes, you still marvel that you even talked yourself into believing you needed someone to love and to cherish for the rest of your days.

It just *had* to be her, didn't it. And she just had to be one who could barely spare any real, true feelings for you. In fact the more you've tried to show her how much you love her, the more she's taken you for granted. And now she's even taking advantage of you, knowing you love her *far* too much to *ever* love anyone else. You are *stuck.*

God, how you used to *dream* about her loving you. You must have been trying to turn wishful thinking into reality.

No longer do you even bother to look out the bedroom window to see what's going on, supposedly "behind your back." Nonetheless, you feel as intensely jealous as ever because it does nothing to allay that jealousy, which has been brewing for *so* long.

The worst part is you can't stop obsessing over what she does to him and how it must feel. He receives that magic touch from her practiced hand, and there really is nothing here on earth, even half as heavenly.

She places a slender hand on his shoulder and gently strokes until she reaches a most sensitive area of his. What being doesn't have at least one of those?

Well, this particular spot is right on the money, every time. She instinctively knows *all* about this, although she once revealed she read a lot of books. She said books were more of a help in personal matters than many people realized. They needed to give books a better chance. She said it was a process of slow but steady discovery. Then, with knowledge learned in that manner, you became confident.

If that sounds like a writer talking, a *proponent* of the written word, then you, the reader, have a real power of perception. Nadia is indeed a writer, although technically a journalist—or nowadays, with the pay raise to prove it, she's an assistant editor at the *Daily Chronicle.* It's no longer a daily paper, however, not since the original owner had major (heart) surgery and handed the responsibilities over to his weedy-looking, sandy-haired nephew. The nephew promptly said it was O.K. to work "any old time," and not only was it permissible to smoke in the office, you could smoke "the good stuff," if you wanted.

The paper is now selling like crazy, since it only comes out twice a week. The people here in downstate Sparks, Indiana, were getting awfully bored with the old format, too.

You're certainly no advocate of long-haired hippies running *any* companies, and definitely not those tied in with the media, but even you have to admit, he's doing one hell of a job. He's got the kids in baggy pants and backward baseball caps, reading the damned paper. Next thing you know, he'll be converting them from rap, back to rock and roll.

But before you go off on a tangent about him, you want to dissect a little more of what goes on here at your speck of property (a mere 10 acres, surrounded by 100's and 100's of acres of corn, hay and soybeans and sometimes winter wheat). It's farmed by Moses Schaeffer and his son Lyle, both decent, respectable folks. You've done business with them on a regular basis, and they've never been anything but straight-up. (There really isn't a complaint to be had when people are so thoroughly honest.) Too bad more of the world isn't like them. A great lesson in humility, they are.

Anyway, as soon as your wife's hand gets tired of all that stroking and rubbing, what's the next thing she does but take a break—but not the usual kind of break, when you *rest* your body. Oh, no. (And she's obviously got a thing about only using her *right* hand, and leaving her left one for doing no more than placing it somewhere or else leaving it at her side.) Yes, she's right-handed, but she doesn't have to be quite so determined to prove as much. You have to admit, however, she *does* use both hands on you. What annoys you is that you can just see she puts more affection and love into one-handed caresses than the ones using two.

It's utter grace, how she moves that hand, and the hand itself is as beautiful as the movements she makes with it. (She was once a hand model, by the way.) She could have probably also been a fashion model, although she's more cute than stunningly beautiful. The time she likes to spend outdoors, keeps her youthful and fit. This helps renew her sexual passion, even if it's repressed, around you.

She wasn't a virgin when you met her. It was a matter of which she seemed to think reassuring you was absolutely necessary. You didn't understand it at the time, but now you do. She knew she was still so childlike in many ways (and still is, at 33), and she feared you wouldn't want to have a thing to do with her. She would be inexperienced or worse, not experienced, at all. (A woman never will understand a man's attitude toward her, will she.) But see, men love to go where none have gone before. A woman's body is, in the civilized world, the *final frontier*.

Anyway, even before you married, you could have watched her doing a number with those hands and immediately would have termed her either experienced or a *real* natural. It was actually more the latter than the former, but that was O.K. with you.

The last thing you were planning on doing was falling in love—at first sight, no less. Who says blind dates are for the birds? Only when you make assumptions do you leave the door wide open for failure.

She later admitted (she was kind of ashamed, as if it proved she was shallow) that she hadn't a single expectation that you could be "so good-looking." But you trusted the mediator, the diplomat, the one who made this meeting (or collision) of the minds, come true. You wanted to believe someone out there besides you, felt this was a perfect match.

You said she's a writer. You called her that, first, because her favorite hobby *is* writing—poetry, mostly. She doesn't mind you calling her a writer, since she's been a journalist her whole life (and now an assistant editor), and that term can cover both her career *and* her hobby.

But please, oh please, don't call her a poet. To her, it brings to mind a pale-faced, dark-haired woman in rimless glasses, who's prematurely aging around the eyes, from too much intellectual toiling, all for a bunch of words nobody understands and for bodies of work that will never get published.

Well she *is* getting some frizzy gray hairs that make themselves very noticeable in her otherwise black head of hair. Are those *premature* or is she indeed growing old? (To think how youthful-looking you just said she was!)

She obviously isn't prepared to meet her fate. She plucks each gray hair individually, crying out every time.

Sometimes you try to picture how she'll look when she's old, really old, and you're horrified. You seriously doubt you'll be able to look her in the face, by then.

You two are close to the same age and as you slide through your 30's, you're really, physically seeing that it *is* better to be a man. Men were made to grow old and become even better looking with age.

Lines and gray hairs really do become you, so much more than her. She bemoans those godawful crow's feet, while you welcome them like a much-needed holiday.

But no kids for her. No way. She'd rather go through the motions, but not "do it" for the reason "it," is really for. Her argument is she has enough to do in her life, and it would in fact be selfish to have kids, because she'd never pay him or her enough attention. Even if you and she *could* afford a nanny, having one would be out of the question for the very reason *she* refuses to delegate a responsibility as basic and intimate as raising a child to some stranger, someone *paid* to care.

You get out of bed to watch her now, as she ever so ably moves that right hand of hers across his back and continually lets it rest in the very middle, as if it's part of some sort of ritual to satisfy a deity. All her actions belie such devotion and love, how can you not get absolutely, totally incensed, so frustrated with pent-up envy you can't think straight? (Have you ever considered possibly you're psychotic?) *Now* you wish you'd stayed in bed, where you belong.

No. You're fine. You're human, that's what you are, and human beings *do* have emotions. *She* appears entirely oblivious to the fact *her* displaced emotions/passions/affection are killing you. *She just doesn't get it.*

You suddenly find yourself so f—ing steamed you know this time there's no turning back. Vengeance feels like it's literally coursing through your veins, elevating your body temperature. Damned if you could work some magic numbers with *your* hands, even though they aren't nearly so blessed with that sensuousness. At least you have *love* on your side. You love her, as much or more so than she loves that—that—*thing*. And so too you have brute strength on your side, which can come in *real* handy.

Know who has the screws loose? Her. She does. So when she comes in the kitchen door, you have a surprise for her. First you let her pull off her "muck boots," the ones she wears to clean Bugs' stall. *He's* her *one*, true, pride and joy, and it makes you sick.

"WHO KILLED WHO"

Death grip on the steering wheel of his new (but dirty, right now) white Corvette convertible, Byron's giving new meaning to the term "Sunday drive." (He's still trying to figure out what was on the road that made his car get so grimy. And no, it didn't rain. He would have known, driving with the top down.)

He's headed south, in the wonderful Mexican countryside, and he's not too far from Los Mochis. (Or did he just pass it?) He can't seem to remember. The whole trip has been that way for him. He feels like he's in a trance. Either that or a really bad B-movie. (He didn't ever aspire to act, but with his telegenic looks, he should have done *something* in the entertainment industry.)

Ever practical-minded, he was a financial planner (and "was" is entirely correct). He was due for a vacation, but this is more like an extended leave of absence, one that just might go on, indefinitely.

Late yesterday afternoon, Byron left his home in Phoenix, Arizona with the bare essentials, his passport and a map. He essentially fled the scene of what was a freak accident, but has probably become the scene of a crime, all because of what he did (or didn't) do.

Still, it seems fated something would eventually happen to that "girlfriend" of his. It just *had* to be Byron. He just *had* to be the one to help ensure her demise. As much as Jenna Mulholland liked to boast about all the people she knew, from seemingly every walk of life, it should have been someone else. That's all there is to it.

Byron has positively wracked his brain by this time, wanting to know, *Why him*? Not only did she know everyone, she'd been through dozens of boyfriends.

Byron himself had a good job, a decent place that was paid for, some money in the bank (all well-invested), not to mention this hot car.

He was making something of himself and proud of it. And proving his ambition, he aspired to be a millionaire by age 40, a mere eight years away. Then along came Jenna Mulholland. She thought she was so "lucky," she found herself a financial planner. (She clearly never had one of those, before.) It sure as hell wasn't as if she wanted his financial advice.

Here in Mexico, Byron probably already *is* a millionaire. The only problem is he as good as said good-bye to all his money, when he left the U.S.

If Byron does happen to be a wanted man (he bets the police at least want to talk to him), he's not imagining he's running from something terrible. (It's easy to become paranoid, after being in Jenna Mulholland's company awhile.)

How can he even begin to explain, there was no point in sticking around—either the scene of the accident or the United States? By the way Jenna's body convulsed and the simultaneous expression on her face, he was certain she was dead.

Good God, he'd never witnessed such a macabre sight, her face frozen into a grin, eyes popping out of their sockets.

Admittedly, however, he did not take her pulse, to make sure. He was afraid to leave any more finger-prints on her, than were already there.

Byron doesn't expect any sympathy (although a *little* would be nice). People are usually jealous of him, before anything else. Well, if it's any consolation, right now he looks like hell. All he can think about is getting where he needs to be (wherever *that* is). He can't let himself think about much else. Otherwise he'll get distracted and won't be able to continue driving. As it is, he's low on gas and so exhausted he can't drive another mile, not right now.

He pulls over to a narrow shoulder, all that separates the two-lane road from a deep gorge. He tries in vain to see what's at the bottom (or *where* the bottom *is*). Maybe if he gets out of the car he'll be able to see.

For the time being, however, he's content to just sit here. He raises a hand to his head, realizing his hair is a mess. There's no doubt he's entered (or *was* in) that state of shock so deep, you're unaware of your basic wants. He can't recall the last time he took a piss, and his jeans might even be soaked, he wouldn't know.

After crossing the border, he breathed a little easier, but he most definitely didn't relax. If anything he became more tense, thinking, *Now it's official. I'm a stranger in a strange land.* Not for much longer could he afford to remain Byron C. MacPherson.

He didn't linger at Jenna's, after the unfortunate mishap, but he spent some time at his place, debating what to do. He even dreamed up some possible scenarios, he could play out (such as returning to the scene of the occurrence and pretending he "discovered" Jenna's body). That was nixed because he knew what a pathetic actor he was.

It was a lousy idea anyway because there was a guard on duty at the Casa de Adobe, where Jenna (or her mother Gina, actually) had a two-bedroom condominium. Jenna lived there, rent-free (pretty good, huh).

The argument was Jenna worked for a florist (she was a flower arranger), and it didn't pay well enough for her to live in the kind of place she *deserved*. She supposedly had some friends in some pretty damned high places. How bad would she look, being paid visits, if she lived in a dump?

Byron didn't even pay attention to some of the things she said, they were such blatant exaggerations. If telling tall tales turned her on, so be it. It was one of the reasons they were so incompatible. She always let her imagination run wild (not to mention her big mouth) and he was practical, if not quite skeptical, as well.

Anyway, if Byron had gone back to the condominium complex later, another, different guard would have been on duty, but that wouldn't have done a thing to simplify matters. The autopsy would have revealed precisely when Jenna died, right down to the exact minute. The guards would have only ended up verifying the premise, Byron tried to cover his tracks.

All in all, he didn't do the right thing, but rather the *only* thing he could, to spare himself a conviction and a jail sentence.

The moment he pulled his hotshot sports car into that place and the security guard let him in, Byron was a doomed man.

The ludicrous part is all he went to Jenna's to do, was to tell her off and give her the final word, their relationship was over. That's what he briefly explained on a note he scribbled and left on his kitchen table—which he'll probably never see again.

Byron really liked the place where he lived. It was one of the tidiest, best-decorated bachelor pads on earth (and he decorated it himself). Hell, he kept it *clean*, himself.

Never one to sweep dirt under the rug, in *any* sense of the word, he doesn't seem like the type to flee the scene of a terrible accident.

But he did, and it's much too late to turn back now. He'd sooner kill himself. That's the truth. At this point, *no* amount of explaining will help.

If he wrote down the details of the whole sordid incident, he wonders if he'd feel any better. The only problem is he's too damned tired. He needs some rest, but God only knows, even if he *did* have a bed to sleep in, he couldn't get any rest.

A tale of two incompatibles, that's how Byron would describe the relationship he had with Jenna Mulholland. Who knows, maybe they should have gone down, together.

With that, he finds himself so intensely curious about the gorge on the right side of the road, he finally gets out of the car to have a look. The first thing he notices is how there's no guardrail. The drivers here, are apparently expected to fend for themselves. He finds that intriguing. And since this is going to be his new home, he figures he might as well start finding things he likes about this country.

He's the only one around here with a Corvette convertible— or any Corvette, for that matter, not that he's done much driving in the daylight.

Where he came from, his car was nothing special (except to him). It was lost in the glut of other Corvettes, not to mention other, more expensive sports cars. (It really did get pretty aggravating.) Now, the last thing he wants is to be seen

That's one hell of a drop-off, by the way. Wherever the bottom is, he can't see it. He'd have to step closer, which he doesn't want to do.

Byron left that note of his, where he knew it would be most easily discovered. He wanted everyone to know that although he ran away, he didn't run from the *truth*.

His mother Adele. His poor mother Adele. Byron and she never did get along very well, and now there's no way to rectify the situation. The best he can do is not think too hard about it.

One day at a time, right now, there's really no other way to deal with this "escape plan" of his. With all the loose ends he left behind, it's almost impossible to even concentrate on the here and now. Plus, he's as exhausted as hell.

He looks around. He really *is* all alone here, on this secluded, scenic stretch of road. He hopes there's a gas station, not too much further ahead. If it's closed on Sunday, which sounds probable around here, he may not be making much more progress until Monday.

Once he'd finally decided to leave Phoenix, it felt like the right thing to do. Despite not believing in supernatural hocus-pocus of any kind, it seemed like a divine spirit were leading him on this journey. For better or worse, he was compelled to follow.

Byron believes he deserves a break because up until this time, he didn't do anything wrong, not to say he's a saint. For a man, however, he really does have a lot of discipline and self-control.

That said, he wishes he'd just stayed away from Jenna's, yesterday morning.

Oh, never mind, reflecting won't do any good, not for the sake of adding up regrets.

Jenna should have given that guy with the red Camaro (the same kind and color of car as hers) a better chance, not complained about him so much. She really was pretty picky, especially for a woman with a seemingly insatiable sexual appetite.

What Jenna needed was a goal, when she was looking for a

man. Or a better goal than the one she had (to fuck and be fucked by the classiest men she could find, in the most out of the way places).

At first, Byron's ego made him want for her, to want only him, to have her decide her "search" was over. Then, as he got to know her, he felt like he was tangled in a web—a sticky one.

And he was exactly right. Extricating himself from her grasp was messy, not even counting the unfortunate accident, at the end.

Her financial security was the icing on the cake of her already overly-confident self. She was an upper-middle class brat who acted like she owned the world, and she could really put on a show. She would have made a great actress.

There were two things about acting, she couldn't have tolerated. One was the rejection, and two was sitting still long enough to be made-up. She had a sort of "as-is" mentality, when it came to primping. Luckily for her, the "natural look" didn't leave her looking undone.

The evening of what was to be their final date together, Byron sensed beforehand, the six-month relationship had run its course. Just the outfit of hers, was a big hint. He wanted to keep her under lock and key (or at least stay at her place and order something in), but you didn't tell Jenna Mulholland what to do.

Since he hadn't made any reservations, they could forget walking right into a restaurant and getting a table, not on Saturday night. One quality Jenna did *not* have, was even an ounce of patience.

Jenna didn't get her way and she would throw a tantrum that would put a spoiled five year-old to shame—the only problem being she was 25.

The dress she wore that night, really did say it all. Its top consisted of a scooped neck and capped sleeves, nothing particularly revealing. No, the nightmare began with the bottom portion of this lime-green silk atrocity. The skirt was spaghetti-thin fringe, cut so high you could see her private area. (And she didn't wear any underwear, either.)

Yes, the outfit alone, stood to embarrass the hell out of Byron, and that wasn't even taking into account her big mouth and her belligerent attitude.

Byron still finds it incredible, he got along with her, at all. Until the unfortunate accident, he would have described himself as a morally upright person, who was polite and completely law-abiding. He really had no business being even remotely interested in someone like her.

And as much as he hates to admit it, at first he found it kind of amusing, the never-ending game she played, of antagonizing others—especially outright strangers.

Considering how incompatible they were, it's amazing they lasted together as long as they did. (It seemed like eons, too.)

So when it *did* end, he failed to see the need to tell her good-bye. Jenna, however, was not in agreement, something he didn't realize at the time. Nonetheless, up until the bitter end, oh, how he *tried* to remain rational and sane. Even the most steadfast of people have a breaking point, not that Byron places himself in that category (but he came closer than *she* did).

Jenna Mulholland had something the matter with her, not that she deserved to die because of it. Byron believes a number of factors contributed to her demise. She certainly was the most "unique" character *he'd* ever met, not that he got around a whole lot.

Still, he never had a chick give him a blow-job as a way of getting to know him. (And he willingly succumbed, loving every second of it.) Luckily they didn't get caught, as this encounter happened in a public place.

Jenna wouldn't have cared if they *had* been discovered. If anything, it would have added to the thrill. Most likely she'd done that kind of thing, lots of times, even got in trouble.

The illicit scene took place in a darkened corridor of Apache Community College, where Byron was taking a computer class. God only knew what course *she* was taking, besides Laws of Lovemaking, 101. She never told Byron the name of the class, and shortly thereafter she dropped it—or so she said.

If Jenna didn't want to attend the class anymore, she simply wouldn't. Formalities weren't her thing, one reason of many, she wasn't in any hurry to get married. Supposedly, however, she once staged a mock wedding, just to see what it was like (and have an excuse to wear white). That was one of her tall tales, he found hard, if not impossible, to believe. It was on par with her claim about some of the well-known people she knew.

A logical explanation occurs to him, regarding what the hell Jenna was *really* doing at Apache Community College. She was hanging around, hoping to meet someone just like Byron (innocent and well-to-do. Who else *could* she want?). She even "admitted" to having first laid eyes on him one day, when he was in the campus bookstore. She followed him to his classroom and waited for the ten-minute break (it was a three-hour class that only met once a week), to "introduce herself."

And what an introduction that was, if he does say to, himself. It wasn't customary for him to meet a woman like her. The females he's used to, would make sure there was plenty of down time, before there was any action (*not* the good kind of down time).

Considering everything (like the fact he would have taken two or three blow-jobs a day, seven days a week), Byron exhibited remarkable restraint, not that they actually ever lived together. *That* situation could have been changed, easily enough. The problem was that he could only stand her company when they were about to have sex (or having it). If he wasn't such an avid fan of dining out, he wouldn't have been able to endure her company, at all.

Byron always did think of himself as a modern-day survivor. If he didn't, he wouldn't have bothered coming to Mexico, to start a new life.

According to his mother, she was told by the doctors, her son might not make it past puberty (but he did, with flying colors, all his ailments miraculously disappearing).

It's hardly any wonder she proceeded to try and spoil him rotten, as grateful as she was to have him alive. He was also an only child, and she soon became a widow when her husband Peter died, following a long illness.

Adele *could* have been overly-protective of Byron, but her instincts told her that would do more harm than good. For that reason alone, she deserved some credit for being a good mother.

Although she was living in the same house Byron grew up in, not far from where he had a place, rare were the occasions they got together. Now he feels guilty about it. (He's glad, however, his mother never had any idea he was dating Jenna.)

Jenna. She really was unique, as Byron described her, earlier. She wasn't a one-night stand type, but she liked sex enough, she would have made one hell of a nymphomaniac, a new man for every day (or night) of the week.

But see, she liked to take her time, finding the next conquest. Doing some "research" was important. (It the guy couldn't afford plenty of dinners and bouquets, forget him.)

The night of the beginning of the end between them, not even a dozen red roses would have saved the date. It was already too late. Plus, she spent her days looking at *all* kinds of flowers.

It was unsettling to think Jenna might have been stalking Byron for quite awhile, prior to that introduction he'll never forget. Unsettling, in regard to the likelihood he was so damned oblivious and unobservant, he hadn't *any* idea. She was kind of spooky, really, how she could be sneaky when she would so choose.

Also, Byron's so handsome (or was, until he hit this crisis in his life), he has become accustomed to being openly admired and yes, even occasionally followed. He never thought anything of it (he just took his god-like status, in stride).

Jenna lucked out because Byron wasn't seeing anyone when she came along (and with that first "greeting" of hers, he would have been a fool to say no). Still, Byron prided himself in his strict monogamy.

If he'd had a little more time to be objective, the first thing he would have concluded about her was, "not my type," and really, she wasn't. Byron liked women long and lean, not that Jenna didn't have a sexy body.

She had those in-your-face kind of features, ones almost too big for her, not that she was petite in any way.

And God, those brown eyes of hers, bulging like they did when she was taking her last breaths, Byron never would have thought they could get any bigger.

A certain *aura* about her (for want of a better word) bespoke of the fact she got around plenty, starting at a young age. So when she told Byron she lost her virginity at age 11, it was one tall tale of hers, he actually believed.

What *is* hard to believe is she was a "flower arranger," the term Byron uses to describe her career. He just couldn't see how someone like her could possible devote *any* of her already limited attention span to something so genteel and which required an eye for details.

Byron could only picture her with some sort of employment that would constantly require her to go full-tilt. (Maybe that's just because he hasn't very much imagination.)

If it weren't for her sex drive, Jenna would have lacked any motivation to exercise and keep in shape. She said so, herself.

Working out bored her (like everything seemed to do. Even sex got to her after awhile).

Conveniently, however, there was an exercise room at the condominium complex where she lived. She also power walked around the perimeter.

If she did too many weight-bearing exercises, she feared her "boobs" (as she called them) would disappear, which made a good excuse, if nothing else. Supposedly, however, that happened to a friend of hers who needed to lose some weight from her hips and thighs. She was too busy paying attention to her shapely "new" legs and lost her chest in the bargain.

Substitute Byron's dick for that woman's breasts, and he can identify with how she must have felt. She probably wasn't exactly buxom, to begin with. (Just like he isn't the most well-endowed man on earth.) But Jenna never made fun of him, so he can't be laughably little. If anyone knew about the relative size of penises, it was her.

Anyway, it was ironic (at least as far as Byron was concerned)

Jenna lived someplace that provided security, around the clock. Byron lived in a pretty upscale place himself, but the gates were electronic, eliminating the need for a guard.

Those guys probably thought condominium number eleven was the passageway to Grand Central Station, given the comings and goings of Jenna and her string of boyfriends.

There had to have been a few dozen, maybe more. If she *had* been a one-night stand type, the total conquered, would be in the hundreds.

Byron admits he did not feel any *real* remorse or regret for her ill-fate, until he'd left her place and started thinking about what happened. Even then, he didn't feel sorry for her, just sorry something bad came to pass.

Maybe it comes down to the fact a man would have had a hard time, truly abusing her. Abuse really didn't exist for her because just about everything, painful *or* pleasurable, turned her on. That alone never ceased to aggravate the fucking hell out of Byron.

Her dying was the first thing that made any impression on her, Byron's sure of it. (Her expression said it all, hideous though it was, not to mention imprinted forever, in his mind's eye.)

The night she wore that awful dress and acted so full of herself, Byron suspected she'd taken something, as she was obnoxious like never before. (He didn't buy her adamant claim she *never* took drugs. Only *he* could say that and have it be the truth.)

Anyway, she was undeniably at her worst. She managed to be hateful, haughty, and indignant. (Did he include everything in there?) He should have fucked her and called it a night.

Byron (also) ought to have known, when he drove out of the walled (and gated) confines of where she resided, asking her, "Where to?" he was allowing her *way* too much freedom. Sometimes she had to be reined in, just like a horse. (More on those in a minute.)

Meanwhile, Jenna could hardly wait to reply, "Any place that's got valet parking," the significance of which was initially lost on Byron. He stupidly thought she was looking out for *his* best interests, a la he could indulge in having his automobile parked by some string bean-legged, 17 year-old who has to move the seat way back to let out the clutch. (So for the next week, Byron would have the distinct pleasure of trying to figure out where he had the seat.)

Little did he know, in short order, those "minor" irritants would no longer be part of his life—a life he missed already. Dying really would be easier at this point, he realizes.

Anyway, that night Byron (once again) humored Jenna, and little good it did him.

He knew plenty of places to eat in the Phoenix Valley, and he knew of one that had valet parking, that wasn't too far away and hopefully wouldn't have too much of a wait, for a Saturday night . . .

Byron and Jenna arrive at the Mesquite Bar and Grill, on Camelback Road, just west of 32nd Street. She won't get out of the car until this kid (and he is, too) opens the door for her. His subsequent display of shock is clearly a thrill for Jenna, and she can hardly contain herself. Meanwhile the kid's face is turning various shades of red, and Byron's trying to ignore the whole incident as it unfolds. It's one time he can't find it in him to even grin a little, let alone laugh. She's so entirely unself-conscious, it's embarrassing to even be in her company. And he flashes back to their initial encounter, in the darkened corridor of the Whitner Building at Apache Community College. His fly was wide open, and she was working her magic on him. Actually, he too could have been accused of not being at all self-conscious, that particular day.

Out of the car, Byron hurries to Jenna's side, as if he can somehow shield her as they make their way into the restaurant.

Of all the nights, on this one she decides to stride up to the door like she's a goddamned runway model, fringe flying everywhere, those platform sandals only encouraging her to walk so much differently than usual.

Byron just wants to make sure she's inside the place before his car is moved even one inch. Even at his age (and plenty of practice) Byron has barely mastered the art of driving and gawking. He pictures his Corvette being rammed into a pillar or two or worse, another car.

A *big* plus for the restaurant, Byron realizes when he opens the door for Jenna and they go inside, is that it's poorly (or dimly) lit.

There's no one waiting in the foyer, but the bar, to the left, sounds jammed. (But then they usually sound that way, don't they.)

The first order of business is to give the tall, blonde, crop-haired hostess his last name. (Demeaning is how he finds doing so. He really hates being put at the mercy of a hostess and her waiting list.) He always was an avid fan of the good old reservation.

"Good evening. Two of you?" she fairly warbles and come to think of it, she does look a little like Tweetie Bird. (This is something Byron could *only* have occur to him, in Jenna's company.)

Speaking of Jenna, it's safe to say she just spent the time, giving the hostess a look that could kill. She happened to hate *any* women who were substantially taller than herself. She also hated natural blondes, and although this one didn't have a whole lot of hair, there was no mistaking the truth.

Anyway, blonde-hostess does a stellar job of telling Mr. MacPherson (could he please spell it?) that there will be a twenty to thirty-minute wait, totally avoiding any eye contact whatsoever with Jenna. She concludes with: "Would you like to have a drink in the bar?" and motions in that direction. *Was that singular or plural "you"* ? he wonders.

He almost tells her, "No, not really. If I slip you a fifty can you seat us right away?" but decides against it. He must be in one of his "cheap" moods.

Even a minimum of alcohol in her system, and Jenna gets as saucy as can be. And on a night like this, God only knows what's already in her bloodstream.

Still, the waiting time doesn't sound as horrendous as it could. As long as things keep moving, Jenna won't have a chance to get bored. That's when the trouble inevitably begins.

If she hasn't eaten all day, she can also get nasty. (She likes to fast when she knows she'll be going out to dinner, that evening.)

Byron braces himself as he watches her straddle her seat of

choice, in the bar—a black vinyl stool. He takes the one to her right and tries not to do too much looking around. He doesn't want to know how many pairs of eyes are glued on *them*. (He really only likes to be seen when he's driving his car down the road.)

She orders a double Scotch on the rocks. *She* knows how to get around the possibility of being served a watered-down drink.

Byron settles for a gin and soda, on the rocks. He's the designated driver, not to mention the only one who can be counted on to stay level-headed through this—ordeal. (Any dummy could have sensed this wasn't going to run smoothly.)

He vows not to order another drink until dinner is on the way. (He knows he's being overly-optimistic, making this plan, but he can't seem to help himself.)

Jenna's bare butt on that stool, it's something Byron can see perfectly, even without so much as a glance in her direction. God, what a mistake it was to follow that dumb blonde's advice and come in here. There was a completely empty brown vinyl bench, out in the Saltillo-tiled foyer.

Byron tries not to even consider what may be going on, behind them. If anyone's talking about them, it's (fortunately) too loud to hear.

The next thing he knows, Jenna has a hand in his lap (and it really is *in* his lap, too), creating a distraction that can't be ignored.

And for a minute or two it seems like maybe he's relaxed. Then, from the other room the hostess' voice can be heard, calling, "Tipton, party of four. Tipton, party of four." From behind Byron and Jenna can be heard the subsequent chair-moving, (and body-moving) as "Tipton, party of four," appears out of the woodwork. Byron now feels like progress is being made. (And eight fewer eyes are no longer beholding a sight fit for a porn flick.)

If so, Byron must be a co-star, given how he enjoys the message on his lower extremities.

Always ready with *some* sort of complaint, Jenna remarks, "That's why there's no tables for couples like *us*. Two couples come here together and hog all the tables. I bet they put all the tables for two together, tonight, 'cause it's so damned busy."

"I doubt it," Byron returns, not really thinking about the conversation.

"You're *doubting* me?" she exclaims. "My friend Tina waits tables at that Tea Tree Café, so I know plenty of shit about how these restaurant-people think."

Right. Got this one in about knowing the waitress. Byron can't keep them all straight, that's for damned sure. Next she'll tell him all about the trapeze artist she just met. (No, actually it was a make-up artist. Someone from Hollywood, who came here, to start her own business.)

Jenna's massage has since changed from relatively gentle rubbing, to some real friction-induced pleasure. Byron starts damning himself for having worn khaki-colored pants. (Why-oh-why didn't he think to wear black tonight?)

The drinks finally arrive, with the bartender's face beholding a cat-ate-the-mouse grin. Byron worries he himself must look like he's completely at the mercy of this slut/nut seated beside him. Or does Jenna *know* him? It's possible she *did* happen to mention she knew a bartender, but she made it clear she *once* knew him. And if this guy's suddenly recognizing her from his past, Byron can't imagine him keeping quiet about it.

Either way, the drinks aren't on the house, and Byron's got a loose fiver in his pocket. Too bad. The drinks alone cost seven bucks plus change. This is the price of drinking in a "dimly-lit" place, that's all there is to it (because it's not like the food here is really great). And through it all, Byron has a sense of humor—so far.

Jenna has already drunk half of the drink Byron has yet to pay for. Not even a double Scotch can slow her down.

Unfortunately for Byron, she abruptly ends the massage, and she stands, announcing, "We're going to sit in the entryway. I don't trust Miss Hostess Cupcake to forget about us."

"She won't. She has my name," Byron counters (even though he knows it's in vain). You don't argue with Jenna. Period.

She tells him, "That doesn't make one shit-hole of a difference. Blondie's a little troublemaker. She's already decided she don't like the sound of your name or the likes of me. Or both."

Aware this is *not* the time to dispense some advice (not that *any* time is), Byron nonetheless can't keep from saying, "Jenna, sometimes you get needlessly paranoid. You have to quit being so hard on people, especially ones you don't even know."

He might as well expect her to up the ante, now that he said that. For the time being, however, she ignores him and is already halfway to the archway separating the bar and the foyer.

Byron finds himself following her, looking just like her little puppy dog. And that's exactly what he's imitating so well. (He said he could never be an actor?)

Drink glass proudly in hand, Jenna plops down upon the bench, just about exactly in the middle. It came in handy she polished off so much of that drink because otherwise she would have spilled it. And had some of it landed on her dress, she *really* would have been mad.

The hostess has so far ignored the presence of the MacPherson party. She's busily scribbling on her name-list. She must be crossing out anyone she doesn't like (proving Jenna to be entirely correct). It's really something, how easy it is to become as paranoid as the person whose company you're keeping.

She next announces, "Gillman, party of three. Gillman, party of three."

Jenna nudges Byron, whispering, "That's two guys and the girl. She's got 'em by the balls, got 'em talked into a threesome. Hard to get a guy to dig one of those, when *he's* the odd-man out."

Well, that may be correct, but as far as the Gillman party goes, it consists of two older women and one older man (and they don't look like they'll be doing any partying, anytime soon). But then, *looks* can be deceiving.

Jenna will get angry, if only because she was so far off in her prediction. These poor, unsuspecting people will have to take the blame.

Giving the Gillman party one hell of a dagger-like stare, Jenna will *not* be able to keep her mouth shut—or so Byron assumes.

Remarkably, she doesn't say anything about them (or *to* them), but she has something unflattering to say about the hostess and how she does her job: "Missy Hostess sure doesn't know how to seat her customers, does she. That blonde hair keeps her in her place, you know?"

Thank God the one thus accused has long gone, the Gillman party trailing her, before Jenna opened her big mouth. Usually Jenna's much more quick with her comments, not that she could ever be called clever.

She takes another hard, long swallow of her drink, this time about finishing it. Then she tells Byron, "And I'm going to have to have a refill, if we don't get a move-on here. Hello!"

Byron rolls his eyes, not even caring if she noticed. But luckily she didn't, as she's busy watching the couple that just came in the door. Some serious class, Byron can see that much, already. The woman is almost too damned beautiful to be real, and the man's level of handsomeness isn't too far behind.

Byron gloomily (and not a little guiltily) thinks, *Why don't I have a babe on my arm?*

Or even, where did his taste go, that certain something that allows him to discern between a girlfriend and a—uh (he glances at her), a slut.

Not to worry, Jenna would have taken that as a compliment. (There really and truly never was any way of putting her down.) She was immune to what could most certainly be termed a criticism—when she would so choose.

The hostess in the meantime must have gotten lost somewhere in the back because she hasn't returned to her post. Barbie and Ken (they really do look like them) patiently wait, as animated as if they really are two dolls. Byron almost feels like openly deriding them (but he assumes Jenna will take care of that honor).

Instead, she appears content to pick on the hostess in absentia, only bothering them in an indirect way: "Don't waste your precious time, waiting. Miss Hostess Cupcake's behind the back kitchen door, getting it on with one of the waiters." She waves in the direction of the entrance/exit, telling them, "You might as well leave because there *is no hostess*. Do you hear me? Hello!"

The woman gives Jenna one of those nervous smiles, like only women of her caliber, can do. They look like they just can't believe God could put them, goddesses in every way, in such uncomfortable positions as these.

Meanwhile, the man tries his hardest to ignore her, altogether (what Byron would do and about how he'd look, in just such a situation). He doesn't wear any expression, hoping this nut-case simply disappears. (This is just about Byron's line of thinking, himself, he realizes.)

Then, surprising everyone, the hostess magically appears from around the corner and greets them: "Good evening. Two of you?" *At least she can't be accused of inconsistency in what she says*, Byron thinks.

And it's not lost on Jenna, who chooses to take it to mean it's time for some sarcasm, not to mention time to drop another hint for Barbie and Ken, to get lost, themselves: "There must be an echo in here. Hello! I don't see *anyone*, except the MacPherson party of two."

Byron figures this did *not* win any points with the hostess. *Their* wait has now been moved up to an hour—if they're lucky.

As the hostess does her best (seemingly) to ignore Jenna, and instead concerns herself with writing down Barbie and Ken's last name, (Jones?) and lets them know the wait will be *twenty* minutes, Jenna turns to Byron to say, "Five more minutes and I've had enough of this shit."

It's been twenty minutes, easily (and feels like a lifetime). But admittedly, the hostess told Byron it would be *twenty to thirty* minutes.

The congenial hostess did her best to try to convince Barbie and Ken to go in the bar and have a drink, but they're obviously *not* interested. They steer clear and wind up seated where else but the bench, as close as possible to the door. They're not *too* stupid, are they.

Unfortunately, they're not so far away, they go unnoticed by Jenna. Tonight too, she decides to have X-ray vision. Byron prefers her when she's blind with fury and rage (so he thinks, at this point in time, anyway).

Right now, the best he can hope for is to have her continue to pick on the hostess. (The damage is undoubtedly already done, anyway, for having antagonized the woman.)

For maybe a minute, Jenna is relatively content to concentrate on getting the rest of the liquor out of her drink glass, rattling cubes like you wouldn't believe. Byron never would have thought that noise could be music to his ears.

No one activity can keep Jenna amused for long, not even sex, truth be told. That's not to say there was ever any lack of enthusiasm on her part.

All Byron asks at this point, is for Jenna to please not catch that woman's eye because it will only set off a whole chain of events. He knows as much from experience, having dated a few women who were easily "distressed." They were magnets for disasters (or so they assumed). And yes, all of them were exceptionally beautiful, although he doesn't think he's ever laid eyes on a woman as gorgeous as this one.

Jenna carefully places her glass to her right and proceeds to remove a cigarette and a lighter, from her purse. Nowhere in plain sight, is there a sign reading "No Smoking," but the hostess warns Jenna, "No smoking in the foyer, ma'am," the words spewing from her mouth. It was pretty plain right there, her low opinion of Jenna. Even Byron's a little put off.

Jenna drops the cigarette and the lighter on the bench and leaps up, shaking her purse and crying, "You bitch. You don't own this place. You don't make the fucking rules. You're just some dumb-ass who's playing fucking games. *I* don't play *any* games I don't think I can win, so fuck you. Me and my boyfriend are outta here."

Outrageous (and embarrassing) though Jenna is, Byron can't help but give her credit for standing up for herself.

Proving things don't *always* turn out the way you might think,

AMY KRISTOFF

Jenna's leading the way out the door. (Byron thought he would have had that honor, for whatever reason.)

Byron leaves his drink glass on the bench, as Jenna did with hers. For a second he almost walked off with it. If the hostess had wanted to nit-pick, she could have called him a thief. (He was once such an honorable citizen, things like this actually bothered him.)

Amazingly, Jenna only smiles and waves at Barbie and Ken, dispensing with any comments.

That leaves one last hurdle, the valet parking attendant. Byron does not see how Jenna won't try one last, goofy antic, and why not, on someone who's a relative "kid" (in regard to experience, if nothing else.)

Byron knows he's getting ahead of himself, going through pizza delivery numbers in his head, but he does so nonetheless. (*What was that place that delivered Chinese food?* he wants to know.) He's always ready for some variety.

It's not even necessary to give the attendant the ticket for his car. He *remembers*.

If Byron felt like a skinflint earlier, when he didn't want to slip the hostess a fifty, the feeling hasn't dissipated. In fact he's reluctant to tip the attendant the customary dollar (Byron's customary dollar).

Realistically, the dollar should come from the hostess' pocket, but since there's no way that will happen, Byron can take solace in knowing he didn't waste fifty bucks. (Or would it have been money well-invested?)

If the attendant can help Jenna into the car without a ruckus, it's worth the buck.

And he's hustling to get the car, making Byron feel sort of like a VIP (which suits him just fine). *This* is what going out, should be about. Byron felt like dirt in that restaurant, all because he didn't have a reservation. Is it surprising he doesn't blame the company he's with? Well, why should he when he has enough class for the two of them?

The car arrives and the attendant hurriedly jumps out and holds the door for Byron. Before getting in, Byron hands the kid a dollar. Now for a million seat adjustments, to make Byron regret his generosity.

Meanwhile, the parking attendant flies (practically literally) to the other side of the car, to help Jenna.

She's already in the car and is about to slam the door. The most that's left for him to do is touch the door with his hand. If he wanted one, last X-rated glimpse, he missed out.

Alas, Jenna isn't *quite* finished with him. While Byron continues to adjust the seat (hurrying) she tells the attendant, "You know, kiddo, you were just a *little* older, I'd offer to go down on you. My pleasure."

She starts laughing her head off and Byron takes that as his cue to whip out of the parking lot, tires squealing, damned effectively imitating the raucous laughter coming out of Jenna's big mouth.

The first light at which they're stopped, Byron turns to her, asking, "Was that really necessary to say what you did, just now?"

She sits up, looking so completely innocent (even if it's but momentary), Byron finds himself amazed. She really *can* play the part of the ingenue. She expresses some amazement herself, (or at least she sounds that way) wanting to know, "What? Who?"

Byron impatiently replies, "The kid with the car," to which she bursts into that hideous, ear-splitting laugh, a laugh so awful, there could never be anyone to imitate it.

Then she cleverly quips, "I *wanted* to say I'd like to *eat* him, since you and me didn't have dinner yet, but I was afraid he'd take me up on it. And right now, I'm needing some *real* food."

Byron can hardly believe what he's hearing. This, from someone who thinks of him as her boyfriend, yet he still can't get himself to think of her as his girlfriend. And at this point, he vows he *never* will.

The light changes, so they're moving again. He asks her, "What'll it be. McDonald's or Domino's?"

Apparently ignoring him (twice in one evening?), she takes

the opportunity to lay a hand in a most distracting place, picking up where she left off, earlier. Any exasperation he felt toward her, temporarily vanishes. But soon it will be back, she'll make sure of it. There isn't a single person she doesn't at least *try* to somehow antagonize. She'll have to do more than ignore him, however, to make him angry.

Massaging away on Byron, Jenna takes the otherwise relaxing opportunity to tell him, "You know, I was just about gonna deck that hussy-hostess, but I knew *you* for one, wouldn't approve of it."

For an instant, Byron feels as if perhaps there's a *reason* the two of them were thrown together, and that reason being he can *teach* her a few manners. He's in fact just about ready to remind her, "You don't hit people, merely for the sake of it." (These massages really do a number on his brain, don't they.)

When he reaches Ocotillo Boulevard, where Casa de Adobe is located, she complains, "You know, you coulda taken me to your place. Or is it so high-class, the Domino's guy can't deliver pizza there?"

She *was* listening, earlier. He'd better watch himself. Still, he really can't win with her.

They rarely go to his place in the Candlearia Commons, and that's all there is to it. (And he just changed the sheets on the bed. He wants the distinct pleasure of being the first one to dirty them.)

One way or another, Jenna will ruin the evening. The hostess helped get things rolling, and now here comes the rest of it. The security guard lifts the gate, not just because he remembers Byron from earlier this evening, but because he *knows* who Jenna is. He's not even one of the regulars, and in fact Byron doesn't think he's ever seen him before. The guy's well-aware, however, of the importance of hitting the "gate-up" switch, not giving Jenna even a second to get impatient and indignant.

And then, here it comes, the comment Byron should *not* have been at all surprised to hear from her mouth: "You know, you need to get a sticker for your windshield."

There it is. Proof of some permanence, in the form of a stupid sticker. Worse, it happens to be something that will only *ruin* his perfect car. (He always was terribly anal about those things, and he just so happens to *hate* stickers, *any* stickers.)

Byron isn't quite sure how to explain himself, since more than anything, he's embarrassed by his own pickiness. He proceeds to make a grave, grave error, by not saying anything at all. He would have been better off, dispensing some more advice. You very simply do *not* ignore Jenna Mulholland.

And sure enough, right away she exclaims, "Well? Turn around and tell that chump what you want."

Much too hastily (and sounding much too exasperated) Byron replies, "Jenna, I'll do it later—on my way out," and beads of sweat form on his forehead. He knows he just got himself into a heap of trouble, and his instincts already reacted.

It's little comfort they've reached her condominium, but here they are. He parks his Corvette behind her Camaro, nudging up close to her bumper because there isn't much room. She can't get the door open fast enough, and once she does, leaps out, screaming, "You son of a bitch. You lousy, stinking son of a bitch. I *hate* you! And here I loved you, too! And like the total idiot I kidded myself *maybe* you loved me a little, too, but hey, you're about *done* with me, and that don't sound like somebody who might be goddamned in love with me. You fucking user. That's *all* you are! You're the worst one, yet. And I loved you? Ha!"

The whole time this has been going on, Byron's been wondering why he didn't just make a U-turn and get a stupid sticker, humor Jenna. He was so desperate and lacking in foresight to get involved with her in the first place, he simultaneously obligated himself to appeasing her neurotic little self, whenever the situation might call for it.

Truthfully, however, he's glad they've finally had this parting of the ways, so to speak. Now (he thinks) he can get on with his life. As for Jenna, he incorrectly assumes this has been but a minor mishap for her. (He obviously doesn't believe she really meant what she said.)

He at least should have figured there'd be some battle scars (because at this point he's still entirely unblemished).

Byron concludes the best thing for him to do, as she proceeds to start stringing together expletives, calling him as many as she can at once, is leave.

He shifts to reverse and starts backing up, only to have her proceed to remove one of her platform-soled sandals and throw it at him. It hits him right on the side of the head. Had she really *whipped* it, she would have knocked him out. And her aim's right on the money.

Now he definitely isn't going to say good-bye (what he'll only regret, later). As far as *he's* concerned, however, this is the end of their "relationship." (Byron just can't help using quote marks. Jenna really was like no other woman he ever knew. And although embarrassed {or is it sorry?} to admit it, the relationship was based entirely on lust.) If there *was* any semblance of compatibility between them, it was based on that.

Byron tosses her sandal (which *is* heavy) back to her, and it lands in the middle of the yard, in front of her condo. She goes to retrieve it, and he makes his final getaway, before she can throw the other one. He can hear her yelling expletives, even as he rounds the turn and the guardhouse comes into view.

Byron kept expecting to hear from Jenna. He'd come home from work, thinking there'd be an obscenity-riddled message on his answering machine, accusing him of avoiding her, of pretending like she no longer existed, etc., etc.

He seriously doubted she had it in her, to call his office and ask the secretary, Carrie Metzer, to speak with him. It was hardly any comfort to Jenna, to have to talk with another female who had an ongoing relationship with him (strictly platonic but better than nothing). A man and his ego, what Byron admits, himself.

And that ego of his was precisely what made him begin to wonder, what was the matter with him, she could let go so easily?

He was a real catch for a number of reasons, even if he could be a bit *too* practical-minded, sometimes.

Jenna should have been begging and pleading to see him again, wanting to make amends (not that he actually wanted any of this to happen).

But then, he couldn't forget she was always ready to meet someone new, and just maybe she had another man in her life.

Byron found that hard to believe because *her* boyfriends had to meet a number of criteria, and they didn't come along, one after the other. (She was more discerning than him, and he was bad enough, about the women he dated.)

Slowly, he began to put her out of his mind. And then he met someone new—or was *introduced* to someone new. She was the daughter of a client's best friend. There was mutual consensus between the two parties, Byron would make a good "friend" for her. (She didn't seem to have many of those, not genuinely nice ones.) She'd had her fill of people, male and female, preying upon her wealth, however, in the form of trying to sell her show hunters at grossly inflated prices. (She was a serious amateur hunter rider, at the "A-rated" shows.)

Her parents (no one said anything about *her*) were desperate for their daughter to meet a kind young man who would like her for who she was—an extremely well-off, twenty-three year old woman, obsessed with competing her three show hunters. So aside from her bank account, there was nothing *too* terribly extravagant about her.

What she needed was to get out of the tight circle of "horse show people" and meet someone new (whether she wanted to or not). It was hardly any secret her parents were forcing this upon her.

Byron fit the bill because he was intelligent, polite, financially secure, handsome as hell, and didn't know a *thing* about horses. That last attribute alone, made him *perfect* for her (much as he wanted to believe his sterling personality was what everyone, Mr. and Mrs. Capshaw in particular, liked most about him).

Normally, Byron didn't care to play the escort (how he referred to himself in this situation), but it was still better than being caught in a round of mutual friends, playing matchmakers.

And the second Byron met Ellie Capshaw, the sparks flew, even though the very last thing he intended to do was fall in love.

One of the beautiful things about her (besides the fact she was a pretty, dear, sweet girl) was the near-certainty she was a virgin. That drove him to the brink of madness (the *good* kind of madness) whenever he was around her.

Quickly, he learned the value of patience and the exercising of his gentlemanly ways. Sure he had his reputation to uphold, but he genuinely *loved* this woman (and lusted after her). He'd just spent six months dating Jenna Mulholland. It gave Ellie's innocence a whole new dimension, making him want her, all the more.

Still, as much as Byron loved her, she only *liked* him. This relationship-stuff was new to her, as she'd devoted her whole life to her horses. There wasn't time for socializing in high school or college because she was too busy competing at the shows.

Ellie needed lots of patience on Byron's part, he'd tell himself. It was fine with him because look what happened to his "relationship" with Jenna Mulholland. It began so intensely, there was nowhere left for it to go.

Dining out was the only thing Ellie and Byron both seemed to like to do. (Sex didn't consist of more than an occasional kiss. Oh, and holding hands. {Does that even count?}.)

Byron was so damned hopelessly in love with Ellie, he was willing to do *anything* to win her heart. Plus, he was scrambling to find a common thread. At the rate he was going, he had more in common with Jenna (if you counted sex, of course).

So all this goes quite a long way (if not the entire distance) in explaining why Byron bought the bare essentials of riding gear (hat, breeches, boots) and started taking lessons. This effort, from a man who never even had a dog (not that he didn't like animals).

Ellie would patiently watch from the sidelines, typically finished riding for the day. Both she and Melinda Blade, the trainer, claimed Byron had an extraordinary amount of natural talent and was a "fast learner."

Byron would think, *No, I'm just in a hurry to get good enough so Ellie and I can ride alongside one another, even if it's just around and around this dusty ring.* (Nothing like the power of love, is there.)

So too, Byron wanted to impress Ellie, show her he could tackle any new endeavor he would so choose. (God, if that didn't turn her on to him, what would?)

Indeed, there was just whispering about it, but Byron heard enough to know another one of the reasons Ellie's parents wanted her to meet and make friends with a real *gentleman,* was they suspected she might have had a foray or two with the same sex. Out of loneliness and desperation, she would have felt there was no other choice, all because she was surrounded by plenty of so-called "friends," but no one she could really trust.

As thrilled as Byron was, to be so passionately in love with Ellie, it was a *tiny* bit frustrating to think he could stand to blow his chance to win her trust (and hopefully, her love) if he said or did the wrong thing. It wasn't like he didn't feel he could be himself in her company, but he definitely had to physically hold himself back. (Sometimes Byron could *almost* feel aggravated by her, he wanted *so* badly for her to want him—not only that, he just *wanted* her.)

Meanwhile, through it all, she acted like she could take or leave the relationship they had. Either way, tomorrow she'd still be at Sandhurst Stables, riding her show hunters, getting ready for the next show.

And Byron thought so much of her, he accepted the circumstances.

Jenna Mulholland must have had a method to her madness, all along. She must have because she found her favorite target (Ellie Capshaw) and spewed all her venom upon her.

Byron wondered how he couldn't have suspected all along, Jenna had a plan up her sleeve.

And it wasn't just Jenna, talking dirty to Ellie, that irritated the hell out of Byron. It was Jenna, explaining in vivid detail the "dirty" things Byron and she did. Not only that, she made it more clear than clear, Byron and she were still together. They were just taking "a break" from one another, Byron was Jenna's man, etc., etc.

In her own strange way, Jenna really did love Byron, just as she said. Byron nonetheless couldn't believe she would stoop *so* low as to smear his name, making him a victim.

Well, he was as good as finished, insofar as ever being more than a chaperone for Ellie Capshaw.

As for the riding lessons he was so dutifully taking, she informed him it was O.K. with her to continue, she didn't mind. (*Gee, thanks*, he would think.)

And even as the eternal friend, the best he'd get was lunch with her, "on occasion." (*Thanks, again*.)

Ridiculous though it seemed, even at the time, Byron actually felt like life wasn't worth living.

Lunch? Lunch was a meal Byron either skipped altogether or else had with clients or business associates. He'd been badly bruised by Ellie's new "rules."

She wouldn't say how or where, but Byron knew where this "conversation" between Ellie and Jenna, came to pass (and made him think he might never eat lunch again, at least *not* at the Tea Tree Café, and not there with Ellie).

This particularly charming bistro was in the same strip mall as the Blooming Field Flower Shop, where Jenna worked. No harm in that alone because the two of them wouldn't know one another, just from plain sight.

The problem was Tina the waitress (remember Tina from the restaurant pointer Jenna gave?) loved nothing more than to eavesdrop. And what great fun it was to eavesdrop on Ellie, who enjoyed lunching alone but talked into her cellular the entire time.

It didn't take Tina long at all to put together the story of Ellie's life, as she casually conversed with whoever was at the other end of the line. (And it helped, there weren't a lot of financial planners named Byron, in this town.)

Anyway, Ellie was more fond of Byron than she cared to admit, and evidently not even she was immune to the feeling of completeness that came with having him in her life. (It also made her appear more "normal" to the rest of the world—i.e.—those outside the horse shows.)

Jenna was more than happy to keep on the lookout for a "tall, lanky brunette, wearing boots and breeches, driving a white BMW convertible." It would be Jenna's *pleasure* to confront the "girl" (as Jenna would refer to her), as she was either going into or coming out of the restaurant. It was sufficiently far from the florist's, Jenna's boss would stand *no* chance of hearing or seeing a thing. All Tina had to do was call and let Jenna know when Ellie paid the bill and was getting ready to leave (before which time she would usually make one more quick call, errand-related, such as calling to ask if something or other was fixed, cleaned, altered, whatever).

But on this day, she left her typically meager tip and departed! Tina had phoned Jenna, telling her, "Be by in a minute or two," but Ellie was already out the door.

Tina didn't know what to do. As much as she liked being friends with Jenna, she was kind of afraid of her. The last thing she wanted to do was make her angry.

But no matter. As it turned out, Jenna simply confronted Ellie as she was about to unlock her car door. Parked well out of sight of the flower shop, it was as good of a place as any to give Ellie Capshaw the what-for, for thinking she *deserved* Byron MacPherson, especially after *all* Jenna did for him (and this is when she went into graphic detail), concluding with the bullshit concerning the notion Byron and she, Jenna, were still a "couple."

Well, of course, that didn't hurt Ellie's virginal ears, half so much as being told the various ways in which Jenna and Byron had been intimate. In fact, she could see the possessiveness in Jenna's eyes and wasn't surprised at all to hear her unconditional claim on Byron.

Byron obviously (as Ellie surmised) had a sexual appetite that took on a life of its own. That positively repulsed her.

Byron's logical conclusion of all this was since he stood little to no chance of ever fucking Ellie Capshaw, he sure as hell didn't want to take another one of those loathsome riding lessons. (It was murder on his butt and his hamstrings.)

It was also entirely logical to Byron to give Jenna Mulholland a piece of his mind and tell her that their relationship was over. Finished.

Byron slept on it, thinking maybe it would be better *not* to see Jenna one more time. He knew there might be a scene, and frankly he was sick and tired of how she treated *everything* like it was a life or death matter.

But Saturday morning, he not only wanted to confront her and tell her off, he was feeling vengeful. He was well aware that wasn't the frame of mind in which to see Jenna Mulholland, but it would be more *bearable*. Acting like her, stooping to her level was the only way to *endure* her. And truthfully, the rare moments in which he almost got along with her? He would be on the brink of imitating her behavior, or at least finding her behavior, somewhat amusing.

Maybe standing up to her, was what she needed. Since there was a time when he actually thought they were together for a reason, it made perfect sense, meaning he was fated to be the one to give her the what-for.

What she could do to him (still) couldn't be denied, if only because memories of erotic ecstasy, died hard. He feared his willpower would let him down, should she come on to him.

But if he'd been involved with Ellie Capshaw? He would have been O.K. He was *sure* of it. The problem was he hadn't had any real *sex*, since Jenna and he were together. Because of Jenna's prowess and her passion (hell, her outright determination to be the greatest lover alive) she had turned him on, more than any other woman he ever knew.

For that reason alone, she had the upper hand. Lust was a mighty tool, possibly enough to make Byron forget, if temporarily, he was in *love* with Ellie Capshaw and Jenna ruined it.

An unannounced visit was what Jenna had coming to her. She'd resent it, especially if she wasn't alone. Even if she was, she had a thing about a fair warning, all so she could plot something wicked.

Byron had decided once and for all, he was going to Casa de Adobe, yet he lingered at home. He got a lot done, however. He washed his car, waxed it, then cleaned house (or condo). By then it was high time he go there or forget it. By afternoon, she'd be off someplace (unless she was in bed with her latest conquest).

After his shower, Byron made sure he put on plenty of cologne. He wanted to taunt (and tempt) her a little, knowing the scent of masculinity, drove her crazy.

Yes, it was awfully foolish for him to do something like that, especially when he didn't trust his own ability to exert self-control. But hell, he was taking a big risk, just by going to her place.

Driving there, the top down, Byron's thoughtful. Thoughtful about what, he can't say. Whatever's on his mind, it's hiding in his sub-conscious.

Once he arrives at Casa de Adobe, he tells the security guard who he wants to see and the number of the condominium she lives in, only to have the guy pick up the phone, preparing to call her. They only usually would do that for repair or delivery men. The guards that work weekends, follow the rules *too* carefully.

Jenna *still* isn't going to be prepared for his visit if this guy calls her place, but Byron really wishes he wouldn't.

As if the guy knows as much, he puts the receiver back and presses the button, to open the gate. Byron's so grateful, he enthusiastically waves back to the guard. The guy must have wondered what in the hell Byron's problem was. (Byron wonders himself, at this point.)

The first indication Jenna's home, is her car, parked under the carport. There's no visitors that he can see. (The only other car is the neighbor's, parked to the left of Jenna's Camaro.)

Can he afford to assume no one picked her up and took her somewhere, or even, she didn't spend the night, here? Yes, those are possibilities, but for all her wild ways, Jenna was always quite the creature of habit. If anything, she's either still in bed, taking a walk around the complex, or else making use of the exercise facilities, provided "free of charge." (And in her case, it really was free, living like she did.)

There's no reason to get edgy, he reminds himself. More than ample opportunity will be coming along, shortly.

He gets out of his car and makes his way to the front door of the tan stucco, Santa Fe-style house. He rings the doorbell but she doesn't answer. The bedroom window shades are closed, but the living room drapes are wide open.

Impatiently, he steps in the dirt under the window (crushing some plants while he's at it) and peers inside. He can see through to the patio and there she is, sunning herself. He never would have seen her, except she just plopped back down, from having been standing. There was a flash of white, the color of her bikini. (Byron got that correct, from only a glimpse. The part he missed, was she had nothing on, on top.) If he *had* known that, you can bet he would have hot-footed it back out of there. The more bare flesh on her body, the lesser his self-control.

But he's still determined, now that he *knows* she's home, to go through with this mission of his. He feels like he'll never be satisfied until he tells her it's *over* between them.

He retraces his steps, past the bedroom window, and follows the sidewalk to the east side of the house, where there's a black wrought iron gate. He quietly unlatches it and walks to the back. There, he must unlatch a second gate, one separating the yard in which he's standing, with the patio—where Jenna is lying, he can plainly see.

He isn't as discreet when he opens this second gate and curses to himself, about his trembling hands. He must get hold of himself, before he proceeds.

At this point he still doesn't realize Jenna isn't wearing anything on top, but that fact is soon made clear to him, once he's hovering over her.

Her face is pressed into the chaise lounge, and she could be fast asleep, for all he knows. She falls asleep easily and sleeps so soundly, Byron could indulge in touching that incredibly smooth skin in the crease of her vertebrae, and she would never know.

The urge to touch her is so great, he can't control himself. It seems like forever since he last laid a loving hand on a woman, really felt her. (And before him lies the very woman with whom he had the steamiest sex, ever.)

If only there was a bikini strap or two, to break that beautiful monotony of skin on Jenna's back, Byron might be able to keep himself in check. Suffice to mention he's temporarily forgotten why he came here.

The same time he reaches down with his right hand, to touch her, he imagines she's someone else. Who, he isn't sure. Or maybe it's still Jenna Mulholland, but she's a likable person, not a selfish little brat.

Just as Byron slowly and tentatively places a hand on her, Jenna ever so slightly lifts her head and turns it to one side, to see him. If anyone's startled, it's Byron. *She's* completely at ease.

A smile creeps across her face and there's a devilish look in those dark brown eyes. She sits up and turns around. It takes all Byron's concentration to keep his eyes on her face and not on anything else.

Meanwhile he must have unconsciously stepped backward, to allow her some room, in case she might care to stand. She patiently waits for him to speak. (Why *wouldn't* she be patient at a time like this, when she *knows* she has the upper hand?)

Byron's mouth as dry as cotton (the only part of him not sweaty or moist), his voice on the verge of cracking, he tells her, "I considered it *way* out of line, how you told Ellie Capshaw all about us. You could have saved yourself the effort, giving her all those explicit details, because we're through either way, Jenna. No, we're *not* taking a break from one another, like you told her. We're finished. Our relationship ran its course, and that's all there is to it. It's history. Finis." He finds he wants to go on and on, never mind he's saying the same thing. It's either that or else scream, "Do you *hear* me?" like *she* would do.

But he doesn't doubt she hears just fine. The trouble is she can't seem to listen, not unless she might *choose* to.

Jenna looks positively mirthful about the whole thing, and her comeback line is, "What's the matter? She *that* bothered by some gooey, messy sex scenes? She just too damned prude? Then be *glad* I got the bitch outta your way. That's how you *should* be lookin' at it."

Byron's fuming. No one does *him* any favors, when it comes to matters of love and relationships.

He can thank Jenna for reawakening all the angry, vengeful feelings he *almost* forgot about. (*Thank you, Jenna, for ruining my chances of ever fucking Ellie Capshaw.*)

Then, Jenna, in one swift, cool move, before Byron can even try to resist the siren's grasp, finds himself entwined by her. His lower extremity reacts in such a way, he knows self-control is completely impossible. If there was a game being played here, he just lost and he resents it. But he doesn't blame Jenna. He blames himself.

Jenna Mulholland isn't stupid, at all (as Byron formerly thought). She knows precisely how to take advantage of each and every situation. And as if to prove it, she hangs onto Byron even more tightly and starts kissing him with utter abandon.

Overwhelmed by her sudden passion, Byron's spontaneous reaction is to push her back, trying to make her fall upon the chaise lounge. Instead, she makes way for it and starts tumbling backward, with nothing to stop her momentum. It's almost like Byron gave her a push, except she did what she did, on her own.

She doesn't start to go down until her head hits the far concrete wall, and then her body too, is seemingly hurled against it by some supernatural force.

Byron watches it all, stupefied. Her body reacts to the force of impact by convulsing every which way, while those eyes of hers, locked a bugged-gaze upon none other than him.

He shudders at that look. Whether or not she's still conscious, she's damning him to hell.

He doesn't remain long. If he was going to do anything before leaving, he would check her pulse. But what's the point? As far as he's concerned, she's dead.

Wait a minute, Byron thinks. Did he leave his car running that day, after he killed Jenna Mulholland? (He's taking the blame for her death, having just reviewed all the events leading up to it.)

More importantly, did he leave it running now, when he stepped out of it to have a look at the gorge? He honestly can't remember, yet it's idling, sure as hell. And there's no one out here, for miles around. Besides, he couldn't have been so lost in thought, he didn't hear the person start the engine—or at least he doesn't *think* so.

He turns around, both curious and afraid to see who or what demonic character might be behind the wheel of his car. As determinedly non-religious as he might claim to be, Byron has no delusions about what deserves to happen to him.

The sun has risen considerably while he's been standing by the gorge, contemplating. He's hardly prepared for it, when he finds himself looking straight at the rays. Quickly he diverts his gaze to the driver's side of the car, but he's been too temporarily blinded to see.

Then he does see and he sees *her*—or should he say—*it*. At first he thinks maybe he's imagining it all. The exhaustion from having driven all night, the stress of knowing he might be a wanted man, the guilt resulting from leaving the scene of a terrible accident, are all making him hallucinate.

But from its mouth comes hideous, choking laughter. And if it weren't for that unmistakable laugh, he would doubt this bloody, beaten thing was actually Jenna Mulholland. Still, it's geographically impossible it's actually her, even if she *didn't* die. By the looks of her, she must have crawled all the way here, maiming body parts and catching her hair in sticker bushes and brambles.

Her loud, obnoxious laughter is drowned by the sound of Byron's screams as he runs in the direction of the gorge and throws himself over the side.

"Make-up!" Jenna calls, just like she's on an actual movie set. It's so much fun to pretend.

"SAME TASTE IN WOMEN: PROOF OF FOREVER— BEST FRIENDS"

In regard to my former best friend Nathaniel Dowling's innate cunning, I was mistaken. Moreover, I was all wrong, there's such a thing as "former" best friends, at least given our identical taste in women. Even more of a giveaway, was the fact we fell head-over-heels for the very same one.

Indeed, Nat could really throw me for a loop, and I kidded myself all these years, *I* was the clever one. So too did I believe he was the "lucky" one of us two, all because he was born into wealth. Up until the very last, I got by on only knowing bits and pieces of the whole story. Small wonder I ended up calling this the "surprise ending." And it turns out I was the lucky one, all along. I sure did feel sorry for myself in the meantime, however.

I was better than anyone, when it came to running the other way, once I'd deemed things, too much to handle.

Please, hear me out, try to weigh all the sides, before you call me gruesome or sick. Perhaps you can spare me some compassion. (I've always had a thing about not wanting to be hated by anyone.)

There was a customer seated at table three in my restaurant, the Sycamore, who had asked to speak with me. It wasn't often they requested to speak directly with yours truly, the owner/proprietor/chef/head-honcho, at least *not* before they even ordered. And that was indeed the case.

I preferred to stay hidden in the kitchen, where I'd lose myself in all the cooking tasks. It helped maintain an aura of mystery about me, which I happened to like.

Fortunately (though it *should* go without saying), I've never had to endure a barrage of complaints. With a place of this caliber, there's not the riff raff, more typical of "lesser" restaurants. My customers trust what they order, will be absolutely the most divine creations they've ever tasted.

Jacques Merced was the one who had come in the kitchen to tell me the customer wanted to speak with me.

Since this was a small restaurant, I categorized Jacques as one of the wait-staff, but actually he was more or less a bus-boy. Seating customers made him nervous and self-conscious. Explaining the menu was bad enough, but sometimes he was forced to do that, too.

Trudy Matthews was principally the one who took care of that duty, as well as hostessing. And on Friday and Saturday nights, a gal by the name of Dinah Cortez worked, too.

I'd also formerly had weekend-bussing help, another guy in his early 20's, Eddie Silvers, but he quit, about a month ago. Finding a replacement presented a difficulty because I was extraordinarily particular about my wait-staff. It wasn't a matter of hiring just anyone with whom to surround myself, given my exacting standards.

I was about as picky concerning who was allowed to work for me, as I was selective about whom I could love. For me, there was but one woman, and her name was Leona Dowling (nee Harker).

Before I looked out the one-way window, which offered a perfect view of table number three, I asked Jacques if "the guy" was one of the regulars. When he replied, "Sorta," I had a premonition, who it might be.

One glance and indeed, there he was, none other than my so-called *former* best friend, the recently-widowed (as of one month ago) Nat Dowling. Actually, *I* was the only one who knew for sure he was a widower.

"What do you know," I fairly muttered. So. Fate was intervening, once again. If I wanted to complete my ghastly little scheme, this was my golden opportunity.

He was seated in the very same place his deceased wife Leona (yes, Leona) occupied, the last time the two of them dined here, about a month ago. That was to be her last dinner, although maybe not her last meal. She came back to the restaurant, however, for something other than one of my gourmet masterpieces—a sort of rendezvous for reconciliation.

What was Nat's problem? Did he expect me to run out there and offer him condolences? I preferred not. Although the Dowlings occasionally dined at my restaurant (their initial visit coincidentally following a huge write-up about me in *Phoenix Home and Garden*), I certainly never intended to be friends with either one, ever again. It was pretty sad in a way, when one of them was once my best friend and the other, my one and only true love. In fact, until the last time the two of them dined here, I'd avoided them both. When Leona finally did lay eyes on me again, she must have liked what she saw.

I was too damned curious about what Nat might want, to be nervous about a one-on-one with him. I used to call him Nat, by the way, back in the olden days (and golden days they were, too). Life really was more simple when I was a struggling investment-firm gofer, working for none other than his father Norton's, Dowling Investment Firm, Incorporated, in Phoenix, Arizona.

I actually used to kid myself, his father wished *I* was his son, as I used to think *I* was the more intelligent one. What Nat inherited from his father, mostly consisted of the man's physical features— an egg-shaped head, with a tendency to baldness on top, a bulbous nose, big brown eyes spaced almost too far apart, and a short, stocky frame. According to popular consensus, neither one looked the part of the highly-driven, iconoclastic, mega-successful businessman. Regarding Nat, he had to *push* himself to be that way. And that's just what he did. Nobody said you couldn't be happy, being miserable—not to say he ever was, even one day in his life. That much I could never say, for sure.

However, I *did* know his elitist friends made Nat out to be someone "less" than they were, if only because of his looks. He had a severe confidence problem and didn't need any more reasons to fall further behind in his self-esteem.

Still, there were members out at Desert Spa Country Club, whom he called "friends," but I could never buy it. They were just too fake and condescending. I was always sincerity itself and through it all, I was his one and only *real* friend. His pal. His best buddy.

What hurt him most was knowing he wasn't the perfect physical embodiment of Adonis, that most women didn't look twice at him.

But this isn't to say he didn't have a sense of humor about his plight. That's in fact what got him through life, made him at least appear happy to the outside world

And he needed his sense of humor, when it came to marriage. He'd married to help appease his father, but he didn't marry the woman Pops wanted him to.

He sure as hell didn't marry who *I* wanted him to, not when up until Leona became "his," she was mine. It was only thanks to me that the two even met.

What hurt me the most was the utter unexpectedness of it. There was no fair warning whatsoever. That's why I wanted so badly to truly even the score.

I never spied on the loving couple when they were here, but I must have done some sort of looking/watching. I could remember the real, true, most appropriate example of her feelings for him— she couldn't even turn her head to talk to him. Instead, she'd address the empty seat across from her.

Still and all, it shocked the hell out of me when she called me at the restaurant, the afternoon following when I finally came fact-to-face with her (and him), again. She wanted to meet with me. She actually remembered me, after so much time.

Typically, the Dowlings would show up on a slower night, like a Tuesday or Wednesday. (The restaurant was closed on Sunday and Monday nights.) They never called first, to make a reservation, just in case. They wanted to remain as inconspicuous as possible. Well then, the feeling was mutual. I guess if fate hadn't intervened, Leona would still be alive, today.

Anyway, I knew she wasn't calling to meet and talk about roast duckling sauces. (She never gave a whit about cooking. She said so, herself.) She needed "inspiration," as she once told me, back when we were together, the brief amount of time that it comprised.

She had better things to do than learning how to cook. She was secretly on her way to snagging Nat Dowling. (I was determined I had a hand in all this.)

God, she was stubborn. But then, aren't most women? I can't speak from a vast array of experience, however, strictly from hearsay.

For example, when *I* knew her, she didn't/couldn't drive. Like me (about all we had in common), she walked to work every day. *I* had a car, but it was such a decrepit thing, I hated even being seen in it. But you can bet, the short amount of time Leona and I were together, I had it up and running, shuttling her to wherever her little heart desired. (And I spent every dime on her, ending up flat broke by the time she left me.)

Having gone straight from the comparatively low-life to the high life, I was certain she never bothered to get a driver's license. Whether by taxi, limousine, her husband as chauffeur, or using her own two feet, she preferred these means to driving herself anywhere. She *loved* knowing someone was making an effort for her. This went a long way in explaining why the night of her clandestine visit to the Sycamore (after the place was closed for the evening), there was no car in the parking lot. That was lucky for me because it was something I failed to take into consideration. I foolishly assumed all the evidence had been disposed of.

There was one thing I didn't understand (but which cleared me of being a suspect, not that I was regarded as such), and it was a quote of Nat's in the newspaper, shortly after the "crime" (how *I* knew it). The situation was described as the "abrupt disappearance," of the wife of finance wizard Nathaniel Dowling. Nat told reporters, "She's done things like this before, but this time I know it's for good. She finally took her car. Fortunately she knows how to take care of herself and I wish her well. She must have finally decided to take that tour of North and South America."

According to the article, however, Mrs. Dowling's silver Jaguar sedan, had yet to be seen on any roads or highways. Both car and driver seemed to have disappeared into thin air. Since Mr. Dowling didn't consider her truly "missing," he refused to file a missing person report. He claimed that would only ensure Mrs. Dowling would *never* return, she would be so incensed.

I didn't buy it. He was pulling *somebody's* leg, and I was wondering *who* he bribed (and how much) to get by, publicly saying this bullshit.

One thing was certain. He and I were inadvertently co-conspirators. He *had* to know she was dead and he was taking advantage of the situation. All I had to do was keep my mouth shut.

With that in mind, here I was, about to face him. I mean, still and all, I killed the guy's wife, for God's sake. Oddly enough, however, I actually did feel prepared to stand my ground. That was definitely a new one for me.

Approaching him, I had a couple seconds to get a pretty good look at him, better than the last time he was in here, when I wasn't paying any attention. (That was when all the attention was focused on me, courtesy of Leona.)

Honestly, he was looking better, just since being freed from Leona's grasp (how *I* saw their union all along). If I could have offered up any sort of greeting, it would have been to comment on just that: "You're looking good Nat." Instead, I found it impossible to decide how I could even address him, what *name* to use, since we were the same as strangers, at this point.

Ah, I might have known. Despite how polite I always considered myself to be, I remained at a loss for any words at all, while *he* jumped right in and said, "Look here, Marc. About that Bachelor Stew? I'm afraid your bus-help wasn't much help, and the gal who seated me, can't seem to be found. I'm curious as the dickens about it."

I asked him, "Did Trudy explain all the entrees to you, already?" as they were written on two separate chalkboards, on either side of the room. (Don't worry, it wasn't a huge room.) The entrees were also written on a chalkboard outside, by the door. In case you didn't see something you were crazy about, if you came back another time, you would see something you'd like. In other words, the

menu was guaranteed to change, regularly. I got bored easily, much
to the advantage of the customers who liked variety.

Bachelor Stew was a take-off on a stew I'd offered only one
time prior to this. I'd concocted a new recipe, based on how I
assumed Leona Harker tasted.

In the interim, when you saw "Bachelor Stew" on the menu,
you would be eating a bird of some sort (sounds appropriate, doesn't
it).

I could hardly believe Nat was taking a particular interest in
the very dish I hoped he would. Was the name the selling point? I
wondered.

Indeed, he wanted to know, "Whatever *is* the reason for the
name? I'm curious to know." His big brown eyes magnified by his
gold-rimmed glasses, he did indeed look curious, in that undeniably
intense sort of way.

I curtly replied (like I had better questions to answer), "No
real reason, at all," and that was the truth. It was also true that
what I wanted to call the dish was "Cherchez La Femme Stew,"
but that was too exotic and too obvious. Besides, this was *not* by
any means a French restaurant, so I wasn't about to use any French
names for dishes. It was *my cuisine* (showing how possessive I was,
of my creations).

I told him, extending this silly conversation, just to be polite,
as I *usually* did with such ease, "I mean, if anything, it's a celebration
of the single man and a reminder of my stew days, those when I
was working for your father and using stews to experiment, as it
was a cheap way to eat and still have unlimited opportunities to
test my imagination."

He said, "I'd like to have it, but I'm wondering. I've never
been much of a stew-man, myself. Could you tell me what meat
you put in it?"

I was thinking, *Yeah. The meat I need to defrost, A.S.A.P.* I would
have to microwave a portion of Leona before tossing "her" into the
stew.

But one thing at a time. I first needed to make sure he was
going to have the stew, and in that respect, my job was not yet

finished. And what do you know, my imagination was about to kick into overdrive, for better or worse. I felt like I'd just entered the set of my very own episode of the Twilight Zone. Believe me, I wasn't enjoying the feeling of floating. This was not the good kind of floating-feeling.

And here I went, off on a tangent: "The meat was specially ordered, after I saw a sample at the wholesale market, where I buy all my meat and fowl. It's pheasant, actually, and I inquired if I might have more than one bird. The manager said yes, of course. As a matter of fact, the son of one of the suppliers, shot these pheasant over the weekend he spent at a game retreat, in Pennsylvania. He had them flown back here. I jumped at the chance to have the whole flock. This is your lucky night." I just had to add the last little bit, when truthfully, it was *my* lucky night. That was my attempt at cleverness, when he always thought he was getting one up on me.

I would have thought he was finished grilling me on the subject, but no. I ought to have known better. When it came to thoroughness, Nat was second to none. He asked, "Would you be able to tell me *where* you buy your meat?" and I looked at him like he was nuts for asking. No chef in his right mind would ever reveal the exact source of the most important ingredient—the meat itself.

I let him down gently, saying, "I'm afraid that's something I *prefer* to keep to myself. If the name leaks out, fine, but it's important to me, to guard *some* secrets."

I really thought I was being clever with the innuendoes, irony, and everything else.

He was just a little too quick to be understanding when he said, "Right. I see. Well, Marc, I've *got* to have this mysterious Bachelor Stew—and the house salad, but no soup, if you please."

Mysterious? Yeah. Sure thing. It was about the same as Leona, popping into my life. I fooled myself, thinking there was some great mystery surrounding her.

He was only messing with me. I mean, didn't I just *explain* to him, the whole history of the stew, the meat, etc. What a lunkhead. Sometimes he seemed almost determined to cancel out his cleverness. He was making it hard for me to continue to be patient and polite with him.

Before I hot-footed it back to the safety of the kitchen, I told him Jacques would be bringing him some warm bread. And would he like another carafe of wine? No, he was fine. Too bad. I wanted him to relax, so he'd forget to ask so many questions—in all apparent innocence, no less.

Having failed to offer him any sort of sympathy or concern regarding his wife said it all, right there. At the very least, if I supposedly hadn't read or heard about Leona's disappearance I *should* have asked him where she was. I felt like this placed me in a major quandary. Should I forge ahead or go back and inquire about Leona?

The former seemed easier because I was already to the swinging door by this time. (This was how I tended to make many of my decisions.)

Simultaneously, however, I was going against my politeness, this failure of mine to at least *appear* concerned. I in fact was once *so* polite, Leona would tell me it was annoying. Well, as much as I loved her, her laugh annoyed the hell out of *me*. And she laughed *a lot*. I don't care if laughing's healthy, how about the damage it does to those who don't want to hear it practically nonstop?

Her laugh was so loud and raucous, the vibrations rang in my ears long after she'd finished—and was started on the next one.

What I ought to have done was rejoiced that I *didn't* end up spending the rest of my life with Leona. Although I found it impossible not to love her with all my heart, getting along with her all those years, couldn't have been easy. She had far too many stipulations. There's reasons for everything, and there was a reason Nat "got" her, instead of me. (I put the quote marks because it was really the other way around.) She got hold of him and used him, big-time.

I loved that woman much more than she *deserved* to be loved. She was far too selfish to even *begin* to be able to reciprocate any of my feelings for her.

And that's the past tense, mind you—a *very* past tense. If she came here, hoping to rekindle something within me, she was only wasting her time. And I made *that* one clear.

Before Jacques went out to serve Nat his bread, I couldn't resist briefly delaying him, to place the white porcelain cup holding the butter, so that it wasn't quite so close to the warm bread. That would only melt it faster. It was this never ending attention I paid to details, that made me proud of what I did for a living. Many people live their entire lives, never finding a niche. I *almost* didn't, since I never believed I could actually support myself (and support myself, *well*), doing what I loved, more than anything (Leona herself, aside).

Oh-so-patiently did I try to drill my perfectionist attitude into my staff, but there was only so far it could go. The rest was up to them, if they had the gumption. I was probably seen by some as a misogynist, but I nonetheless unfailingly believed women were more prone than men, to take the time to remember details, at least when it came to food.

I really did think the Silvers "kid" quit, because I got on his nerves. I mean, the commute to and from work couldn't have gotten to him, when he lived with his mother Eugenie in a one-story bungalow, but one block from the Sycamore.

He attended ASU in Tempe, just like Jacques. Although the two weren't what I called *friends*, they happened to see one another quite frequently, either on campus or else in the vicinity of it—at least according to Jacques.

Jacques held a definite contempt for Eddie's new, flamboyant style of dressing. It sounded like Eddie was spending more money than he ever got paid working for me, just on clothes. The thing was, he didn't get a new job, at least not so he claimed. Why would he lie about a thing like that? All I could think was he was either blackmailing someone or running some sort of illegal business. I wasn't being ridiculous, but rather *realistic*. This kid was no dummy. So too, he had nothing against breaking some rules, undoubtedly a reason why he had his fill of working for me, me and *my* long list of rules and regulations.

Anyway, Eddie wasn't talking about it, merely giving Jacques these sly grins. He always did think he was hot stuff. I told Jacques to just ignore him, it wasn't anything personal (as if *I*, of all people, really *knew*).

Jacques was made of firmer stuff than Eddie, so he didn't take offense to me, "adjusting" the butter holder. (That was also part of the problem, why he wasn't *becoming* a perfectionist.) Eddie meanwhile, would have quit over something like that. The exact reason for is departure remained uncertain to me, however. If there was a specific incident that served as the "final straw," I couldn't recall it. Worse, I took it kind of personally, he left.

Where the hell *was* Trudy, by the way? I couldn't afford to have this be her "off" night, when *I* already laid claim to that one. Thank God it was (so far) a slow night. I never believed I'd say this, but it was welcome to stay that way. If I lost some money tonight, so be it. I just wanted to avoid a nervous breakdown. I knew there'd come a point at which I overworked myself, and I'd need a break. The time was now, only I couldn't up and disappear (as much as I wanted to, for a variety of reasons). This would really stand as a test of my willpower, since I had an inherent desire to run from anything I didn't care to endure.

My career was my life, simple as that. I'd even put a bid in on a restaurant that was soon to be closing, a few miles west of the Sycamore. Currently it catered to a lunchtime crowd, as it happened to be wedged between two high-rise office buildings. With a suitably able wait staff at each location, I could shuttle my much-in-demand self, between the two. I would keep the Sycamore strictly a low-key, five-nights-a-week, gourmet bistro, while the other place would only serve weekday lunch. It sounded like a workaholic's dream come-true. I wasn't absolutely certain, however, the deal was a "go." There was still some negotiating to do.

Meanwhile, I continued to have my hands full, what with the time required just to shop for food, let alone prepare everything. I also had a cookbook, *slowly* in the works (although I already had a major New York publisher, eager for it). I needed to quit procrastinating working on it. Part of my problem was I refused to publish any of my really *best* recipes. Those were altogether too

sacred to me. So, I had the unenviable task of trying to conjure up
"new" classics. It wasn't easy.

Just to get through tonight would be a feat, and it wasn't even
a Friday or Saturday night. I was currently doing nothing but
standing by the stew pot, when what I needed to do was hurry up
and grab a frozen portion of *meat*, from the freezer. No one was
around to witness me doing so, although Trudy in particular, was
so spaced-out, she could have watched the actual murder and would
have assumed it was a hallucination.

Was I possibly jealous because she was lost in the dreamy state,
bitten by the *love bug*? Not a chance. The beginning of the end for
me, was to lose myself in a sea of bliss. I vowed that would never
happen to me, ever again.

Trudy fell (and fell hard, so it would seem) for none other
than her dessert-instructor at the cooking school she was attending,
three mornings a week. Guy Everest was his name, a balding, mid-
fortyish connoisseur of confections (and God only knew what else,
to have won Trudy over. She seemed pretty hard to please).

I was suddenly tempted to do something that was entirely
contrary to my character (since I was typically a proud, stubborn
S.O.B.), and that was call Eddie and *casually* (as in don't grovel)
ask him if he wanted his job back. Me, the dictator, was actually
volunteering to play the diplomat. Right this minute, he was
probably sitting there, doing nothing or watching TV, same
difference.

I went back to my makeshift office and dialed his number on
my cell phone. Because of my most excellent memory, I had no
trouble remembering it.

When I got the answering machine rather than a live person, I
was relieved. I decided calling him at all was the same as begging,
and the last thing I wanted was for *him* to think I was desperate for
his help. Of all the wait-staff, he was the one I didn't really miss.

At this point, it appeared the remaining wait-staff had
disappeared off the face of the earth. Actually, it was in keeping
with the whole Twilight-Zoneness of the evening. Typically, Trudy
and Jacques went back and forth through that swinging door so

many times, it seemed like they enjoyed doing it, for the simple sake of it.

Finally, amazing though it seemed at this point, I got Nat's *special* order of Bachelor Stew on its way. Yes indeed, preparations were underway, and I could even prepare Nat's salad—especially since it appeared no one else intended to do so.

I shouldn't have gotten so far into the "pheasant story." He didn't believe one word of it. But that didn't matter. I still maintained he didn't know he was going to devour his wife (or a portion, thereof).

The extent of how much Nat doubted my story? Only that the pheasant weren't nearly as exotic as I claimed.

Surprise, surprise, I got the salad ready and before I knew it, Jacques came through that swinging door and practically yanked it out from under my nose.

Rather than hand him the pepper grinder, I found myself following him to Nat's table, with it. I couldn't believe I was doing this. I felt like it was my duty or something, I really didn't get it.

Finally, however, I did catch sight of Trudy. She was fielding questions (literally) concerning the entrees she just spent the past half hour, explaining. I hoped to God nobody wanted any specifics from *me* about the Bachelor Stew. I'd *never* be able to recall the spiel I told Nat. Worse, he'd hear every damned word of the latest rendition. There were definitely things to be said against such a small room.

Why didn't I stay hidden, like I usually did? was what *I* wanted to know. This was *so* far out of character for me, it *almost* wasn't.

I asked Nat if he'd like some ground pepper for his salad and he said, yes, please, of course, so I started grinding away. I kept waiting for him to say, "when," hesitating every few seconds. Finally I just outright stopped and asked him, "Is that enough yet?" having covered about every bibb leaf by this time.

He jumped, as if awakened from a dream, only he'd looked anything but asleep. He exclaimed, "I thought *you* knew when to stop!" meaning either I was the headmaster here, or else I *once* knew him and his preferred tastes. Well, tastes changed, so what of it?

One thing didn't change, however, not with me—and that was I *hated* to see food go to waste. And if he told me the salad was now inedible, I was going to tell him where to put it. So much for being polite.

Teeth gritted, I nonetheless sounded like politeness itself, offering to bring him another salad. He replied, "Oh, no, Marc. That won't be necessary. If I remember correctly, the house dressing here, could use some spicing up."

Ouch. That *really* hurt. Why didn't he tell me this, long ago? Oh, that's right. There was never any real *opportunity*. Well, admittedly, I've never been much for salads or desserts. However, the least I could do was take some time to experiment with some new salad dressings. As for the desserts, that was where Trudy came in—if she *cared* to. She could be promoted from the wait-staff to the full-time dessert chef for my *two* restaurants (provided I bought the other one, as well).

I left Nat to suffer with his salad, returning to the kitchen with the pepper grinder, before I knocked him over the head with it. Just kidding. I had more self-control than that, although it was still true, I was intolerant of food waste. Clever though Nat was, he could never identify with my feelings on the matter. He was born, surrounded by richness.

Never for a moment, however, did I ever want to be him. There *were* times I wished I could live his life, but I was perfectly happy, making do. It taught me to take pleasure in the simplest, seemingly most inconsequential things in life.

I made daily visits to the "Fresh For U" supermarket, which was on the way back to my apartment. It made the walk seem more worthwhile, when I had something to show for it.

"Fresh For U" didn't cater to a rich clientele, but the store did happen to stock many hard-to-find items, ones you wouldn't expect. In those days, I owed much of my sense of adventure to that store. A unique ingredient alone, whether it was a condiment or a kind of meat, was inspiration enough, to experiment. I never purchased more than a few items at any given time, if only because it was all I could afford. (Plus, it kept the walk enjoyable.)

I wasn't actually "friends" with any of the cashiers, as I wasn't prone to striking up conversations. (Wasn't that how it worked?) I mean, the cashiers were expected to be friendly, but they didn't have to fall all over the customers.

Well, one way or another, naturally flirtatious-looking Denise had developed quite a rapport with one of the customers. They could have been next-door neighbors for all I knew, but I had it in my head, this was a check-out line romance. It had developed with time, slowly but surely, the best way to a lasting romance. (What I didn't have the maturity to realize, when Leona jumped me.)

Handsome though I was, my looks didn't even register with Denise. At that age, around 24, I was already accustomed to going unnoticed, for the most part. I obviously lacked that lusty spark in my blue eyes.

Denise was definitely a woman of few words toward me, as if she didn't want to disturb me. I didn't harbor any sort of grudge against her because of this treatment—quite the contrary. The one against whom I had the grudge (and perhaps even a certain amount of hatred, if you will), was Mr. Don Juan, with his "six-six" frame, his swarthy looks, his easy smile, and his goddamned nerve. His nerve was the *most* annoying when he physically tried to hurry me out of there, all by pushing his cart right up to my butt.

And Denise had her *own* nerve, which consisted of carrying on a conversation with Loverboy while checking out *my* handbasket's worth of groceries. Worse, she *shoved* them all in one paper bag that would never survive the trip home.

And the most deplorable part of all? I was so incensed I was in the way of their banter, I paid *no* attention to how she overstuffed the bag, until I was walking out the door with it. Did I go back inside and have her give me another bag, if not separate some of the items, herself? Hell no. Now *that* was definitely stupid. However, lingering around what was formerly my favorite place, simply wasn't an option.

The ultimate punishment was walking back to my apartment, trying to walk fast and keep the bag from giving way. Of course, I secretly *wanted* it to, so the entire contents would spill all over the sidewalk, and I could blame womankind for it (most especially Denise the cashier).

My "love life" was *not* exactly at a high point, at this particular time of my life. (O.K. I hadn't gotten laid since I couldn't even remember. Probably something like high school—senior prom night.) I thought I'd been doing a pretty damned good job of channeling that sexual energy, but you know, it can come out inadvertently— i.e.—there's no way of stopping an unwanted tantrum or two.

But my lack of a sex life was the most important tie that bound me to Nat. He wasn't getting it either, for his various reasons, not the least of which he was shy, like me. Then, what do you know, the woman who broke me free of that long term of sexual self-exile, would be the one to do the same for him.

Climbing the stairs to my second-floor, one-bedroom apartment, I heard that annoying laugh of Leona's. *Any night but this one*, was all I could think. With her apartment right across the hallway from mine, it was almost too convenient. And up until this day, she had treated me as if I didn't exist. I mean, to be even remotely acknowledged by her, would have been a big deal. She took some sort of cruel pleasure in treating me like this. At the same time, I doubted she knew what I felt for her. She was merely playing her own little game and having one hell of a great time.

I certainly wasn't *jealous* of whoever was giving her the time day (and who knew how to make her laugh so loud. I mean, I assumed it was a boyfriend who was the comedian wannabe, making her laugh like that).

Leona was the unattainable woman, simple as that. A man like me, at that time in my life, saw her as such. I didn't think for a second, in terms of compatibility, practicality, etc. Unfortunately, I also had an apparent obsession with considering any relationship I might possibly enter, as *The One*, to last me until my dying days. That didn't especially include holy matrimony, but I hoped it figured *somewhere* in the equation.

My feet dragged as I *attempted* to ascend the stairs. It was suddenly too much, to tolerate that obnoxious laugh of hers. Interspersed with the laughter there was relative silence, since she was talking on the phone or listening to the next joke. Anyway, her speaking voice certainly wasn't loud, or I would have heard *something*. It proved the volume level of her laughs, was pretty damned high.

Quiet, somber me didn't stand a chance of making Leona Harker happy because apparently laughing was *very* important to her. She'd force a laugh from herself, if necessary.

Well, I proceeded to do it again, twice in a day, I let a little annoyance turn into a great disturbance. Leona's laughter ringing in my ears prevented me from remembering to have my key ready, once I *did* finally reach the top of the steps. The door might not have even been locked, and I easily could have laid the ailing bag down to check. I had a habit of forgetting to lock it.

But no. I had to hold onto that damned bag, as if my life depended on it. It was about like a shipwreck victim, hanging onto a piece of floating driftwood, in the middle of the Atlantic. And if that allusion sounds corny and trite, well, *nothing* was more trite than me that evening, letting the whole entire female species, get the better of me.

There I was, trying to balance *and* hang onto this breaking bag, while I fished for my key. That just *had* to be when Leona really let it rip with the laughter. Neither before nor since have I ever heard anyone laugh like she did, that night. It not only made my skin crawl, it got *under* my skin, so to speak. I let my mind go into frustration overdrive, and it was *not* a pleasant sensation. I was about nine-tenths out of control at that point, although at the time, I didn't have *any* idea the potential for vengeance, inside me.

In the next few seconds, I abandoned trying to find the key and found myself trying to stop what was by this time the inevitable—the contents of the bag, ending up on the tile floor.

With a loud crash (it sounded much worse than it was), everything hit the floor at once. The celery was the single unbreakable item, yet *nothing* broke. It would have otherwise really been a mess. And I didn't want to do things to antagonize Mory Landau, the superintendent? Luckily I *didn't* buy that carton of eggs I was thinking maybe I needed.

Well, I was right, when I said it sounded worse than it was. It succeeded in ending Leona's phone conversation, so she could investigate what the hell just happened.

Her door was flung open and there she stood, peering down at me, looking like she might burst into laughter, at any second. It figured. Making a fool of my self was the only way *I* could possibly get her to laugh. She said, "I thought for sure Landau finally fell down the stairs."

He *was* kind of clumsy, come to think of it, but still. She knew who the doofus was. I was only kidding myself if I seriously believed she was really referring to him.

I was suspended in disbelief, once and for all, when she proceded *not* to slam her door and disappear back inside her apartment, but to get down on her hands and knees and help me gather my items. Even if I *had* broken some eggs, she would have helped me that day. Now I can be sure of it because she had an ulterior motive, all along.

At this point, however, I was still pretty skeptical her helpfulness was even something you could have called "neighborly." As I mentioned before, up until this time, I was about the same to her as a piece of lint. She must have finally seen Nat pick me up in his Porsche. He liked to go in the crescent driveway in the front, which Leona's apartment overlooked. (My apartment overlooked the dumpsters.)

I *thought* I was maintaining the correct, haughty attitude toward her, but it would only end up melting in a flash when she said, "Speaking for *everyone* on the floor, Marc, if not the entire building, the dishes you make, smell *so* good. I need to take some lessons from you, sometime, if you have a chance."

Was she inviting herself to spend some *quality* time with me? I wondered. I was too surprised to even consider it with any real seriousness, but I did tell her she was most welcome to come over and "observe."

Meanwhile, I was intoxicated by the scent of her perfume, speaking of pleasant smells. That was having as much or more of an effect on me, than the gorgeous view of her breasts, barely concealed by her black cotton, V-neck sweater and sheer, natural-colored bra. If I'd had more *sexual* experience at that time of my life, I would have taken the initiative, right then and there. So too, I'd gotten so used to exercising restraint, it was impossible *to* let go, at this point.

The most unbelievable part of the story (if you knew how *few* favors Leona Harker did for people), was she *insisted* upon carrying the broken bag of food into my apartment.

Following me, she made me incredibly nervous. I was also panicking because I couldn't recall how messy I'd left the apartment, that morning. As long as she didn't look around, I could be safe because although the kitchen was overflowing with gadgets and utensils (which didn't fit in the limited shelf space), it was very neat and orderly.

I still didn't know for sure if the door was locked, but I went through the motions of unlocking it. At this point, I didn't want to *know* if I had failed to lock it.

Inside, I told her to set the bag on the kitchen table, a piece of secondhand furniture that managed to look like it had some charm. It obviously added *something* to the atmosphere, for she commented, "Cute place, Marc." She must have been expecting the worst, but I still thanked her for the compliment.

I was sweating like hell, just feeling the air of expectancy (although I seriously doubted anything was going to happen, unless of course I initiated it).

Her chore completed, Leona didn't linger. She turned on her heel and said, "I'll leave you be, to work some of that magic. And I may just take you up on those cooking lessons." With that, she was gone, only after patting my shoulder. It wasn't a pass, only a friendly gesture, but it still made my day. That was when I *knew* I was hopelessly in love with her.

The whole time I spent cooking that night, I couldn't stop thinking about Leona and what she said. This was the first time my concentrative powers had been corrupted, at least when it came to cooking. Even if nothing happened after this initial, brief encounter with her, I was perfectly happy, replaying the scene, even including the contents of the bag, ending up on the floor.

That particular night, I just so happened to have been creating a stew that was the predecessor to the very same "Bachelor Stew," Nat was having, over twenty years later. It goes to show you the enduring qualities of a real classic, a dish that I was very proud of having created. In fact, at the time, I'd been working on a sort of "vegetarian" stew, one that tasted like it had meat in it but actually did not.

Then I started thinking maybe Leona *expected* me to make a move of some sort, since she had actually made the first one. I guessed I needed to invite her over, for a cooking lesson.

I was in agony by the time the stew was finished because I couldn't decide how long I should wait, before I asked her over. I felt like a real idiot, one whose lack of confidence forced him to lead a sheltered existence. And when it came to making a move on a girl, I obviously lacked the necessary wherewithal.

And here came Jacques, back into the kitchen. He looked like the soldier who had been given the what-for and humiliated beyond repair. In his mitts he carried an uneaten salad and an empty bread basket. I even recognized that same leaf of bibb lettuce. It hadn't even been subjected to a push of a fork. If I'd had any appetite at all that night, I would have eaten the salad, myself. That was how much I hated seeing food go to waste. I did *not* want to be tempted to go out there and give Nat the what-for. I had to keep in mind he was a customer, and if he didn't want to eat the salad, that was his prerogative.

Shame on me. I needed to feel some sympathy for the poor man. After all, he was still deeply mourning the "disappearance" of his wife, his one true love, just like she was, for me. And in his case, he'd also invested a lot of time (and money) in her. Living alone for as long as I had, there was an initial tendency to be a bit narrow-minded.

Jacques could see me scowling at the salad, so he hesitated, awaiting specific orders as to what to do. If not, perhaps I expected an explanation from him.

I didn't do or say anything. I was trying with all my might, to keep from throwing a godawfully embarrassing fit. Jacques would stand there the whole time, slack-jawed, which would *really* infuriate the pants off me.

Ever so calmly, I told Jacques to please take the man at table number three, another loaf of bread. I'd get that smart-ass S.O.B.'s stomach filled, one way or another. I didn't even care if he ended up rejecting the stew. At least I'd know I'd tried.

Despite my all-out attempt at appearing calm and aloof, Jacques was eyeing me strangely. Did a slip of the tongue just throw him off? I might have mumbled something as he turned to leave with another basket of bread. It didn't surprise me to have come *all* this way and have my very own self, deceive me.

I really needed to be careful. Jacques was one of those who paid more attention to what you said under your breath than to his face. Small wonder he started plodding if you gave him too many tasks to do, all at once. Unlike that Silvers kid, however, at least he didn't get offended easily.

If I could work with my usual fervor, everything would be all right. You'd think when I was in the midst of carrying out such a devious deed, I would be working a mile a minute. Instead I couldn't concentrate enough to even *think* about working.

I looked out the one-way window and expected Nat to be trying his damnedest to see in. No, actually, he looked entirely placid, staring straight ahead. He was seated in what was formerly Leona's seat, the one that offered a side view of her (and now, him). It was the table that kept them most squarely in the limelight, the way they both must have liked it to be. (Even though Nat was shy as compared to his deceased wife, he wasn't *too* shy.)

When I took Leona out, she expected me to pay. She knew I wasn't well-off, or she wouldn't have trampled me, on her way to whom she *really* wanted. Not *one* time did she even *offer* to pay her share, yet my salary was no more than hers, probably less. So flattered was I, she even wanted anything to do with me, I wouldn't have let her pay, anyway. Was that a man in love, or what?

The relationship she and I had was so brief, it might as well have never happened. Unfortunately, I have the mental scars, to prove it did. She would have left me, even if she *did* know how much she meant to me. That's just the way she was.

And once she was finished with me, all I wanted was to get as far away as possible from her. That was why I essentially abandoned my life. There was no possible way I could live with all the reminders of her. I'm embarrassed, still, that I threw away a chance to make something of myself in the business world, even if that was never where I felt even remotely happy.

I considered returning to the Midwest, where I was originally from, hoping that would help relieve me of this affliction called rejection-depression—or so I termed it.

Having abandoned my job, my car (not missing much), and my apartment (meaning I lost all my possessions), a bench at central Phoenix's Acacia Park, became my home for a time.

That was when I was most grateful I kept all my recipes in my head. And as much as I wanted to complete that cookbook I was working on, unconsciously I couldn't help procrastinating. I wanted my recipes to remain with me, in my head, like they were, way back when. They were *all* I'd salvaged, from my "other life."

Finally, I noticed the order Trudy'd left me for the table of four, the ones who needed each entree described in explicit detail. Three of them were having the stew. Of all the nights, when I had an extra-special order in the works, there were *more* potential takers. One taste of Leona and they might all be hooked, you never knew.

But I couldn't do that to Nat. His wife ought to be saved for him and only him. This was only the beginning. Already I was imagining the ingredients for the fillet sauce I could serve with another portion of her.

Leona's last meal here at the Sycamore, she acted differently. That was even before I made my unexpected appearance at her and Nat's table. I was *not* spying on them, even on that particular evening. As usual, I was minding my own business, and nobody did that better than me. I was told the "Odd Couple," as Trudy called them, were more aloof than ever, toward one another. She had an ongoing fascination with them, most probably because of their local renown. They were socialites who attended every damned charity dinner that existed. That was their way of satisfying their philanthropic side.

As I mentioned earlier, what must have prompted their initial visit to the Sycamore, was the highly complimentary write-up about it, in *Phoenix Home and Garden*. The wait-staff was said to be, "as courteous and efficient, as the chef-proprietor Marc Jerred, is reclusive." The Dowlings assumed they could sneak in here, unnoticed by me and satisfy their curiosity about the place. They didn't want a single one of their friends to be given a negative response, when asked if they had been to the Sycamore.

But see, they ran into a glitch because the cuisine is so stupendous, they couldn't resist coming back.

The desire to avoid *them*, was sure as hell strong for me. Short of telling them to leave (which I *never* could have done), all I *could* do was stick to my reclusive ways and stay in the kitchen.

However, devotion to the smooth-running of my restaurant, was of primary importance. That was what forced me to make an appearance that night. It just so happened to be on the same one as when Leona was behaving differently. She had it in her head, if she finally did meet me again, perhaps we could rekindle what I called a lost hope (and those, you do *not* resurrect).

The day following this evening when Leona and I locked eyes on one another again, she phoned me at the restaurant. There was urgency in her voice, when she begged to meet with me, "in private." I assumed that meant *sans* Nat. Fine with me. Putting her off would be entirely impossible. I mean, the woman was *crying* over the phone. I don't think she was faking it, either. She wanted to see me so badly, I wasn't going to begrudge her. (I was secretly flattered as hell *she*, of all people, the one-time, oh-so-briefly love of my life, wanted desperately to have a rendezvous with me.)

I stipulated we would have to meet at the restaurant that night, after closing time, about eleven. By then all the wait-staff would be long gone, and we'd have the place to ourselves. (I did *not* have *any* plan in mind, believe me. I definitely didn't think I'd be strangling her, by night's end.) She shouldn't have mistaken my roughness for a return of her advances, or she might still be here, today. I *hate* being misunderstood. However, she was the kind of woman who would second guess you, if only because she thought she could change your mind, that way. I wasn't as stubborn as she was, but I was certainly set in my ways. She should have kept that in mind before executing her little scheme, to re-seduce me. She must have left all her cleverness back at age 23, once she no longer had any use for it.

What I *should* have done was called Nat and told him to pick up his adulterous wife. She was at my restaurant, wanting a late-night snack.

But I didn't know his number, I was certain it was unlisted, and furthermore, we were no longer friends. He was the same as a stranger at that point in time.

Once I strangled Leona, at the very same table she used to dine, I found myself with the body of an adulteress, of which I needed to dispose. The last thing *I* wanted to do was get caught. At the same time, running some risk, really turned me on. That was how I decided to cut her up, boil the meat, and freeze it. Only later did I think of actually putting her in a dish—to be fed to none other than the heartbroken, grieving widower. Poor man.

Obviously I was in a manic frame of mind, the night I committed the horrific deed of strangling and cutting up *and* cooking Leona Harker. (She will always be *Harker* to me, even though she married Nat Dowling and took his name. That's my way of thinking of her, separate from Nat. She was *mine*, before she became his, even though *that* was a permanent arrangement.)

To say I was "temporarily insane," would be ludicrous. If anything, my mind was more clear and sensible than it had ever been, if only while I carried out the deed, from the strangulation to the freezing of the portions of meat, carefully cut from her body.

The entire time, I felt like I was not only living my life, but watching it on a 3-D movie screen. I definitely didn't feel like I was doing anything wrong, not even something gruesome. (I always did have kind of a morbid sense of humor.)

But I *never* would have described myself as a potential murderer. I guess this proves that given the motivation, *anyone* can do it. However, I'm *not* condoning the act, not me.

If I could blot out but one incident in my life, it would be meeting Leona Harker for the first time. Ah, the terrible price for receiving *exactly* what you want. The beginning of the end was when the obsession with her, set in—and *that* took place even before we met. Of that I'm certain, looking back on it all.

That night I never worked so hard. There was plenty to clean up afterward, and it was dawn before I had a chance to rest.

I sat myself down in Leona's favorite seat, the one Nat would later occupy. I'd made myself a cup of instant coffee, not that I needed to worry about staying awake. I knew it was the only thing I could have, that would go down and stay there. I didn't have even a nibble of dinner the night before, yet I certainly wasn't hungry. That was about the only indication what I did had a profound effect on my nerves.

To serve Nat his very own order of Bachelor Stew, it truly was the culmination of this deed. The more I thought about this *final* chapter, the more excited I became about it actually happening.

And now was the time. I would ladle his serving (a generous one) into a bowl, let it cool for a minute or two, and serve it to him myself, with pleasure. I didn't even care if he suspected anything, because I was suddenly showing my face so much.

Neither Trudy nor Jacques was around, so there was no bothering with having to shoo them out of the way. I made my own grand passage, from the kitchen to the dining room, pushing the swinging door for all it was worth. I felt like I was on a mission— a good kind of mission. I did not feel the least bit of guilt.

Barely was the stew placed before Nat when he commented, "Gee, that looks good. I can hardly wait to dig in."

I thought, *Better you than me.* I went totally against my credo and didn't taste-test it. It was quite a wonder I could even *serve* something I'd never before tried. I had to count on my instincts for this one, when it came to which ingredients best complemented Leona.

Lingering by his table, Nat had every right to wonder what the hell my problem was. He commented, "The chef looks hungry to me. He'd better save a bowl of this, for himself."

I nervously cleared my throat and said, "I just wanted to make sure you liked it, before I went back to the kitchen" (since the salad obviously didn't go over, too well).

"Thoroughness. Conscientiousness. They're both positive attributes to have, as a chef," he said, but I wasn't really paying any attention. I was watching him as he prepared to place a spoonful of Leona, his *wife*, in his mouth. I felt like a kid again, back to the days when you made a "friend" unknowingly devour something, while the rest of the "friends" gathered around and watched (and preceded to fall on the floor, in utter hysterics).

But this time, I found I really couldn't watch. I might otherwise throw up. Laugh, I could not, that much was certain. It wasn't because I didn't find it funny, however. It was *too* funny (and too good) to be true.

Then I turned away, only to have Nat order me, outrightly *order* me to come back. He didn't say it like a customer talking to the proprietor, but rather like a condescending sounding "friend," just like he used to do, in the old days. Every once in awhile he'd treat me like that, as if to put a check on me, let me know I wouldn't have any fun, no extravagant pastimes, if it weren't for him. (Rides in his Porsche, golf at *private* Desert Sage Country Club, fishing weekends up north, etc.)

I'd tolerated the treatment because I knew that he couldn't help himself. He was nothing but an insecure little dweeb, at heart. There just wasn't a whole hell of a lot to him.

Just like Leona, as a matter of fact. Why did I let her be the ruin of me? If the woman was indeed truly special in any way, it was because she knew how to break hearts. What kind of redeeming quality was that?

There was only one other thing she might be special for.

I turned around and returned to Nat's table, grabbing a fork from another place setting, at a nearby table. *I* saw it as only fitting to use a fork. The stew was definitely thick and meaty enough.

"Thatta boy," Nat said, watching me. "Help me polish her off."

"I thought you'd never ask," I returned, fork poised.